THE

JON CLEARY, the Australian whose books are read
throughout the world, is the author of twenty-eight
novels including such famous best-sellers as *The
Sundowners* and *The High Commissioner*.

Born in 1917, Jon Cleary left school at fifteen to
become a commercial artist and film cartoonist – even
a laundryman and bushworker. Then his first novel
won second prize in Australia's biggest literary contest
and launched him on his successful writing career.

Seven of his books have been filmed, and *Peter's
Pence* was awarded the American Edgar Allen Poe
prize as the best crime novel of 1974.

JON CLEARY

The Long Pursuit

FONTANA/Collins

First published by William Collins Sons & Co. Ltd 1967
First issued in Fontana Paperbacks 1969
Second Impression October 1969
Third Impression January 1979
Fourth Impression November 1982

Made and printed in Great Britain by
William Collins Sons & Co. Ltd, Glasgow

TO MARK AND SARAH

Farewell, the long pursuit
And all the adventures of his discontent.
                                    Elinor Wylie

CHAPTER 1

Jack Case lay on his back in the Singapore mud and dreamed of Texas. Occasionally he raised his head, took a swig from the bottle of Johnnie Walker, mumbled an apology to the mosquitoes he had disturbed, then lay back. He was past the point of distinguishing between comfort and discomfort; he had taken enough punishment over the past few years to have become almost immune to such minor irritations as carnivorous mosquitoes, cold slimy mud and a stench that might have warped the nostrils of someone more sensitive. The mangrove swamp smelled no worse than had the oil fields around Beaumont and the mosquitoes here might have been blood cousins, *his* blood, to those along the Neches River. Twelve thousand miles and twenty years from home, nostalgia suddenly made him drunker than the whisky had. He began to sing *Deep in the Heart Of Texas*, getting the clap-clap of the song by slapping his palm flat on the wet mud. Once, two rifle shots from somewhere over near the Causeway came in on the appropriate beat and he stopped and nodded his head appreciatively. Someone might have died from the rifle shot, but the thought did not disturb him. Even the thought that he himself might be dead by morning did not agitate him, at least not now. Whisky and nostalgia were proving to be ideal sedatives.

He lifted his head once more when he heard the sound of footsteps padding across the mud. Well, here they come, he thought; and began to sing louder. He ran out of the words of *Deep In The Heart Of* and switched to the *Yellow Rose Of Texas*; Stephen Austin and Sam Houston would be proud of him when he joined them in the special Heaven reserved for Texans. Jack Garner and Sam Rayburn might even drink a toast to him if ever the word got back to Washington about how he had died. Still singing, he tried to get to his feet, to die like a true Texan.

'For God's sake, will you *shut up*! Who do you think you are—Gene Autry?'

Gene Autry! Whoever said he was a true Texan? Indignation almost succeeded in sobering Case. Kneeling in the mud, he peered around in the dark for the sacrilegious Jap who spoke English so well. Then the voice said behind him, 'Who the blazes are you?'

5

Case tried to turn round on his knees, lost his balance and fell on his face in the mud. He rolled over scraping at his eyes with one hand, and looked up at the figure standing above him. Whisky and mud hadn't improved his vision, but he was not so blind that he could not recognise that this was no Japanese.

'Who are yo', po'dner?' When he was drunk he was the Texan of all Texans, accent thick as the mud along the Rio Grande.

'I asked first.' The stranger looked back over his shoulder to the black wave of mangroves; behind it the sky glowed red from a burning village on the Bukit Timah road. Then he turned back to Case, keeping his voice low. 'Who are you?'

Case considered a moment, then he said, 'Jack Case. From Beaumont, Texas.' For an instant there was an echo in his ears from out of the past: a hundred announcers shouted his name and tens of thousands of fans roared their approval.

But now there was only the croaking of frogs and a quizzical silence from the man standing above him. In the darkness it was impossible to see his face, but his build was slim and short; no more than a bantamweight, thought Case, accustomed to putting men into weight divisions. The stranger was dressed in a dark suit and carried a suitcase that was heavy enough to pull him down at one shoulder.

'What are you doing down here?' His accent was English: North of England, Case was to learn later.

Case was relaxed again. He lay in the mud and looked up at the Englishman. 'Thass a good question.' He pondered it a while, then shook his head. 'Unforshunally——' His tongue slipped on the word. 'Unforshunally, Ah don't have a good answer.'

'My name's Garrick.' He awkwardly shifted the suitcase to his other hand and looked nervously back over his shoulder again. 'What are you planning to do?'

'Plans Ah don't have, muh friend.' Case struggled up into a sitting position, then clumsily got to his feet. He stood swaying, trying to bring his eyes into focus. 'But if yo' got any plans, Ah'm willing to help yo' with them.'

Garrick fidgeted, tapping his free hand against his side. Then he said, 'Just my luck. Me a teetotaller and I get landed with a drunk!'

Drunk or sober, Case had learned to ride insults just as he had learned to ride punches. 'Don't think Ah got any pride, muh friend. Ah'll go with anyone.'

'Come on, then,' Garrick snapped, and began to make his way

across the mud flats towards where a line of mangroves curved out like the sea-eaten wreckage of a breakwater. Case looked after him, then he shrugged and began to plod after the Englishman, the whisky bottle held up in front of him like a candlestick. He was not so drunk that the image didn't occur to him and he giggled. This was just what he needed: an unlit candle to guide his way into the darkness ahead.

Up ahead Garrick stalked along, bent over to one side under the weight of his suitcase. His shoes were full of slime and his feet were threatening to slip out of them at any moment. Cripes, he thought, why did I ever leave Leeds? But he knew why he had left, and the question only made him grin sourly. He felt no homesickness, even now when he might never see home again. All he felt was a regret that he probably would never see Tahiti. He shifted the suitcase to his other hand, slipping in the mud and almost losing his balance as he did so, and wondered if he should have bothered to bring it along.

Suddenly he dropped flat in the mud. 'Down!'

Case went down in a limp heap, collapsing like a man with no bones. That was something else he had learned over the past few years: to go down when he was told to.

'Nips!' Garrick whispered hoarsely, and pointed out towards the water. A small boat was coming down from the direction of the Causeway, visible only as a moving silhouette against the string of lights that connected the island with the mainland. A searchlight in the prow of the boat suddenly blazed on; Garrick started, as if the bright burst of light had been an explosion. The beam swept across the mud flats, throwing the mangroves into relief: the contorted trees stood frozen, like primitive dancers caught in some savage rite. Then as the light moved on the trees seemed to move into each other, became a dark crowd of bystanders waiting for something to happen, the only outsiders in this war that had finished tonight.

Garrick and Case stretched themselves flat in the slime, trying to sink into it. An urge for survival had come alive like a flickering spark in Case; perhaps the cold mud had begun to sober him. He became aware of the mosquitoes, the smell of the mud; discomfort was suddenly like smelling salts. He tried to drain the substance out of himself into the mud, to become a flat patch of skin and hair, a piece of flotsam, as the light beam crept towards them across the shining flats.

The beam went over them, stopped and came back. It played over them and it was almost as if it were a ray of fire; Garrick

7

could feel the hair on the back of his neck beginning to curl and his whole body seemed to shrivel. Case waited for the bullets to chop into him; he knew he would be dead before he heard the sound of the machine-gun. He could feel the mud against his face, taste it on his lips; something slid over his legs, cold as the finger of death. What a way to go, he thought; and all at once wanted to weep for all the lost opportunities. He was only thirty-six and even old Phil Frisco, the seventy-year-old punchie in the gym on Fourth Street in downtown San Francisco, would die with no less dignity than this. *You'll come to a bad end with all that money and that sort of company,* Josef Czeicinski had said. Well, the old man had been half right. Only there was no money and you couldn't call this young Limey stranger company. Leastways, not the sort of company the old man had been talking about.

Then the beam abruptly swung away from them, swept quickly on across the flats, swept back once more and was switched off. The motor of the boat was speeded up and the boat turned and began to churn its way back towards the Causeway. It was as if the Japanese were already becoming careless. The war in Malaya had finished tonight; the war in the Pacific would be over in a matter of weeks. The Japanese patrol was evidently on its way back to the celebrations that must be going on.

Garrick scrambled to his feet and without looking back at Case began to stumble at a run across the flats towards the screen of mangroves. Case raised himself up, stood swaying like a man caught in a wind of indecision. Then he, too, began to run towards the mangroves, jogging along as if he were once again doing roadwork.

Garrick reached the tree, dropped his suitcase and began to run up and down the long line of twisted trunks. Case stopped and stood watching him, grinning with the idiot amusement of a good-tempered drunk.

'What you looking for, muh friend?'

'A boat. There should be a boat here! I paid that thieving Chinaman——'

'That it?' Case pointed, his finger stabbing through a singing veil of mosquitoes.

It was a small boat, wedged between two trees, held tight by their gnarled limbs as if caught by two old men who hated to give it up. Garrick jumped towards it, had to grab hold of it as his feet slipped in the mud; then he began to haul on it, trying to pull it out from between the trees. His breath came

8

in great sobs as he almost wept with exhaustion and panic.

'Help me, for God's sake! Just don't stand there!'

Case moved across to the boat, set his whisky bottle carefully in the bottom of it, then took hold of one side of the boat and heaved. The boat remained stuck fast for a moment, the old men trees refusing to let go; then abruptly it slipped out, went sliding down over the mud. Case and Garrick fell back, each losing his grip and sliding across the mud like beginners on an ice rink.

Garrick struggled to his feet, dropped his suitcase into the boat and began to push the boat towards the water fifty yards away. He was making almost no progress at all till Case joined him; then the boat began to slide smoothly across the slime. They pushed it out into the water and clambered in. Garrick picked up the one set of oars and stroked the boat out into deeper water.

Case lay back on the bottom of the boat, leaning against one of the seats. He shivered a little as a cool breeze came up the water from the west, and took a swig of Johnnie Walker's liquid warmth. 'Where we headed now?'

'Kiepang, up the coast. I can buy a bigger boat there.' Garrick, as he rowed, was staring back at the gradually fading lights of the Causeway, as if expecting every one of them to turn suddenly into a blazing searchlight.

'Where you headed after that?' Case had woken up a little, throwing off some of the effects of the whisky. Texas was not so thick on his tongue.

Garrick rested a moment on the oars, getting his breath. Gradually he seemed to be relaxing, the nervous irritability going out of his voice. 'As you say, that's a good question. Any suggestions?'

'Miami is always good this time of year.' Case had another drink, then offered the bottle to Garrick. 'Sorry. Forgetting my manners.'

'I told you, I'm a teetotaller, or almost.' Then Garrick, too, apologised: 'Sorry. That sounded pretty stuffy.'

He began to row again, rowing west, down the Straits of Johore and out towards the Straits of Malacca and the open sea, moving at no more than six knots on the ebbing tide on a journey that might take them forever. Because he had no idea where they might head after Kiepang. He looked at the dark figure in the bottom of the boat, but could make out no recognisable feature. The two men were still just silhouettes to each other in the darkness. Cripes, Garrick thought, here I am escaping from Singapore with a chap whose face I've never seen. They always told me at the bank I'd never make it to manager, I was too trusting. Why can't I be cautious and suspicious just once in a while? My dad always did say the blood in me couldn't be good Yorkshire stuff, thick as treacle with suspicion of strangers.

'Where did you get the bottle?' he asked. 'I thought they confiscated all the grog on the island?'

'Not all of it.' Case grinned like a schoolboy, but Garrick couldn't see the smile; he could only hear the chuckle in the voice. 'Why did they do it? Who's in charge of Singapore? The Women's Temperance Union?'

'I heard they were afraid of what happened in Hong Kong. The Nips got drunk there, ran amok and had a right old time.'

'So the army brass *did* have an idea the Japs might take over Singapore?'

Garrick looked shrewdly at the man sprawled in the bottom of the boat. 'You're pretty sharp for a chap who's supposed to be drunk.'

Again there was the chuckle. 'I get drunk occasionally, but I ain't stupid.' There was a pause, then: 'Well, occasionally I'm stupid too. But not about this. I know a balled-up mess when I see one. You notice? There ain't a trench anywhere on this side of the island, though they knew the Japs were coming this way. They don't dig trenches, but they start destroying all the booze. I ain't prejudiced——' He lifted the bottle and in the darkness winked at it. 'But I think they got their priorities wrong.'

'We all make mistakes.' Tolerance was a weakness with Garrick, and he knew it. Anger was something he had to work on, stoking it up over days sometimes; but even when it burst out of him, it was only a small blaze and more often than not he was embarrassed by it. He knew that later on he *would* be angry about what had happened in Singapore; but not now. Even disaster took time to have its effect on him. *You'll never make a cricketer*, said his father, who could be made angry by a change in the wind, *you don't have enough guts to hate the other chap*. What his father had meant was, *you'll never make a man*, but Charlie Garrick had always seen the whole world as a cricket field. The thought of his father brought a spark in him and he said, 'But they'll pay for it.'

'They already have,' said Case, and turned in the bottom of the boat and looked back at the red glow in the sky. 'If I never see another army sonofabitch, it'll be too soon. Wars might be tolerable if it weren't for them bastards.' He looked back at Garrick and chuckled again. 'Head somewhere, friend, where there ain't any army. If a man can help it, he ought never get himself involved in someone else's war.'

Garrick wondered whose war the American thought this was. He himself had never disowned the war in Europe and over England; he might have disowned Leeds, but his mum and dad and sisters still did live there. Sometimes he had felt a twinge of conscience at being in the safety of Singapore, though it had not been enough to drive him back home. But after to-night there would be no need for conscience: Leeds at least still belonged to England, Yorkshire and his mum and dad. Suddenly he grinned. 'How about Tahiti?'

They were getting close to the open sea now. Stars were caught in the bracken of clouds, and there was a hint of moonlight below the horizon. A damp breeze came in at them, insinuating itself into their bones; both men shivered and Garrick turned up the collar of his jacket, his Sunday suit. He had dressed for his escape from the island as if he had been going to a sherry party at the bank manager's home; that had been his mother's influence. *Always dress for the occasion*, she had said when he had left Leeds; and even at a remove of nine thousand miles he had always tried to please her. He had always dressed for the occasion: sherry parties, funerals, escape from the Japanese.

He put down the oars, scrambled to the back of the boat and with some difficulty lifted the small outboard motor into place. Case lay watching him, not attempting to help him. Garrick fumbled with the starter, but nothing happened. He tried again and again, but got not even a cough from the engine. Then Case raised himself up and without a word took the starter cord from Garrick. He gave it one flick and the engine at once burst into life.

The two men sat close together on the rear seat of the boat, seeing each other clearly for the first time in the light of the rising moon. Garrick saw a blond man in his mid-thirties, solidly built with shoulders whose strength was apparent beneath the torn blue shirt. The face might once have been good-looking but now it was worn at the edges; the cheeks seemed to have been flattened, the nose was slightly crooked, the good-humoured eyes were hidden under brows made heavy by scar tissue. Case saw a boy in his early twenties, black-haired and thin-faced; he might have been ugly but for the warm friendliness in his eyes and the curve of his mouth. They looked at each other and each committed himself.

'Well, here we go,' said Case.

Then they saw the tracers, like deadly fireflies, coming out at them from the dark shore.

2

The voice was unsteady, as if the speaker were drunk or was trying not to weep: or both, thought Maynard.

'. . . As of twenty-three hundred hours last night the war in Malaya has ended. All our forces are to lay down their arms at once. Anyone who disobeys this order and continues to fight will be punished by death by our'—the voice faltered just a moment—'honourable foe, the Nippon Army. We repeat, lay down your arms and surrender to the nearest troops of the glorious Nippon Army.' One of the men listening to the radio made a rude noise with his mouth. 'This is our final broadcast. The war in Malaya is over.'

'Like hell it is!' said Maynard.

The men looked up to him, indifferent to his anger. He was the only one on his feet among the sixteen men here in the clearing in the rubber plantation. The others, exhausted and dispirited by six weeks of fruitless fighting, lolled in the coarse grass or lay back against the trunks of the rubber trees. Despair had drained all resistance from them: they were as indifferent to Maynard's anger as they were to the insects that crawled over them. They were dead men, past caring about defeat or insect bites.

The English voice went off the air and was replaced by a Japanese voice speaking a sibilant sort of English: 'And now something to keep up your spirits . . .'

Strains of music filtered through the plantation, then Bing Crosby began to tell the men he was dreaming of a White Christmas. They had reached this abandoned rubber estate last night, had slept in the house, then moved down into the cover of the plantation at first light. During the night they had heard trucks passing on the road bordering the estate, but no one had disturbed them. But none of them had dreamed of a White Christmas.

A short grizzled man, with a long sharp face and the lean build of an Australian cattle dog, pushed back his broad-brimmed hat and spat disgustedly. 'Wouldn't it tear you?' He reached across and switched off the field radio. 'Well, that's the end of our little gallop. Now we better start learning Japanese. What's Jap for, *Up You, Jack?*'

'I think I might ask them to ship me to Tokyo.' Another Australian, a boy with a bandage round his head, began to roll a cigarette. 'Those Nip sheilas ain't bad. Great stuff with the massage. They take their shoes off and run up and down your spine in their bare feet. Very sexy.'

'You dirty-minded bugger,' said Polo Murphy, the first man who had spoken. 'Always got your mind on it.'

'What else is there? Especially now the war's over.'

'The war isn't over!' Maynard had been about to walk out of the circle of men, but now he turned back, staring hard at the young Australian. Tall and well-built, he looked even bigger than he was as he stood among the sprawled boneless men. 'They still have to take us. We're not going in with our hands up like a bunch of schoolgirls——'

He looked around belligerently at the men. They were a mixed bunch: nine Englishmen, all of them from Maynard's own unit; four Australians, each wearing the A.I.F. Eighth Division colour patch on the puggaree of his slouch hat; and two Sikhs, their tin helmets looking incongruous above their bearded faces. Circumstances had thrown them together a week ago when their respective units had finally disintegrated before the Japanese as they came down through Malaya. Maynard, the only officer in the party, had taken charge and even the Australians, from whom he had expected trouble, had accepted him. Up till now . . .

'You couldn't of been listening to what the bloke said.' Polo Murphy took out a battered packet of Capstans, extracted a cigarette and lit it, and shoved the packet back in his ammunition pouch. Maynard, an impatient man, waited patiently, aware that some sort of rebellion was brewing. 'The Nips will carve us up soon's they catch us, if we go on playing soldiers.'

'I'm not suggesting we *play* soldiers,' Maynard said coldly. 'I'm suggesting we *be* soldiers.'

Peters, the young wounded Australian, whistled a martial tune, somehow managing to make it sound sarcastic. Some of the Englishmen smiled, but the two Sikhs, like bearded schoolboys, looked uncertainly from the English officer to the careless, scornful Australians. They were not accustomed to this sort of disregard for discipline. But the elder of them, Corporal Singh, privately thought the Australian, Murphy, had something. He would have been willing to die with pride, almost with gladness, in the Punjab; but not here in Malaya. In the last couple of months he had lost all the respect he had once had for the British Raj.

'Your Pommy brass shoulda thought of that a coupla months ago.' Polo puffed on his cigarette. 'I never seen a shambles like this campaign——'

Suddenly there was a piercing whistle. Maynard spun round, looked up to where an Australian was perched high in the branches of a rubber tree. 'Nips! Coming down the road!'

'How many?'

'Coupla hundred at least. On bikes.'

Maynard raced up through the plantation to the estate bungalow. He bounded up the steps to the wide veranda, ran along to a corner that looked down over a shallow valley. He took his binoculars from their case, adjusted the focus and at once picked up the blue line of the main road as it scrawled its way down through the rubber trees and looped up the ridge on the far side of the valley. The Japanese, at least two companies of them, were coming down the road a couple of miles away, riding three abreast on bicycles, the wheels of which glittered in the sun so that at this distance the column looked like a long shining snake.

Maynard turned as the other men came up on the veranda behind him. 'We'll ambush these blighters. Murphy, you and Singh and Barrow——'

Polo stubbed out his cigarette, put the butt away in the battered packet. 'Not me, sport. You heard what the bloke said on the wireless. The war's over.'

'I'm giving you an order, Private Murphy.'

'You know what you can do with your order. I'm in the A.I.F. I'm not in your mob.' Polo looked around at the men gathered behind him on the veranda; then he looked back at Maynard. 'Look, mate, I ain't a dingo. I'll fight as good as the next bloke when the odds are good enough. But what's the point now of getting our throats cut, just to kill a few more Nips? We kill those bastards down the road there, it ain't gunna win the war.'

'We kill as many as we can!' Maynard knew he was losing his dignity and his authority by snarling, but he couldn't help it.

'Like I said, your brass shoulda thought of that months ago.'

'Don't lump Captain Maynard in with the base wallahs.' Hutton, Maynard's sergeant, stepped forward. He was a big ox of a man who looked as if he might have spent all his life till the war locked in the second row of a rugby football pack; his nose was flattened and his ears looked as if they had been screwed flat to his head by the hips of hundreds of brawling forwards. In fact he had been in the army for twenty years and hated all kinds of sport except beer-drinking and brothel-visiting. 'He doesn't think any more of them than you do.'

'Well, why the blazes didn't he do something about it?' Polo demanded.

'In the British Army,' Maynard said, 'captains don't tell their generals what they can do with their orders. Even when we feel like it.'

'Well, you're all lumped in together, far as I'm concerned.' Polo unslung his rifle, as if he were already preparing to surrender to the Japanese, now only a mile away. 'Don't talk about trying to win the war now. Your mob chucked it in ages ago.'

'Not all of us have *chucked* it in.' A vein quivered in Maynard's temple as he struggled to keep control of himself. He knew that once he lost control of himself he would also have lost control of these men. 'I was taken at Dunkirk—but I'm not going to be taken again! I'm continuing the war—and anyone who doesn't like it had better start moving now.'

He looked around the men, challenging them, challenging *himself*. Because deep within him he could feel the slowly growing cancer of doubt: was it really worthwhile going on? Then the men began to answer him. One of them picked up the Bren gun he had set down on the veranda, turned and pushed his way through the men, went down the steps and ran lumbering across the road. Other men followed him, moving reluctantly at first as if a little ashamed of what they were doing. Singh looked at his fellow Sikh, nodded, and the two men, faces expressionless, turned and ran down the steps and up behind a line of pink-flowered oleanders.

Maynard looked at Polo. 'You'd better go if you're going.'

Only Polo and Peters remained on the veranda with Maynard. The older Australian looked at the younger man and shrugged. 'I want me bloody head read. The missus would kill me if she knew I was staying here, shoving me neck out like this.'

'You mean you take orders from your missus?' Maynard said drily.

Polo eyed him quizzically. 'I don't think you and me are

15

gonna get on, mate. Not if this private little war of yours keeps up too long.'

Then he and Peters turned abruptly about and, now that they had committed themselves, moved briskly down the steps and up through the bungalow garden towards the road. Maynard took a last look at the approaching Japanese through his binoculars, then he too left the veranda and took up his place for the ambush. This was the fourth ambush they had staged in the past week and every man knew the drill. Maynard might be irritated by the independence of some of the men he commanded, but he admired their ability. Most of them might be volunteers, amateurs to a professional like himself, but in the past two months they had acquired a professionalism that two years of peacetime manœuvres could never have given them.

He lay behind a bank, sheltered from the fierce morning sun by a clump of bougainvillaea that, supported by a tall tree stump which it had enveloped, rose up like a towering pillar of purple fire. The estate garden had run riot since the plantation workers had moved out; temple flowers, Croton, Indian laburnum covered the ground like floral lava. He took off his cap and wiped the sweat from his brow; he wondered how Ruth would be enduring the winter at home. English-born but Kenya-reared, she hated the northern climate. They had met and married within six weeks; then a week later war had broken out. Since then they had spent only two months together . . . He put his cap back on and looked down the road, trying to forget England.

The Japanese were approaching the top of a slope. Below them was a narrow bridge that crossed a small stream bordering the plantation. Now he could see them clearly without the aid of his binoculars: a bicycle club out for a jaunt, the only false note the rifles slung over their backs. They rode sitting up straight, legs moving in unison, the wheels spinning a moving mirage beneath them. They were singing, happy victors on their way to collect the club's prizes. The song floated over the valley, the wild, lilting chanty that Maynard had heard several times since he had made contact with the Japanese: *Tai Hei Yo*, which someone had told him meant *O Great Pacific*. The song had almost a Western rhythm to it and sung by almost three hundred men it had the perverse effect of stirring Maynard's blood. All military men love a martial song, even those of the enemy. Damn it, thought Maynard, and tried to shut his ears against the song.

Then suddenly at the top of the rise above the bridge the song ended on a dissonant note. For one horrifying moment Maynard thought the ambush party had been spotted; he waited for the Japanese to fall from their bicycles and dive for defensive positions. But they kept coming and next moment they were singing again, this time another song. Then he remembered that *Tai Hei Yo* always ended on that abrupt discordant note, almost the only Oriental dissonance in the whole song. He recognised the new song, the Sousa-like *Ai Koku Koshin Kyoku*. The Japs were certainly happy this morning.

They came down the slope, gathering speed, some of them breaking off the song to laugh out aloud like schoolboys. The first ranks of them swept across the bridge, rose up on their pedals for the push up the rise on this side of the stream. Then Maynard opened up with his Thompson gun.

In a moment the song had been lost in the roar and chatter of the ambush party's fire. The Japanese fell off their bicycles, some of them with their mouths still open, but screaming now, not singing. They went down in a wild tangle of men, bicycles and rifles. As the first ranks went crashing down, those behind, unable to stop their speed down the slope, ploughed into them. The Japanese sprawled like crippled ducks in the fire of the ambush party. And Maynard, son of a clergyman, product of a public school, revelled in the slaughter. Frustration, anger and hatred had stripped the veneer from him. England was another world, forgotten now, and everything in him was concentrated on the bridge below where the Japanese were being massacred.

A few of the Japanese had fallen off the bridge into the stream; red streaks dyed the water. At the rear of the column some of the enemy had dived for cover behind the bodies of their dead comrades, had unslung their rifles and were returning the fire of the ambush party. Maynard suddenly stopped pumping his Thompson gun, took control of himself again. The ambush had achieved its aim; if they stayed any longer it would develop into a fixed battle. He put his whistle to his lips and blew it.

At once the firing from up here on either side of the road stopped. The Japanese continued to shoot, but they were firing blindly, still unable to see the ambush party. Maynard slid back through the grass, got to his feet and, crouching over, ran back towards the house. Hutton and three of the men were already there waiting for him.

'Everyone all right, sergeant?'

Hutton shook his head. 'We lost Prosser, Barrett, two of the Aussies and one of the Indians. Lucky shots got them, sir. Our blokes must of got careless.'

Maynard wasn't sure why he asked, 'Was the Australian that chap Murphy?'

'No, sir. The young cove, Peters.'

Maynard said nothing, but all at once he was aware of a great heaviness seeping through him. He looked at the three men standing silently behind Hutton; their faces were blank and it was impossible to read their thoughts behind their dull eyes. But their very silence was a judgement, he felt. He turned quickly away, busying himself with being a soldier, trying to bury the man he was. Other men were now running up through the garden, and he felt a physical sense of pain when he saw that two or three of them were limping. One man suddenly stopped, sat down and looked as if he were about to take off his boots. Then all at once he keeled over and died, his bloody head lying like a bouquet among the fallen temple flowers. Polo Murphy stopped beside him, knelt down and jerked off the dead man's meat-tags, then stood up and came running on, his bowed legs looking as if they might collapse at any moment.

'Where to now?' He stopped beside Maynard, breathing heavily, wiping his nose with a bloodstained finger. 'You better get us outa here, sport, or I'm likely to hand you over to the Nips meself. If they take us, I'm gonna tell 'em what rat-bag organised that little picnic back there.'

There was still some spasmodic firing going on down along the road, but the Japanese were evidently not yet organised enough to start seeking out the ambush party. Maynard quickly counted the survivors. 'Ten of us. Righto, we'll make for the hills that way.' He pointed. 'We'll split up, go in pairs. There's a village called Kiepang on the coast, about twelve miles from here. I was up there once on a recce trip. We'll try and grab a boat.'

'Where to then, sir?' asked Hutton.

'Sumatra,' said Maynard; then he glanced at Polo. 'After that, we might try for Australia.'

'Two thousand bloody miles away?' said Polo. 'You want your bloody head read.'

At dusk that evening Maynard crouched among the low semi-circular stones of a Chinese cemetery on the edge of Kiepang. With him were Hutton and six other men.

'That leaves Murphy and Singh to come, sir,' said Hutton. 'Unless they've run into some Nips on the way.'

'If they have, Murphy will talk his way out of it.' Maynard looked out to sea where dark ropes of clouds were strangling the setting sun. 'We'll give them five more minutes——'

Then they heard the voice. 'I tell you, Gandhi, it's years since I felt as crook as this. Once I had German measles, caught 'em from the missus——'

Two figures loomed up out of the dusk and Maynard said, 'All right, Murphy, that's enough of your troubles.'

Polo and Singh flopped down beside the other men. Polo took out a cigarette, went to light it, then stopped when he saw the other men weren't smoking. 'Nips in the village?'

'We don't know,' Hutton said. 'Captain Maynard and me are going down for a recce.'

'We'll stay away from the village,' Maynard said. 'All we want is to grab a boat.' He pointed down towards the beach below the village where a line of fishing boats was clearly silhouetted against the rose-gold water. 'We'll have a look at that big one on the end.'

Polo stood up. 'I'll go with you.'

'Why?' said Maynard.

'Just to check you know what you're doing. I ain't going two thousand miles in some leaky old rowboat. Fair enough, mates?' Polo looked around at the other men, didn't seem disturbed that none of them nodded in agreement.

'It's unfortunate for you, Private Murphy,' said Maynard, 'but we don't have trade unions in the British Army. We'll do it my way. When I need your advice about leaky old rowboats, I'll ask for it. Come on, sergeant.'

He moved off before Polo could continue the argument, Hutton keeping close behind him. The sun had dropped suddenly, the ocean turning all at once from gold to dull cast-iron. The village was not a large one: a long line of atap-roofed native huts backing on to the beach and, on the other side of a narrow road from them, half a dozen more solidly-built houses, the homes and stores of Chinese traders. In the suddenly damp air the smell of the sea and rotting fish came up the beach at them as they moved past the hundred trunks of a banyan tree and stepped out on to the sand. They ran quickly down towards the water, keeping an eye on the backs of the huts. But everyone seemed to be inside the huts preparing or eating their evening meal, and Maynard and Hutton reached the line of boats without being hailed.

In the pattern of shadows made by the boats, Maynard straightened up. 'This one should do,' he said in a low voice. 'I'll be big enough for all of us. And there's a sail.'

The boat was about twenty-five feet long, strongly built and with a tall mast from which hung a rattan sail, a prahu built for going far out to sea. 'What about food and water?' Hutton said.

Maynard looked back up towards the village. 'I'm wondering if we should risk it. Some of these villagers might give us away to the Japs——'

Then he heard the sound of the motor boat out at sea. He spun round, straining his eyes to peer out into the darkness.

'Nips?' Hutton muttered.

Maynard shrugged. He dropped down on one knee, crouching below the level of the gunwale of the prahu; and Hutton followed his example. Maynard had left his Thompson gun with one of the men in the cemetery; now he took his pistol from its holster and thumbed back the safety catch. Hutton had his Thompson gun and Maynard heard him check the magazine.

'Do we jump them, sir?'

Maynard shook his head. 'Only if we have to.'

The engine of the motor boat cut out and there was silence but for the lap-lap of the water against the sand. Up in the village a dog barked and someone shouted at it. Then Maynard heard the sound of oars. He raised his head above the gunwale of the prahu and looked out to sea. Dimly he saw the boat sliding in out of the darkness, one man on the oars and another sitting in the stern. He looked at Hutton, nodded at the sergeant's Thompson gun and shook his head. He put his own pistol back in its holster and took from his belt the *tumbok lada*, the small Malayan knife he had bought in a bazaar in Port Swettenham. The owner of the stall had told him that it was a lover's knife, designed to strike deep at the heart. He tightened his grip on the carved handle and got ready to drive it into the heart of a Japanese.

The motor boat, engine silent, came drifting in. There was the sound of the oars being shipped, then the boat had grounded on the sand. The man at the stern of the boat half-fell over the side, giggling to himself at his own awkwardness. He went down on his knees in the water, hanging on to the side of the boat. He made a noise, a sort of giggling snort, and the man who had been rowing hissed at him. Then the man in the water turned and saw Maynard and Hutton.

Maynard moved swiftly. He went round the back of the prahu and across the space between himself and the man in the water in two steps and a dive. He hit the man with all his weight and the two of them sprawled down in the water. Maynard brought up his arm, ready to drive home the knife.

Then, 'I surrender, Tojo! You just won the war!' said Case, and fell back beneath the water.

Maynard stopped the knife half-way down towards the other man's chest. He spat with disgust, stood up and looked across at Hutton, who had Garrick bent back over the gunwale of the boat.

'What's yours, sergeant?'

'Another civilian, sir,' said Hutton. 'Not a very good speci-men, either.'

Garrick straightened up, spluttering with indignation. There had been little commotion, but people were already running down from the village, followed by the soldiers from the ceme-tery. Maynard, on edge now, took out his pistol and looked beyond the approaching villagers to see if any Japanese were behind them. But there appeared to be only children and dogs bringing up the rear.

He looked back at Garrick. 'Who the hell are you?'

Garrick, his indignation already spent, introduced himself. 'I'm from the British Singapore Bank. This is Case.' He indi-cated the American as the latter, spitting water, struggled to his feet and leaned gasping against the boat. 'I don't know where he's from or what he does.'

Case, sun-blistered from the long day in the boat, head aching from his hangover, looked around at the small crowd. In the darkness it was impossible to see their expressions, but he could tell from their attitude, that of the Malays and soldiers alike, that he and Garrick were not too welcome. He grinned, as much at himself as at the crowd. 'Yo' can go home, folks. The bout's over.'

He saw the army officer, the one who had attempted to knife him, look hard at him; then the officer had turned away to face the villagers. 'Who is the head man here? We want a boat and some food and water.'

A young Chinese pushed his way through the crowd. 'I own all the boats. These people work for me.'

I might have known it, Maynard thought. The Chinese had begun their quiet invasion of Malaya long before the Japanese had thought of the same thing. 'How much for the biggest boat?'

The young Chinese sucked on his teeth. 'What money do you have? English pounds or Straits dollars?'

'We don't have any money,' said Maynard, angry at being made to feel foolish by this profiteering young Chinese. 'I'll write you a chit.'

The Chinese laughed, a laugh made more irritating by its high harsh note. 'And who will collect it? My grandchildren? Sorry, mister. Try somewhere else.'

'Righto, we asked him.' Polo had stepped to the front of the group of soldiers as they stood to one side. 'Now let's blow his head off and take the boat. We mucked about long enough.'

There was a growl of assent from one or two of the men. The Chinese had been about to turn away, but he stopped and looked across at the soldiers. The Malays had been pressing around him, but now they backed away, leaving him exposed. Some of the later arriving villagers had brought oil lamps with them and the flickering yellow light seemed to make the soldiers bigger and more threatening. The Chinese for the first time seemed to realise that these men were desperate, no relation at all to the servicemen with whom he had bargained in his store before the Japanese had entered the war.

Pessimistically Maynard thought, Perhaps we'll never come back here to Malaya. We can't leave here as murderers. 'I don't want to steal your boat, but if I have to——'

'We'll pay him for it,' said Garrick stepping forward, taking money from the inside pocket of his jacket. 'There's about a hundred Straits dollars there.'

'It's not enough,' said the Chinese, but there was not much argument in his voice; he was looking at Polo rather than at Garrick or Maynard. 'The boat is worth double that at least.'

'I'm afraid you'll have to take it and like it.' Garrick stepped up to the Chinese and thrust the money into the other's shirt pocket. 'We'll want food and water for it, too. Enough for all of us.'

'Who said you two were coming with us?' Maynard demanded.

'No, you're coming with me and my friend.' Garrick was amazed at his own temerity. I'm showing off, he thought. This is how money goes to your head. 'I'm the one who's paying for this little trip.'

'Attaboy,' said Case. 'Those army guys think they never need us civilians.'

Then his legs buckled and he fell back into the motor boat. Maynard looked down at him, then turned disgustedly away. 'Who would ever need the likes of him?' Then he looked at Garrick. 'All right, Garrick. We accept your offer. I'll write *you* a chit.'

'No need,' said Garrick airily, for the first time in his life a big time spender. 'It's on me.'

'Where are you headed for?' The Chinese stood sullenly to one side, nursing his money and his resentment, while the Malays ran giggling up towards his store.

Maynard shook his head. 'That's our business. I don't trust you. If there are any Japs in the neighbourhood you'd give us away without any compunction. Am I right?'

The Chinese stared at him, then nodded. 'I hate you English. You are finished now.'

'Let's see how you like your new masters.' I should blow his head off, Maynard thought, just as Murphy suggested. It would be wanton murder, but he had reached a stage where wantonness might be the only valve to release the anger and frustration he felt. His hand, as if unfettered by any conscience, had already begun to move towards his pistol when he was interrupted by Hutton.

'They have some fruit here, sir. Shall we take it? It might go rotten.'

He turned quickly on his heel, suddenly glad of the interruption, and strode down over the sand to the prahu. He stopped by the motor boat where Garrick was trying to get Case on his feet.

'He seems to have passed out,' Garrick said. 'He had a lot to drink——'

'Then leave him.'

'*Leave him?*'

'He looks like a derelict to me, just a drunk. He'll give us nothing but trouble.'

Garrick stood up, letting Case fall back into the boat. 'Look, who the blazes do you think——'

Then there was a shout from up by the village and a Malay came running down the beach. He was shouting in Malay, but Maynard caught the word for *Japanese*.

He swung round, ran to the prahu. 'Everybody here?'

'Murphy went up to one of the stores for some cigarettes.' Hutton scooped up the heap of fruit at his feet and dropped it into the prahu. There were also two water-cans and he dumped those on board. Then he turned round and yelled in his parade ground voice: 'Murphy!'

The beach was now a confusion of scattering figures. Polo came running down the beach and the last of the soldiers were scrambling aboard the prahu. The Malays had doused their oil lamps and were fleeing for the jungle farther along the beach. Garrick, burdened by his suitcase and Case, was stumbling through the shallow water to the prahu. Only the Chinese stood still, gazing up towards the village like a man waiting for the police to arrive to break up the antics of some troublesome schoolboys.

'I think a bullet up his backside might do him the world of good,' said Hutton, as he pulled Maynard into the prahu.

Then there was a sudden sound of a shot and the Chinese spun round and fell over. A moment later there was a fusillade of shots from up near the huts and bullets smacked into the rattan sail above Maynard's head. Some of the men jumped overboard and began to push the prahu out from the sand. Others picked up oars and began to paddle furiously. Hutton was bending over the engine in the bottom of the boat, cursing it as he tried to kick some life into it. The Japanese were still shooting, but they were firing too high; the rattan sail was disintegrating, falling on the men in a rain of splinters. Then one of the men, struggling to get into the prahu from the water, suddenly gasped and fell back. Maynard made a grab for him, but was too late. The engine all of a sudden coughed into life and the prahu gathered speed, seeming to shoot out from the beach towards the black night sea. The dead or wounded man, Maynard would never know which, fell back beneath the dark water.

The prahu was racing through the water, bucking the slight swell coming in from the sea. Maynard saw one or two of the men raise their rifles to shoot back at the Japanese and he yelled, 'Don't shoot back! If they can't see our fire, they can't pin us down!' Even as he spoke there were further smacks as bullets hit the mast and sail and more splinters rained down on the men. Maynard could see the quick pinpoints of fire along the black shore, but the Japanese seemed to have lost the range. Occasionally there would be the loud smack of a bullet ricochetting off the water, but nothing was now coming near the prahu.

Maynard sat up, shifting his buttocks uncomfortably on the narrow seat that ran along the side of the boat. He looked around at the dark figures of the men crowded together in the boat. Then he became aware of the man slumped beside him. He looked across Case at Garrick, sitting with his suitcase resting on his knees.

'I thought I told you to leave him?'

Case raised his head, spat something from his lips. 'Ah heard you say that.' He spoke slowly and deliberately, like a man trying to control a loose tongue. 'Ah told muh friend Ah didn't wanna come, but he insisted.' His tongue slipped on the last word and he repeated it. 'Insisted.'

Maynard stared at him for a moment; then he said, 'Sober up then. There's no room in this boat for anyone who can't pull his weight.'

'Yo' don't have to worry, buster.' Case sat up, carefully and with some effort. 'Ah'm as good a weight-puller as you'll ever be. Better maybe.'

Maynard said nothing, not wanting to continue the conversation. But Case seemed intent on proving that he was now sober, concerned for people other than himself. He grasped Maynard's arm and the latter, even through his own irritation, was surprised at the strength in the American's fingers.

'What's gonna happen to those natives back there?'

'I don't know,' said Maynard, taking Case's hand and lifting it from his arm as he might have removed a crab. 'But we can't help them by going back.'

'Well, that's a goddam non-committal attitude, ain't it?' Case was still speaking carefully, almost as if he were using a foreign language. He looked around at the other men, but it was impossible to tell whether they were interested or not in what he was saying. 'We walk into their place uninvited, draw the flies like a piece of candy——'

Then one of the men let out a shout. 'Back there!'

Everyone turned to look back at the shore. A sudden blaze leapt out of the darkness, beginning as a small flame, then quickly spreading. The whole village was all at once visible as it went up in fire; huts stood out for a moment and then were gone as the flames swallowed them. The scene was reflected in the water along the beach, the village dying twice. Small dark figures could be seen flitting in silhouette across the leaping yellow background. The prahu was too far out for any sound to be heard and the village and its people seemed to be dying in silence.

'The bastards,' said Polo, and for once Maynard agreed with him.

Maynard turned to say something to Hutton and saw Case staring at him. Even in the darkness he knew that the American was accusing him. All of a sudden the whole past two months burst out of him: the stupidity and selfishness of those in charge of Singapore, the senseless sacrifice of men and ships and aircraft, the continuous fighting, the heat and discomfort and exhaustion, and finally this merciless slaughter of a harmless people and the destruction of their homes: 'Do you think I don't bloody well care! Good Christ, who are you, an American, to pass judgement——!

Reason went, and he lunged at Case. But the latter almost casually threw up an arm and warded off the blow. Then Hutton and another man had pulled Maynard back.

'Steady, sir.' Hutton spoke as he might have to a child. 'We're all a bit on edge. Take it easy, sir.'

Maynard simmered down. Breathing heavily, he made himself relax. For Christ's sake, don't talk to me like some bloody nanny, he thought; but all he said was, 'I'm all right now, sergeant. You can stop trying to throttle me. It isn't conducive to good order and military discipline.'

He heard Case chuckle and he wasn't sure whether the American was laughing at him or with him. Why am I allowing this drunk to get under my skin like this? He was exhausted enough by his responsibility for the other men, by the doubting antagonism of the Australian, Murphy. Why take on another opponent, expose himself to the jibes of a beachcomber? He looked again at Case, saw the American was watching him, and turned quickly away. And knew even that was a confession of weakness.

Hutton stepped back and almost fell over Garrick's suitcase, which had slipped off the latter's knees as he had tried to get out of the way of the scuffle.

'What the hell have you got there?' Hutton said.

Garrick hesitated a moment. 'Love letters.'

'Well, keep 'em to yourself, matey. This boat is too crowded as it is.'

Maynard looked about the boat, trying his best to be an officer again. The commandant at Sandhurst would have thrown the book at him for that display of temper and lack of self-discipline a moment ago. And his father, the clergyman, would certainly have found a quotation aimed at both shaming and improving him.

26

'We'd better have a head count,' he said. 'There should be twelve of us. Counting you two.' He looked at Garrick and Case as if he would have preferred *not* to count them. 'We'll have a roll call, Sergeant Hutton?'

'Sir.'

Maynard went through the names, concentrating to remember those of the men who did not belong to his battalion. 'Garrick—is that your name?'

Garrick nodded. 'That's it.'

'Any relation to Charlie Garrick plays for Yorkshire?' asked one of the men.

'Let's get this finished first,' Maynard interrupted. 'Then we'll have the biographies. What's your name?' He looked at Case.

Case told him. 'And we'll skip the biographies. I don't wanna get to know you that well.'

'It's mutual, I assure you,' said Maynard; then looked up towards the silent figure in the bow of the boat. He counted all the heads again, then once more looked at the man in the bow. 'Thirteen. Who the blazes are you?'

The man fumbled in his pocket, then passed something to the soldier next to him to hand to Maynard. 'My card, signore.'

'Signore?' Maynard heard his voice crack with incredulity.

He took the small business card handed him and Hutton, shielding the light with a huge hand, switched on a field torch.

'*Vittorio Cabrolini*,' Maynard read. '*Fiat Representative.*'

'Holy Nellie!' said Polo. 'A bloody Eyetie!'

One or two of the men laughed, some growled, but all of them stared with disbelief at the nervous figure sitting up straight in the bow of the boat.

'I am sorry I had to board your vessel unannounced.' Cabrolini's accent was not unpleasant; he had obviously learned English from a good teacher. 'But those Japanese were chasing me——'

'Where did you come from?' Maynard demanded.

'I have been the Fiat representative in Indo-China for four years. My headquarters were in Saigon——'

'One of Musso's spies, I'll bet a quid on it,' growled Polo.

Cabrolini shook his head, almost too fiercely. 'No, signore. I am not interested in politics. Just motor cars and aeroplane engines. When the Japanese landed in Saigon, I went to them, told them I was a friendly alien, that we were on the same side——'

'Throw him overboard!' someone snapped.

'Please, signori!' There was panic in Cabrolini's voice now; his accent suddenly got thicker. 'All I want is to get back to Italy.'

Maynard told the men to keep quiet, then looked back at the Italian. Who else am I going to be stuck with? he wondered. 'Go on,' he said, and kept his voice cold, determined not to encourage the Italian till he could see him in daylight.

Cabrolini hesitated, then he went on: 'The Japanese would not listen to me. They threw me into a prison camp with everybody else. But I managed to escape, and I ran away, all the way down through Siam into Malaya.'

'That's all you Eyeties are good at, running,' said Polo.

Cabrolini suffered the insult in silence: he was in no position to start defending national pride. He waited till Maynard told him to continue, then he went on: 'I got to Kuala Lumpur. By then I was exhausted—any prison would have been a rest camp. I told the English I was an *enemy* alien, would they please put me in an internment camp. But they told me they had troubles of their own, would I please not bother them. Then the Japanese arrived and I started running again.' He looked in the direction of Polo and said, 'Just like you gentlemen are doing now.'

Polo made a move, but Maynard snapped, 'All right, that's enough!'

'Throw him overboard!' someone said, and Maynard whirled in the direction of the voice. And found himself looking at the dark stiff silhouette of Case.

'Throw him overboard,' said the American quietly, 'and you gotta throw me over, too.'

Maynard drew a deep breath. 'Don't tempt me.' He was aware of the tension in the boat, the black mood of the men who wanted to work off their anger against someone, *anyone*. More to gain time than anything else, still trying to sort out his own confused thoughts, he looked at Garrick. "Are you volunteering for the water, too?'

Garrick swallowed. 'All I want is to stay alive.' He looked up towards Cabrolini, at all the men, then finally back at Maynard. 'But that's all *he* wants, too.'

There was another murmur from some of the men, but Maynard had now made up his mind. "All right, Cabrolini, you stay with us. But try anything, and you go overboard.'

Cabrolini leaned forward eagerly. 'I could help, signore.'

'Don't call me signore!'

'Capitano, commandante—whatever you wish, sir. I could help. I know engines. This one could break down—it sound very sick——'

'Don't start jinxing it,' said Hutton, 'or you'll go overboard right away!'

There was a soft laugh from Case. Maynard and Hutton both turned their heads to stare at him, but he seemed undisturbed by their hostility, and not just because he could not see it. This man doesn't care a damn, Maynard thought. And they were always the worst of the lot to handle.

Maynard turned and looked out to sea. The moon was just coming up over the horizon, striking sideways across the faces of the men, turning them from anonymous silhouettes into individuals. *Thirteen of us*, he thought. And wondered when the veneer had been washed so thin that superstition could worry him.

CHAPTER 2

'My dad is a county cricketer,' Garrick said. 'Something like one of your baseball players.'

'Big time?' Case said. 'Like Joe DiMaggio?'

'I've read about him. No, my dad was nothing like that. Seven or eight quid a week, and doing some coaching on the side. He was just county standard, nothing better, but cricket was his whole life. We lived in this back street of Leeds, and my dad would never move from there. I was eighteen before I found out why. He was a prince there. Anywhere else he'd have been a nobody. He was the only one from the council school who'd got his name in the papers for something besides throwing bottles at the coppers.'

'So what did you do? Throw bottles at the cops?'

'I had to get out of Leeds somehow,' Garrick grinned. 'Every day I had off from school, my dad made me go and watch him play. He wanted me to be better than him. But I couldn't even hold a bat. My sisters were better than me.'

'From Leeds to Singapore,' said Case. 'That's a long way to come to dodge a game of cricket.'

Garrick shook his head morosely. 'It didn't work. I got a job in London in the bank. They offered me a job out here in Singapore and I jumped at it. The day I landed I found I was down to play for the bank cricket team. They knew who my dad was and that was why they asked London to send me out here.'

Case smiled sympathetically. Then he remembered his own father, who had never insisted on taking him anywhere but had been glad to be rid of him. He remembered going to see the semi-pro ball teams playing in the sun-baked, shabby field in Beaumont, sitting alone in the bleachers, munching on pralines, not feeling sorry for himself even then but wondering why his father should be so determined to avoid the simple joys of living. Josef Czeicinski had brought a bitterness with him from Poland that he had never attempted to explain to his son, a lack of love and understanding of other people that had even extended to his wife and boy. Case had never understood why his father had married, and his mother, dying when he was ten, had never tried to tell why she had given herself to the sour, dour man who, silently but effectively, let everyone know that he needed no one but himself.

Garrick had taken a small book from his pocket and was flipping through its pages. 'A Japanese phrase book,' he said in answer to Case's look of inquiry. 'I got it in Singapore, even when they were telling us the Japs couldn't take the island. Always be prepared, my mum used to say.'

Case reached into his own pocket, took out a pair of dice. 'Maybe I should've met your ma. I've always depended on these. They ain't reliable.'

He shifted a little trying to ease himself into the sparse shade flung by the rattan sail. He looked out at the blue glare of the sea, seeing the flying fish moving across it like motes in his aching eyes. It was now late morning and they had been out of sight of land from just after dawn. The men lay listlessly in the prahu, the Australians, in their broad-brimmed slouch hats, envied by those who had no hats or had only their tin helmets to protect them from the blazing sun. Case looked up as Hutton, carrying a water can and a tin cup, stopped above him. The sergeant poured out half a cup of water and held it out to Case.

Case squinted up at him, then nodded to the Sikh, Singh, who lay beside him. 'What about him?' He had seen Hutton step over the Sikh, ignoring him as if he were no more than a sleeping dog.

'He'll get his,' said Hutton, thrusting the cup down at Case. 'When we've all drunk from this.'

Case took the cup, staring up at the burly sergeant, then

nudged Singh. 'Here, Mac. Have one on the British Army.'

Singh hadn't moved, but his dark eyes had opened and were watching the two white men. He ran his tongue over his lips, but it was impossible to tell whether he was thirsty or nervous. He was a lean-faced man, his cheekbones prominent above the black mask of his beard. He had been fifteen years in the Indian Army and the habit had been driven deep into him not to question or antagonise an n.c.o. with three stripes on his arm; especially one as hard-bitten and prejudiced as Hutton. Yet he knew that the American was trying to do something for him. Whatever he did, his pride would suffer. So he hesitated, uncertain whether to let Hutton keep him in his place or whether to accept Case's offer of equal status.

'These chaps suffer from all kinds of disease,' said Hutton. 'Cholera, smallpox, all those sort of things.'

'How about imperialism?' said Case. 'How's that for a disease?'

'Look, matey. I ain't getting into any arguments with you about things like that. But you better get it straight—the Army's running this boat. If you don't——'

Case almost lazily transferred the tin cup from his right to his left hand and bunched his right fist. 'If I don't——?'

'You just might get a bunch of knuckles up your snout.'

Case looked him up and down. 'I don't think you could beat my grandma. And she was only a flyweight.'

All the men in the boat were now watching the encounter. Hutton glanced around, very aware of them; but Case seemed oblivious of them. He stared at Hutton a moment longer, then he turned and offered the cup again to Singh. The Sikh hesitated, then he sat up and took the cup. He looked up at Hutton, his face expressionless; he drank, then handed the cup back to the sergeant. The latter snatched it, slopped water into it and thrust it at Case.

'Try it for cholera!'

Case took the cup, grinned, raised it to Singh and drank from it. Then he handed the cup back to Hutton, who grabbed it, held it over the side of the boat and washed it in sea water, then dried it with the sleeve of his shirt. He went through all the motions, not looking at Case but at Singh, as if to impress on the latter that he should not get any ideas, that the American's gesture was not going to change the way the Army was run.

He moved off towards the bow of the boat. Case looked after him and saw Maynard staring at him. He was tempted to throw a mock salute at the officer, but he held back. His gesture towards Singh had not been just an act of rebellion against the army; his ire had been aroused by the deliberately insulting way Hutton had ignored Singh. He knew that he himself had been guilty plenty of times when he was still young and in Texas of drawing the colour line; but he had beaten and been beaten by a dozen coloured men since those days and learned tolerance at the end of an eight-ounce glove. His world after he had left Texas had been made up of dinges, kikes, wops, heinies and Polacks, all made brothers by the hungry gut. His one prejudice in this boat was against the men in uniform, or anyway the ones in authority. But he was not stupid, he knew he would have to live with them at least till they reached Sumatra or some other landfall. A mocking salute to Maynard would be a petty gesture and he knew he would only get a sneer as an answer.

He turned away and then saw that the Australian, Polo Murphy, was watching him closely. 'Case?' said Polo. 'From where'd you say?'

Case hesitated, aware at once that the other man already knew him. Even while he regretted the recognition, he was pleased by it: it meant that something worthwhile had been achieved in the old days. 'Did I say?'

'I remember.' Garrick leant forward, resting his arms on the suitcase on his knees; he had not relinquished his hold on it since he had come aboard the prahu. He seemed eager now to break up the mood that had settled on the men after the business between Case and Hutton; he was eager to help Case, but the latter didn't thank him for it. 'You said you came from some place in Texas. Beaufield. No. Beaumont. That was it —Beaumont, Texas!'

Polo clicked his fingers. 'Texas Jack Case!' He shook his head in wonder at the smallness of the world. 'Well, waddia know! Way out here in the middle of bugger-all, and you turn up! Whatever happened to you, sport?'

That's a question you should never have asked, sport, Case thought; but said nothing. He sat looking straight at Polo, conscious that the other men had begun to lean forward, grateful for anything that broke up the tedium and discomfort of being here in the boat. Garrick looked at him, then at Polo. 'Who's Texas Jack Case? A cowboy film star or something?'

Polo shook his head at all the ignorance there was in the world. 'They just never know what goes on, do they?' he said to Case. He looked around at the other men. 'He was a top middleweight, one of the best. He fought all the good 'uns. Mickey Walker, Vince Dundee, Freddie Steele——' He looked back at Case, nodded his head appreciatively. 'You might have been the best of the lot of 'em.'

Case shook his head: he knew the truth. Then he said, 'How do you know so much?'

'I used to do a bit meself one time. I was a lightweight. Never any good—I never got out of the preliminaries. The missus made me give it up when our first kid come along. But I never give up reading about the game. I got a stack of magazines that high——' He held up his hand.

'You should've burned them,' said Case. He had burned his own scrapbook, tossing it on to a garbage dump fire the night before he had sailed for Bangkok, burning his life and his bridges behind him, burning his shame. He had been cold sober when he had gone out to the garbage dump, but he had been blind drunk when Sammy Bern, the agent who had booked him, had put him aboard the ship. He had been at sea twelve hours before he had woken, and he had lain in his bunk tasting the booze and the sadness of a farewell that had never been said. He had meant to say good-bye to Sammy, to Sammy's wife and kids, to Turkey Bones, the old coloured man who had once been his second and had ended sweeping up other people's cigarette butts in the gym down near the Southern Pacific depot in 'Frisco. But he had said none of those good-byes and his last memory of the States was of his life turning to ashes on a city garbage dump while the birds swung above him like vultures.

'Did you ever fight for the title?' one of the men asked.

Case looked up at Polo, knowing the other man would answer for him. My biographer, he thought: a guy who would blow off the head of a Chinaman and toss an Italian overboard. 'You would have fought for it,' said Polo. 'But when you lost your licence——' He shook his head again, his way of acknowledging the world. 'I read all about it. But I'll never understand why you——' He looked at Case, his voice trailing off.

'Why you what?' Garrick looked at Case.

'Why I retired,' said Case, and stared at Polo. The Australian stared back at him, then he nodded almost imperceptibly, granting the unspoken plea. How many fights did you lose, Case wondered, ones that you were expected to win?

He turned his head, looked up towards Maynard to see how much the Englishman had heard. Already it was as if the officer was the only man in the boat who counted; and he was annoyed at himself for giving Maynard such a status. Maybe he was still a creature of habit: he still nominated his opponents. But what had made him nominate Maynard?

The Englishman was staring towards the east, his binoculars to his eyes. He took them down, turned back to face the men in the boat and said almost casually, 'There's a plane coming. It looks like a Zero.'

The men spun around. 'Christ, what're we going to do?'

'There's not much we can do.' Don't be so goddam calm, Case thought, yet admiring Maynard even though the latter's nonchalance seemed studied. He's been seeing too many goddam British movies. 'Except that those who still have the gift might start praying.'

The plane, no more than a translucent insect in the glare of the sky when Case first saw it, was now growing frighteningly bigger, as if it were not approaching but was having a magnifying glass slowly but steadily adjusted on it. In the vast expanse of blazing sky there was no suggestion of movement by the plane; the only movement seemed to be in the focus of one's eyes. The horizon was lost in haze and the plane came towards them out of bright blue nothingness, the only perspective that of sound as the engine all at once began to bore in at them, first a droning, then a sharper, whining hum, then at last and suddenly a loud, ear-splitting roar as the plane swept low over them and the prahu rocked wildly in the wake of its passing.

The men swung round, some of them shouting obscenely at the plane as it went on up in a steep curving bank. Again for a moment there was the illusion that the plane was not moving; it seemed to hang at a point in the sky as if pinned there. Then it had swung down and was coming back and this time the men could see the popping red flashes, like exploding light globes, along the edges of the wings. The shells came pang-pang-panging across the water, smashing into the prahu and the men. Two of them stood up, their fists raised in defiance of the Japanese pilot, but they were already dead; the plane swept over and the men fell out of the prahu, toppled by the sudden sharp gale of wind. Other, live men followed the dead, going over the side in panic-stricken dives as the Zero swung up to come back a third time.

Case crouched in the bottom of the boat. Beside him was Singh, knocked unconscious by a piece of falling timber from the smashed mast; beyond the Sikh, Garrick lay spread-

34

eagled, trying to squeeze himself down behind the tiny bulwark of his suitcase. Maynard, kneeling in the bow of the boat, was yelling to the men to stay low, not to go overboard.

The plane came back, the shells chopping the water ahead of it. Case winced as a piece of timber flew off the side of the prahu and he shut his eyes as splinters sprayed against his face. When he opened them he saw Garrick standing up, one foot on the side of the boat. Case yelled, dived across the unconscious Singh and grabbed Garrick by the leg. The boy struggled to break free, then fell back into the boat. And in that moment Case heard the terrified shout: 'Sharks!'

Still holding on to Garrick, he sat up and looked over the side. The water was a threshing mess of flailing arms, sharks' fins and bobbing heads screaming in panic. Even as he looked, Case saw one man throw back his head, his mouth wide open in a terrible scream, and disappear beneath the water. Case heard the chatter of a gun and he ducked, thinking the Zero was coming back in again; but it was Maynard, standing up in the prow of the boat and shooting at a shark as it rolled over, white belly flashing in the sun, to strike at one of the men. Case flung himself at the side of the boat, grabbed at the man's hand and tried to pull him in. But the man suddenly shrieked, his hand was jerked out of Case's, and he fell back, disappearing beneath the blood-streaked water.

The Zero came roaring back, guns silent this time, and Maynard suddenly swung round, shooting at it with his Thompson gun. He fired wildly, like a crazy man, shouting incoherently as he did so. Then the plane had gone, climbing towards the sun and disappearing into it, and suddenly Maynard stopped firing. He stood, the gun held in his arms like a skeletal baby, and looked about him. His mouth was working, but it was difficult to tell whether it was with rage or despair. He stared around at the live and dead men in the boat, then down at the blood-dyed water. The sharks had also gone, as if they had been part of the attacking force along with the Zero. A man floated on his back in the sea, his dull eyes staring up at those who had remained in the boat.

Case sat up, moving stiffly, as if he had been crouched in the bottom of the boat for hours instead of only a few minutes. He saw Maynard put down his gun, then the Englishman leant over the side of the boat and grabbed the floating man by the hair. He pulled the man towards him, gazed down into the blank face, then opened his fingers and let the man's head slide out of his grasp. The corpse sank slowly beneath

35

the surface, its mouth opening in a final silent appeal for help that it no longer needed.

Case had picked up one of the water-cans, but he was still watching Maynard. He was moving down the length of the boat. He stopped by a dead man, bent his head and murmured silently; then he lifted the man and gently pushed him overboard. He moved on, did the same to a second, third and fourth man. Then at last he sat down and, hollow-eyed, looked along at the watching Case.

'Well, what would you have done?' he said with sullen defiance. 'Taken them home for a military funeral?'

Case said nothing, wanting no responsibility. He lifted the water-can; there was a hole right through it. He turned it over, but no water ran out. Then he saw Hutton, at the other end of the boat, holding up the other can. It, too, had been hit by cannon shells.

2

Case watched the sun go down, then turned towards the east and welcomed the darkness as if it were a long cool drink of water. His head throbbed from the day-long hammering by the sun, his eyes felt like hot jelly in their sockets, and his swollen tongue seemed to be trying to force the teeth out of his gums. It will be worse tomorrow, he thought; and wondered who would be the first to die. He looked about at the stiff figures in the prahu, all of them sprawled in postures that suggested agony. There were only seven men aboard now: himself, Maynard, Garrick, Polo, Cabrolini, Hutton and Singh. Strangers with whom he might share a common way of dying. How the hell did I get here?

A Polack boy from Beaumont, Texas, one who had had his name changed to Case ('They don't like foreign names in Texas, son,' his first manager had said. 'Who the hell would believe Texas Jan Czeicinski?'), who had had his first fight for five dollars in a tank town in the Panhandle and by the end of his first year had made five thousand; who three years out of Beaumont had fought Ace Hudkins to a draw in Madison Square Garden and been told he would be the next world champion: how the hell did I get way out here in the Straits of Malacca? But the question did not distress him. He had become philosophical at an early age, the only defence against the indifference of his father; somehow he had

36

never been able to hate the old man, but had pitied him. A shrug had become his acceptance of what life offered him, and it had saved him from the bitterness that had pickled his father. But, now he came to think of it, maybe it was the reason he was way out here in the middle of bugger-all, as Polo had described it. Fighters had become title-holders with left hooks, right crosses, combination punches; none of them had ever made it with a shrug. He grinned, but his cracked lips hurt and the expression turned to a grimace. He lolled against the tiller, but the prahu, motionless on the still sea, needed no one to steer it.

It was dark now, the night rushing at them out of the east. Maynard stood up, stiffly like an old man, and one by one the other men followed his example, the prahu rocking as they did so. They stretched their arms and legs, the bones of some of them cracking.

Maynard picked up a Thompson gun, took out the magazine. 'Empty,' he croaked. 'Does anyone have any ammunition at all?'

Case picked up the Thompson gun beside him, one that had belonged to one of the men who had died. 'Nothing,' he said, and the other men made hoarse echoes. 'You got a boatload of military eunuchs, captain.'

Cabrolini had moved awkwardly to the engine, squatted down beside it and looked at it, running his hand over its oily, rusted surface. He could not see it in the darkness, but his hand told him what he already knew, had been brooding about most of the day. There was a hole as big as his fist right through the block.

'I cannot fix it.' His voice was harsh and thick, his swollen tongue having difficulty with the words.

'You already told us,' Polo said irritably. 'Don't keep bloody well harping.'

Hutton stumbled down the length of the boat, handing out food to the men. 'This is the last of it,' he growled as he handed Case a durian.

Case took the fruit, peeled the prickly rind from it and almost vomited at the smell of it. He held it away from him over the side of the boat, and Maynard, beside him now, said, 'Don't throw it away! If you don't want it, someone else will eat it.'

Case tried to close his nostrils as he put the foul-smelling fruit up to his mouth. He wanted to gag, but he forced himself to eat it. The juice ran down his throat and almost at

37

once his tongue seemed to begin losing its thickness. He ate the pulp, chewing on it while still trying not to smell it. Then he had finished. He leaned over the side of the boat, washed his hands and chin, then straightened up. Maynard, having done the same thing, sat down beside him.

'Stinks, doesn't it?' The juice of the fruit had taken the croak out of Maynard's voice. 'But it's the smell of heaven to some people. According to legend out here, there's no better aphrodisiac anywhere in the world.'

'That's just what I need right now.'

Maynard looked curiously at the Americans. 'What else do you need?'

Case, puzzled, turned his head. It was impossible to see Maynard's face, but the Englishman's tone of voice was not antagonistic. 'You figure I need *something*?'

Maynard nodded. But he did not elaborate, as if he had suddenly decided he had already intruded too far into the other man's life. Their antagonism had lain dormant all day, stunned by the tragedy of the morning and then the almost intolerable heat of the sun during the afternoon. To invade Case's privacy further might only stir the antagonism into life again; and Maynard had had enough war, large or small, for today. Instead he turned and looked back to the east. 'We'll have to post a watch in the morning. Just in case the Japs send out more patrol planes. If we see them coming in time, we can go overboard, hide beneath the boat. Perhaps then they won't shoot us up.'

'What about sharks?'

'That's a risk we'll have to take. Those sharks this morning were already following us when our chaps went overboard.'

'Maybe they were Jap sharks,' said Case, but Maynard's silence told him the Englishman didn't think the joke was funny. He studied the lean profile silhouetted against the first of the evening's stars, with its long well-shaped nose and the bony chin that looked as if it could not take a punch but did suggest that the man would fight. 'You make a real business of this, don't you?'

Maynard looked at him, puzzled for a moment. 'What? Oh, the war? That's what war is—a business.'

He looked up, then stood up and fingered the shredded rattan sail. 'This isn't going to be any use to us, even if a breeze does spring up. Perhaps we'd better try a turn on the oars— we may not feel up to it tomorrow in the sun. You and I will take first go.'

'Is that an order?'

Maynard looked down at him. 'Take it how you like. But I'm in charge of this boat. Even if your friend,' he nodded up towards Garrick, '*is* financing it.'

'Okay, so you're in charge. But you and me'll get on better if you *ask* me, not order me. I'm allergic to orders.' He stood up, looked around for someone to take over the tiller. The nearest man was Hutton. 'Here, sarge. Steer clear of cholera areas.'

Hutton snorted, but Case had already stepped over the sergeant's legs and moved up to sit down beside Maynard. Each of them took hold of one of the long-handled Malay oars and began to row. Case was awkward at it, but Maynard rowed with a long smooth stroke as if he had been doing it all his life.

'I believe there's an American term for chaps like you. Is it Philadelphia lawyer?'

'We've got one for *chaps* like you, too,' said Case. 'Toffee noses.'

'Well, that's the introductions over.' Maynard bowed his head in mock politeness. 'How do you do?'

They rowed for a few strokes, as formal as oarsmen in a royal barge. Then Case, still having difficulty with his oar, said, 'Did you ever crew at Oxford or Cambridge?'

'Crew? Oh, *row*. No. And not all Englishmen go to Oxford or Cambridge. I went to Sandhurst.'

'Sandhurst? What's that?'

Maynard raised his eyes to the stars. 'God forgive me for the description—it's the English West Point.'

'I wouldn't know the difference. I went to Texas State.'

'What's that? A gymnasium?'

'What did you major in at Sandhurst—insults?'

'I majored, as you call it, in this business of war.'

'And you think you're pretty good at it?'

No, thought Maynard. If I and all the rest of us who were supposed to be the professional British soldiers were any good, we should not be losing the war as we now are. We are a war behind in our thinking and that is one war too many. But he said, 'Yes. That's why I've taken charge. A soldier just doesn't only learn how to kill. He learns how to survive, too.'

'With some of us that's a natural instinct,' said Case.

'That's not enough. One needs discipline, too.'

'Maybe some of us don't care for discipline.'

39

'I've noticed that,' Maynard said drily.

They rowed then in silence and after twenty minutes Garrick and Cabrolini took over the oars. Case lay down on the bottom of the boat, trying to make himself comfortable, but it was not easy. He stretched out, looked up at the stars and for the first time saw that they had gone. The night sky was entirely black now and even as he looked he felt the first drops of rain hit his face. He sat up at once, but the other men were already reacting to the rain. They were standing up, as if trying to expose themselves fully to the onslaught of the rain as it suddenly began to pour in a tropical downfall.

Polo was yelling like a schoolboy, rocking the prahu as he jumped up and down. 'Oh, you bobby-dazzler! Send her down, Hughie! Send her down!'

The rain had drenched them in a few moments. It was almost as if they were standing under a waterfall; it fell out of the sky in a great cascade. Case threw back his head, opened his mouth and let the water run in. In the splatter and hiss of the rain it was hard to distinguish any other sound, but it did seem to Case that he could hear Garrick giggling hysterically and Singh shouting something in his own tongue that might have been a prayer. Case leaned back against the mast, his face still thrown back; the rain blinded him, ran up his nose so that he could not breathe, choked him as it poured down his throat. I'm going to drown in rain, he thought; and could not have cared less.

Then Maynard had stumbled by him, slipping in the pools of water gathering in the bottom of the boat. 'Find something to catch the water in!' he shouted. 'Anything will do!'

Then he fell over something in the bottom of the boat. In the darkness he groped for it and stood up holding Garrick's suitcase. He fumbled at the locks, but couldn't open them. 'Garrick!' he yelled, water running out of his mouth. 'Open this! Quick!' But Garrick hesitated, and Maynard, putting his fingers under the lid, tried to wrench open the suitcase. 'I shan't read your blasted love letters. But give me the key!'

Still Garrick hesitated, till Case put a hand on his arm. 'Come, on, Reg! Your girl won't mind.'

Garrick stood stock still a moment longer; then he put his hand in his pocket, took out a key and thrust it towards Case. The latter took it, dropped down beside Maynard who was now kneeling in the bottom of the boat. Hutton produced his torch and by its yellow glow Case, still blinded by the water in his eyes, fumbled with the locks. Then he had flung open the top of the suitcase.

'Holy Pete!' The suitcase was packed tight with coloured bundles of paper. 'How many girls do you have writing to you?'

Maynard tipped the suitcase over and the bundles fell out into the bottom of the boat. Hutton picked up one and flashed his torch on it.

'This isn't love letters! It's money!'

He swung the light on Garrick. His sun-blistered face dripping water, the youngster grinned like a small boy caught smoking.

'I was going to open a branch in Sumatra,' he shouted against the rain, and suddenly began to laugh hysterically, the rain running down his thin cheeks like tears.

3

'They told us we had to burn all the money we held,' Garrick said. 'They burned something like five million Straits dollars at the Treasury.'

'How did you come by this?' Case asked.

'The manager of our bank and I were burning our stocks. But then he skipped out, left me holding the kitty. I went on burning it, and then I got frightened. The Nips were only a few streets away, I could hear the shooting outside. Well, I wanted to save my own skin and I'd have been disobeying orders if I'd let what was left fall into the Nips' hands. So ——' He looked around at them all. 'I don't think I'm an embezzler. I'd call this salvage, wouldn't you?'

It was morning now and Garrick was laying out his money to dry. It was spread all round the boat and he had been moving around, turning over the wet bundles like a cook taking care of baking dough. The rainwater caught in the suitcase last night had been carefully stored in the water-cans, which had been plugged with pieces of canvas cut from ammunition pouches. The men had breakfasted on another durian each and half a cup of water, and Maynard had decided that while they were fresh and had the strength they should keep rowing.

So now Maynard and Hutton were on the oars, Polo was on the tiller, and Case, Garrick, Singh and Cabrolini were taking a rest. But none of them was relaxed, because every now and again each of them would steal a glance towards the east, half-expecting the planes to come up out of the soft white clouds that lay like snow drifts along the line of the horizon.

'That is a lot of money,' Cabrolini said. 'What are you going to do with it?'

Garrick shrugged. Then he picked up a bundle and held it out to Cabrolini. The Italian shook his head, looked around at the open sea. 'What is there to buy?'

'Stick to it, son,' said Polo. 'I might want to borrow a quid or two if this war goes on too long. What about you, Gandhi?'

'Do not call me Gandhi, please,' said Singh, and glanced towards Hutton, as if expecting the sergeant to make some comment. But the latter turned his head away, pointedly ignoring the Sikh.

'Sorry, sport.' Polo was not entirely insensitive, but he had known nothing of the world beyond the New South Wales coalfields till he had enlisted in the A.I.F. and been sent to Singapore. He could recite the ring record of a hundred foreign boxers, but he knew nothing of the conditions that had spawned them, the prejudices that they had had to overcome, or the reasons for the obscurity to which they had to return. He had sometimes wondered what had happened to Tiger Flowers, Benny Bass (yes, Texas Jack Case), but the thought had never bothered him. The world beyond Cessnock and the mines was a spotlighted ring, a clean, well-lit arena where men met on equal terms. Then he had come to Singapore and found out that all foreigners were not equal.

He looked out across the blue glare of the sea, wondering what Mum and the kids were doing now. They would have heard of the fall of Singapore; and he wondered if Mum would be weeping, thinking him dead. Neither of them had been much for a show of affection, he had been embarrassed when she had kissed him goodbye in front of the kids. But in the darkness of their bedroom, in the comfort of their lumpy bed, she had often wept: at the death of young Billy, at the debts that always faced them, at the arguments they had had. Good old Vi, he thought; and found his own eyes beginning to water. He closed his eyes, seeing the glare of the water even through his lids, and a love came alive in him that had been dead for years. He and Vi had lived without love for the past ten years, each of them just part of the furniture of the other's life, but now he remembered everything as it used to be between them. Good old Vi, an old bag now but still the only girl he had ever loved.

The day wore on, a furnace whose only dimension was time. A few clouds floated like smoke across the sky, but they did nothing to relieve the glare of the heat. Case could feel his body beginning to dehydrate, his life being soaked up by the sun; he closed his eyes and his skull became a stew of memories, dreams and hallucinations. The sun became the lights above a hundred rings; he heard the cheering and himself grunting as the punches, weightless in memory, hit home; *You'll be the best*, his manager had said, but Teddy Yarosz had knocked him out in one round on a broiling summer's night in Chicago. He remembered the bodies and faces of a dozen girls, but no names; and he dreamed of a girl who had had no name, no face, no body, but was as real as any of the others because she had been his ideal. The sweat ran out of him like blood, and again he wondered who of them would die first.

Then the sun, foiled that it had lost them for another day, began to cool, foundering on a reef of dark cloud along the edge of the sea. A breeze sneaked in, the whisper of a blessing, and the tattered useless sail creaked in the current it was powerless to use. Case opened the oven-lids of his burning eyes, saw a red world and for a panic-stricken moment wondered if this, and not blackness, was the colour of blindness. Then his eyes cleared and far off, like a splinter laid across his eyeballs, saw the dark strip along the horizon.

It took them another two and a half hours to reach the shore, with everyone taking a ten-minute turn on the oars and rowing at a good speed. Slowly Sumatra came up out of the sea, the dark line gradually taking colour and shape as they crawled towards it across the desert ocean. They were still a mile or so from shore, able now to see the beaches, the mangrove swamps, and, farther back, the rising hills, when they heard the plane. They turned and looked to the north-west and saw the flying-boat skimming in low towards the coast, no more, it seemed, than a few feet above the water.

'What is it? A Jap?'

Maynard had managed to get his binoculars focused on the plane, a giant homing bird against the red sky, just before it disappeared behind a low headland. 'It looks like a Catalina! There could be a base there!'

Case swung the tiller over, heading the prahu up along the

coast. Polo and Garrick were on the oars, rowing now like men in a quarter-mile sprint; but they gave way to Case and Maynard, who in turn gave way to Cabrolini and Singh, before they had reached the end of the headland. The exertion and excitement had the men trembling as the prahu nosed its way round the low spit of land. The sun had gone down, leaving only a wash of pale red light in the sky that was dying even as they looked at it. The breeze increased, bringing with it the dank smell of the land, one which was not pleasant in the men's nostrils but which they welcomed as if it were the perfume of some woman.

'Smell those mangroves!' Case exclaimed. 'Ain't they great?'

'Quiet!' Maynard snapped.

They were round the headland now, moving slowly in towards the shore. Darkness fell like a storm and in the black night they could see nothing more than fifty feet from them. Then from across the water they heard a voice, one that cut off as sharply as it had first spoken.

'That wasn't an English voice, was it?' Garrick whispered.

'Didn't sound like it,' Maynard said. 'Ship the oars and paddle in with your hands.'

With Case at the tiller, the other men leaned over the side and began to stroke the long boat closer towards the shore. Fortunately the tide was running in, and slowly but surely they moved into the still water within the curve of the headland. They could now hear the soft slap of the water on sand ahead of them, but there was no other sound. This part of the coast of Sumatra could have been dead men's land; the voice they had heard could have been only an echo from the past. The silence was like the heat they could now feel coming out from the land, heavy and oppressive; they began to sweat, as much from fear as from the humidity. Case's hand began to cramp as it held tightly to the tiller and he had to use his other hand to free his stiffened fingers.

Then suddenly the prahu was bumped from either side and a voice snapped, 'Righto, one peep and you're gone!' Almost at the same moment a heavy guttural voice said something in Malay from the other side of the prahu.

Case, sitting in the stern of the prahu, had the best view. He saw Maynard and the others look quickly from side to side, not sure from where the attack was going to come. He saw them bring up their empty guns in a reflex action, but at the same moment there was the sharp click of rifle bolts being shot home.

'Don't try it,' said the first voice, and now Case recognised the accent, 'or you're a goner, sport.'

Case grinned and said, 'Friends of yours, Polo?'

Everyone in the prahu relaxed with nervous giggling laughs. The tension of the last few minutes, the strain and exhaustion of the long hours at sea, slipped out of them as if they had been bled. Garrick began to gabble incoherently, looking from right to left, reaching out his hands to the dark figures in the rubber dinghies on either side of the prahu. Everyone was talking at once, their relief babbling out of them as it might have out of the mouths of children. The warm night air, smelling of invisible mangroves, was full of the happiness of men who knew they were safe at last, were only one step away from home.

Then the Australian voice said, 'Righto, break it down. We don't want the Nips in here. Bring your boat into the shore.'

By the time they had run the prahu in on to the beach, the men's eyes had become more accustomed to the darkness. The stars had now appeared and the night was not so intense. Case and the others fell out of the boat and on unsteady legs stumbled through the shallow water and up on to the sand. One or two of them fell down and remained there, still overcome by relief and exhaustion. Case stood swaying a little, feeling as if he had been through forty rounds with a heavyweight, and looked at the people on the beach.

There was a large group of them, men, women and children, all of them speaking softly in a guttural voice that he guessed was Dutch. There were also four Australians, the crew of the Catalina flying-boat moored just off the beach. The leader of the Australians was speaking to Maynard.

'We have to get off from here within the next fifteen minutes. The nearest Japs are supposed to be twenty miles away, but they could have patrols out.'

'Who are these people?' Maynard asked.

'The last of those who got out of Medan. There are some VIP's amongst this lot.'

'Where will you take us?'

'Us? You've got it wrong, captain. I can't take you. The aircraft is going to be chockablock as it is. There are five more bods here than I'd been told to expect. I'm going to stuff them in somehow, but there'll be no room for you blokes.'

Polo, one of those who had flopped down on the sand, suddenly straightened up but remained on his knees. 'Stone the bloody crows, you can't just leave us here! What about the Nips?'

'I'm sorry, mate, but I have my orders.' Lucas, the flight-lieutenant, was a young man, no older perhaps than Garrick. A year or two ago he might have been responsible for no more than the mail in some office; now he was responsible for a couple of dozen lives. He pushed back his cap, and in the light of the moon now coming up above the rim of the sea Maynard could see the deep lines of worry etched in the boyish face. The war was proving more complicated than he had expected, had been led to believe. 'Looks like you'll have to find you own way home from here.'

Polo got slowly to his feet, one knee cracking like that of an old man. His rifle was slung over his shoulder and almost casually, as if the sling itself had slipped, the weapon slid down into his hands. 'What would you do if we took the plane over from you?'

'That's enough!' Maynard snapped.

But the young pilot hadn't appeared even to blink. His voice was just as steady as before as he said, 'I doubt if any of you could get it off the water. But even before that, none of you would get near the aircraft.'

He nodded around him. The other three members of the flying crew and several of the Dutchmen had guns trained on Maynard and the others. There was silence for a moment, broken only by the whimper of a child somewhere at the back of the group.

Then Case said, 'Your army is getting out of control, skipper. How about a little discipline around here?'

Maynard ignored him, just stared hard at Polo. 'That's enough, Private Murphy.'

Polo hesitated, then he slung the rifle back on his shoulder. He looked at Lucas. 'Sorry, mate. Dunno what got into me.'

The young Australian waved an embarrassed hand and the crew and the Dutchmen lowered their weapons. To help break the awkward moment Maynard said, 'How much of Sumatra have the Japs taken?'

'The lot, as far as we know,' Lucas said. 'They're in Java, too, but there's some pretty stiff fighting still going on there.'

Case had withdrawn from the group, moving down the beach away from the boats. He passed a young woman standing with a baby in her arms and two small children holding to her skirts. He nodded to her and ran a gentle hand over the head of one of the children.

'Good luck,' the woman said, and he stopped, startled from

46

his introspective mood by her speaking in English and by her sentiment. She was the first woman he had spoken to in seven months whose feelings towards him had not had to be bought.

'And to you, too.' He looked down at the children, small pale wraiths in the moonlight. 'Is their father here?'

'He is back there somewhere.' She nodded towards the impenetrable blackness of the hills.

'Then *he* needs your luck, not me.'

'He has my prayers,' she said simply, and there was no answer to that.

He moved on, smelling the mangroves, aware of the mosquitoes now as they came foraging out of the thick-smelling darkness, settling on his arms and face in whole colonies. He slapped viciously at them, but it was like trying to trap floating clouds of dust.

He had reached a nadir of despair that he had not felt for a long time. His remark to Maynard about the lack of discipline on Polo's part had sounded light-hearted, but his own shock and disappointment at their being left here on the beach had, he knew, equalled that of Polo. As he had stood on the beach, looking out at the floating Catalina, its tail raised high like that of some stately bird, he had already been thinking of the States. Not of any place in particular, just America: a dozen Main Streets had run together in his mind, even Broadway had not meant just New York to him. Going home, as he had thought then, he had become homesick. Now, for the first time in his life, he had a sense of dread. Now, when he had nothing to live for, when death should have been welcome, he suddenly wanted to live. And the lifeline, that flying-boat, was being jerked away from them.

He turned suddenly, angry now; and saw Garrick coming towards him through the moonlight. 'Quick, Jack! That RAAF chap thinks he can squeeze two more on the plane!'

Case broke into a run and the two of them jogged back along the beach through clouds of mosquitoes, oblivious of them now. 'I suggested we throw for the two places—those dice of yours. You still got them?'

Case had the dice in his hand when he and Garrick reached Maynard and the other men. The rubber dinghies were ferrying the last of the Dutch group out to the Catalina, and the young pilot stood waiting impatiently by the water's edge. 'You've got two minutes, fellers,' he said. 'Hurry up and decide who's coming.'

Case looked at Maynard. 'Who throws first? And what'll it be? Two highest throws?'

'One thing,' said Polo, and looked across at Cabrolini. 'He ain't in the game. I'm barring him.'

'We're all in this together,' said Maynard, but was ashamed at the lack of argument in his voice. He was just like Polo, he wanted the odds shortened as much as possible.

'Not him,' said Polo. 'I ain't giving up my chances of going home to some enemy Dago. If he throws, I'll put a knife through him. To stop me, you'll have to put a knife through me.'

There was silence for a moment, then Hutton said, 'I think he's right, sir. We're not in this war to save the likes of him.' He nodded at Cabrolini.

The latter stared at the men for a moment, then abruptly he turned and walked away into the darkness. None of the men looked after him, nor did they look at each other; but each knew there was now a skeleton in the game.

'Well, thank Christ he's got some decency in him,' Polo said.

'Yeah,' said Case. 'Where would we be without that?'

Garrick coughed, but it could have been a chopped-off laugh. Then Maynard abruptly swung and moved along the beach away from the RAAF pilot, and the men followed him. Case looked back, but Cabrolini was lost somewhere in the darkness.

Maynard held out his hand for the dice. 'I'll go first, then you'll all know what you have to beat. We'd better have a little light, sergeant. But keep it shielded, otherwise none of us might win a ticket.'

The six men squatted down and Hutton switched on his torch. A cobweb of mosquitoes hung in the light, but none of the men noticed it: their eyes were only on the two dice held in Maynard's open palm. Polo smoothed out a small patch of sand, then looked up at Maynard.

'Go for your life, skip.'

Maynard looked at him, wondering if the other had caught the double meaning in his own words; but Polo's face showed no expression at all. Maynard looked down at the dice, rolled them in his palm, closed his fist and threw. The torch beam swung down on to the patch of sand, as if it were the one eye of all the men.

'Bad luck, sir,' said Hutton, but it was difficult for him to keep the elation out of his voice: his own chances had just improved. 'Two ones.'

Maynard's face was impassive, but inside he could feel the sickness welling up in him. There were tears of anger behind his lids, but somehow he held them back. But Jesus Christ, when was his luck going to turn? If he survived, if he ever saw him again, he would have to ask his father, the pious clergyman, when one stopped praying.

Garrick picked up the dice, gingerly: they might have been someone's eyeballs, the way he held them in his hand. He was sitting on his suitcase, and all at once he looked down at it, staring at it for a moment. Then he looked up and around at the men. 'Would anyone think I was a swine if I offered them all this for their place on the plane?'

The men just looked at him. Nervously he raised a hand and smacked at a mosquito on his cheek. Then he nodded. 'I'd have thought the same myself.'

With a quick throw, as if suddenly he now wanted to be rid of them, he tossed the dice on the sand. Two threes.

Polo looked around, silently inquiring who wanted to be next; then he reached out a hand and picked up the dice. He was strangely quiet, his thin tanned face yellowed and old in the glow from the torch. He muttered something that sounded like, 'Mum'; then he threw the dice. A four and a one.

Nobody seemed eager to pick up the dice, and Lucas called from down by the water's edge, 'Get a move on, fellers!'

'You'd better go next, sergeant,' Maynard said.

Hutton, sullen and tense, his thick lips pinched tight between his teeth, picked up the dice. 'I never was lucky at this sorta game,' he said, and almost casually, already resigned to bad luck, he tossed the dice on the sand.

At once his broad, chipped face split apart in a wide smile. 'Two sixes! Oh, bloody marvellous!' He scooped up the dice, shoved them at Singh. 'Here you are, mate!'

Singh took the dice. He looked around at the other men, smiling almost shyly, as if he felt they were doing him a favour by letting him take his chances with the rest of them. Then he threw: a five and a two. He looked up and around at the men again and there was something like fear in his eyes this time: he had done the wrong thing, had thrown the second highest score so far. He picked up the dice quickly and handed them to Case.

Case rolled the dice around in his hand, blowing on them.

He remembered a hundred other games, in Chicago, Kansas City, Memphis, in tank towns that as far as he knew had no names; sometimes the stakes in those games had been high, but none as high as this. 'Come on, baby. Texas is calling your daddy back home!'

He threw, the dice rolling over on the yellow spotlighted patch of sand. Then he looked up at Singh. 'Sorry, pal.' He had thrown a six and a one.

Singh said nothing, but his lip quivered just a little. Hutton, the one safe member of the party now, picked up the dice and held them out.

'Come on, make it quick! We haven't got all night.'

Case looked across at him. 'You got all the time in the world from now on, sarge. We're the ones who may be running short.' Then he looked at Singh. 'You married?'

Singh blinked, surprised at the question. Then he nodded.

'Any kids?'

'Three, sir.'

'Don't call me sir. You and me could never be more equal than we are right now.' Case looked down at the dice he had taken from Hutton, then he held them out to Singh. 'You throw first.'

Singh hesitated, then took the dice. He swallowed, murmured something the others didn't catch, then tossed the dice away from him almost as if with distaste. The torch had to search for them, found them: two and three. A look of pain swept across the Sikh's face, but he said nothing. With a formal movement, as if he were presenting a gift, he picked up the dice and passed them to Case.

'Good luck, Mr. Case.'

Case stared at the Sikh for a long moment. I haven't done many worthwhile things in my life, he thought; don't let me bugger this one. He cupped the dice in his palm, holding them with two fingers; then abruptly he dropped them into the full glare of the torch. He looked at Singh's face before he looked down at the dice, but the look on the Sikh's face told him he had done the right thing.

'Snake's eyes,' he said, picked up the pair of ones and put the dice in his pocket. He stood up, easing the stiffness out of himself, feeling a queer sense of relief now that the gambling was over. He looked around for Cabrolini, but the Italian was still not visible.

Singh put his hand on Case's arm. Hutton had switched off his torch and only the moonlight lit the Sikh's face. Above the black shadow of his beard his eyes glimmered. For a moment Case thought he was going to break into tears, but Singh had too much dignity for that. His fingers tightened on the American's arm, digging into the flesh; Case felt the other man's gratitude as a stab of pain that almost made him cry out. Then Singh had let go and turned away.

Hutton, his British Raj attitude now forgotten, a brother to the world now that he was on his way to safety and White Australia, grabbed Singh by the arm. 'Come on, matey, they're waiting for us!'

Hutton and Singh went down to the water's edge, followed by Garrick and Polo. Case started to follow them, but stopped when he saw Maynard staring at him.

'Where did you learn to do that?' Maynard asked quietly.

'Do what?'

'Throw the number you wanted.'

Case hesitated, wondering how much any of the others might have guessed. 'It's a gambler's secret. They teach it at a school in Memphis, Tennessee. Part of higher education in America.'

'If you can do it, how is it you're not a rich man?'

'I only went to one semester. They just taught us how to throw the low numbers.'

Maynard shook his head. 'You're a mystery to me, Case.'

'I am to myself sometimes,' said Case, took the dice out of his pocket, juggled them, then put them away again. 'That's why I never get bored with my own company.'

Then he went down to join the others at the water's edge, cursing himself for his surliness, wondering why he had rejected Maynard's attempt to approach him. There was too much of his old man in him; Josef Czeicinski was not entirely dead. He wondered how his father, a bigoted anti-gambler, would have reacted to the suggestion that he should throw dice for his chances of rescue.

Hutton and Singh were already in the dinghy with the RAAF pilot. Hutton, going on a picnic, all hearty cheerfulness, had given Maynard his torch. 'I shan't need it, sir. Not from now on.' He waved good-bye as the dinghy pulled out. 'Good luck, mates! You won't have long to wait. I'll see someone comes back for you. Keep your pecker up, mates!'

'Can you send someone back for us?' Garrick had to raise his voice as the dinghy pulled quickly away from them.

The pilot's voice floated back across the water. 'I'll ask, but I wouldn't bank on it. They won't risk aircraft this far again.'

'Where are you headed now?' Their voices, across the water, had a forlorn sound to them, the sound of final farewell.

'There's a new rule. Never tell anyone anything. If the Japs captured you, you couldn't tell them anything. Because you wouldn't know.' The last words drifted away, faint as a sigh.

'I just hope the Japs appreciate it,' Case said quietly. 'If and when we meet them.'

'We ought've asked 'em to leave us their ammo,' said Polo.

'They wouldn't have given us any,' Maynard said. 'They don't believe they're safe themselves yet.'

'I just wish I was as safe,' said Garrick.

They watched Hutton, Singh and the pilot board the Catalina. The dinghy was deflated and pulled aboard, the hatch was closed and a moment later the flying-boat's engines stuttered, then began to roar. The pilot lost no time. He turned the Catalina out to sea, opened up the engines and took the aircraft out across the lagoon and up into the death's head moon.

Then Case turned and saw the prahu pulling out from the beach, Cabrolini working an oar in the style of the Malay fishermen.

CHAPTER 3

Case opened his eyes as soon as the morning sun hit him. For a moment he wondered where he was, his skin hard and scaly as that of a crocodile; he moved his head and something slid off his cheek like a loose scab. Then he remembered: they had caked themselves thick with mud last night as a protection against the mosquitoes. They had gone into the mangrove swamp behind the beach, suffering the hordes of mosquitoes while they painted themselves with the foul-smelling mud. It had been uncomfortable but the idea, Maynard's, had worked.

Case got to his feet, the mud falling from him like dead skin. He looked down at Maynard, who opened a live eye in a dead mummy's face and looked up at him. 'You never looked better,' Case said.

Maynard smiled, his grey outer face cracked and falling off him. He stood up, but by then Case was already down at the water's edge. He watched the American shake his body like a dog, a fine dust of mud spraying off him, then he had dived into the water. Garrick and Polo were sitting up as Maynard ran down the beach and dived in alongside Case.

As Case and Maynard came up to the surface again there was a shout from Polo. Case turned his head and saw the prahu coming round the end of the point. Garrick and Polo ran down to the water, dived in and came up to stand beside the other two. The four men stood there, streaming mud, as Cabrolini, still working the one oar, brought the prahu in beside them and ran it into the beach. Case ducked under the water again, quickly washed the mud from himself, came up and followed Maynard, Garrick and Polo out of the water and up on to the beach.

Cabrolini still sat in the prahu. He said something in Italian, then lapsed into silence as if his tongue were not capable of dealing with the situation in English. None of the other men said anything, even Polo remained silent. Case, keeping his own silence because he felt the encounter concerned only Cabrolini, Maynard and Polo, wondered why the latter two did not speak. Then he saw the look on their mud-streaked faces and knew. There had been angry curses at Cabrolini last night and if Maynard and Polo had had any ammunition for their guns they would have shot at the Italian. But somehow their anger had leaked out of them during the night and they had woken this morning knowing who had driven Cabrolini to take the prahu. And now he had brought it back.

'I had to come back,' Cabrolini said at last. 'I am hung round your neck like an albatross.'

'Albatross?' Now the other man had spoken, Polo's silence cracked. 'What the bloody hell are you talking about?'

'Coleridge?' Maynard asked Cabrolini, and the Italian nodded. 'It's a poem, Polo. About bad luck.'

'If he thinks he's bad luck, then he better piss off again.'

'No,' Maynard, quietly emphatic, determined not to repeat last night's mistake. 'He stays. He's one of us from now on.'

Case turned away with relief. He had developed no real feeling for any of the men except perhaps Garrick, but he wanted to be involved in no more arguments. Arguments meant commitment, and he meant to leave these men before being bound so tightly to them. He had no plans where he might go, indeed was in a part of the world where destinations meant nothing because he knew the names of none of them. But he had been without destinations before and had survived.

He stared down the lone empty beach, wondering what lay there for them beyond the wall of brilliant light thrown up by the glittering sand. Sea birds hung as white splinters in the bright glare and a flock of them moved across the sands like a pale shadow. Then suddenly the birds on the beach exploded into the air, breaking the glare as if shattering a pane of glass, and out of the white world came the dark stumbling figure. Case, blinded a little by the glare, shut his eyes, afraid that they were playing a trick on him. But when he opened them, the figure was still there, still stumbling towards them.

'Who the hell is that?' he heard Maynard say beside him.

Then he and Maynard were running down the beach, recognising the figure as that of a woman now. When they reached her she had fallen to her knees. She looked up at them out of cavernous eyes, then she fell forward and lay still.

Case dropped down beside her, turned her over and brushed the sand from her face. Polo, half-way down towards Case and Maynard, turned and yelled back to Cabrolini to bring some water; and in a moment or two the Italian had arrived with the plugged-up water-can. He poured water into the tin cup and while Case held the girl's head, forced some water between her lips, murmuring to her in Italian.

The girl coughed and opened her eyes. She looked up at the men, the fear going out of her face as she realised that, for the present at least, these men meant her no harm. She drank some more water, then she said something, forcing the words out past her cracked and swollen lips.

'Are you Dutch?' Maynard asked, and the girl nodded. 'I'm afraid none of us speaks Dutch.'

The girl sat up, then allowed Case to help her to her feet. She looked out to sea, then back at the men. 'The plane has gone?' Her English was only a little guttural. 'Is it coming back?'

'No.'

'But it has to!' She looked down the beach at the prahu, then looked sharply at Maynard again. She took the cup from Cabrolini again and wet her lips, running her tongue round them. Then she handed the cup back to Cabrolini without looking at him, just holding out her hand as if she knew that he would take the cup. 'Is that your boat? Do you have radio?'

Maynard shook his head. 'They wouldn't come back even if we could contact them. I'm afraid you're like us, miss. Out of luck.'

The girl's mouth tightened, as if she were not used to being told her condition. This baby makes up her own mind

54

whether she's in or out of luck, Case thought. Beneath the straggling blonde hair, the scratches and bites and mud on her face, and the torn shirt and skirt she wore, there was only half-hidden a beautiful girl. One who knew she was beautiful, Case guessed, and liked to be reminded of it. But it was not her looks but her manner that intrigued him. She looked around at the five men, then said in a sharp peremptory voice, 'And just who are you?'

Case could see the reaction on the faces of the men. Even Cabrolini, the one who by tradition should have been most accustomed to dealing with women, looked affronted by the girl's imperiousness. Case grinned and said, 'We're the Swiss Family Robinson. Who are you?'

The girl looked him up and down, dismissing him at once as the least presentable of the five men. 'I am Elisabeth Brinker.'

She said that, thought Case, as if she has an echo in her ears, too. Who was she? An actress, maybe? He couldn't remember ever having seen or heard of a Dutch actress, but he guessed there must be one or two: even Holland must want an answer to Joan Crawford and Ginger Rogers. None of the other men seemed to recognise the name, and because of that he did not feel so ignorant.

Maynard said, 'Were you supposed to be on the flying-boat?'

'My father and I——' She stopped, catching her breath; then she nodded. 'Yes, we should have been here.'

'Where is your father?'

'The Japanese caught him. He is dead.' Her voice, too, was dead; but there were no tears in the pale grey eyes. But there was pain there, and the men were aware of it and felt pain of their own.

'Did they catch you, too?' Polo asked, and the girl nodded. 'How'd you manage to get away?'

'I killed the guard. He was careless with his knife.'

Case whistled softly. 'Nice going, honey.'

'Do not call me honey.' There was the imperiousness again; Case bowed his head, subtly mocking her, but she was too intent on memory. 'And it was not nice going, as you call it. I did not enjoy it in the least. It was ugly and sickening——' Abruptly her voice broke and her eyes suddenly melted. She put a hand up to her mouth, holding her fingers against her trembling lips. 'I saw what they did to my father. I did not want it to happen to me.'

'Did they torture your father?' Maynard said. 'Why? They haven't been doing that in Malaya. At least we hadn't heard of it.'

'They wanted to know if we had been in touch with Australia.' She took her fingers away from her mouth, but kept them close to her face as if afraid that her lips might at any moment need their support again. She was suffering the migraine of some terrible memory, but she would tell the men about it. They sensed that she was coming to accept them now, convinced that there was no one else on whom she could rely. She looked out to sea again, at the empty sky and the promise of nothing, then back at them. 'We were leaving our place when one of the estate workers told my father there were a great many Japanese in Belawan Deli.'

'Where's that?' Garrick said.

'It's where I'd hoped we were headed,' said Maynard. 'It's the port for eastern Sumatra. Am I right, Miss Brinker?'

She nodded. 'But the Japanese have it now. And the man was right—there seemed to be thousands of troops there. Marines, my father said they were. We went down into the town to check and that was when we were captured. My father went to a man's house, a Eurasian, to find out why all the ships were in the harbour. And the man gave us away to the Japanese, told them who my father was.' Her lips trembled again, but this time with anger as much as horror. 'My father had given the man his first job.'

'Who was your father?' Cabrolini said, remembering something now. 'I came down here to Sumatra, oh, three years ago. We were trying to sell trucks to a company named Brinker—they seemed to own everything wherever we went.'

'That is my family,' said the girl without any false modesty. 'Joachim Brinker was my father. You may not know who he is—was, but the Japanese did.'

'But why would they torture him?' Case asked. 'So he saw a lot of Japs in this place Belawan whatever-it-is. If the Japs have taken over Sumatra, they wouldn't care who spotted their occupation troops.'

'They weren't occupation troops,' said Maynard. 'Not if they were marines. The Japs aren't like the Americans, Case—they don't use marines as occupation forces.'

'Don't complain to me,' said Case. 'Write to Congress. I always did say we should have stayed out of the Caribbean.'

Maynard pursed his lips, then looked back at the girl. 'Did you and your father find out anything?'

'The Japanese are using Belawan Deli as a staging post. They are on their way to Hollandia in New Guinea.' She looked around at the men, then said without any hope at all in her voice, 'We must find a radio.'

Polo looked up and down the beach, at the mangrove swamps and finally at the low hills inland. He spat in the sand and said, 'You're the one who might know where we could get one. But I ain't too flaming hopeful meself.'

Maynard said, 'Do you know Sumatra well, Miss Brinker?'

'My family have been here for three hundred years.' Again there was no attempt at modesty: she was stating a fact of history, her family was part of Sumatra.

'That doesn't answer the question,' said Case, who had never known even his grandparents.

Elisabeth Brinker stared at him for a moment, then she looked at Maynard. 'I know Sumatra, captain.'

'How far is it to the nearest town?'

'Subayang is thirty or forty kilometres down the coast from here. It is a trading kampong—a village—for the rubber workers.'

'Would they have a transmitter there?'

'I don't think so. But——' She considered for a moment, as if deciding whether to trust them. Then: 'My brother is with some soldiers in the hills—guerrillas. They would have a radio.'

'Where are they?' Polo asked.

Elisabeth Brinker shook her head. 'I don't know. They keep on the move. But someone in Subayang might know. The police sergeant—if he is still alive.'

'Are there any Japs in Subayang?' Garrick said.

'The Japanese are in the towns and kampongs all down the coast.'

'Then I'm for staying out of Subayang,' said Polo.

'Me, too,' said Case.

Maynard ignored Case, but looked at Polo. 'If the Japs get as far as New Guinea, it's only a stone's throw from there to Australia.'

Polo hesitated, then shrugged. 'Maybe you're right.'

'You two can go, then,' said Garrick. 'I'm with Jack here. I've finished fighting the war. All I want is to stay out of the way of the Japs.'

'For how long?' Maynard said, contempt curdling his voice. 'For ever?'

'We haven't given it a try yet.' Case looked around at the empty world, the sun now striking off the sea to wash out all distance, the hills lost in a great wave of cloud that only seemed to give perspective to infinity. Which way to go? he wondered; but knew that he least of all had the answer. But he sensed that Garrick and Cabrolini were with him: better to run anywhere at all than go looking for a hopeless fight. He had always been cautious about mis-matches, even in the days when he had had less than his life to lose.

Maynard said angrily, 'If we can get to a transmitter, perhaps it'll be our best chance of getting off Sumatra. If we can get in touch with Australia, they might tell us where they can pick us up.'

'And they might not,' said Garrick. 'You heard what that pilot said. They won't risk planes this far again.'

'And they'd be right,' said Case.

2

He was looking down towards the headland, at the small boat materialising out of the sea glare. The others all turned and Maynard put his binoculars to his eyes. He saw the patrol boat and the five men in it, and at once felt the sick hollowness inside him. Without looking at them he was aware of the empty guns he and the other men held, and once again the old doubt came back. Was it worth going on?

Then Case said, 'We better make ourselves scarce.'

He was already leading the way towards the mangroves. The others followed him, Maynard taking Elisabeth Brinker's elbow and half-supporting her as she stumbled on weak legs across the sand. They ran into the thin shade of the trees, tripping over the rascal roots, slipping and sliding in the pools of mud. Mosquitoes rose up like thin mist, humming with delight at the unexpected meals presenting themselves. Case stopped and looked back at Maynard.

'How far do we go? This swamp could go on for miles.'

Maynard looked back through the screen of twisted trunks. 'We'd do better if we can keep a sight on them. We'll cut down that way, keeping parallel to the beach.'

They moved on through the trees, sloping through the mud, sometimes sinking as far as their knees. Once Case lifted his foot to step on a glistening root and it turned into a snake and slid effortlessly away among the real roots. They could hear birds somewhere in the swamp, but could not see them. They heard the grunting, and Case, leading the way, pulled up dead.

'Holy Christ!' said Polo right behind him. 'I thought they were dead logs!'

No more than thirty feet in front of them the crocodiles, a dozen or more of them, lay in patches of sunlight that filtered through the trees. Even as they watched, one opened the saw-toothed trap of its mouth, and Case felt the involuntary shiver run up his spine. Another of the evil-looking beasts waddled a few feet, then slid off the mud bank into a dark shallow stream that wound its way through the mangrove. But as it went two others crawled up out of the water on to the mud.

Case turned back. 'If I got a choice, I think I'll take the Japs.'

There was no argument from the others. Maynard led the way now, still holding Elizabeth Brinker by the arm. They stumbled back towards the beach till they came to the last line of trees.

'Down behind the sandbank,' Maynard said. 'We can keep an eye on them from here.'

They all flopped down, sweat pouring out of them as they gasped in the thick heat here beneath the trees. Mosquitoes settled on them, covering their hands and faces, and they slapped mechanically at the gnats, streaking themselves with blood, as they stared through the trees at the Japanese.

The patrol boat had come into the lagoon. They could see the Japanese quite clearly now: an officer in the bow, three soldiers sitting stiffly behind him with their rifles at the ready, and a fourth soldier operating an outboard motor at the stern. The boat moved in by the beached prahu, the officer stood up and looked into the native craft; then he looked up and down the beach, said something to the soldiers, and the patrol boat moved off in a line parallel with the shore, going away from where Case and the others were hidden.

'He's playing it safe,' Maynard said. 'He won't come ashore till he's sure there's no one around.'

'Oh, my God!' Garrick suddenly exclaimed. 'There's my suitcase!'

All at once he leapt to his feet, fell over a tree root, picked himself up and started running through the trees. 'Stupid sonofabitch!' said Case, and got to his feet and went after Garrick.

He caught the boy before the latter had gone fifty yards, grabbed him by the back of his braces and pulled him down. They fell together into the sand, Case having to throw out his arm so he would not fall on his Thompson gun. He spat sand from his lips and snarled at Garrick, 'You crazy or something? That dough won't buy you anything if you're dead.'

Garrick, sweating and gasping, lay flat and buried his face in his arm. 'I didn't stop to think——' He raised his head and looked over the tangle of roots in front of them towards the suitcase lying where he had slept last night between two hummocks of sand. 'But after carting it all this way——'

Case wanted to call the boy greedy and stupid, but then he saw the look in the thin ugly face and he stopped. Garrick had told him something of what life had been like in Leeds; he himself had seen the back streets of Gary, Indiana, and of Pittsburgh. If Garrick had cherished an impossible dream of Tahiti, Case could not blame him for wanting to save his ticket money. Most men's dreams had a foolishness about them that led them to do foolish, even stupid things.

He watched the patrol boat come back, then slide in beside the prahu. The Japanese got out and moved up on to the sand, one man holding their boat by a long rope. They were still alert, looking suspiciously around; they brought a picture to Case's mind of terriers sniffing around for a trail. They were examining the fandango of footprints left by last night's evacuees, occasionally snapping a comment at each other in their high light voices. Then one of them moved up the sands away from the prahu, stopped, said something over his shoulder to the others and pointed straight up the beach at the spot where Case and Garrick lay in the mangroves.

Case saw the footprints leading right up to himself and Garrick. They were lying right where the whole party had run into the mangroves, lying there like bait dropped in the tracks. Beside him Case felt Garrick stiffen and he put a restraining hand on the boy in case he jumped up and ran. Then he heard the movement to his right and out of the corner of his eye saw Maynard drop down behind the gnarled roots of a tree. What the hell's he up to? Case wondered. None of them had any ammunition. Was Maynard going to take on the Japanese barehanded? He could feel the sweat coming up through Garrick's shirt under his hand; it ran down his own forehead and hung in tiny globules from his brow. His face flat on the sand, all perspective fore-shortened, he saw an insect, a giant dragon, crawl up the black mountain ridge of the mangrove root in front of him. It moved on out of the corner of his staring eye and he looked straight down the beach and saw the Japanese, guns held ready, stalking straight up the track of foot-prints towards himself and Garrick.

He felt Garrick's back arch beneath his hand, and he took his hand away, ready himself to surrender. Then suddenly the Japanese swung round as Maynard barked, 'Hold it!'

The Japanese didn't fire. It was obvious they were uncertain how many of their enemy were in the mangroves; perhaps the mess of footprints down by the prahu led them to believe there might be a platoon hidden in the trees. They looked anxiously around, but did not drop their weapons. The man down by the boat brought his gun up, but he looked up towards the officer waiting for an order.

'Can you hear me, Case?' shouted Maynard.

Case blew the sand off his lips. 'Yes!'

'Keep them covered while I take their guns.'

Don't be a goddam fool! Case almost shouted; but Maynard, his empty Thompson gun held threateningly, had already stepped out from behind the mangrove. He kept the officer and the three soldiers between himself and the man down by the boat, but the latter still looked as if he was afraid of being shot down by the invisible platoon or company. Case, watching the Japanese officer, saw the latter's eyes flick a glance along the line of trees, as if trying to guess how many men were hidden behind the grotesque trunks and twisted roots. He's going to wonder in a moment, Case thought, why we aren't all stepping out into the open like Maynard.

Suddenly he stood up and stepped out on to the sand, his own Thompson gun held as threateningly as Maynard's. The Japanese officer stared at him a moment, glanced at Maynard, then abruptly snapped an order. He dropped his pistol on the sand and the three soldiers behind him followed suit with their weapons. Maynard swung round, aiming his gun down the beach, and the man down by the boat got the message. He dropped his rifle and shook his head violently, asking not to be shot.

Garrick came quickly and awkwardly out of the mangroves, picked up the weapons of the officer and the three soldiers, then scurried down the beach and grabbed up the rifle lying in front of the man by the boat. The latter was only a boy, younger even than Garrick. They glanced at each other, afraid of each other yet bound by their youth. War for each of them was still a brand new experience, and amazement at their own involvement was as much part of their feeling as enmity.

Polo, Cabrolini and Elisabeth Brinker now came cautiously up the beach from where they had been hidden. Polo and Cabrolini each held his empty gun in the same threatening way as Case and Maynard, contributing to the bluff that so far had been so successful. Elisabeth Brinker, having nothing to bluff with, did her best to hide her apprehension and somehow succeeded in looking more confident than the Australian and the Italian.

'What now, skipper?' Garrick came back with his arms full of guns, a military sheaf.

'Hand out those guns,' Maynard said, and took the officer's pistol from Garrick.

Garrick handed round the guns, a rifle each for himself and Cabrolini, an automatic weapon each for Case and Polo. The men dropped their own weapons in the sand, and Polo moved around, relieving the Japanese of their ammunition. Case, just before he dropped his Thompson gun, glanced up and saw the Japanese officer watching him. He took out the magazine, showed it was empty and grinned broadly at the look of chagrin on the officer's face.

'Do you speak English?' Maynard asked, but the officer did not answer him, just stared straight ahead with dull pained eyes. He was older than any of his men, perhaps in his mid-thirties, and there was a long scar down his left cheek; it was a relic of the rape of Shanghai, one he bore with honour and that he used to boast about. But honour was dead now and all he wanted was to die. Maynard looked hard at him for a moment, wondering if the Japanese did speak English; then he turned and went down and looked at the patrol boat, and came back. 'We'll take their boat. There's more ammunition and some extra tins of petrol in it. It will get us to Subayang. We'd better start moving now.'

Garrick looked at Case. 'I think I'll go with them, Jack.' His voice was apologetic. He owed something to the American, but he knew that the way to Tahiti was not through those swamps behind them. 'There might be miles and miles of those damned crocodiles.'

Case nodded, being sensible if not enthusiastic. Then he looked at Maynard. 'What you gonna do with these Nips?'

Maynard looked around at the Japanese, drew a deep breath

and said quietly, 'I'm afraid we're going to have to shoot them.'

Even Polo looked surprised. 'That's a bit bloody drastic,' he said, and rubbed the grey and ginger stubble of his beard. He would shoot the Japanese if it had to be done; he was primitive enough to be more concerned with his own life rather than those of others. But he looked around at the other men and at Elisabeth Brinker, hoping one of them might have an alternative.

'What you gonna do?' Case said. 'Line 'em up and mow 'em down? Let 'em run along the beach and we'll take pot shots at 'em, a prize for the guy with the best score? Is this what you call the business of war?'

'What would you suggest?' Maynard said angrily. 'Leave them here, let them get away and sound the alarm? We'd be gunned down by a plane before we'd gone five miles down the coast.'

'Maybe that's a risk we gotta take.'

Dear God, Maynard thought, why did you have to saddle me with a humanitarian? His father was a humanitarian, a man who believed the British Empire had been won by the kindly nature of English Christian gentlemen; Maynard himself believed in the Empire, but he was a realist and knew it had been won by men with a certain streak of ruthlessness in them. Men who would have seen the realism of what he was proposing: 'It's a risk I don't want to take. We've been shot up once—I don't want to go through it again. But what is just as important—we have to get to that wireless transmitter! If we're the only ones who know that convoy is on its way to New Guinea, then it's up to us to see we get the information through to Australia!'

'I thought you English bastards were supposed to be civilised,' Case argued stubbornly. 'Where's all that goddam respect for human life you're always telling the rest of the world about?'

'We weren't the ones who started this war.' Maynard could feel the anger and impatience bubbling up inside him. 'Dammitall, can't you see I'm just trying to be practical? I don't want to kill these men just to be rid of them. In a way, if we shoot them it will be the most humane thing we could do. If we tie them up, perhaps they could starve to death, go out of their minds with the heat and thirst, anything.'

'We could take them with us,' Garrick said without any thought of logic.

'And what will we do with them when we get near Subayang?' Maynard demanded. 'Throw them overboard to the sharks?'

'The skipper's right,' said Polo, and even Maynard was surprised at where his support came from. 'Being practical is the only way you stay alive in a war. I vote with him. Let's shoot 'em.'

Case shook his head, unable to accept the cold-blooded callousness of it. But he looked at Garrick and said, 'What about you?'

Garrick, too, shook his head. 'I never was very practical.' Then added with uncharacteristic bitterness, 'Especially about killing people.'

Case looked at Elisabeth Brinker. 'What do you say?'

She came up out of some dark memory, looked at him blankly and he repeated the question. She looked at the Japanese, hating them with a passion that none of the others had yet had cause for; but something, a foreboding of guilt perhaps, made her say, 'I am sorry. I do not wish to vote.'

'Don't want to——?' Case was angry now, a stranger to the men who had been with him for the past two days. He's not so casual after all, Maynard thought, he does give a damn about something. But it was not going to make him any easier to deal with. We're trying to decide the lives of five guys and you don't wanna vote! Goddam it, what the hell d'you think this is? An election for a bridge club or something?'

Elisabeth Brinker said nothing. She had made her decision and decisions with her were like actions: one could not recall them. Pride threw up hurdles behind her, left her isolated.

'Leave Miss Brinker alone,' said Maynard, knowing that Ruth, his wife, also would never have voted on such an issue. 'That leaves the voting split, if we're going to vote on it at all. And if it is a toss-up, I'm afraid practicality has to win.'

'We haven't finished voting yet,' said Case, and looked at Cabrolini.

'You can't ask him!' Polo protested vehemently. 'Righto, we were wrong last night, not letting him have a go with the dice. But Christ, this is different. He's on their side!'

Case was still looking at Cabrolini. 'Are you?'

Cabrolini did not even look at the Japanese, but he did look at Elisabeth Brinker before he said, 'Do I have to vote, signore?'

'You can join the non-voters,' said Case, still angry; he

was trapped, had been made to commit himself, 'But I was hoping you'd have the guts to make a decision!'

Cabrolini flushed; then he looked steadily at Maynard. 'I do not think we should kill them, captain.'

'We don't care what the hell you think!' Polo snarled.

Maynard looked at Case, Garrick and Cabrolini, then turned and faced the Japanese. Then he lifted his pistol, saying over his shoulder, 'You had better go, Miss Brinker. But please hurry!'

Before Elisabeth Brinker could move, Case had stepped in front of Maynard, grabbing the Englishman's wrist and pushing the pistol up. The two men stared at each other, the sweat of agony shining on the face of each; neither of them wanted this situation nor the decision he had had to take, but they were trapped as in a quicksand. Trapped so deeply that they might kill each other before they would kill the Japanese.

'Who do you shoot first?' Case said, and nodded at the pistol, aimed now at his own head.

'Don't—*please!*'

Maynard turned his head as Elisabeth Brinker suddenly spoke; and the moment was broken. He slackened his arm, and Case, recognising the surrender, let go of Maynard's wrist. The two men stood back from each other, and behind him Case heard one of the Japanese hiss softly with relief.

'I just hope you're right,' said Maynard, trembling a little, glad inside himself that he did not have to shoot the Japanese, but knowing inside himself also that it would have been the most sensible thing to do. And added, because there was still some of his father's piety in him, 'I *pray* you're right.'

3

'You'd have shot *me*, wouldn't you?'

Maynard looked down at the Japanese officer. The latter did not speak English, but he had understood what had gone on and now he understood the question, the scar on his cheek twitched, then he nodded. He's a professional, too. Maynard thought, he understands the business of war. He bent and checked the bonds of the officer and the four soldiers; they had been bound with ropes from the prahu and the patrol boat. Then he straightened up and said, 'You poor devils. It would have been better——'

'What?' said Garrick. Case and the others were down by the patrol boat, but Garrick had come back to gather up his suitcase. 'Why would it have been better?'

'They're going to die anyway. My way would have been quicker.'

Garrick said nothing, looking down at the bound Japanese, then he nodded. 'Perhaps you're right. But the other was too much like execution.' He looked up and said almost irrelevantly, 'I'm against hanging.'

'I'm not,' said Maynard. 'But this wouldn't have been an execution. It would have been more a mercy killing. Or are you against that, too?'

'I'm a Catholic,' said Garrick. 'I'm against that, too.'

'What are you *for*? Winning the war?'

'Of course.'

'Then you are going to have to swallow some of your principles. You don't win wars playing the game one's own way. You win them playing them the other chap's way. War isn't cricket.'

'You should talk to my dad then,' said Garrick, unable to argue: he would always be out of his depth in the rules of war, even if the war lasted another two or three years and he was involved in every moment of it.

Maynard took a last look at the Japanese, then he and Garrick went down and joined the others in the patrol boat. Cabrolini pushed it out, clambered aboard and started up the outboard motor. They went out across the smooth blue lagoon, turned round the point and headed south-east. The men looked back at the last moment at the prahu, its shredded rattan sail hanging like a tattered flag from the splintered mast. It sat forlornly just above the water's edge, the marker of the first stage of their journey home.

'You had better sit low in the boat, Miss Brinker,' Maynard said, turning back, facing the next stage of their journey. 'The rest of us put on the Jap caps and try and look like a samurai. Keep your face turned away from the shore. It's only a rough chance if someone picks us up in the glasses, but we may get away with it.'

The men pulled on the Japanese field caps, none of which fitted. 'The bloke who owned this one must've had a pin head,' said Polo. 'Where'd he carry his brains?'

Cabrolini looked at Maynard. 'If we strike trouble in Subayang, captain, what happens then?'

'We stick together, no matter what happens,' said Maynard, and looked at Case. 'It's our only chance.'

'I ain't arguing,' said Case. 'Not yet, anyway.'

Elisabeth Brinker, sitting on the floor of the boat, said, 'We have a rubber plantation about twenty kilometres inland from Subayang. My brother used to live there.' She used the past tense without realising it.

'That will be our alternative then,' said Maynard, then glanced towards the shore, keeping his face tilted down beneath the peak of his cap. Sumatra, dark green, hard as an emerald, seemed to stare back at him, if not hostile at least uninviting. It had never been a gentle land; the Dutch had not conquered it by acting as Christian gentlemen. Maynard glanced across at Elisabeth Brinker and wondered how hard her family had had to fight to remain there for three hundred years. Then he said, 'But I hope we find what we want in Subayang. I don't fancy running around Sumatra for the rest of the war.'

Polo took out his battered packet of Capstans, extracted one and lit it. He blew out smoke and looked around. 'I'll share me tucker and water with anyone. But I ain't gunna hand out any of me smokes. This is all I got left and if the skipper's right and I'm gunna be running around Sumatra for the rest of the war, I'll need 'em for me nerves.'

'But the war might last for years, Mr. Murphy,' said Elisabeth Brinker.

'My word, it might,' said Polo. 'But if it does, I won't see the end of it. I'll pack it in when me last smoke is gone.'

Elisabeth Brinker stared at him a moment, as if not sure that he was joking. Then she turned away, took a handkerchief from her pocket, reached over and wet it in the sea, then proceeded to sponge the dirt and sweat from her face and arms. She seemed unaware of the men watching her till she took a comb from her pocket and went to run it through her hair. As if reading their minds, but not sounding as if she were on the defensive, she said, 'I do not expect any favours because I am a woman.'

'We'll try not to embarrass you with any,' said Maynard. 'But having a woman with us does change the situation a little.'

'Didn't they make allowances at Sandhurst for a second sex?' Case asked.

'I can forget my sex if you can,' said Elisabeth.

'I am an Italian, signorina,' said Cabrolini. 'It would be a

67

biological impossibility to attempt to be so absent-minded.'

'Then you had better forget you're an Italian,' said Maynard, not sourly, because he was coming to like the Italian.

'I don't know what it was like at Sandhurst, skipper,' said Garrick, 'but fifty percent of the rest of England is female. And I was brought up to appreciate it.'

'So was I,' said Maynard. 'Despite what Mr. Case may think, I didn't marry my wife as a military exercise.'

Case grinned, conceding the point. He knew now that he was committed to the company of these men and he did not relish the thought. Something would unravel from the fabric of each of them and intertwine itself with him; it had happened before with managers, trainers and seconds, and all the relationships had gone sour. And the fault had been his. He had chosen isolation, or had had it forced on him, when he was only a child; and the habits of childhood, like certain ailments, are not always outgrown. So far, of all these men and this girl, he felt most at home with Maynard, even though the Englishman irritated and at times even angered him with his uncompromising approach to any situation. It had been that way in the old days: he had always felt more at home with an opponent in the ring than with the subtler, more complicated relationships with his friends outside it. Maynard was an opponent, one capable of scoring points with his tongue.

'End of the round,' said Case. 'You took that one on points,'

Maynard stared, not understanding at first; then he nodded, accepting that this might be a long bout. 'I'm sure you won't throw in the towel. Or will you?'

'Not with you, buster,' said Case, and took some strength from the promise of the encounter.

Maynard had begun to sort out the weapons and ammunition they had taken from the Japanese. 'Two machine-carbines —these are copies of the German Solothurn. They fire 8 millimetre ammunition.' The others said nothing, watching him while he, the professional, went on as if giving a lesson to new recruits: 'These rifles are 6.5 carbines made by Arasaki. And the pistol is a Nambu 8-millimetre, fires eight rounds.'

'Where did you learn all this?' Case asked.

'It's part of the business of war.' Maynard's sarcasm was only thinly veiled. 'Didn't you always try to find out what armaments your opponents had, the sort of punches they favoured?'

"Your round again,' Case conceded.

'Our own weapons are useless without ammunition. And

we're not likely to find any.' Maynard picked up his Thompson, looked at it almost affectionately, then dropped it overboard. Case and the other men hesitated, then they followed his example with their own weapons. Maynard went on: 'From now on we'll depend on this Jap stuff. And every chance we get, we'll steal ammunition for it.'

'How many chances do you think we'll get?' Garrick asked.

Maynard shrugged. 'I haven't the faintest idea.' He looked inshore at the flat swamps stretching away to the haze-distorted hills. 'My father, a man of infinite ignorance, used to say, "When you don't know", which was most of the time with him, "then pray." I think I might follow his advice this time.' He looked back at the others. 'I'm sorry I can't be more decisive.'

'Don't apologise, captain,' said Elisabeth. 'There might be some of us who do not look upon prayer as only a last resort.'

The sun began to burn them, making their mosquito bites itch, and before long they all were looking with longing eyes towards the distant inland hills under their pale canopy of clouds. The coast, miles upon miles of mangrove swamps, appeared deserted of kampongs and they moved at a steady rate towards Subayang, having no milestones but Maynard's watch. He looked at it in the early afternoon and said, 'We can't be too far from Subayang. We'd better find somewhere on shore and hide up there till dark.'

Cabrolini swung the tiller over and they moved in towards the shore till they were riding the swell off a small, dark-stained beach. They went in at one end of the beach, Cabrolini shipped the motor, and dragged the boat up on to the sand. They cut branches from the mangroves with a parang they had found in the boat and covered the boat with them. Then they retreated to the shade of the trees. It was still blazing hot and the mosquitoes, drowsy with the heat, did not come out of the swamps to attack them.

'I shall be back in a moment,' said Elizabeth.

'Where are you going?' Maynard said.

'There are certain things, captain, that a person, man or woman, likes to do alone.'

Maynard blushed, something Elisabeth had not done when he had asked her the question. 'Sorry.'

Elisabeth walked away, disappearing into the trees, and Polo said, 'You're gunna have to get used to her, skipper. She's worrying you more than the rest of us put together, but we're stuck with her and you're gunna have to get used to her.

If she wants to go for whatever she wants to do, we're gunna have to turn our backs and make out we don't notice. Women are touchier about them sorta things than men are.'

'You don't have to lecture me about women,' said Maynard, touchy himself now.

'No offence,' said Polo. 'Only I been around my missus longer than you been around yours.' Then added with a moment of clear insight into himself, 'I never done the right thing by the missus, never took her flowers or anything like that. But I learned one thing, to respect her privacy. And I don't just mean when she went to the dike.'

Case looked at the Australian, seeing for the first time the other men that populate the skins of all of us. None of us is one man, thought Case; but why are we always so surprised when the strangers emerge? We are aware of the secret men within ourselves, but never anticipate the surprises in another man. He looked with new interest at Polo and said, 'How did you come by the name Polo?'

Polo grinned. 'I used to work down the mines, the coal mines, back home. Went down 'em right after I knew I'd never make good in the ring. They put me in charge of the ponies——' He stopped for a moment, remembering the thick smell of the ponies, the way he could recognise each of them, like humans, in the gloom of the galleries, the way he had cried in that same gloom, away from the eyes of the other miners, when four of the ponies had been killed in a fall-in. He suddenly grew wistful for all that he had been yearning all his life to escape. He went on, 'Working down the mines, you start dreaming about what it could be like up top. I used to dream about having me own string of polo ponies. It's bloody silly, I know——' He stopped again and blushed, embarrassed more by the admission of his dream than he had been by the admission of his inadequacies as a husband. 'I used to read about them, too, the polo players, I mean. Fighters and polo players. Great combination, eh? I knew all the handicaps of blokes like Tommy Hitchcock, Harriman, Bob Skene, just like I knew your record, Jack. I was gunna be Ten-Goal Murphy, the polo-playing miner from Cessnock. The bloody silly things a man dreams about.' He shook his head. 'Bloody silly.'

Then Elisabeth came back, unembarrassed, and said, 'If we can contact the police sergeant, I think we should ask him if he can get us some quinine. Just in case some of us should go down with malaria. And we should be careful what we eat, otherwise we might get dysentery. I had it once and it is not very pleasant.'

'I'm more worried about Jap bullets than I am about malaria and dysentery,' said Garrick.

'Then you don't know Sumatra,' said Elisabeth. 'This country can kill you just as easily as the Japanese.'

CHAPTER 4

'We're getting close,' Maynard said. 'Cut the engine.'

Cabrolini cut the motor, tilting it out of the water but leaving it in position on the stern of the boat. Garrick and Case took up the oars, sitting facing the bow, and began to scull the boat slowly through the darkness. Each of them had his rifle, one of the Japanese Arasakis, across his knees. Up in the bow Maynard and Polo each had a machine-carbine; Maynard also had the Japanese officer's pistol. Maynard had debated with himself whether to give Elizabeth the pistol, then had decided against it. She now crouched behind him, between him and Case. No one spoke again as the boat glided up the river, keeping close to the bank that they sensed rather than saw. In the darkness on their right, the nearer bank, thin harsh cries occasionally ripped the silence, chilling the blood of all of them but Elisabeth, who must have lived with such sounds from the day of her birth. Night, upon which they depended so much, was no comforting ally.

Polo touched Maynard's arm and pointed up ahead. The gesture also was sensed rather than seen by the others in the boat; they all leaned forward and Case and Garrick stopped rowing for the moment. The skyline ahead, no more than one deeper darkness against another, had changed; the casual scribble of treetops had given way to more definite silhouettes, the sharp prow-like roof-tops of native houses. They had reached Subayang.

Before they had left the last beach Elisabeth had sketched roughly in the sand the lay-out of the large kampong. The men knew now that a majority of the houses were built on stilts out over the Subayang River, that the main wharf was two hundred yards upstream from the first house they must pass, that the police station faced immediately on to the wharf. Elisabeth had surprised them with her detailed picture

71

of the place, but she had told them she had known Subayang when she was a child and a young girl. 'These kampongs do not change,' she had said. 'If the house falls down in a storm, they build another exactly like it in the same place.'

'Isn't anyone interested in progress around here?' Case had asked.

'I thought you would have been the last to ask that question,' Elisabeth had said, looking him up and down, convinced now that he was no more than a beachcomber.

'You got me wrong,' said Case, unperturbed by her insult. 'Subayang might be just the place I been looking for. Under this bum's exterior there beats a very conservative heart. You might even call me a reactionary.' But then he had exposed the tongue in his cheek by adding, 'Just like you Dutchmen.'

'Not Dutchmen,' she had said, disturbed by his careless attitude towards her. All her life men had courted her, even as a child; women, especially beautiful women, were always in short supply in colonial life. She had come to expect homage and admiration, sometimes even adoration, as she expected good manners and respect; she was not accustomed to men who looked at her with amusement bordering on contempt. Especially men who would have been thrown in gaol in the society in which she had lived. So, wanting to shut him out, to have the last word, no matter how petty, she had said, 'Not Dutchman. We call ourselves Hollanders.'

'Is the police sergeant in Subayang a Hollander?'

'Naturally.'

'Then I'll bet there's been one change in the kampong,' Case had said. 'I wouldn't bet on him still being there. Progress or no progress.'

'We shall still have to risk it,' Maynard had said, wanting no more argument. He had to work according to a plan; Sandhurst had not taught him improvisation. It would be against his whole nature and training to wander around Sumatra hoping for an accident that might help them escape; better to risk capture doing something planned. Unlike Case he believed in destinations, depended on them. 'We need to find that transmitter.'

Now they were within two hundred yards of where they hoped the transmitter might be. The boat slipped in beneath the houses and at once came to a halt; something fell on those in the boat and they all gasped with shock. Case went down, feeling Garrick wrestling beside him; Case stayed still, waiting for a light to go on and the Japanese voices to bark at them. He could feel the wet net wrapped round his face and body like a hundred clammy hands, could hear the others struggling softly but frantically to free themselves. He found the edge of the net, lifted it and sat up from beneath it.

He patted Garrick reassuringly and the boy stopped struggling. Case freed him from the net, pulled it in towards himself, freeing the others and then dropped it over the side of the boat. He leaned forward, his eyes accustomed to the heavy darkness now, and tapped Maynard on the shoulder. He pointed up ahead to where other nets hung down from the houses' platforms, outlined against the paler darkness beyond the houses like some sort of climbing sea ivy. He put his mouth against Maynard's ear.

'Fishing nets. But where are the folk upstairs? They must've heard us.'

Maynard shrugged, glancing up at the floor of the house above them. The people in the house must have heard the commotion, stifled though it had been. Why hadn't they come out on to their platform to investigate? Something was fishy and it wasn't just the net. He smiled without humour at the weak joke, the sort his father would have made. He found Case's ear with his own mouth, hissed softly, 'Everything's too quiet.'

'You wanna turn back?' They were as intimate as lovers whispering obscene endearments; they turned their ears to each other's lips.

'It's too late now. Ship the oars, use your hands.'

They moved on, slipping between the stilts. Once the boat bumped gently against a stilt and they all froze; above them a child whimpered and a board creaked as someone moved quickly across the floor; the child was quietened, those in the boat waited a moment, then they moved on. They could smell domestic smells now, the lingering odours of tonight's meal; they swung cautiously past a rope on which washing hung like a line of flattened carcases. They heard a dog growl and again they stopped, holding their breath; but like the child, the dog also was quietened and nobody came to the edge of the platform to see who was beneath the house. Their nerve-ends began to tingle; their skin rubbed irritatingly against their salt-stiffened clothes. They knew now that someone was waiting for them. But where? They had come so far now that it could be as dangerous to turn back as to go forward.

Then, as they were about to move out from one house across

73

an open water lane towards another house, they heard some-one padding in bare feet across the floor above them. Case put out a hand, grabbed hold of a stilt and held the boat steady, his arm almost pulled from its socket as the weight of the boat and its occupants swung it round on the current. He held on, gritting his teeth, and waited for the bare-footed man to come down the rickety steps ahead of them. But the footsteps stopped at the edge of the platform. They waited for the challenging cry, Maynard and Polo with their fingers already on the triggers of their guns, eyes strained as they peered into the darkness. Then they heard the tiny musical sound of water hitting water, saw the thin string of urine falling from the edge of the platform. Everyone giggled silently, their mirth taking some of the tension out of them. The man finished his bladder-relieving, padded back across the floor and in a moment there was silence above them again.

Maynard jerked his hand forward, Case and Garrick pushed against the stilts and the boat shot quietly out across the water lane towards the black cave beneath the house opposite. And in that moment the searchlights, two of them, burst on them. They threw up their arms, cowering back as if they had been hit physically. Case, from under the shade of his arm, saw everyone in the boat literally reeling, made groggy by the smashing impact of the lights. He drew in his breath, then flung himself towards the back of the boat. He fell over Cabrolini, pushed the motor back into the water, grabbed the starter and jerked it.

Next moment the boat had shot forward out of the lights into the blackness beneath the house in front of them. Bullets smashed into the stilts, but somehow missed the boat. Case, blind now in the darkness after the glare of the lights, steered only by chance. The boat crashed into a stilt, there was a loud cracking sound and shrieks from above; the house tilted crazily and a man plunged by them, followed by a yelping dog. The boat ploughed on, cannoning off more stilts, while the Japanese searched frantically for them with their fire. Everything was a confusion of noise: the roar of the boat's motor, the chatter of automatic fire from the Japanese, the thin screaming of women and children in the houses above the racing boat.

Then the boat smashed head-on into a flight of steps. Maynard was flung forward right out of the boat and on to a small platform. He scrambled to his feet, looked up and saw the stars in the polygon of the sky between the roof-tops.

'This way!'

The others followed him, oblivious of the bruises and lost skin they had suffered as they had been flung off-balance by the collision. They were aware of nothing but the desperate urge to escape, though Garrick, almost as an automatic action, did grab up his suitcase. Even Case, who would never understand why he had been the first to react in trying to get away, did hesitate but jumped out of the boat and clambered up the steps, caught up in the momentum of his original involuntary action.

They ran along a long platform, like a sidewalk above the water street. It swayed and bent under the pounding of their feet and several times one of them almost plunged off into the water below. Dogs, chickens, even a small pig impeded their progress; but Maynard, leading the way, crashed on, oblivious of cruelty to animals. The Japanese had stopped firing, but the searchlights were still seeking the fugitives. The lights were mounted on two launches which had now pulled out into the river; their beams swung up and down the long row of houses on this side of the water. Maynard saw the yellow boom of light swinging down the houses towards them and abruptly he turned down a narrower platform between two houses, pulling the others with him as on an invisible rope.

Case, bringing up the rear, bumped into Elisabeth, felt her stumble and begin to go down. He grabbed at her, even at that moment aware of the softness of her body beneath his rough hands. He heard her sob as his hands closed on her breasts and lifted her up; but he knew it was not a sob of indignation but only of despair. He could feel the surrender in her, the exhaustion and fear that had taken all strength from her.

'Get up!' he yelled savagely. 'Keep running!'

They ran down between the houses, turned left and found they were off the shaky platform and on firm ground. They were running past a line of stores, atap-roofed huts with signs hanging outside them. For the moment they were cut of the line of fire from the Japanese down on the river; then suddenly they saw the tiny spurts of fire up ahead. Bullets smacked into the stores near them; a sign splintered and flew off the roof like a hit bird. Maynard lurched to the left and Case, running behind him, thought he had been hit. But the Englishman had flung himself at the door of a shop, gone hurtling in, yelling to the others to follow him. Somehow they all made it without being hit, while the Japanese fire raked the front of the store.

Case pulled Elisabeth down beside him, feeling her shudder as bullets crashed into the wall above them. He heard a child cry out and he swung round. A small oil lamp burned in one corner at the back of the shop, and there a Chinese family, a man, a woman and three small children, cowered in the one small tight group, their faces puckered in the same grotesque expression of fear.

'Get down!' Maynard yelled at them, gesturing to the floor, but they were blind and deaf with terror. He moved swiftly towards them and pushed them down behind two large bags of rice. He handled them roughly because, illogically, he knew he was angry at their being here: he did not want to be responsible for more lives. He turned back and shouted to Polo and Cabrolini, 'Cover the front while I'll scout the back!'

Then he blew out the lamp, but not before he had had a quick look around the shop. It was a typical Chinese store, the sort he had seen so often up-country in Malaya. Barricades of goods cluttered the floor space; the ceiling was hung with a jungle growth of nets, ropes and lamps. A small harvest of brooms grew in one corner; dried fish were stacked like giant leaves. Everything that a villager was likely to need was here: this was a jungle department store. Maynard blew out the lamp, turned round and fell over a stack of tin saucepans. The small silly accident saved his life. A burst of automatic fire chopped through the slats of the front of the store, sprayed the shelves just above his head and sent glass tinkling to the floor.

Polo and Cabrolini were at the front of the store, shooting out through the open door at the Japanese farther up the alley that divided the row of stores from the houses on the river. Case and Elisabeth were down behind a counter, he still with his arm about her, afraid that she was exhausted enough to want to surrender. He was still under the impetus of his own involuntary urge to escape. Behind him he could hear the Chinese family whimpering with terror and he turned, wanting to comfort them too, but he could not see them in the darkness. Despite himself he was reaching out to people, committing himself to them. But there was no time to think

76

about the change in himself. Bullets crashed into the shelves above the counter and he and Elisabeth ducked beneath a rain of rice and nuts.

Maynard had wrenched open the back door, found a narrow alley there. He shouted to the others and Garrick, suitcase in one hand, gun in the other, led them out the door on the run. Case pulled Elisabeth to her feet and dragged her after him towards the rear of the store. They ducked as another spatter of bullets ripped along one wall. When he looked up he saw a familiar shape outlined against a window at the back of the store. He grabbed the bottle, hoping it *was* Vat 69, and pushed Elisabeth ahead of him out into the alley. Maynard took one last look at the dim shapes of the Chinese family lying on the floor behind the rice sacks. Poor blighters, he thought, yelled 'Sorry!' at them, and went out of the doorway after the others.

They were half-way down the alley when the Japanese soldier came round the corner ahead of them. The Japanese raised his gun to shoot. Garrick flung himself to one side, his reflexes not conditioned to bringing up his own rifle to shoot back; Case, the bottle in one hand and his rifle in the other, flung himself against Elisabeth and the two of them crashed down against the wall of the hut. They heard the shots rip down the alley from behind them, saw the Japanese stiffen and go down. Then Maynard, Polo and Cabrolini were running past them, Maynard reloading his pistol as he ran. Case pulled Elisabeth to her feet and they followed the men down the alley.

Maynard stopped, waiting for them by the body of the dead Japanese. As Case, Elisabeth and Garrick reached him, he looked down at the dead man at his feet. Then he looked again, dropped on one knee and turned the man's face up to the starlight. There was no mistaking the long scar down the sallow cheek. Maynard looked up at Case, but said nothing. His mind was a confusion of queries as to how the officer had got here from that beach forty kilometres up the coast. Had another patrol found him and his men? Or had they managed to undo the ropes that had bound them, found their way inland to some road and somehow got a lift to Subayang? There were a dozen conjectures, none of which could now be answered. The one unarguable fact was that he *was* here, must have been the one responsible for the ambush into which they had fallen. He stood up, looked again at the stunned and puzzled Case, then started running again.

It was Elisabeth who reversed her role with Case. She grabbed at his arm. 'Keep running!'

Case, recovering, took one last look at the dead Japanese, the man who had betrayed him. Then he followed Elisabeth down the alley towards the black jungle that stood waiting for them like another betrayer.

2

It began to rain when they were no more than ten minutes outside Subayang. They were moving down a path that wound through thick jungle, Maynard occasionally flashing his torch when they blundered off the path and into thick bushes. There was no sound of any pursuit behind them, but they moved as quickly as the darkness would allow them. Then the rain came down.

It came accompanied with lightning and thunder, a storm for the end of the world. It fell with the fury of a barrage, leaves and vines becoming part of the downpour as the rain hammered like shrapnel at the upper terraces of the invisible trees. Thunder exploded in tremendous blasts, as if mountains had risen up and collided with each other, and great swords of lightning tried to slash the world apart. Sometimes the party came out into a clearing and had to fight their way across what seemed to be a waterfall, each of them choked and blinded by the deluge of rain. Humanity ran out of them with the water and they became animals, fighting the storm, shouting at it with miserable anger as it tried to beat them into the muddy grave of the ground. In the eruptions of lightning they glimpsed each other's faces, green and skull-like, and saw their own hopelessness mirrored in the dead eyes that stared back at them out of the water that was drowning them. They stumbled on, lifting their feet out of mire that grew deeper with every step; leaves, branches, even dead birds fell on them as they bent closed to the waiting earth. They were ready to collapse when they came to the flooded stream.

Maynard, still in the lead, almost walked into the stream. He felt the path beginning to slope down and he grabbed at an invisible bush, his hand having luck of its own and landing on a thick branch; his feet went from under him in the mud, but he hung on and stared down into the darkness ahead of him. The expected flash of lightning came and he saw the stream, greenish-brown, rolling by only feet below him. Cabrolini slid into him, slumping down on his behind in the mud, but the others managed to pull up.

Maynard turned his head, shouted into the thunderous darkness, 'Sit down where you are! We can't go on!'

Everyone sank down, surrendering gratefully to the cold slimy comfort of the mud. Case stretched out, shivering, his teeth turning to chalk in his chattering mouth, felt for the neck of the bottle he still carried, opened it and lifted it to his mouth. He was not even sure that it was whisky; it could be turpentine, rat poison or varnish; but he didn't care. He was not going to query why there should be a bottle of Scotch whisky unopened in a Chinese store in a kampong in a remote part of Sumatra. There were too many questions crowding his mind, ones that he would have to find an answer to if and when this storm let up and day was allowed to dawn. In the meantime, if he was going to die it did not matter whether he died quickly from poison or with Scotch comfort in the wet bed of the mud.

It *was* whisky. He felt the warmth of it at once, took a second swig and found the mud almost endurable. He reached for Elisabeth, shoved the bottle at her; the lightning flashed again and he saw her take the bottle and raise it towards her mouth. She did not hand it back to him; he waited impatiently for it while it moved around in the darkness from hand to hand, from mouth to mouth; it was Garrick who finally gave it back to him. He lifted it again to his own mouth, cursed that it now seemed only a third full. Cold, miserable and exhausted, he cursed himself too for his generosity. And did not feel ashamed by his lack of charity. Misery does not breed charity and he knew with certainty that all the others, shivering and spent as himself, would have been just as selfish.

The rain stopped as abruptly as it had begun. Though the trees continued to drip water and the stream hissed below them in the darkness, something like deep silence prevailed after the tumult of the storm. They all sat up from where they had been lying on their stretchers of mud, but none of them stood up. Soaked through so that even their flesh seemed to squelch with water, they were no longer aware of the slime in which they sat. They rested gratefully on it, feeling that even its viscosity could support them better than their own liquid legs.

'We'd better stay here till daylight,' Maynard said. 'We

79

'can't cross that stream or river or whatever it is, in the dark.'

'What about the Nips?' Garrick asked.

'They won't move around in the jungle before daylight. That was one thing we learned about them in Malaya. They don't like the jungle at night.' He peered into the darkness, then saw Elisabeth in a departing slash of lightning. She looked like a mad woman, Ophelia a week after drowning. 'Are you all right, Miss Brinker?'

'Yes,' she said, feeling the leeches already coming up out of the mud on to her legs, but determined not to complain, not to be a woman.

She drew the darkness about her like a blanket. Shivering with memory as much as with the dampness of her body, she tried to look at the future, but it was no more penetrable than the black night that enveloped her. And so she fell back on all that she knew, the past; because she did not know the present, was only experiencing it and still had to absorb it and find the meaning to it. Life in the circle in which she had moved had not prepared her for tragedy; Sumatra could be a cruel country, but she had been protected from it. She knew the dangers of its fauna and its climate: she had seen rubber workers who had been killed by tigers, had had an uncle whose face was pitted with monkey-pox, had nursed her father when he had gone down with his periodic bouts of malaria. But she had been insulated against that other pox, nationalism; and her father and his friends had lightly dismissed her fears about the Japanese. The Dutch, like the British, were here in the East to stay; the nationalists and the Japanese would make noises, but there was no call for worry about them. And so, still confident of the future, still insulated by three hundred years of complacency, she had been bridesmaid at a wedding on the day the Japanese landed in Sumatra and were welcomed as liberators by some of the more violent nationalists. The wedding breakfast had broken up in a panic and the bride and groom were dead within the hour, still in their wedding clothes. The wedding gifts had been looted and had disappeared, but that was not all: a way of life, too, had disappeared.

So now she sought refuge in the past, but that did not help. Tears wet her already wet face, she trembled with grief, not fear. She lay back in the mud, too exhausted to care about the leeches, and sleep wrapped her like a mercy. The storm retreated, the lightning no longer frightening but pale and beautiful in the distant sky, and the moon came up, skull-like among the black shrouds of cloud. Everyone slept, too spent to care about discomfort or even death, and water dripped from the trees like seconds in the clock of the night.

Maynard woke to the gossip of monkeys. He opened his eyes and saw them swinging through the trees, their flight almost a musical rhythm, tiny men whose antecedents in the mud beneath them had much less dignity and were no less ugly. He had often debated Darwin's theory with his father, but had got nowhere. Peter Maynard would never allow himself to believe that a middle-class Christian Englishman might have had an ancestor who had lived in a tree. Man had emerged, walking upright and with a hairless body, in the Garden of Eden, and the full flower of that development now sat in the Archbishop's chair in Canterbury Cathedral. And if they taught otherwise at Sandhurst, then God help England, the Empire and the human race. Maynard smiled, cracking the dried mud on his face, sat up and saw at once the dozens of bloated leeches that had attached themselves to him through his tattered clothing.

It took them all of a quarter of an hour to burn the leeches from themselves. Polo was the only one with matches; they used two of them to light four dollars bills twisted into a long wick. Elisabeth, with the Dutch habit of minding her own business, had not asked what Garrick carried in his suitcase; she had been amazed when he opened it to reveal the stacks of money, but she had said nothing. She had not asked how much was in the suitcase; rich as she had been all her life, Garrick's wealth would not have impressed her. But she was impressed when the boy, without any complaint, joking even, had wound the four bills into a twist and lit it with the matches. Even her father, the richest man in northern Sumatra, had never been that profligate. They burned off the leeches, sometimes singeing themselves as well as the thick, blood-gorged worms, then washed the blood from themselves in the dark brown waters of the swollen stream.

'Righto,' said Maynard at last. 'We'd better get cracking. Which way is this plantation of yours, Miss Brinker?'

Elisabeth shook her head, lost now. 'I don't know. Which way is Subayang?'

'Christ knows,' said Polo, puffing on a damp cigarette. 'But we ain't going back looking for it, my oath we're not!'

'I think we oughta try and find the coast again,' said Case quietly. 'We're gonna get nowhere wandering around in this jungle.'

Maynard looked at him for a moment with cold, contemptuous eyes; then he turned back to Elisabeth. 'Where is the plantation? Is it on a main road? Up in the hills?'

'What does it matter?' Case interrupted before Elisabeth could answer. 'Let's get the hell out of this and down to the coast. Maybe we can grab another boat——'

'Will you shut up!' Maynard's anger made the bones stand out in his face; his whole body became angular with emotion. 'We listened to you once—and it's only by the grace of God we're all still alive!'

Case's own anger was less fierce, because it was diluted by doubt. 'I don't give a goddam what your military mind thinks! And I dunno how the hell that Jap got down to Subayang. But I know I was right about what we did back there on that beach. We couldn't have killed them—not the way you wanted to do it!'

'I'm not going to argue with you about it,' said Maynard, holding tight rein on his temper. Above him he could hear the monkeys chattering excitedly; he could imagine their eyes wide open with fright and curiosity, like those of children about to witness a fight between adults. Ridiculously, the chattering also angered him, and he strove to hold in the violence that surged in him against the monkeys and this man in front of him. He could feel the temper quivering in him and every nerve in his body seemed to become exposed. 'It's past and we'll forget it. But from now on we'll do it my way, and there'll be no voting!' He looked around at the other men, at Polo, Garrick and Cabrolini. None of them shook his head, but neither did they look at Case. Maynard felt the temper in him go down, doused by the flush of a victory of sorts. He even forgave the monkeys their derision, and looked back at Case. 'We'll get out of Sumatra somehow. But first we have to find a transmitter!'

'You're not gonna find it on some rubber plantation,' said Case, but the argument had gone out of his voice. All during the trek last night he had wondered and worried about the Japanese officer? How had he escaped from that beach? Should he have been shot? The first question puzzled Case; the second tormented him. It had writhed in his brain all through his sleep last night, a nightmare as unfathomable as any bad dream. He looked around at Garrick and Cabrolini, from whom he might have expected some support, found none, and did not continue the argument with Maynard. He picked up his gun and the almost empty bottle of whisky, walked several paces along the bank of the stream and stood there, alone but with the others still very much aware of him. It was a situation that was somehow the image of his life.

Maynard then said to Elisabeth, 'The plantation—is it in the hills?'

Elisabeth, disturbed by the friction between Case and Maynard, had to recollect herself. 'No, it was on the river.'

'Then we'll follow this stream,' said Maynard, and looked down to see which way the current ran. 'It probably joins the river somewhere.'

'And if it doesn't?' Garrick felt he had betrayed Case; he put the question as some sort of recompense.

Maynard looked first towards Case, as if he felt the question had been prompted by the American; then he looked back at Garrick. 'If it doesn't, we'll just go on looking till we find the plantation.'

'Miss Brinker's brother won't still be there,' Garrick persisted.

'No, but the estate workers should be,' Maynard said, irritated now by Garrick; with Case's capitulation he thought he had won them all over. 'Perhaps they can tell us where to find Mr. Brinker.'

I hope so, thought Elisabeth. She and her brother had not been close over the last few years, he being twelve years older than she and with a wife and two children; he had made his own life on the rubber estate on the Subayang River while she had spent her time at Medan, Palembang, Batavia and other places where her father's business interests had taken him. Now all at once she remembered her brother as she had seen him as a young man; she remembered him with the eyes of a young girl of eight or nine, saw him as tall, blond and exploding with laughter. She knew that now he was balding, running to fat and most of his laughter he found in a bottle; it happened to so many of the beautiful young men who grew up here in the Indies. But already she was retreating farther and farther into the past, dreaming the saddest dreams of all, those that are already gone.

Polo stubbed out his cigarette, put the butt away in his packet. 'I think we better get moving.' Like so many argumentative men, he was not interested in other people's differences. He had made his own commitment to Maynard and all he wanted now was to be on his way. 'Some of the Nips might be out on early shift.'

They started out along the bank of the stream, Maynard

leading with Elisabeth, Case bringing up the rear. Garrick, still conscience-stricken, dropped back and walked beside the American in awkward silence. At last Case said, 'You voted with me back there on the beach.'

Garrick slipped in the mud and Case had to catch his arm to steady him. The boy nodded his thanks, swallowed, then said, 'I know I voted with you, Jack. But if some of us had been killed in Subayang——'

'No one was killed but the Jap.'

'That was just luck.'

'Sometimes luck is all you have going for you,' said Case, remembering fighters in the later years who had been too good for him.

'That's not much encouragement when you're trying to decide what's right and what's wrong.'

'If you had your vote over again, you'd have voted with Maynard.' Case felt a sense, not of betrayal, but of disappointment. He knew he had been right to spare the lives of those Japanese on the beach, but he needed to be told he had been right. He was not accustomed to making moral decisions; they fitted him like a bad gum-shield. He looked reproachfully at Garrick, but the boy was looking straight ahead, concentrating on where he put his feet on the muddy, slippery bank.

'I didn't say that, Jack. But Maynard did show us there's something to being——' He looked at Case, uttered the word tentatively, as if he were afraid it was some sort of insult: 'Practical.'

Case said nothing, turned his face away and plodded on, putting his own feet down carelessly but never slipping; his footwork had always been good, had often enabled him to go the distance with men who had had the power to nail him in the first if they could have got near him. But footwork would not be enough to take him the distance on this journey ahead of them. A rusty conscience, one that had not been used in years, was beginning to shackle him.

CHAPTER 5

It was eight o'clock by Maynard's watch when they came to the rubber estate. They had reached the river an hour earlier and turned upstream, tramping on past the debris brought down by last night's storm. A bloated pig went past, lying on his back, its four stubby legs sticking up like the stumps of four tiny masts. Logs and branches went swirling by on the yellow-brown current, and once, incredibly, they saw a dog swimming down the middle of the river, a peasant's straw hat grasped in its mouth. Dragonflies hung above the surface of the water, rubies waiting to be strung together, and water-hyacinths drifted by, some of them strung like a wreath round the haunches of the dead pig. Birds and monkeys screamed at each other and Maynard kept glancing up at them apprehensively, wondering if some Japanese patrol in the neighbourhood might come to investigate the uproar in the trees.

Then Elisabeth said, 'We're almost there.' She nodded at the first of the rubber trees as they came up past the last tangled patch of jungle. 'There's the bungalow.'

It was not what Maynard would have called a bungalow. It was a brick house surrounded on all four sides by wide verandas, with high moulded gables such as he had seen on some of the Dutch-styled houses in London. The Brinkers might have been here in Sumatra for three hundred years, but Holland was still home. The English were not the only empire builders who suffered from a lack of imagination when it came to adapting themselves.

'*Bella*,' said Cabrolini admiringly. He had an open mind: the Italians were still new as empire builders. 'Your brother must have been very happy in such a house, signorina.'

'Yes,' said Elisabeth, noticing the past tense of Cabrolini's remark.

'It looks deserted,' Maynard said, 'but we'd better make sure. You and I will go in, Polo.'

Polo spat into the thick grass. 'Skipper.'

Maynard had begun to move forward, but he stopped and looked over his shoulder. 'Yes?'

'In future let me do me own volunteering.' Polo stared hard at Maynard for only a moment, then he unslung his gun, checked the magazine clip, and looked up, his thin, lined face abruptly wiped of its sourness. 'I'll take the back.'

He moved off through the trees, flitting like a scrawny, ugly wraith down through the plantation, an amateur soldier, who, having made the point of his independence, was now acting like a professional. Maynard looked after him, not resenting the Australian's small rebellion, only cursing himself for not having been more diplomatic. He had authoritatively taken charge of the party, but he could not afford to offend the one man who was wholeheartedly with him on the question of practicality. Sandhurst before the war had not taught what allowances should be made for the ranker who saw himself as good as his master. There was no such animal in the British Army.

He left Case and the others, going down through the trees and up through the garden towards the house. A wide lawn stretched across the front of the house but it looked as if it had not been cut in weeks; the foot-high grass was flattened in sections where people had trampled their way through it. The garden was a small jungle. Flame of the forest trees blazed with tongues of fire, a thick line of oleanders was like a banked hearth, and just below the front veranda, the final Dutch touch, tulips, broken and tattered by the heat and rain, stretched in a yellow moat. Maynard, moving cautiously down through the gloomy silence beneath the rubber trees, his nostrils thick with the sweet stench of the decaying vegetation underfoot, began to pray that the bungalow was deserted. He had not realised how tired he was, how little fight he had left in him.

Then he saw Polo come out the front door of the bungalow, stand on the veranda and look around, a caricature of a Dutch Resident; the little man had an unconscious air of arrogance about him, lord of all he surveyed, the ten-goal miner. Then he saw Maynard, grinned and bellowed, 'She's jake, skip! Nobody home!'

Then Case, Elisabeth, Garrick and Cabrolini came down through the rubber trees and joined Maynard and Polo on the veranda. All the men stood aside while Elisabeth entered the house first; it was more than just a gesture of politeness. This was some sort of homecoming for her; they were now her guests. She went in through the wide teak doors with their brass knobs, once highly polished but now already pitted and blotched like mouldy fruit, and the men followed her. Maynard and Polo, the only two with hats, took them off

86

in what seemed a parody of good manners. It was the sort
of house that demanded such formality.

Elisabeth paused in the wide hallway that went right through
to the back of the house. Then, memory coming back to her,
she turned to the right and led the way into a big living-room.
She stared at it for a moment, then a sob escaped her and she
put her hand to her mouth, holding her lips, as she had done
that first morning they had met her.

'They've made a mess,' said Maynard.

The room was furnished with a mixture of tropical cane
furniture and heavy oak pieces: the Indies and Holland
were mixed even here in the house. All one wall was lined with
bookshelves; a second wall had been a glass-fronted gun
case. A grand piano stood in one corner; beside it were two
giant native drums. Above the big stone fireplace there hung
a picture of Queen Wilhelmina, motherly rather than regal-
looking; she was flanked by a picture of a sad-eyed young
woman and one of an arrogant-looking young man with an old-
fashioned moustache. From the beamed ceiling, tinkling softly
in the breeze that came in an open window, hung a huge
chandelier.

'My oath they have,' said Polo. 'A real mess.'

Case looked first at Elisabeth, saw her control come back,
saw her straighten up and take her fingers away from her
mouth. She has class, he thought; and had to grin at himself,
wondering how he would recognise it: there had been no
class girls around the rings where he had fought. Then he
turned away from her and looked about the room.

The furniture had been overturned, the cane chairs slashed
and broken so that the cane stuck out like so many ribs. A
tracing of bullet holes marked the wall above the fireplace:
Queen Wilhelmina had a bullet hole right through her forehead. The picture of the young woman was untouched, but
the young man with the moustache had a small parang pro-
truding from his throat. The piano had its lid torn off and
its wires sprayed out like the exposed bones of some giant
fish. The gun case had been smashed open and all the guns
were gone; books had been pulled from the shelves and flung
about the room as if someone had rebelled savagely against
knowledge. On the far wall of the room, splashed in red
paint, was the word *Merdeka!*

'What's *Merdeka* mean?' Case asked.

'Freedom,' said Elisabeth, but there was a note of query
in her voice, as if it were a new word to her, one that she

did not understand should be scrawled here on a wall inside her brother's house.

'We'd better scout around,' Maynard said. He walked to a smashed window and looked out at the silent, deserted plantation. 'Where are all the estate workers?'

'Gone through,' said Polo. 'Maybe we better do the same, soon's we got some tucker in us. Think there might be some around, love?'

'Tucker?' Elisabeth still seemed dazed.

'Food. I reckon we'd all feel a bit better if we had something inside us. Have a look in the kitchen, will you?'

Elisabeth looked around the room once more, then she nodded and went out into the hall. They heard her going down the tiled floor of the hall, then Polo looked around at the other men. 'Better if we get her doing something. Otherwise she's likely to get a bit moody about what she's seen here, you know what I mean?'

Case's glance happened to meet Maynard's, and each man guessed the other's thoughts. Each was surprised at the occasional sensitivity that came out of the crude-mannered little Australian; Old Vi, or whatever her name was, must have had her influence on him. But neither Case nor Maynard exchanged any comment; their mutual reaction to Polo's gesture towards Elisabeth did not lessen the antagonism between them. Each was not prepared to make any gesture of his own.

Cabrolini had been wandering about the house, admiring the big rooms, looking with warm-eyed sentiment at the signs of family living that still remained: a child's cradle, some toys, a woman's robe hanging on a hook behind a bedroom door. His wife and his two girls had sailed for Italy three months ago; he prayed each night that they had reached there safely. If they had, then they would be in the villa on the hill behind Lerici and his wife would be opening the shutters, letting out the mustiness of three years' neglect of the villa, putting the house on herself as she might a garment, making it part of her, making it home. His eyes watered as he thought of Valentina standing at a window murmuring, *Mia casa*. She would make it sound like a song.

He came back into the living-room as Maynard was about to go out on to the front veranda. 'Captain, I have found these.' He held out some cartridge shells. 'Are they Japanese?'

Maynard took one of the shells, shook his head. 'The Dutch use an M-95 rifle. This ammunition would fit it.'

Then Garrick came in another door from the rear of the house. He held up a water bottle with a hole right through it. 'This was in one of the back rooms, under a window. There's some blood on the floor in there, too. Looked as if someone might have been shooting out of the window and was hit.'

'Then the guerrillas must have been here,' Maynard said.

'Sure,' said Case. 'But when? Yesterday? Last week?'

'This is one time,' said Maynard sarcastically, 'when your guess is as good as mine.'

Polo, Garrick and Cabrolini looked uncomfortable, standing on the outskirts of this private war. Maynard saw their discomfiture and at once was sorry for his petty sarcasm. But Case took no notice of it, just looked around the room and said quizzically, 'Who chased the guerrillas out of here? The Japs or someone else? *Merdeka* ain't a Japanese word.'

'We shan't know that unless we can find some of the estate workers.' Maynard tried to sound more amenable, but without offering any truce. He did not trust Case; give an American an inch and he would take a yard. Then he chided himself; he was condemning an entire people because of one man. It was the way his father, the English Christian gentleman, would have thought. He wondered how many men had brought abuse on England because of their own personalities; then remembered several he had met in Malaya. He would have to stop thinking of Case as an American. But it would not be easy; most men's nationality was part of their personality, they wore it like a second skin. Though Case seemed to have a refinement of it: he was a Texan American, whatever distinction that was.

'Well, we better go looking for the buggers,' said Polo, and headed for the door. 'Looks like they ain't gunna come looking for us.'

Maynard, Garrick and Cabrolini moved after Polo as he went out of the room, but Case remained standing by the disembowelled piano. Maynard stopped and looked back. 'What are you going to do?' He kept his voice even.

'I thought I might give our girl friend a hand. I used to be a short-order cook once. A long time ago.'

Suddenly Maynard heard himself say, 'You're all right, Case. Why do you have to be such a bastard at times?'

'Same reason you gotta be such a sonofabitch. You don't like me and I don't like you.' Case turned away, closing the conversation. 'You better go and hunt up your rubber workers.'

Maynard's face had relaxed, had been almost ready to smile. But now the muscles tightened; the vein quivered in his temple. Abruptly he wheeled about, his heels grating on the parquet floor and stalked out of the room. Case turned his head and looked after him, then he shook his head and reached for the bottle of whisky he had set down on the piano. Christ, he thought, why do I have to work so hard at being an isolationist? I'd make Hiram Johnson sound like a One Worlder.

Then he heard the footsteps on the tiled floor of the hallway and Elisabeth came into the room. 'Oh, where——?' She looked around, as if she half-expected to see the other men sprawled at their ease in the cane chairs.

'They've gone out looking for the rubber workers,' Case said.

'Why didn't you go? Or were you left here to protect me? I told you, I don't expect any favours——'

'Relax, honey.' He saw her brows come down, and he grinned apologetically. 'Sorry. That slipped out. No, I wasn't left here to protect you.' Maybe she's another isolationist, he thought. And, perversely, felt better about his own irrational behaviour towards Maynard. One's sins seemed somehow reduced when duplicated by someone else's. He looked away from her and up at the pictures on either side of that of Queen Wilhelmina. 'Relatives?'

She accepted that he was trying to be friendly, but wished he had chosen another avenue. She looked up at the photographs and felt the tears prick the corner of her eyes. 'My mother and father when they were first married. She had just arrived from Holland.'

'That why she looks so sad?'

'You noticed it, too? I used to ask her about it, but she would never tell me. She was very loyal to my father, but I think she hated Sumatra. She died when I was only ten. My father, he never explained why, he took her home to be buried in Holland. But I think I know why.'

Case reached up and pulled the small parang out of the picture of Joachim Brinker; shards of glass fell out of the frame and tinkled on the floor. 'Looks like someone was trying to hex your old man.'

'Hex?'

'Put the evil eye on him.' Then he said, his voice soft with sympathy, 'Maybe they did. He didn't have to die the way you said.'

She looked at him, silent for a moment, as if surprised by

his concern for her father. Then she nodded. 'No. No one should die the way he did.' Then added with despair, 'But I don't suppose he will be the last.' She turned away, somehow forced the tears back into her eyes, once again retreated to the past: 'I used to come here for holidays when I was a little girl. I learned to play on that piano. An American jazz song, *The Sheik of Araby*. I used to play it with two fingers, and my father used to sing it.'

Then she fell silent again as she mentioned her father, and Case said, 'How's breakfast coming?'

She looked at him gratefully, recognising he was trying to help her forget her grief over her father. 'That was why I came in here. Would you help me? There are tins of meat in the kitchen, but nothing to open them with.'

'We'll use this,' said Case, bouncing the parang in his hand.

They went out to the kitchen, a room big enough to have accommodated the kitchen staff of a small hotel. The floors were black and white tiles, the carved wooden cupboards featured windmills and tulips, the crockery was blue and white delftware. This was a Dutch kitchen: one expected to look out of the window and see barges on a nearby canal.

'They have smashed nothing in here,' Elisabeth said. 'My brother's wife would be pleased to know that. This was her favourite room.'

Case, wielding the parang with some skill, had opened half a dozen tins of meat. Then he reached for the whisky bottle he had put down on a shelf, took the cork from it and saw Elisabeth looking at him. 'I have it every morning instead of fruit juice,' he said. 'It cleans the suede off my teeth, too.'

'Whisky isn't good for you in this climate, Mr. Case.' She said it without any primness.

Case recognized that she was trying to be friendly, so he grinned, determined not to repeat the error he had made with Maynard a few minutes ago. 'I never drank to do me good. That ain't what liquor's for.'

But he put the cork back in the bottle and put the bottle back on the shelf. Elisabeth said, 'Why *do* you drink?'

No woman had asked him that before, only managers and, once, a State boxing commissioner. He took a fork and began to scoop the corned meat out of a tin. 'I once went on a bender for two weeks. I ain't bragging, just telling you some history. They put me in the ring against a young guy, but forgot to tell me how good he was. He was twenty-two years old and I was pushing thirty-two. He had two strong legs and I had a coupla rubber stilts. He coulda put me down in the second, but he liked hitting me. Finally I went down myself in the ninth. I looked around for the floor and I fell on it. They said I took a dive. They were wrong. I just had nothing left.'

Elisabeth said nothing, feeling that this strange man perhaps was talking more than he had in years. She had never suffered the confessions of men before. Beautiful women, unlike plain women, do not have to splurge their sympathy. But she listened to Case because he had listened to her. And she could not remember ever before having talked to a stranger as she had talked to him.

'I went on the bender that same night,' said Case. 'When I woke up I was in Kansas City six hundred miles away.' He scooped the meat out of a tin, dropped the tin with a clatter into a waste bin beside the big black stove. 'That's what liquor's for.'

'And then they took your licence away.' Polo stood in the doorway leading out to the back veranda.

Elisabeth saw something like a flush rise up behind Case's stubble of beard and his knuckles showed white as his hand tightened on the fork in his hand. But when he looked at Polo he was smiling and his voice sounded half-amused. 'You oughta do something about that memory of yours, Polo. It's too good.'

It was Polo's turn to flush. Elisabeth would not have believed it possible, but the lined, weatherbeaten face suddenly seemed to crumble in on itself. 'Sorry, sport. Didn't mean to butt in.'

He moved on along the veranda, his army boots scratching grit beneath them: they seemed, too, to scratch the silence in the kitchen. Elisabeth did not move for a while, even after the sound of Polo's footsteps had died away, then she looked carefully at Case. 'I don't think he meant to be unkind.'

'Neither do I,' said Case. His face had a tentative look to it, a mixture of puzzlement and regret. Regret for what? Elisabeth wondered but she did not dare ask. Then he looked at her and said, 'Most of us don't mean to be. Unkind, I mean. It's just our tongues. They don't always belong to us.'

Five minutes later all the party but Garrick was sitting in the living-room eating their breakfast. Garrick had taken up a post just inside the back door of the kitchen where he could watch the rear approach to the bungalow. Maynard was by one of the front windows and Polo was by the door of the living-room where he could see out through the front door of the hall. Cabrolini sat in a deep leather armchair that, besides being slashed so that its horsehair stuffing bulged out like an exposed tumour, had gone mouldy; but Cabrolini found it comfortable because it reminded him of a leather chair in his own home in Lerici. Nostalgia, he mused, was a form of upholstery.

Case sat at the piano, his plate of cold corned meat balanced on the closed lid of the keyboard. He looked up as Elisabeth, sitting down at a small card table, said, 'I can remember once when I was very young, my father held a banquet here for the Governor-General. There were ten courses, and seventy people sat down to the table in the dining-room.'

'The good old days, eh?' said Polo.

Elisabeth nodded. She had often heard her father and his friends use the expression, but this was the first time it had ever had any real meaning for her. She said it to herself and it tasted bitter on her lips; at twenty-four one should not pine for the good old days. The pattern of her life had been set for her at her birth; she was only to repeat the lives of generations of Brinker women before her. It had been as predictable as human affairs will allow, but she had not rebelled: safe and dull though it was, it had at least promised luxury, something she had enjoyed. Now, suddenly, the pattern, and the luxury, had gone.

'All Hollanders, I suppose?' Case said.

'What do you mean?' There was a touch of imperiousness in her voice again, an echo of the good old days. She suspected his question was not an idle one and she began to throw up her defences at once.

'How many of the local natives did your father ever ask to eat with him?' Case went on eating, as if making casual dinner-table conversation. He was aware of Maynard watching him now from the window.

'The people here were not educated.' Elisabeth would have

ignored Case's question if they had been alone. But the other men seemed to be waiting on an answer from her, and she felt she had to defend her father in front of them. 'They would not expect to be asked to eat with my father. But they respected him.'

'You think so?' Case said.

'What do you mean by that?'

Case nodded up at the slashed picture of her father, then reached across and flipped one of the broken wires of the piano. 'This wasn't done by anyone who respected your old man. And it wasn't done by the Japs. They didn't paint that on your wall.' He nodded towards the scrawled *Merdeka!* at the far end of the room.

'What are you trying to say?' Maynard said, without moving from his place by the window.

'Another empire heard from,' Case murmured, but only Cabrolini sitting close by him heard him. He swallowed the last of his corned meat, put his plate up on top of the piano and said, 'I'm trying to say, Who are we gonna be fighting if we stay here in this part of the world? Just the Japs? Or are we gonna be battling these *Merdeka* jokers, too?'

'We shan't have to worry about the locals,' said Maynard. 'If they're not on our side, then they won't have gone over to the Japs. Not yet. They'll want to see which way the wind is going to blow.'

'You mean they wanna see if it's gonna blow the Hollanders back in here?' Case shook his head. 'I'll give you ten to one the wind ain't gonna blow that strong ever again.'

'You don't know us Hollanders, Mr. Case,' said Elisabeth.

No, thought Cabrolini, he doesn't. But it will not take him long to learn: the Dutch are not hard to know. They are obstinate and they are as unimaginative as the English; they are formalists and they believe, as the English do, in their Divine right to rule. One of their Governors-General (the one who had dined here perhaps?) had said to the nationalists, 'We Dutch have been here for three hundred years. We shall remain here for another three hundred years. After that we can talk.' People with that confidence in their destiny were not hard to know. Case would soon learn about them. That is, if he met any besides Miss Brinker. Cabrolini looked across at the Dutch girl and wondered if she had ever heard what the Governor-General had said. And wondered, too, where the present Governor-General was. Waiting somewhere for the wind to change direction?

'I take it you're anti-imperialist?' Maynard said.

'I hadn't thought about it till a coupla weeks ago,' Case said. 'But if you're gonna hang labels, yeah, I guess I am.'

'You are just fortunate, Mr. Case.' Elisabeth continued to eat. Even defending her countrymen could not reduce the hunger she had. The stomach has no patriotism, Cabrolini thought, watching her closely.

'How come?' Case was puzzled.

'You Americans have never been called imperialists.'

'Not so far,' said Case, and could not imagine the possibility.

'There is still time. Not even American—what do you call it?—know-how can plan history in advance.'

'I'm a Texan,' said Case, and again Maynard noticed the definition. 'We believe in minding our own business.'

'You've been going against the Texas grain lately then,' said Maynard.

'Attaboy,' said Case. 'Fancy punches never get you anywhere. Always get in there with the good low ones. Right in the gut.'

He's pulling my leg, Maynard thought; but refused to let the American bait him into losing his temper. He said, 'Imperialism has its virtues. You've been defending your own position in the Philippines long enough.'

'Not me. Mine was the voice you didn't hear.'

'We've done a lot of good in Malaya,' Maynard said, as if he had not heard Case. 'We've taught them administration, improved their health, brought wealth into the country.'

'You've taken some out, too,' said Case mildly. 'Or were the tin and rubber companies run by the Salvation Army?'

Cabrolini smiled behind his hand. The Italian empire was too new for him to have been influenced by it; for all he knew the Italian empire could already be dead. Abyssinia and Somaliland were places he had never mentioned, for fear Fiat might have sent him there; he was not a conqueror who looked for new territories, a sales Cæsar. He had welcomed the posting to Indo-China. The French were civilised and even the Indo-Chinese had a suggestion of being civilised, though their French master might have denied it. And there had been the side trips to Siam, Malaya and the East Indies. The English and the Dutch were not as civilised as the French, but they had their pretensions.

He studied Maynard carefully as the latter put his argument for empire. He liked the man: he might be stiff-necked at times, too much the military man, but he was less hypocritical than many of the English Cabrolini had met in Malaya. He had never been to England, so he did not know what the English were like at home; he had heard a visitor to Malaya say that there were two breeds of Englishmen, and perhaps the visitor had been right. Those in Malaya indulged themselves to a degree that Cabrolini knew they could never have achieved at home. They treated the local natives as uneducated children, but their own education had stopped when they had left school or university; they could recite the history of the Harlequins or the M.C.C., but they were not interested in the history of Malaya before the time of Raffles. They clapped Eurasian cricketers with Portuguese names but never bothered to wonder if the de Silva who had just scored a century might be descended from Albuquerque's captain at the siege of Malacca. And if someone had told them that there had been a sophisticated civilisation here in the East when England was still struggling out of the Middle Ages, they would have thought the fellow had been drinking too much in the sun.

The colonial Englishman never saw himself as others saw him; when he looked in a mirror he never remarked the quizzical face of the local native staring over his shoulder. He was self-deprecating and casual when he talked with other Europeans; he would not have believed that those same Europeans might have noticed his air of superiority when he talked with the natives. He believed, with some justification, that his sense of justice and his honesty in government were the best in the world. He would have considered it bad taste to have mentioned the barbarities and cruelties of the early English rulers in the East; that was another day, old boy, and how's your pink gin? Cabrolini had met them all, hated them and yet admired them, and had wondered if any of them had ever pondered the thought that the sun *might* set on the empire some day. Probably not, because that thought would have called for more imagination than the colonial Englishman possessed.

But Maynard was not unimaginative; he defended the empire but he was not blind to its faults and limitations. 'All right, yes, we have neglected education,' he was saying. 'We've neglected a lot of things. But we brought peace to this part of the world. Pax Britannica is more than just a phrase, you know.'

'Maybe the local folk were happier fighting than working for some white foreigner,' Case said. Ah, thought Cabrolini, there's the one who is blind. Americans are always wanting to do good. What is it that pricks their conscience so much when they come abroad? Is it their treatment of their own Negroes and Redskins?

Maynard sighed, 'I just hope you Yanks never have to take over from us.'

'Or us,' said Elisabeth.

'And the French and the Portuguese and the Belgians,' said Cabrolini, and they all looked at him in surprise. I'm an outsider, he thought, still the alien not entitled to an opinion. But he persisted, said with a smile that disarmed them all, 'Or even us Italians.'

3

Out by the back door Garrick could just hear the murmur of the voices in the living-room. He did not resent having been posted out here by himself. He was naturally gregarious, but since early this morning he had wanted to get away on his own. The small disagreement with Case had upset him. He knew in his heart that Jack had been right, that they could not have killed those Japanese in cold blood. But their narrow escape from Subayang had frightened him even more than had the strafing by the Zero in the open boat. The strafing had been unexpected and they could have done nothing to prevent it; his survival of it had been purely an act of God and he had mumbled an almost incoherent prayer of thanks as soon as the Zero had disappeared. But the ambush and escape from Subayang had been something else again. They *could* have prevented the ambush if they had followed Maynard's advice; he had no doubt of that. And that was what disturbed him as much as the disagreement with Case. Because all the time he had been running for his life along the platforms of Subayang, hiding behind the counter in the Chinese store, crouching low while the bullets smacked into the shelves above him, he had been wondering if the Japanese had got away from the beach. And had not been surprised when, out in the alley, Maynard had turned the dead Japanese's face up to the star-light and they had recognised the scar-faced officer. At that moment, trembling with fear and the exhaustion of running, he had wished they *had* killed the Japanese back at the beach.

He was confused now. Though the war in Europe had been going for over two years, though Singapore itself had been full of troops for almost all that time, he had never been able to put himself into a belligerent frame of mind. The bank had had him exempted from military service; they had convinced the authorities that business was more important than defence. He had not argued with his classification; his patriotism was not as strong as his fear of being killed. He had believed everything he had been told, that Singapore was impregnable, that the Japanese would never dare to come down into Malaya, that there was nothing to worry about. He had gone to dances at the Adelphi Hotel, listened to Reller's Band play *We're Going to Hang Out Our Washing On The Siegfried Line*; he had only been tolerated at the dances in the past year because there was then a surplus of army officers and the local girls had no longer had to depend on bank clerks as partners. But he had established his position at the dances before the invasion of the officers and, showing a social doggedness that was new to him, he had turned up each week at the Adelphi. Had been there the night when news had come through that the Japanese had landed on Singapore Island, and everyone had gone on dancing—'Just as they did in Brussels on the eve of Waterloo,' someone had said. 'Jolly good for the old morale, eh?'

But he had gone home that night to the flat he shared with two other clerks, and had lain awake till dawn wondering what he would do when the Japanese took Singapore. Because, though he never voiced his opinion to anyone, he had known the Japanese would take both the island and the city. He had lain awake listening to the snipers who had already infiltrated into the city, shooting at those late going home from the parties and the dances that had been held to keep up morale. He had added up his stock of courage and had not shied away from the truth: he had very little. He had made up his mind then that when the Japanese finally came he would not fight them but run away. He had told no one what he was going to do, and his sense of shame was not lightened when he saw hundreds of others, many of them men with much more responsibility than himself, already preparing to leave Singapore. He *was* ashamed, but he was honest: he did not dream up excuses for wanting to leave, as so many of the others did; he did not write home to his parents and tell them he was doing prodigious defence work, digging trenches, working round the clock with the civil defence units. He went quietly about his business of getting away, choosing his route of escape, finding the Chinese who would supply him with a boat. The suitcase full of Straits dollars had been a windfall and he had appreciated the irony of it: it was not just the brave who were rewarded. He had fled Singapore on the night of the surrender, knowing full well what he was: a coward who had no stomach for fighting.

And now here he sat in the back door of a Dutch bungalow, a rifle in his lap, committed to the responsibility of other people's lives. He was still afraid, still a coward, but he had to stay with these people: he was too afraid to run any farther on his own.

He put down his empty plate and wished for a cup of good strong tea to wash away the dry saltiness of the corned meat. He was sitting on his suitcase and he leaned back against the door jamb, stretching out his legs. He saw a punai pigeon shoot out from among the rubber trees, a small green jewel that dashed in the sun, then was gone among the shadows again. The morning sun streamed in on him, warming him, making him feel sleepy. He could sleep for a week, if Maynard would only give the word that they could stay here in the bungalow that long. . . . He saw the movement down in the plantation and he blinked awake. He stared hard, not sure that he had not just seen the stirring shadow of a tree branch. Then he knew what he had seen.

'Skipper!' It seemed to him that Maynard was beside him almost before the call was out of his mouth; he was not the only one whose nerves were on edge. 'Down there! In the trees!'

They were coming up out of the lines of rubber trees, fifty or sixty of them, dark shadows being born out of other shadows. They came silently, even the very young children among them making no sound. Then they were standing in the open space behind the house, an old man in a purple-striped sarong at their head.

'Are they the estate workers?' Maynard asked.

Elisabeth and the others had come down from the hall from the living-room. 'Yes,' said Elisabeth. Most of the men carried small parangs, the tool of the rubber tapper. 'I recognise the old man. His name is Sitanala.'

'Would he recognise you? When were you last here?'

'Two or three years ago. He would remember me.'

'Okay, keep us covered, just in case there are Japs down in the trees,' Maynard said to the men behind him. 'Cabrolini, you go through and watch the front of the house. Righto, Miss Brinker. Let's you and I go down and see what we can find out about your brother.'

He and Elisabeth went down the back steps, cautiously yet sedately, like a newly arrived vice-regal couple going down to meet the native guests at a garden party. The guests moved a little closer together, their sarongs merging so that their brown bodies seemed to be standing waist deep in a red, purple, blue and brown pool. Brown eyes watched suspiciously as the two Europeans stopped in front of the old man. A small boy at the edge of the crowd giggled and Maynard looked at him and smiled. But before the boy could smile back his mother, without looking at him, had clipped him under the ear. Maynard looked back at the old man.

'Do you speak English?'

The old man just stared at him, and Elisabeth said, 'Why should he? Do not be stupid, Captain Maynard. You are in Dutch territory now.'

Maynard flushed. 'Sorry.'

Elisabeth spoke in Malay to the old man. 'Do you remember me, Sitanala? I am Mr. Dirk's sister.'

'I remember you, Miss Elisabeth.' Sitanala's face was expressionless.

Several young men, all in new red sarongs, were arrayed behind him. Their faces were not expressionless; all at once Elisabeth was aware of the fact that they hated her. 'Hollander bitch!' one of them said, and leaned past Sitanala to spit at her feet.

Maynard brought his gun up and the young men transferred their look of hatred to him. 'What was that for?' Maynard snapped.

Elisabeth could feel herself trembling with shock as much as with anger. She had heard of demonstrations against the Dutch, but she had never witnessed any; the Sumatrans who had been invited to her father's house had minded their manners. What had these people against her? Their hatred of her was too much to accept; here on her own brother's estate she was no more than a bewildered stranger. But arrogance has its compensations, it is its own defence. She ignored Maynard's question and said to Sitanala, 'Your young men have no manners. Can't you keep control of them?'

The old man's face, gullied as a dried-out gourd, still showed no expression. 'No, Miss Elisabeth.' History was moving too fast for him too; Elisabeth realised she was not the only one who was bewildered. 'The old men do not count for very much any more.'

'That's right,' said the young man who had spat at Elisabeth.

'What is your name?'

'Chairil.' He was taller than his companions, but more than height had made him their leader: authority was stamped on his face like a birthmark. He looked with contempt at Sitanala, then back at Elisabeth. 'There are no police to give my name to. We are the masters here now.'

'Masters of the Japanese, too?' Elisabeth had never argued with a native before: the words were like stones in her mouth. But all at once she hated this young man as much as he hated her and she had to try and put him back in his place. But even as she spoke she knew it was hopeless: she had nothing to fight with but words. Her father and all the Brinkers before him had left her no other weapons. She could not even attack the young man through his sense of gratitude: he had none.

The young man's eyes flickered for just a moment when she mentioned the Japanese: he had his doubts as well as his hopes. 'We shall talk with the Japanese. We were never allowed to talk with the Hollanders.'

Maynard said impatiently, 'What's going on?'

Elisabeth looked at the rows of sullen dark faces, then she turned to Maynard. 'They do not want to have anything to do with us.'

'Why, for God's sake? They worked for your brother, didn't they?'

'Yes.' The other men had come down from the veranda of the bungalow, stood now in a line behind Elisabeth and Maynard. Elisabeth saw Case out of the corner of her eye, watching her as carefully as Chairil and the other young men. She hesitated a moment, but she had never learned to dodge the truth: 'They do not want to have anything to do with us because I am a Hollander.' She looked back at Chairil and said in Malay, 'Do you belong to the PNI?'

Chairil nodded proudly; behind him the heads of the other young men went up and down like a dozen reflections of him. 'I am the party leader in this district.'

Elisabeth said to Maynard, 'They belong to the PNI. The Indonesian National Party.'

'Huh-huh,' said Case behind her. 'Then these are the guys who did that paint job on that wall inside.' He looked at Chairil and said, 'Merdeka?'

Chairil and the young men stared at him with sudden interest. Then they all nodded enthusiastically.

'Do they want us around here or not?' Polo said. 'If they don't, then I think we better skedaddle.'

'Ask the old chap where your brother is,' Maynard said.

Elisabeth ignored Chairil, who had now pushed himself into the foreground, and looked past him at Sitanala. 'Where is my brother?'

The old man glanced nervously at Chairil, then said, 'We know nothing.'

'He says he doesn't know,' Elisabeth said. 'But I don't believe him.'

'Maybe a good kick up the behind would shake his memory,' Polo said.

Maynard stared at the group, looking from face to face to find some crack in the brown wall of sullen silence. Dark eyes stared back at him, promising him nothing; through fear or hope, it was hard to tell which, these people had committed themselves to the young men in the red sarongs. Grudgingly, Maynard thought there was a nobility about them, even if they themselves were unaware of it: simple people like these could bring about the birth of a nation. He doubted its chances of success; the Japanese were not likely to encourage too much independence. And there was always the possibility the Dutch would come back. The war had not been completely lost yet. He looked at Chairil. There was no nobility about the young man; he was too arrogant, too full of himself, for that distinction. He would be the one to whip up the wind of nationalism, drive the others into being perhaps a new nation. But his eye would always be on the main goal: a high post for himself in the new government wherever it might be. Maynard knew from English history that not all patriots were altruistic. They looked for other dividends than honour.

He took the Japanese pistol from his holster and held it against the head of Sitanala. There was a gasp from the natives; even Case and the others were shocked. 'What the hell's that for?' Case said.

'Ask him where your brother is,' Maynard said to Elisabeth.

'You can't threaten him,' Elisabeth protested. Her father's paternalism came out in her: you didn't hold a pistol to the heads of children. Then she remembered the pistols that had been held at the heads of those at Den Pasar in Bali: two hundred and fifty men, women and children had died and there had been no paternalism there. She had heard the story a dozen times, all from the Dutch angle; but her sympathy had always been with the Prince of Badoeng and his palace household, dying in their best clothes with a splendid fatalism that had shamed the Dutch who had shot them down. This old man, Sitanala, was no prince, but the look on his lined face told her he would die with the same fatalism. Paternalism, like hatred, needed acceptance if it was to be effective. She could not help Sitanala if he did not want to be helped. A bullet in his head would help him more than it would the Europeans. His now useless life would have a last moment of glory: he would welcome death in order to shame the young men who had deserted him. 'It's this other man, Chairil, who's the real leader here.'

'I know that,' said Maynard, his pistol still held at the head of Sitanala. The old man's eyes were fixed on a point behind Maynard's shoulder and his face was still expressionless; only the tightening of his neck muscles showed that he was under any strain. 'But the young chap might call my bluff if I tried it on him.'

'You won't shoot the old man?'

'No. But he doesn't know that.'

'I don't think he cares very much,' said Case. 'He might be gonna call your bluff, whether you like it or not.'

'You just keep quiet,' Maynard snapped; then looked at Sitanala and pressed the pistol harder against the old man's head. 'Ask him where your brother is!'

Elisabeth repeated the question in Malay, but the old man remained silent and it was Chairil who answered, 'We know nothing. And if we did, we should not tell you.'

Suddenly Case stepped past Maynard and Elisabeth, pushed aside the young men and grabbed hold of a man. He pulled the man out of the crowd, jerked up the long sarong he wore. Round the man's ankles, looking ridiculous above his bare feet, was a pair of canvas gaiters.

'They're the same sort of gaiters you're wearing,' Case said to Maynard. 'Have the Dutch got some British equipment?'

'It's more than likely,' said Maynard, annoyed at himself for having missed what now seemed so obvious, doubly annoyed because it had been Case, the civilian, who had been the sharpest-eyed among them. He took the pistol away from the head of Sitanala and placed it against the head of the man in the gaiters. 'Righto, chum, you've heard the question.'

He was a small man with an ageless sort of face: at fourteen he had probably looked forty and he would wear the same face if he lived till he was eighty. It was unlined, bland as the faces one saw on travel posters, the sort of face that promised no trouble, no inquiry; only the eyes showed the years of experience, but suggested that at another time they, too, might be as bland as the face. They were frightened eyes now, rolling from one side to the other as he looked from Maynard to Chairil and back to Maynard again. Then he said in only slightly accented English, 'I can tell you what you want to know.'

At that Chairil spun round, pushed aside the young men behind him and, holding up his sarong like a woman her skirt, sprinted towards the trees fifty yards away. Polo swung up his machine-carbine, flicked it on to single shot, took quick but careful aim and fired. Chairil went down, rolling over and over in the grass like a tumbling acrobat who had botched his act. Then he lay writhing in agony, both hands clutching his thigh. There was a gasp from the crowd and a child screamed, went on screaming while its mother stared frozen-eyed at the moaning Chairil.

'What the hell did you do that for?' Case shouted.

Polo ignored him, looked directly at Maynard. 'He'd have been back here in no time with the Nips, skipper.'

Maynard nodded. He had turned his pistol towards the fleeing Chairil, but his finger had had a reluctance of its own. He had been relieved to hear Polo's shot ring out before he had had to force himself to pull the trigger. Christ, he thought, what sort of soldier am I turning out to be? What do I care about these bloody Sumatran nationalists? 'We'd better get moving, in case some Japs heard that shot.' He swung back to the man in the gaiters. 'Righto, where's Mr. Brinker?'

'They left here yesterday.' The man looked wildly from side to side as there were angry murmurs from the young men in the crowd. The child had stopped screaming, but it was whimpering, an animal sound that made the Europeans look at each other with corner-eyed shame. Now we are making war on *actual* children, Elisabeth thought; but said nothing, just looked at the man in the gaiters as he went on, 'Your brother, Miss Brinker, and twenty other men.'

'Where did you get the gaiters?' Maynard said.

'We buried two of the Hollanders. I took the gaiters from one of them. As your English proverb said, Waste not what you want.'

Maynard was in no mood for tangled proverbs. 'Who killed them?'

'Not these people. There were Japanese here.'

'Where are they now?'

'I do not know. They perhaps have followed the Hollanders.'

'For Christ's sake, skipper!' Polo exploded. 'Get it out of him—where the hell are these guerrillas?'

The man looked over his shoulder at the people behind him, then across at Chairil. The latter had stopped writhing, now lay in the grass, staring at the man in the gaiters. Suddenly the man grabbed Maynard's arm. 'Please, mister, take me with you! I can show you the way—I know where the Hollanders have gone! Please don't leave me here. They will kill me!'

'We don't want him,' Case said.

'What's the choice?' Maynard said. 'Who else knows the way? Or do you want me to shoot it out of him?' His anger began to rise: 'You're always ready with the bloody advice! What's your suggestion this time?'

Case regretted what he had just said; he should have left it to someone else to reject the man in the gaiters. He said lamely, 'Okay, we take him. But he's your responsibility.'

'Who isn't?' said Maynard, and for the first time Case noticed the note of despair in the other man's voice. But Maynard had turned away at once, spoke to Polo: 'Get into the house. You and Cabrolini grab what food is left in there. We're moving out now.'

Two minutes later the party was assembled ready to go. Polo and Cabrolini had found more tins of meat and some tins of vegetables. The food was in string-bags and a woman's fancy brocaded carry-all; with a grin Polo handed the latter to Case. 'It goes better with your outfit than mine.'

Case looked down at his tattered shirt and trousers; the custom-made moccasins, all that was left of the days when he had been a sharp dresser, were cracked open across the instep. He took the bag and said, 'A Texas man can sink no lower. A carpetbagger.'

Polo looked puzzled. 'I didn't mean anything, sport.'

Case shook his head, patted the little man's shoulder. 'I'm in your corner, sport. Let's go.'

They began to move across the grass towards the trees. The group of natives still stood close together; no one had broken off from it to move across to the fallen Chairil. The young man still lay in the grass, his hands, still clutching his thigh, now covered with blood. He looked up, his face contorted with pain and hate, at Maynard as the latter stopped beside him.

'I am sorry,' said Maynard. Even if the young man could have understood the words, they would have been inadequate. As it was, neither of them speaking the other's language, the words meant nothing at all. Which was just as well, Maynard realised belatedly: the last thing Chairil wanted was sympathy or an apology. That would only reduce him in the eyes of the other young rebels. Their rebellion was still too young to withstand magnanimity; regret and forgiveness would white-ant their hatred. Chairil stared up at Maynard, then raised his head and spat on the Englishman's boot.

Maynard's expression did not change. He looked down at the spittle on his boot and thought, And that's the answer to three hundred years of Dutch rule. And wondered if spittle was already being gathered in the mouths of Indians, Malayans and Africans, being held ready to be spat at the English when the time was ripe. Christ, he thought, how many enemies do we have? Quite deliberately he turned over his ankle and wiped his boot on the long grass, returning Chairil's stare as he did so. Then he strode away through the grass, past Case and the others and in under the gloom of the rubber trees.

Case, standing with Elisabeth on the edge of the plantation, looked at the girl. 'You better say good-bye to it. I don't think you'll be back here again.'

Elisabeth gazed across the open space at the bungalow. The crowd of natives had now spread out, stood like a long multi-coloured frieze below the veranda. Some of the young men had moved to Chairil, had picked him up and were already carrying him up the steps and into the house. They had taken possession, bailiffs in red sarongs, armed with warrants of nationalism. She felt the tears prick her eyes again, and she hated the arrogant young men and their ambitions. She had never felt any patriotism before, but now suddenly she loved Sumatra as much as Chairil and his friends did.

'This is my country as much as theirs,' she said, speaking to the disappearing young men as much as to Case. 'I was born here. There is some Sumatran blood in me—my great-grandfather married one of their princesses.'

'It's not enough,' said Case gently. 'You could be as brown as they are, but you'd still be a Hollander.'

She looked at him, expecting arguments; but he was only trying to tell her the truth. And after a moment she recognised it and reluctantly nodded. She took one last look back at the bungalow, at her childhood; then she spun round and went quickly down into the thick-smelling morning dusk of the plantation.

Case followed her, his rifle slung over his shoulder, his brocaded bag clinking with the bottle of Scotch and the tins of food, an American still innocent, like America itself, of the image he created.

CHAPTER 6

'What's your name?' Maynard demanded. 'Where did you learn to speak English?'

'My name is Kamar.' The man had taken off his gaiters and stood with them in his hand, as if debating whether to offer them to Maynard. 'I worked as a steward on the ships, sir. For the Netherlands Steamship Line,' he said, and drew himself up as if he were being inspected by one of the line's captains. 'There were many English passengers.'

'You didn't learn to speak as well as you do just from talking to English passengers. Where else did you learn it?'

Kamar held out the gaiters, like dried bloaters. 'Would you care for these, sir? It is very handy to have a second pair.'

Maynard wanted to laugh at the man's cheek, but kept his face grim. 'Don't beat about the bush, Kamar. Where else did you learn English?'

Kamar hesitated, still holding out the gaiters. He looked around at the Europeans gathered in a tight circle about him, realised that till his wiles were sharpened enough to compete with them it would be best to tell the truth. Otherwise they might abandon him to the Sumatrans.

'I went to school in Singapore, sir.'

'Why didn't you say so in the first place?'

'I was not supposed to be there, sir. My father was a smuggler.' He said it without embarrassment: smuggling was a trade like any other occupation. 'He wanted me to help him when I grew up, be his agent in Singapore. Like father, like offspring. Unfortunately he was shot.'

'By the Dutch or the English?'

'By the English, sir,' Kamar said, then added hurriedly, 'No offence, sir.'

'If anyone was offended, it should have been your father,' Maynard said. 'Righto. But what was wrong between you and the other people back at the bungalow? Why would they want to kill you?'

'For helping you, sir. And I am a Javanese. The Sumatrans do not like us. I was Mr. Brinker's head house-boy and the other boys never liked me giving them orders.'

'You're wearing a red sarong, like those young men,' Elisabeth said. 'Do you belong to the PNI?'

'Oh no, miss!' Kamar threw up his hands in horror; she might have accused him of sleeping with his mother. 'I am not interested in politics. I had my red sarong long before the others started wearing theirs.' He beamed, tilting his head in an almost womanish gesture. 'Red is my favourite colour.'

'Mine too, sport,' said Polo. 'I used to carry the flag in the May Day processions.'

'Up the workers!' Case murmured, and looked at Maynard. 'What you say we keep moving? Those guerrillas ain't gonna wait on us.'

Kamar had led them back down to the river and they had crossed it by a narrow wooden bridge suspended between trees on either side of the stream. On the far bank Maynard had called a halt while he interrogated the new member of their party. Polo and Cabrolini had gone back and chopped at the vines that held the bridge in place, then watched the latticework of rough planks fall into the water and swing downstream, still held by the vines on the other side of the river. They had just rejoined the group as Kamar mentioned that red was his favourite colour.

'Righto, Kamar, you lead the way.' Maynard put his hand on his pistol in its holster. 'And if you lead us into any sort of ambush, you'll get a bullet in the back of your neck. I'll stay alive long enough to make sure of that.'

Kamar's smile was sketched on the bland face, a muscular spasm rather than an expression of mirth. 'You can trust me, sir.' He held out the gaiters again. 'You want them, sir?'

Maynard shook his head. 'All I want is to find Mr. Brinker and the other Hollanders. The sooner the better.'

'This way, then, sir,' said Kamar, and led them, like a cinema usher, up an aisle between the trees while monkeys chattered in the galleries above them.

An hour later they were climbing out of a narrow valley, up a narrow track that wound its way through a series of water terraces. A buffalo stood like a horned rock above its glass reflection, gazing at them with dull bituminous eyes. A kapok tree raised an arthritic arm to hold an elegant white crane, and a stand of bamboo, moving in the slight breeze, made a dry music. The terraces stretched below them, giants steps of water that caught the light and flung it back up the hillside in a green glare. They had seen no one as they crossed the valley and now they moved up the hillside of still water, like ants in a glass landscape. Nothing else appeared to be moving anywhere; the valley was just a giant glittering bowl of silence. War had come to Sumatra but it was difficult to believe it.

Case stopped and waited as Garrick, burdened by his gun, his string bag and his suitcase, came labouring up the track. The boy stopped, put down his suitcase, and gasped for breath. 'Now I know what they mean by the burden of the rich!'

Case grinned. 'You wanna share the wealth?'

Garrick wiped the strings of sweat from his face. 'I used to believe in that. My dad was a socialist. He wanted to start a cricketers' union, but he got nowhere. He read only two things, Wisden's—that's the cricketer's bible—and the Daily Herald. And he had only two heroes, Maurice Tate, who played for England, and George Lansbury, who led the Labour Party. I was brought up on two principles, keep your bat straight and share the wealth. Well, I never kept my bat straight,' he grinned, 'and now I've got the wealth, I want to hang on to it.'

'You'd be at home in Texas. They wouldn't know what a cricket bat was, but they know how to hang on to their wealth. What are you gonna do with all that loot?'

'Buy a yacht and sail round the world. And finish up in Tahiti.'

'Why Tahiti? The girls there?'

Garrick gazed out on the shining green world below them. 'If you saw where I grew up, you'd understand. A back street in Leeds isn't anyone's idea of heaven. I didn't see the sun till I was twelve years old.' He grinned at his exaggeration. 'It popped out of the smoke and fog one day and I thought I'd seen the New Coming of The Lord. I ran up the street yelling Hallelujah! Then I bumped into this old chap, he'd been a sailor, and he told me what it was. Said he'd seen it every day when he was in Tahiti.'

'So how did you finish up in Singapore?'

'It was the nearest I could get.' Garrick looked up the track. The others had halted about fifty yards up, were getting their breath after the long climb. He looked back at Case, glad of the opportunity to talk to the American again. He treasured the company of older men; he drew on their experience, as on a bank to augment his own meagre existence. This American boxer could supply a bottomless overdraft. He must have known Joe Louis, Schmeling, Baer. Suddenly Garrick, who had never shown any more interest in boxing than in cricket, saw that this ragged, unshaven man sitting on the bank beside him had an aura of glamour about him. The aura might be in worse condition than his clothes, nonetheless it was real. 'What about you? Where did you want to finish up? As world champion?'

Case looked down into the valley, down into the years gone. 'I don't even know if that's what I wanted,' he confessed. He wanted to talk to this boy, out of friendship; or out of a growing sense of his own loneliness? he wondered. Each of them felt he was in the other's debt; but that was something neither of them would ever confess. He grinned, but not with much mirth: 'Don't tell Polo, but I don't think I'd have ever made it. I had a punch and I had footwork.' He was still staring down into the valley, regretful now. 'I didn't have enough ambition, that was the trouble. You gotta be hungry or ambitious to be champ.'

Garrick took a chance: 'What happened to you, Jack? I mean——?' He gestured around him. 'You must be the first top boxer ever finished up on a hill in Sumatra.'

Case stood up, picked up his rifle and his carpet-bag. 'You just start to slide. It's kinda gradual, you don't always know it's happening. You fight a guy and he puts you down, you say it was just a bad night and you'll take him next time. Maybe you do fight him again and you do take him, but it was harder than you'd reckoned. And the promoters notice it. And the next fight you get, the guy you're up against, he's a young feller on his way up. You fight him and you beat him, maybe. Then the next guy and the next, they're all young fellers on their way up. But you take 'em on because you need the dough. Then one day you wake up. You're in a town you never seen before, Allentown, P.A., or Little Rock, Arkansas, you're fighting a guy you never heard of. And all of a sudden you wake up, they're using you. You're the yardstick to see how good the comers are. They don't want you any more, not for the big time.' He couldn't remember when he had last admitted so much. He suddenly realised he was weakened, as if he let blood run from himself. Christ, he thought, who said confession was good for the soul? But then knew that it was. He looked up and Garrick was staring at him with sympathy, something he found, to his surprise, that he did not resent. Pity he would have resented; but this was something gentler, a gift not a favour. Suddenly he smiled, the first real opening of his face that Garrick had seen; and Garrick smiled back. It was like a warm clasp of hands between them. 'I wonder how good the young guys are in Tahiti?'

Garrick picked up his things. Case had shown him nothing glamorous, but he didn't mind. In some vague way he knew that Case had shown him something more, a part of himself; and something told him Case had not been as revealing as that to many people. He was grateful for the American's confidence. 'We'll see when we get there,' he said, including Case now in his own ambition.

'If we get there,' said Case, looking down into the valley. Then he turned and yelled up at Maynard and the others farther up the track. 'There's someone following us!'

By the time he and Garrick had caught up with the rest of the party, Maynard was taking his binoculars away from his eyes. 'They're Japs. About twenty of them. We'll make it over the top of that ridge, then leave the track and head for the trees.'

They had gone no more than twenty yards up the track when they saw the bobbing heads moving down the skyline ahead of them. They could not see the bodies or even the faces of the newcomers, only the helmets moving down the line of the ridge like so many convulsive turtles.

'More Nips!'

'Scatter!'

The party broke up at once, Kamar moving fastest of them all. He plunged off the side of the track, stumbled through the water of the rice paddy and fell into a ditch running along a side bank to the terrace. He grabbed a reed, shoved it into his mouth and lay back beneath the water, like a man lying down to sleep. The others followed suit, some of them climbing to the terrace above the track, others dropping down to the terrace below.

Polo was one of the last to go down. He dropped his gun and string bag into a ditch, grabbed a weed, and almost dived beneath the surface of the water as he saw the first Japanese come into full view over the top of the ridge. And swallowed a mouthful of dirty water as he screamed in pain. He rolled over on his back, his hands clutching his thigh where the sharp stump of cane had stabbed him. He threshed a moment in agony, choking on the water he had gulped, his teeth biting right through the reed in his mouth. He sat up, almost blind with pain and water but able to see the seven Japanese as they came into view farther up the track. He could feel his stomach fluttering and he wanted to vomit; if he had been alone he would have stood up and might even have welcomed a bullet from the Japanese. But he was not alone. Even in his agony he remembered Maynard and the others. He broke off another reed, put it into his mouth, resisting the temptation to close his teeth tight as another spasm of pain raced through him, and lay back in the water.

He lay on his back looking up through the green-brown surface of the rice paddy at the glare that he knew was the faraway sky. There was no more than six to eight inches of water above him, but it was as if he were at the bottom of a deep still sea. A log floated across his vision, huge against the light above him; one end of it trailed beneath the surface, brushing his nose, and he knew then it was only a bent reed. He was gasping with the pain in his thigh and he was having difficulty in breathing through the reed in his mouth. Several times it seemed to him that he moaned, but the sound was only in his skull; beneath the water he could hear nothing, not even the footsteps of the Japanese as they came down the track. Something moved in the water beneath him, perhaps a snake, but it did not disturb him. He could feel himself growing faint and in a moment he knew he was going to black out.

Then he saw the shadow floating on the water above him. He drew in his breath sharply through the reed, waiting for the Japanese bayonet to come stabbing down through the water and into his gut. The shadow darkened, grew larger; the Japanese must be bending over, making sure he would not miss. Polo tensed, was about to sit up; then he saw that the shadow was coloured, was dark red. He relaxed, letting out his breath. He was looking up at his own blood floating on the surface of the water.

But had the Japanese seen it? There was only one way of knowing: when the bullets or the bayonet hit him. Again he tensed, wondered whether to sit up. Despite the chill of the water in which he lay, he could feel himself sweating. He moved his hand slightly, trying to hold together the edges of the jagged wound in his thigh. He thought of Chairil lying in the grass of the plantation holding *his* thigh. There was a word, something like iron, that fitted this muck-up. Whatever the word was, it didn't matter now. In a moment he would be dead, and that was a four-letter word you couldn't argue with.

Then he saw the other bigger shadow beyond the shadow of the blood. It bent towards him; and he thought, No, I'm not gunna die under this dirty stinking water. He sat up, spat out the reed, looked blindly through the water and blood running from his face at the figure above him, and groaned his last defiance: 'Get stuffed, you bastard!'

'Who, me?' said Case. Then his grin died as he took in the blood that stained the water. He turned to Maynard and Cabrolini. 'Give me a hand, quick!'

Maynard and Cabrolini came floundering through the water. Cabrolini grabbed Case's and Polo's gear, while Maynard helped Case get Polo to his feet. Between them the American and the Englishman carried the wounded Australian up on to the path, the Italian staggering along behind them with the extra guns and gear; four nationalities together in the one small rice paddy on a hill in Sumatra, but none of them aware at that moment of the difference between himself and the others. The four men, which was all they were, were intent only on getting away from the common enemy. Waiting for them on the track were the Dutchwoman, the other Englishman and the Javanese.

'Where's the Nips?' Polo gasped.

'Down the hill somewhere,' Maynard said. 'Make for that cane-brake up there. Hurry!'

They climbed up through the terraces, ignoring the winding track now, wading calf-deep through the water, clambering up the banks, reckless of whether the Japanese could see them. Once they made the stand of cane they would be all right; beyond it lay the forest again and they could soon lose themselves in that. Maynard knew that once they were within the shelter of the trees the Japanese would be careful about approaching them across the open rice paddies.

Luck was with them. Just before they passed behind the screen of the cane Garrick looked back down the hillside. There was no sign of the Japanese. The valley was silent and deserted again, its glass sides reflecting a thousand suns. Garrick looked down into a vast bowl of green sunlight and said, 'We're safe. For the time being, anyway.'

They moved on into the trees, found a small clearing and Case and Maynard put Polo down. The little man had now almost lost consciousness; his mouth hung open in his thin yellowed face like another wound itself. Maynard ripped open the torn trouser-leg and exposed the gaping hole in Polo's thigh. The others gasped in shock and sympathy; and with relief, too, that the wound was not theirs. Cabrolini's hand went to the St. Christopher's medal on the chain round his neck and behind him Kamar put his hands together in the Moslem gesture of thanks.

'It needs cleansing.' Elisabeth had dropped on her knees beside Maynard as he leaned over Polo. 'With that mud and water in it——'

Maynard looked up at Case. 'Is there any of that whisky left?'

Case took the almost empty bottle from the brocaded bag. Elisabeth had already begun to wash the wound with water from Garrick's canteen, using a strip of cloth she had torn from her skirt. Polo had opened his eyes and lay looking at her as she worked. Case handed the whisky bottle to Maynard, then took his parang and turned to move away.

'Where are you going?' Maynard said.

'We'll need to make some sort of stretcher. We'll have to carry him.'

'Pull your head in, sport.' Polo's voice was weak, but there was no mistaking his determination. 'Nobody's carrying me, my oath they're not. Make me a crutch, but forget any bloody stretcher.'

Case looked at Maynard, who hesitated, then nodded. Case moved off into the trees and Cabrolini followed him.

'Do you think we are going to make it, Signor Case? All of us, I mean.'

Case had chosen a thick straight branch and was hacking it from a tree. 'Why ask me? Maynard is the boss.'

'I asked you because Americans are always such optimists.' Cabrolini shook his head ruefully at himself. He was an Italian who saw himself clearly; he had always looked in mirrors for the truth, not out of vanity. 'Perhaps I just needed reassuring.'

'Have I sounded optimistic?' Case had begun to strip the branch.

'Not always, but sometimes.'

'What about Maynard?'

'The captain sounds determined, not optimistic.' He had an ear for nuances; it was why he had been such a good sales representative here in the East. 'There is a difference.'

'In the fight game it was the determined guy, not the optimistic one, who usually got the decision.'

'I think you might be both, Signor Case.'

Case stopped with the parang in mid-air. He was cautious, eyeing the other man carefully, like a boxer assessing an opponent who had shown an unexpected punch. But Cabrolini was only threatening him with friendship: 'I should like to have known you when you were in America, at the —what do they say?—top of the heap? A man should always first be met in his own environment.'

Case went back to stripping the branch. 'What was your environment?'

Cabrolini leaned back against a tree, watching the American shaping a crude crutch out of the branch. Case worked methodically, almost with pleasure, as if he enjoyed working with his hands. Then Cabrolini remembered: of course his hands had been his tools of trade. But he said, 'Were you always a boxer, Signor Case?'

Case did not reply at once. Then, feinting, he said, 'Did you always work for Fiat?'

Cabrolini recognised the counter, but he was not offended. He knew he was still the outsider here, not really entitled to ask questions. 'Always, ever since I left the university. My father was a professor and he wanted me to follow him into the university at Bologna. But I had fallen in love with a girl ——' He smiled, at himself and at Valentina, seven thousand miles and almost twenty years away. Mussolini and his *squadristi* had just marched on Rome, but the young lovers had not been interested in politics or the future of Italy. They had fumbled their way through the politics of love and had made a future for themselves: one that had come to an abrupt break three months ago in Saigon. 'I needed more money than the university paid. Professors are poor men in Italy. Everyone pays them respect, but that is all they pay them. So I went to Torino. Fiat employed me and I have been with them ever since. If I survive this——' He nodded at the crutch Case held, as if it were a symbol of the plight of all of them. 'If I survive this, I shall have a nice pension to retire on and a villa on the hill above Lerici. That's where Shelley, the English poet, lived. I might even write poetry, too.'

'What if you do get home,' Case said, 'and Italy loses the war?'

'We have already lost it,' said Cabrolini. 'We lost it the day we joined forces with Germany.'

'You think the Nazis are gonna lose the war?'

'I don't know. Perhaps they will win it. But whoever wins, the Italians will be the losers. That I know. We do not have enough ambition to be world conquerors. Mussolini has, but not the rest of us. Italians are not the Romans of old. Caesar would have a hard time raising his legions today. We are not cowards, despite what people say. We are like Captain Maynard, only more so. We are practical about lost causes. The English are not.'

'And Americans?'

'You haven't found your causes yet. You will, but not yet.'

Case held up the crutch. He had shaped a fork in it and though it was rough, it would be serviceable. 'We need some padding.'

Cabrolini took off the jacket he was still wearing and with some difficulty wrenched a sleeve out of it. 'The right arm. The one Signor Murphy thinks I raise to Mussolini.'

Case took the sleeve, made a pad of it and tied it with a vine to the fork of the crutch. 'Don't be hard on Polo. He needs his prejudices as a crutch. If he didn't have 'em, his inferiority complex would bowl him over.'

Cabrolini looked at him curiously. 'Where did you get your education?'

Case grinned. 'From *The Ring* magazine. All fighters ain't bums, you know. Tunney used to read Shakespeare.'

They went back to join the others, arriving just as Maynard handed the whisky bottle to Polo. The little man, his thigh neatly wrapped with a bandage from Maynard's field dressing, squinted up at Case. 'There's only a mouthful left, Jack. I don't want it if you wanna hang on to it.'

'Go ahead,' said Case.

Polo drained the bottle, coughed, then wiped his lips. 'I been a beer drinker all me life,' he said apologetically, as if he felt Case's whisky had been wasted on him. He got awkwardly to his feet, took the crutch Case handed him and shoved it under his armpit. He screwed up his face in pain as he put his weight on his injured leg, but he made no complaint, tried hard instead to smile and only succeeded in grimacing. 'I feel as useless as a three-legged dog.'

The others all smiled and turned away, embarrassed because he had so aptly summed up what they were all thinking. Cabrolini picked up Polo's string bag and Case took his gun; the two of them moving off up the path between the trees before Polo could object. Polo looked around at the others with a belligerence as shaky as his stance. 'I'll be all right! Don't anyone hang back for me.'

Nobody argued with him. Maynard nodded absently and turned away, began to gather up his gear. He moved awkwardly and stiffly, like a man suddenly afflicted with arthritis. But only his spirit had become arthritic. In his mind he had already begun to accept the probability that they would have to abandon Polo. Not abandon him alive, but dead. For Polo was surely going to die. He would die by degrees, step by step to a grave, as he dragged himself over these hills for the next . . .

'How long?' Maynard snarled at Kamar. 'How much farther?'

'Not far,' said Kamar. 'Only another day's walk.'

'Another day!' Garrick almost dropped his suitcase in his surprise. All at once his body was heavier than everything else he carried; he sagged under the weight of it. 'What's your idea of far?'

'Australia,' said Maynard, his voice still sharp. 'And we're going to make it there. Right, Polo?'

'My bloody oath,' said Polo, and, making an unconscious mockery of his words, began to hobble up the track after Case and Cabrolini.

Maynard looked at Elisabeth, saw the pity and despair in her eyes that he knew were in his own. But in her eyes the look was deeper, darkening the grey irises to ashes. Tending the jagged hole in Polo's leg she had been wiping the blood from her father, the dead man whose wounds only his living daughter could now feel. Her pain had been as great as, if not more than, Polo's.

2

'I suggest someone should keep watch,' said Elisabeth. 'There are tigers in these hills.'

'I don't think I'd miss it if a tiger took a bite outa me,' said Polo. 'I'm all aches and bloody pains. I know what the missus would say. A good hot cuppa tea and a coupla Aspro, that's what you want. She took it for everything. Headache, backache, labour pains, the lot.'

He lay on his back on a bed of leaf mould, his voice the only live thing in his skeletal body. He seemed to have lost all his flesh in the eight hours' walk since he had been wounded that morning; he had had very little to begin with, but now his skin hung on him like a badly-fitting garment. The dark buttons of his eyes looked up out of the wrinkled yellow silk of his face at the ceiling of trees above them. He could see tantalising glimpses of red sky beyond the stencilled leaves and he wished that they had camped out in the open. He did not want to die here in the black mine of the jungle; he sniffed deeply and imagined he could smell coal dust. He'd make bloody sure he'd live till morning, even if he had to stay awake all night. If he was going to die, it would be with the sun shining on him. Otherwise he might just as well have stayed at home and been buried with the pit ponies.

'Are all tigers man-eaters?' Cabrolini asked.

'Not all. There are some rogues, killers just like some men are. But most tigers, if they are getting enough game to eat, stay away from people. Man-eaters are usually old tigers or ones that have injured themselves. They've become too slow to catch game, so they attack people.'

'Time for chow,' said Case, then grinned at his bad timing.

He had chopped the tops off two tins of meat with his parang. Maynard scraped portions out with his small Malayan knife and handed them to the others. They ate the dry salty meat with their fingers, then washed it down with water from their canteens. For dessert they had rambutans gathered by Kamar, prickly-shelled nuts that had a sweet fruity taste. When they had finished Elisabeth got up and moved away. The men turned their backs out of politeness, but then looked curiously at each other when they heard her still moving around somewhere in the bushes. Then she came back and held out a handful of large dark shiny leaves.

'Do you have any quinine?' she asked Maynard, and when he shook his head she give him two of the leaves. 'Chew these. They are an antidote against malaria.'

Maynard bit on a leaf and at once spat it out. But Elisabeth insisted he keep chewing. She handed leaves to the other men, then began to chew on a leaf herself. The taste was almost unbearably bitter, but they all chewed resolutely, even Polo, grimacing like children as they did so. Then Kamar, grinning broadly, passed around more rambutans and they all ate them to bring back some juices into their dry soured mouths.

'Where did you learn about those?' Case asked.

'We Hollanders did not live an entirely useless life here, Mr.

Case. We did try to learn a few things from the people.' She looked at Kamar. 'And you taught us a lot, didn't you, Kamar?'

'Not enough, miss,' said Kamar.

'What do you mean?'

But Kamar had already retreated behind his smuggler's smile: he had been brought up to deceive, not to venture too far out into the open. 'The Indies are very old. You could be here a thousand years and there would still be things for us to teach you.'

Elisabeth gazed at him for a moment, uncertain whether the Javanese was being evasive or just polite. But she was too tired for polemics. She nodded, finished the short conversation with a noncommittal remark and got up to move across to where she had put down Polo's string bag, which she had insisted on taking from Cabrolini during the day's march. She saw now that Case's own gear was beside hers, and at that moment he came up beside her.

'Two singles,' he said. 'I've registered us at the desk as Mr. and Mrs. Smith.'

For a moment she was irritated, then she saw that he was trying to be friendly. 'In Sumatra that should be Mr. and Mrs. Schmidt.'

'I'll remember that next time.' He lay down, scooping leaves into a pillow and laying the empty brocaded bag on top of it. It was dark now in the clearing and they could barely see each other. The other men had already lain down and Cabrolini, who had volunteered for the first watch, was sitting on a fallen log at the edge of the clearing. A bird somewhere was farewelling the day with a harsh mournful cry and high in the trees a family of monkeys went home wind-bagging amongst themselves. 'Where did you learn all that about tigers? And that quinine bush or whatever it was?'

Elisabeth had made herself comfortable. She was tired enough to want to fall off to sleep at once, but she could not shut out Case. The fact surprised and annoyed her; she was not accustomed to men who intruded themselves into her consciousness. She had not consciously thought of him during the day's long march, but she had always been aware of him. Sometimes she had looked back and seen him watching her, a faint enigmatic smile on his lips that could have been friendly or mocking: either one made her uneasy. The men she had known had all been simple in their approach to her: some had been in love with her, but all of them had wanted to go to bed with her. She was sure that Case was not thinking of her in that way, despite his small joke about Mr. and Mrs. Smith. Though she was arrogant she was not vain: she was not offended if a man did not want to go to bed with her. But she wished she could fathom this man who was such a strange mixture of cynicism and charity, of educated viewpoint and bad grammar, who had fought for a living yet didn't seem to want to fight for his freedom. The East, she knew, was a haven for misfit white men, yet she did not have the feeling that this American was fleeing from anything. It was almost as if fate or events had pushed him to this part of the world and he had gone along, uncomplaining, unworried, perhaps even smiling that puzzling smile of his.

'One of our homes was in the hills where there are a lot of tigers. Our plantation workers taught me.'

'Another home? How many homes do you have?'

'Five. They were not all really homes, just places my father owned. We lived mostly at our house in Medan. Is there something wrong in having five homes to go to? I think I was fortunate,' she said innocently.

'Yeah, that's a good word for it,' he said with gentle sarcasm. She heard him chuckle in the darkness, then he said, 'But who needs all those homes?'

'Are you a Communist or something, Mr. Case?'

'That was how I got started. I won the Moscow Golden Gloves.' She heard him chuckle again.

She was annoyed, at him and at herself for wanting to continue the conversation: 'Is everything a joke to you?'

There was no chuckle this time, just a long silence. Then he sighed and said, 'Not everything.'

She was silent herself for a moment, then as if her curiosity was a thing with a will of its own, something she could not control, she heard herself say, 'Do you have any family back in America?'

He did not reply at once and she thought, I have gone too far. These beachcombers never want to tell you about the people they left behind them. Had he a wife? she wondered; then further wondered what sort of woman this man might have loved. She had begun to think he had finished the conversation for the night, when he broke in on her thoughts: 'I got nobody.'

'What did you do before you became a prizefighter?'

Again there was a silence before he replied. 'Fought with my old man, mostly. He was from Poland, one of the old type.

Our name used to be Czeicinski. He worked in the oil fields and I used to traipse around after him. But we never got on. We were the original opposite Poles.'

'So you ran away?' Her own father had spoiled her, had done everything he could to make up for the mother she had lost.

'No.' There were pauses in Case's replies. He was giving himself away piece by piece, grudgingly, like a bankrupt paying off creditors. Yet compulsion had taken hold of him: he had to reply as she had to ask questions. The jungle night now hid them both completely, the darkness of the confessional. He remembered the visits to the priest long ago, the tortured confession of bad thoughts, bad actions, eating meat on Fridays. Sin was no longer a burden and he hadn't been near a priest in twenty years. This was just as difficult as those other confessions had been, but he had to keep on talking, as if he were looking for some sort of absolution for all the wasted years: 'No, I didn't run away. Not right off. I went to college. In those days I was a pretty fair quarterback—I played high school football. They gave me a scholarship.' Again there was the cynicism: 'It's an old American tradition. Every boy, no matter how poor, or dumb, is entitled to a college education. Especially if he can play football.'

'Did you study anything? Or just play football all the time?'

'Oh, I studied. Funny thing was, I didn't like football. You don't know our game, do you?'

'I have seen it in films. I cannot understand it. All those funny little conferences every two or three minutes.'

'Huddles, we call 'em. No, I didn't like it. I never knew why till these last few days. It was because it's too much like war. It's all strategy and tactics. The coach, he's the general, he sits on the bench, and the troops go out and do everything he's mapped out. It's no game for an individualist.'

'Was that why you took up boxing? Because you're an individualist?'

He chuckled again. 'I didn't think of it that way at the time. No, a guy saw me fighting in the inter-college tournaments. I dunno why I tried out for the boxing team—just something to do, I guess. It was all so long ago,' he said, and attempted that most difficult of tasks, to try and remember the reasons for the decisions of one's youth. And failed, because youth, like the heart, has reasons of its own. 'This guy said he could make me a champion and I believed him. I was a sucker for flattery in those days,' he said, and she could imagine him grinning to himself in the darkness.

'What did you study at the university?'

'Geology.'

'Why geology?' She did not know what she had expected him to say. Public education was a mystery to her. She had been taught by governesses, then taken on a Grand Tour of Europe, only dimly aware that, young as she was, she was a relic of a social age now gone.

'I grew up on the oilfields. Beaumont, where I was born, is right in the middle of the biggest oil industry in the world. I was born not ten miles from Spindle Top, that was where the first big gusher in Texas blew in 'way back in 1901. I worked on the oilfields during vacations. My old man was a rigger, but I wanted something better than that. I listened to guys who'd worked on fields in Arabia or even out here, and I thought that's what I'd like to do. But I wanted to be more than just a rigger. So I took up geology.'

'And why didn't you keep on with it?'

'Laziness, I guess.' He was old enough now to admit the faults of youth. At thirty-five or six one could face the truth of oneself at nineteen or twenty; distance lent indulgence. 'Studying was a grind for me.'

'So you threw up a chance to be a geologist to be a *prize-fighter*?'

'I like the way you curled your tongue around that last word.' He laughed, more than a chuckle this time, and the laugh disturbed Garrick on the other side of the clearing: the boy uttered a strangled cry in his sleep, then was quiet again. 'I made five thousand dollars my first year as a *prize-fighter*.'

'Is that all you wanted out of life—money?'

'Only someone who's never had to think about money would say that.' His rebuff was gentle. He had never envied anyone their wealth; then remembered that she now was quite possibly as poor as he. 'No, that wasn't all I wanted.'

'What else did you want?'

'That's a good question,' he said, but as so often happened, he didn't have a good answer. He had always lacked ambition, even of happiness. He had never forced himself to seek something: love, fame or money, *ersatz* ambition was like *ersatz* coffee, it could turn to sawdust in your mouth. But he had always been aware of a hollowness in himself, a need for

122

identification; even Texas Jack Case had been someone else, a twin who he knew was only a transient. The twin was dead now, but for the echoes: he could expect no help there. He had made no investment for the future, not even of a dream, and now all at once in the damp womb of this night he felt chill of the blank loneliness that lay ahead.

'Good night,' he said abruptly, and turned over. He fell asleep almost at once, as if hopelessness were some sort of drug.

Elisabeth lay staring up at the blackness above her for a while. Stars occasionally showed through the stormclouds of leaves like dagger points of lightning; because they appeared only momentarily their brilliance seemed heightened. Somewhere down the hill below them she heard a grunting: a wild pig, a danger she had forgotten and one which could be worse than a tiger. She shivered, turned over and began to weep. The tears came unexpectedly; it was as if an unsuspected boil of grief had burst within her. But the pain had been building within her all day, ever since she had taken her last look at the bungalow, turned and walked away from it into the deadening shadows of the rubber trees. It had come to a head when she had asked Case what he had wanted out of life. Because she had realised, with a final stab of pain that was almost physical, that she herself did not know what she wanted. It had not occurred to her, up till now, that there might be something better for her than what her father had planned for her. It was as if she had been sleeping all her life without even the poorest peasant's luxury of a dream. Having everything, as she had imagined, she had been denied the dream of wanting *something*. She wept, for her father, the happy man who had spoiled her with his love, and she wept, ashamedly, for herself. Self pity was one of the few luxuries she had not known up till now.

On the other side of the clearing Maynard had been listening to the murmuring of the voices and had felt jealous. Not sexually jealous: the Dutch girl, beautiful though she might be in other circumstances, did not attract him that way. He liked his women small, dark and vivacious, in the image of his wife. If ever he were driven by physical lust to be unfaithful, it would be with a woman like Ruth: the act of adultery would be in a way an act of fidelity. No, the jealousy was a petty one, and he knew it. Why should it prick him that Elisabeth should talk to Case and not talk to him? Did he really want whatever confidences she was giving away? Perhaps not.

But she might have listened to *him*; he might have been able to talk to her as he would have to Ruth. There was no one else here in the party to whom he could talk. Case, Polo and Cabrolini were ruled out because of their nationality; he was the sort of Englishman who was sure he could not confide in foreigners; there was more of his father in him than he cared to admit. He would not have been able to talk to Garrick, and was ashamed of the admission; he was not a snob, but Garrick, in a way, was as much a foreigner to him as the others. Education and class had drawn their boundaries around him: Garrick, a North Country grammar school boy, had the wrong visa for heart-to-heart talks.

It had not been Maynard's fault that he was a separate Englishman from Garrick and his kind. In his first year at Sandhurst the Jarrow marchers had come to London and all his sympathies had been with the thin silent men who, with a dignity that grew with every step they took, had walked from the North of England to the South to ask, not for charity, but just the opportunity to work. His father, comfortable on a private income, safe in a parish where the first five pews in his church held no one but landed gentry, had believed, with the Bishop of Durham, that organised mob pressure was no way to relieve misery.

'The government will solve the problem in its own good time,' he said, sipping China tea and eating a slice of Harrods best fruit cake.

Maynard had gone back to Sandhurst, angry at his father's blind cruelty, but political discussion had not been encouraged at the military college. One discussed the rise of Hitler's new army but not the army of the unemployed. And so, trapped in a sea of at the best apathy, at the worst callous disregard, he had sunk himself in his studies. And despised himself for his only half-hearted effort to reach out to those other men who, like him, helped to make up England. He could not remember all the route of the Jarrow marchers, but he wondered if they had passed through Leeds on their way to London. Some time, if he could find a way to open the subject, he would ask Garrick if he had seen the marchers.

He dropped off to sleep and dreamed of ranks upon ranks of thin, poorly dressed men drawn up on the parade ground at Sandhurst, singing God Save The King while his father walked among them handing out fruit cake and crumpets.

CHAPTER 7

Case, the last man on watch, came sharply awake from the doze that had been creeping over him. He could hear the voices coming up the hill, the light high voices that he knew now were Japanese. He moved swiftly, waking the others, clamping a hand over their mouths as they opened their eyes in alarm. Then they got silently to their feet, gathered up their gear and slid into the bushes. Case helped Polo up and half-carried the little man into the dense screen of the jungle. Maynard was the last to leave the clearing. He had barely had time to grab up Polo's crutch and his own belongings and slip into the bushes before the Japanese, ten of them, came in single file up the track.

The party had camped off to the side of the track, but to Case, crouched behind a bush and looking out at the clearing, the evidence of the camp stood out like newly planted landmarks. The grass and leaves had been crushed into the shapes of the seven bodies that had slept there; Elisabeth's pillow of leaves was still covered with her empty string bag. Case glanced at Elisabeth and saw the latticed pattern on her cheek where she had lain on the string bag. She saw him looking at her and she stared back at him, still only half-awake, still half-submerged in the intimacy of last night's confidences. She smiled tentatively and he smiled back, though he did not know why. This was no moment for smiling.

Beside him he felt Maynard raise his gun and he looked at the Englishman, raising his own gun in a gesture of inquiry. He did not know if he would be able to shoot if Maynard gave the order, but he was not going to argue about it this time. He was surprised when he saw Maynard shake his head. Then he looked back at the clearing.

The Japanese had come to a halt. A sergeant had been leading the column and he had stopped and looked back at an officer who was coming up to join him. The sergeant said something, but the officer, a young man with a thin wispy moustache, shook his head. The soldiers had stopped, were ready to relax; it was obvious now that the sergeant had suggested that they should halt for a rest here. But the officer, an eager beaver just like Maynard, Case thought, had other ideas. He snapped an order, the soldiers straightened up and moved on, grumbling among themselves in the manner of soldiers in every army. As they went out of the clearing the last man looked back. He missed his step and for a moment the sweating Case and Maynard thought he was going to stop and come back. They then saw him shrug and go on, disappearing among the trees.

Case let out his breath in a long gasp and looked at Maynard. 'For a minute I thought you were gonna start pumping bullets into them. They were sitting ducks.'

'I organise my ambushes better than that. We'd have got only half of them. And the other half would have eventually got us.' He nodded back over his shoulder. 'We have nowhere to retreat to.'

Case turned round, then nodded his head and grinned weakly. The jungle finished only a few yards behind them. Through the trees he was looking out on a sheer drop of several hundred feet.

'We'd have been on the ropes,' he said. 'Only there'd have been no ropes.'

'It was one of the things they taught us at Sandhurst. Always have a good place to retreat to before you think of attacking.' Maynard smiled, glad of the opportunity to talk to the other man without some rancour between them. He had become aware of the fact that the bickering between them was having an effect on the others in the party. 'It was something we learned in the American Revolution.'

They had all gathered up their belongings and had begun to move out of the bushes again on to the track. 'Which way do we go, skipper?' Garrick asked. 'Do we follow the Japs down this track?'

Maynard looked at Kamar. 'Do we have to?'

Kamar had been the quickest to dash into the bushes, moving with the speed of a natural, unembarrassed coward. 'There is another way, but it will take us longer. I think we should take it, captain. We should not meet the Japanese, if it is possible.'

Maynard smiled. 'No, we shouldn't.' He glanced at Polo. 'How's the leg?'

'Pretty crook. But I'll be jake, skipper. Don't you worry about me.' Again there was the shaky belligerence. He's fighting *his* war of independence, Maynard thought, remembering the other moments of Polo's belligerence; but this time did not mind. Polo was at least consistent.

Maynard looked back at Kamar. He did not like the obsequious little Javanese any more this morning than he had yesterday, but now he trusted him. If Kamar had been going to betray them he would not have had a better opportunity than a few minutes ago when the Japanese had been about to enter the clearing. 'Righto, Kamar. But get us to wherever we're going before nightfall. I don't want to stumble on these guerrillas in the dark. It's bad enough risking Japanese bullets without having to take a chance on Dutch bullets as well.'

'They hurt just as much, captain,' said Kamar, then smiled at Elisabeth. 'No offence, miss. If I have to be hit by a bullet, I'd prefer it to be a Dutch one.'

'Why?' Elisabeth was puzzled by the small dark man, uncertain as to whether he was mocking her. His smile was open and cheerful, as innocent and friendly as a child's; it did not have the annoying secretiveness of Case's. Yet somehow it was a fixed smile, at the same time as puzzling and unrevealing as the smile of a skull. I'm too suspicious, she thought, I've suddenly had my eyes opened and now I'm going to distrust all the natives. But why should she distrust them? Was not the great majority of the people happy with the Dutch? She asked the question of herself, the one who could least tell her the truth. But whom else could she ask? Kamar, she was sure, would not tell her. The truth, she suspected, would be for him almost an impediment in his speech. 'Why would you prefer a Dutch bullet?'

Kamar's smile was still friendly, but (was she imagining it?) his mouth seemed a little tight at the corners. 'It is better to keep it in the family, miss. I might get compensation.'

The other men laughed. At first Elisabeth was annoyed by their laughter, as if they were siding with Kamar against her and the Dutch; then quickly she chided herself, told herself she must not start distrusting these men, too. 'If you should be so unfortunate, Kamar, I'll personally guarantee you get compensation.'

'You got nothing to worry about then, Kamar,' said Case. 'You might be dead but you won't be broke.'

Kamar's smile wavered for just a moment, then he nodded. 'My father would be pleased. He used to say that only a fool died a poor man.'

They moved off then, pushing their way off the track into a narrow pad that led down through a tall stand of bamboo. It began to rain steadily and with a force that stung their faces as they plodded on through it. They were still in the hills and the sky seemed just above their heads; several times during the morning they walked through cloud that swirled about them like damp smoke. It rained for two hours, a steady drumming on the foliage above their heads, a sound that after a while entered their heads and became a part of the sound of themselves, part of their heavy breathing, their curses as they slipped and fell, the pumping of their hearts as they laboured up steep slippery paths. The jungle had lost its various shapes, had merged into the one green-black plastic tunnel through which they trudged.

Clase felt as if his body, like his ragged clothes and his brocaded bag, was becoming sodden. He looked at his hands and to his bleared eyes they appeared green: he was turning to mould while he still lived. His teeth felt loose in his mouth and his ears were full of the sound of water. But whatever he felt, he knew he was better off than Polo.

The Australian, still brandishing his belligerent independence, had limped and crawled all through the mud of the morning with a determination that the others had to admire, even though they could not comment on it. He looked even thinner to-day than yesterday; but the bones stuck out of his paper-thin flesh like challenging fists. The wound in his thigh had begun to bleed again and the crutch had chafed his skin till his armpit, too, was now bleeding. He had fallen at least once every hundred yards, slipping in the thick mud and going down in a tangle of legs, arms and crutch, his curses fiery enough to have brought steam from the sodden earth into which he had fallen. *Oh Vi, love*, he cried once into the mud that was smothering him; then he lifted his face, clawed the mud from it and climbed awkwardly to his feet again. He looked up the track and through the hissing curtain of rain saw Case waiting for him. He shivered with cold and exhaustion, wanting to cry out to the American to help him; indeed he opened his mouth, but his tongue was dumb and all he could hear was his teeth rattling in the water-bowl of his skull. He was forty-four years old and he had never asked for help in his life. If he had asked he would not have known how to accept it. He was a simple man whose rigid simplicities made life sometimes too difficult for him.

He finally caught up with Case, blinked at him through the rain and said flatly, too weak now to be belligerent, 'I ain't gunna throw in the towel.'

'I wouldn't pay you your purse if you did,' said Case. It was easier to talk to Polo in the boxing vernacular; somehow it took the edge off what they really meant. 'You got only a couple rounds to go.'

Polo leaned on his crutch, wiped the rain off his bearded fleshless face and stared straight at Case. 'You don't believe that, do you, Jack?'

Case looked out from the ridge on which they stood. They were above a wide shallow valley that was still hidden in a grey lake of rain, but on the far side of the valley the clouds were supported by long golden pillars as the sun burst through. Sodden, deadened, he found it was as difficult to express hope as it was to believe in it. 'I gotta believe it, Polo. I was never a guy who had any time for a fight to a finish. Ten, fifteen or twenty rounds, I always like to know how I had to pace myself.'

Polo spat in the mud, managed something that passed for a grin. 'Right now I couldn't go one round with the missus.'

The rain suddenly stopped. For two hours their heads had been full of its steady drumming; now the sudden silence was almost like a sound in itself. Case and Polo looked around, a little bemused, as if they had heard something they did not recognise. Then they looked at each other and smiled, their teeth falling out of their green, dripping faces. A lance of sunlight smote them and it was as if their drowned bodies came alive again.

Polo looked up at the patch of blue sky, straight into the face of the sun. 'Good on you, Hughie,' he said gratefully and with true religion. God was someone he would have found it impossible to mention, but he believed in Him. Hughie was the Australian working man's vernacular for The Lord, though Polo did not know why. He never prayed, but occasionally he spoke to God in such a familiar way, and only Judgement Day would tell whether Hughie minded or not. Polo had never bent his knee to anyone, but he knew the meaning of respect and he was capable of it in his own unconventional way.

It was mid-afternoon when they heard the firing. There was the flat sound at first of rifle fire, then a long harsh burst that sounded like a woodpecker. 'That's a Jap machine-gun!' Maynard said.

'Oh, that's lovely,' said Garrick, sinking down on to his suitcase. He looked at Kamar. 'How far are we from where you're taking us?'

They were in a long narrow valley surrounded by hills like broken battlements. There was no jungle here, only patches of gently waving bamboo, a heath of thorn bushes and occasionally long flat stretches of lalang grass. The rain clouds had disappeared now and the valley was a steaming trough in which they felt they were being slowly boiled. Despite the climb that faced them they had looked forward to being up on the cool height of the hills again.

Kamar pointed up ahead to a steep ridge where they could now see puffs of smoke. 'That is where the Hollanders should be. Belan Koup.'

'What's Belan Koup?' Maynard said.

Elisabeth answered him: 'I've never been there, but I've heard of it. It's an ancient Buddhist temple, or rather the ruins of it. One was never sure whether it was a myth or not.' She looked at Kamar. 'The temple is really up there on that hill?'

'Oh, it is there, miss.' Kamar was casting nervous glances towards the distant ridge, as if he were wishing the temple was somewhere else. The firing was still going on, almost without interruption now as if the battle was getting desperate. 'I went there once with Mr. Brinker.'

'Do we go on, captain?' Cabrolini, slumped on a moss-covered rock in the lalang grass, was staring at the ridge, occasionally flinching a little as there was a particularly savage burst of firing.

'Not till that shooting stops.' Maynard, too, was staring at the ridge, chewed absently on his lips. 'But we've come too far now to turn back. We'll just have to hope that the Hollanders win that little skirmish.'

'I'd say that's more than a skirmish,' said Case. 'It sounds more like a main bout to me.'

Even as he spoke there was a succession of dull crumps and they saw larger bursts of smoke appear like grey flowers on the top of the ridge.

'Mortars,' said Polo, put down his crutch and stretched out flat on the ground. 'I think I'll go home to Mum.'

Maynard looked down at him. 'It would be nice if we could all go with you. Does your wife mind people dropping in?'

'The front door's always open.' Polo had tilted his hat forward over his eyes, but now he pushed it back and squinted up at Maynard. 'Skipper, do you know anything about the lay-out of Australia?' Maynard shook his head. 'I been thinking about it while we been on this little hike. The front door to Australia is wide open. If the Nips ever get to New

130

Guinea, they oughta be able to walk right into Australia. From Cape York right around to the West, there's bugger-all to stop 'em. You could land an army on parts of the north coast and nobody ud know it was there.'

'We need to get that transmitter then, don't we?'

Polo sat up, looked up towards the ridge. As he did so the firing abruptly stopped. Everyone stared up at the now silent ridge, their own silence adding to the brittle tension that seemed to hang over the valley, as if the air itself had been stretched to snapping point. Even the breeze had dropped and the stand of bamboo just ahead of them had turned to a battalion of spears, stiff and threatening. They strained their eyes, trying to pierce the blanket of forest that covered the distant ridge, but the hillside, dull green enamel, revealed nothing.

'Looks like there's been a decision,' said Polo. 'What do we do now, skip?'

Maynard hesitated. He knew how exhausted everyone was; his own legs seemed to have no more strength in them than the spears of grass amongst which he stood. He had heard RAF men in Malaya use the term, *the point of no return*; he knew now that they had passed that point. He spoke carefully, as if afraid that he might exhaust them even further; he was not even sure of his own reserves, so how could he be sure of what strength the others had left? 'We'll go on. We'll stop at the bottom of the ridge, then I'll go up and see what happened.'

He was relieved when no one disagreed with him. He had looked at Case, expecting some argument there; but the American, avoiding making a gesture of it, was busy helping Polo to his feet. 'Here's your wooden leg,' Case said, and shoved the crutch under Polo's arm.

It took them almost an hour to reach the bottom of the ridge. The thorn bushes, which had been ripping at their legs and arms as they had pushed through them, gave way to taller bushes, then they were in under the wide umbrella of a thick forest. Wild rubber, wild bananas, banyans, fought for possession of the earth; the hundred trunks of the banyan, a company of long grey-green tentacles, was winning the fight. A narrow jungle pad, showing no trace of recent footmarks, disappeared among the trunks of the biggest banyan as if into the bloodless entrails of some giant who had died here and been shrouded by the forest.

'I'll go on from here,' Maynard said.

'I'll come with you,' said Case, and Maynard looked at him in surprise. 'You might need a messenger, just in case something happens. I used to work for Western Union one time.'

'Is there anything you haven't done?' Maynard's tone was only gently sarcastic.

'I was never a soldier,' Case grinned. 'But you probably gathered that.'

2

The two men took only their weapons with them, each of them carrying one of the machine-carbines they had taken from the Japanese on the beach. (Was it only the day before yesterday? Maynard thought; and wondered that time could be stretched so much.) They left the others and went up the twisting narrow path, ducking under the trunks of the banyan and coming into a dense jungle of lichen-covered trees where the gloomy silence pressed down on them almost as tangibly as the dank dark leaves. Lianas hung like hangmen's ropes from which the corpses had been cut: leaf mould covered the path like a long line of dead wreaths. Occasionally an orchid offered itself to them, pale and fragile as a baby's tiny hand, but it, too, only added to the atmosphere of death here in the silent forest.

Case was not surprised, then, when they came upon the dead man lying on the path. Barefooted, dressed in faded green shirt and trousers, he lay on his back, one arm flung up around his head, like a sleeping man trying to ward off a nightmare. An orchid of blood glistened dully on his breast. 'He's not a Jap,' Maynard whispered, peering down at the dead Sumatran. 'He must have been unlucky and run into them as they were coming up this track.'

'What's he doing with a gun?' Case leaned close to Maynard to whisper. For men who disliked each other, they were often in situations of intimacy.

Maynard rolled the man over, pulled out the rifle that had been half-hidden by the body. 'It's a three-o-three. He might have been with the guerrillas and tried to get away.'

He slung the rifle over his back, stripped the dead man of his bandolier. 'I wonder where the hell he got this?' He examined the bandolier: it was still more than half-full of cartridges.

'You want to have a kit inspection or whatever you call

it?' The need to whisper was making Case irritable and edgy.

Maynard looked at him, but said nothing. They left the dead man where he lay and continued the climb up the steep tortuous track. Sweat was pouring from them and their legs were trembling by the time they reached the top of the ridge. They came suddenly out of the thick forest and at once pulled up, standing in the shadow of a wild rubber tree.

'It's a lost world,' Maynard said in a soft amazement.

The top of the ridge was flat, a wide wild meadow that led up to what looked at first like a ruined fort. A row of tall kenari trees lined each side of the approach, sentinels who had gone to seed. Between the trees small stone figures, green-skinned with mould, sat beneath the undergrowth. At the far end of the avenue Belan Koup rose against the sky, struggling to beat back the jungle that was crawling over it from the other three sides.

'We better be mighty careful from here on.' Case looked around the meadow, then up towards the temple. 'Can't see anyone, but that don't say they ain't still around.'

'Stick to the trees. They'll at least give us some cover.'

They moved cautiously but quickly out from beneath the rubber tree, waded through the tall lalang grass as if into a lake and came unchallenged to the shelter of the first kenari tree. They crept forward, stopping once with their hearts in their mouths as two monkeys rose up in the grass, looked at them indignantly like disturbed lovers, then skimmed away and disappeared between the far trees. Somewhere they could hear a bird, with a call like that of a cuckoo, but there was no sign of any bird movement here on the narrow plateau. Maynard stopped behind the thick buttressed trunk of the last tree before the wide broken steps that led up into the temple itself. The stillness was like an ache against his eardrums; he would almost have welcomed a burst of firing. He had the skin-itching feeling that he was being watched from every angle, but no matter where he looked he could see no sign of anyone. The long grass was unbroken and unmoving; if it hid anyone they must be coiled like snakes among its stalks. The walls of the temple, so thickly covered with vines and creepers that they looked like no more than huge mounds of vegetation, offered no hint that they might be hiding anyone. Maynard, his hand resting on the tree trunk beside his head, was conscious of the loud ticking of his watch.

'I'll go up first. You cover me. If they jump me, get out of here as quickly as you can.'

Case nodded, looked back down the row of trees to note his line of escape. 'Don't stay around for any medals. At the first shot, come a-running back this way. This ain't any place to win the war.'

Maynard grinned, though it was difficult: he could feel the tightness within himself, as if every nerve had enlarged itself, was trying to break out through his skin. 'It's my turn not to argue. You're right—I'd rather win the war somewhere else but here.'

Then he left the shelter of the tree quickly, running crouched over across the open space before the steps, only his head showing above the long grass that swayed like a green wake behind him. He came to the steps, ran up them, once stumbling on the vines that covered them, then he was at the entrance to the temple, flattened against the end of one creeper-hidden wall.

He was looking down into the main open courtyard of the temple. The jungle had almost taken over, having no respect for men or gods, but there was still much evidence of the magnificence that had once reigned here. The temple must have been a hundred yards long, a walled courtyard surrounding a central monument that looked like a mausoleum. The inner court was sunken and along the terraces on either side, for the whole length of the temple, stretched a line of stupas, huge cages of latticed stonework each of which held a seated figure of the Buddha. Parts of the walls showed through the creepers and Maynard could see the intricate carvings, that, grey-green with age, looked like another, deeper layer of foliage.

There was no sign of any life. Then he saw the white man, clad in khaki shirt and trousers, sitting against one of the stupas and staring across at him. Maynard looked quickly around, then ran down the steps, crossed the well of the courtyard and climbed the steps to the far terrace. He was still thirty feet from the man when he realised the latter was dead. His blond head lay back against the stupa, caught in an angle of the latticed stone, so that he was held upright. A bullet had gone right through his left eye; the other was closed as if in sleep. Behind him the stone Buddha, worn smooth by centuries of weather, looked with bland smugness over his shoulder.

Maynard turned round, then saw the other dead men. There were a score of them lying about the temple, some half-hidden where they had fallen among the jungle growth, others sprawled on the far steps like sightseers overcome by the heat and the long climb up here. There was no one else in the courtyard. Belan Koup was a temple of the dead.

Maynard went back to the entrance, whistled softly to Case. The American came up, looked around as Maynard pointed out the dead, then said, 'One of them must be Elisabeth's brother.'

Maynard nodded. 'You'd better warn her what to expect.'

Case looked around again. 'Will you be okay here on your own? It'll be half an hour before I'm back with them.'

'There's no one here. I don't know why, maybe the Nips are superstitious about staying in a temple, but they've gone. It'll be dark in another hour or so. I don't think they'll be back tonight.'

Case left him and Maynard began to move about the temple. He inspected it methodically, moving along one terrace, stopping to make sure each man he passed was dead, then back along the far terrace. The walls showed signs of the intense firing that had gone on and at the far end of the courtyard the steps had been shattered by two mortar bombs. He had moved down into the well of the courtyard, was passing the central monument with the carved figure on its walls staring balefully out at him through the screen of vines and creepers, when he heard the moan. He stopped in midstride, every nerve alert, his finger at once on the trigger of his carbine. Then the moan came again, deep and louder, as if it were being amplified. He could feel the back of his neck prickling and he slowly turned his head, a part of his mind marvelling at his own superstitious fear. The temple had already begun to work on him.

Then he understood why the moan sounded so loud and hollow. It was coming from the monument. He could now see a small low entrance to the tomb or whatever it was, hardly big enough to be called a doorway and half-covered by foliage that had been snapped off as someone had gone into the monument. The low doorway was magnifying the moans of whoever was lying wounded in there.

Bent double, Maynard moved cautiously into the entrance of the monument. The whole structure, of what he had at first thought to be a solid block of carved rock, was no more than eight feet high. The entrance, a doorless hole some four feet high and topped by an elaborately carved lintel, was raised about a foot above two steps that led up to it. Maynard knelt with one knee on the entrance step, the other leg poised to swing him away out of line if he should be attacked. He brought his carbine forward, finger already squeezing on the trigger.

'I'm English,' he said, and even at that moment wondered if anyone in this part of the world now cared. 'Who are you?'

He was answered by another moan, the sound going out past him like a voice from an echo chamber. There was a cough and a bubbling sound, then a voice murmured, 'Please—help ——'

Maynard scrambled into the monument, his nostrils almost choked by the thick musty smell of centuries. Dimly he made out the crumpled figure of the man lying across an oblong box. He went to lift the man, but the latter coughed, spluttered blood and shook his head weakly.

'Please—do not move me——' The blood in his mouth and the guttural accent made his English hardly understandable. 'I am dying——'

'How many Japanese were there?' Maynard could hear his own voice booming in the dark dank room, a spirit's voice. 'Where have they gone?'

'No Japanese——' The man breathed deeply, a terrible sucking sound. He said nothing further for a long moment, only the bubbling sound coming from his lips. Then in a voice that already sounded weaker he said, 'No Japs. Natives. PNI. Would not come into temple—shot us from outside.'

'The PNI? Where did they get their weapons?' But the man was either too weak to answer or did not consider it worth squandering his strength on a reply. He lay still and silent but for his sighing breathing in the green gloom of the tomb, a man already assuming the dim shape of his own shade. Maynard put out a hand to comfort him and accidentally touched the box on which the man lay. 'Is this a transmitter?'

He sensed rather than saw the man nod. 'Brought it in here —not want them to get it. Code book——' He stopped suddenly, coughing blood again.

Ashamed of the sudden desperate impatience in his voice, Maynard said, 'Is there a code book? Where? Tell me where!'

'Stupa—under Buddha——' Again there was the bubbling cough.

'Have you a code sign? What do I call?' Maynard could hear the frantic note in his own voice echoing in the chamber of the tomb.

'Frangipani—call Waratah——' Maynard had to lean close;

the whisper now was too weak even to be magnified by the room. 'They——'

Maynard sat back, feeling the life go out of the Dutchman almost as if a tangible thing were leaving the tomb. A heavy silence enveloped him, the cold stillness that must have been the atmosphere of this monument for centuries till the dying Dutchman had crawled into it, a Christian seeking a Buddhist haven in which to die. The Dutchman, rescuing the transmitter and leaving it now for Maynard and the others, had, in the right surroundings, achieved unwittingly the status of some sort of Bodhisattvas. Maynard, who had spent six months in southern India before being sent on to Malaya, knew something of the Buddhist teachings, of Mahayana in particular, which taught that one obtained salvation in order to confer it upon others. The Dutchman had obtained his own form of salvation, death, and conferred another sort, the means of rescue, on Maynard. The Englishman looked up and for the first time saw the statue of the Buddha, seated on a stone lotus, gazing down at him with unseeing eyes, lost in a state of tranquillity that the pale green stone suggested more than living flesh ever could have. A complacently habitual Anglican, going to church as a matter of social form, he knew suddenly that the eyes of the stone saints in the cathedrals of England had never looked into his soul as did these green eyes staring down at him now. He was not converted to another religion, but suddenly made aware of his shabby, careless approach to his own.

He lifted the Dutchman, laying him back gently at the feet of the Buddha. A ray of light came in through the entrance, winking on a silver medal hanging on a chain round the dead man's neck; Maynard wondered how St. Christopher would feel about finishing up here; for a moment he thought of taking the medal from the Dutchman's neck, then decided against it. Even to his own mind it suggested some sort of bigotry, a disease he had always done his best to avoid.

He took hold of the transmitter and dragged it out of the tomb into the daylight. The sun was low, its last rays striking through the entrance of the temple, throwing into relief these carved figures that had escaped the bonds of the vines, so that, moulded by the golden light and their own green shadows, they looked like living creatures watching him carefully from their colourless eyes. He carried the transmitter up to the entrance and set it down on the terrace there. It was a British army set, a type 62. It was undamaged and he could feel himself trembling with excitement as he extended the aerial, switched on and began to turn up the volume dial.

He waited for the familiar crackling; but nothing came. He fiddled with the dials, cursed the set, hit it with the butt of his palm; but the transmitter was as silent as the watching stone figures. He had never been mechanically-minded, and now he was angry at himself for his inattention in the R/Toc classes at Sandhurst. He could send and receive Morse with the best of them; he could code and de-code as quickly as any but the most expert. But many schoolboys could have taught him a lot about a wireless transmitter.

He stood up, cursed once more, then turned away from it as if, were it left alone, it might right itself. He went up on to the terrace, began to move from stupa to stupa, looking carefully for the hidden code book. He found it under the ninth Buddha he examined, a small leather-covered book that, for the moment, was as incomprehensible to him as Sanskrit. It was coded in Dutch.

He waited impatiently till Case arrived back with Elisabeth, Garrick and Kamar. As soon as they came up through the entrance of the temple he said, 'Does anyone know anything about making a wireless work?'

Case said, 'That can wait a minute, can't it? Elisabeth would like to see if her brother is here.'

Maynard flushed. 'Sorry.' Then he looked past them down the avenue between the trees. 'Where are Polo and Cabrolini?'

'Polo was having a bad time getting up that track. Cabrolini is giving him a hand.'

'Polo's accepting it?'

'I think his independence is starting to run down a bit. He'd never make that climb on his own.' Case then looked at Elisabeth. 'Do you want one of us to come with you?'

'Where are they?' Elisabeth already had the controlled mask of a mourner who was determined to keep her grief private.

Maynard gestured. 'I left them where I found them. Twenty-one of them. There's one down there in the central stupa. He was alive when I found him, but he died about twenty minutes ago.'

'I shall look at them alone,' Elisabeth said, left them and went down the steps, walking stiff-legged and stiff-backed as if prepared to withstand any shocks.

'Any of them ugly?' Case asked. 'Mutilated?'

Maynard shook his head. 'Nothing like that. But it isn't going to be pleasant for her. Dead men, especially ones with bullet holes in them, aren't attractive. Perhaps one of us should have gone with her.'

'I don't think so.' Garrick was watching the silent figure as it moved about the courtyard, standing for a moment above the body of a man, blessing itself, then moving on. Above certain bodies Elisabeth stood a little longer, as if she had recognised an old friend. 'I remember my mum saying, some women like to weep alone.'

Maynard looked at him, a little surprised, as if Garrick had uttered some great truth. 'I didn't think you knew anything about women.'

'I don't,' said Garrick. 'But I got three sisters and a mother. One thing you learn is when to leave them alone.'

He stood at the entrance to the temple like a traveller at the door of a hotel uncertain as to whether his booking had been confirmed. His rifle was slung over his shoulder; in one hand he carried his string bag of food, in the other his suitcase; he could have been a salesman, one who might sell anything, but could not sell himself. He looked around and said, 'Are we going to camp here?'

Case looked at the sun almost on the rim of the hills, then at Maynard. 'Might as well.'

For the first time Kamar spoke. He had been glancing nervously into the temple, not at the dead men sprawled about the courtyard but at the figures carved on the walls and the Buddhas sitting serenely in their cages. 'It would be better if we camped somewhere else, captain. Belan Koup has spirits.'

'What sort? There are good spirits as well as bad.'

'These are evil, captain. There is a story. Years ago, many years ago, two Hollanders got drunk and fought a duel here. They killed each other, some said the *spirits* killed them. But after that the people said the temple had been defiled. They would never come here again because they knew the evil spirits had taken over.'

Maynard looked around at the ruins. 'So that's why it's like this. That's why the nationalists wouldn't go right in.'

'The nationalists?' Case, who has been watching Elisabeth, jerked his head round. Garrick put down his suitcase and string bag, unslung his rifle and held it ready in his hands as if he expected to be attacked. Kamar stiffened, went to say something, changed his mind and stood watching the three white men carefully.

'It was that political crowd—what is it, Kamar?'

Kamar's voice was dry and husky. 'The PNI, captain?'

'That's the one. It wasn't the Japs did this.' He gestured towards the courtyard, then stopped with his arm raised as he saw Elisabeth coming back towards them.

'Do we tell her?' Case's voice was just a murmur.

'Better not.' Maynard's own voice was low. 'She looked shocked enough at what they'd done to her brother's house.'

Elisabeth came up the steps, her face a mask but paler than when she had gone into the temple. 'My brother is not there.'

'Then he either got away,' said Maynard, and paused for a moment, then nodded down towards the monument. 'Or he is the one down there.'

'I should like to see.'

Maynard and Case hesitated, looked at each other, then followed her as she turned and walked carefully, almost primly, down the steps and across to the monument. Maynard caught up with her. 'Let me go in first.'

He ducked his head, clambered in through the entrance to the tomb. Case stood beside Elisabeth, aware of the stiffness in her; she was staked with a self-control that made her almost rigid. She did not glance at him, but just kept staring at the entrance to the stupa, waiting for Maynard to re-emerge. He came out, awkward with contorting his height in the low doorway and with the situation he now had to handle.

'I think it better you don't go in there.'

'If he is my brother, Captain Maynard——'

He held up a small photo of a young woman and two children. 'Is that your brother's wife and children?'

Elisabeth nodded, took a pace forward, but Maynard remained in front of her, blocking her way into the tomb. In his other hand he held the silver chain and its medal and a leather wallet full of papers. He held them out to her. 'You might like to keep these.'

'First I want to see him!'

He shook his head. 'It wouldn't do any good, Miss Brinker. You've already identified him.'

'I want to be sure!' Her voice, though low, was fierce. She was like most women: she could not bury her menfolk, even in her mind, till she had seen them dead. The man in the stupa could be someone else, someone who had her brother's papers . . .

'You better let her go in,' Case said quietly. 'You've done all you can.'

Maynard hesitated, then he stood aside. Elisabeth stopped only a moment at the doorway to the tomb, took a deep breath like a woman about to plunge into a well that might drown her, then she ducked her head and disappeared into the stupa. Case looked at Maynard, the look of inquiry on his face eloquent enough.

'He'd hæmorrhaged,' Maynard said. 'The place is covered in blood.'

Case wrinkled his nose. 'You did all you could,' he repeated, and Maynard nodded, glad that the other man had agreed with what he had tried to do. They both looked sharply at the entrance to the tomb as there was a faint sound, like a soft moan sharply cut off. Maynard glanced at Case, but the latter shook his head.

Then Elisabeth came out of the entrance. Both men moved to her, took an arm each and helped her down the two steps. She looked at each of them as if they were strangers, then down at her bloodstained hands. She put out her hands, palms upwards, and stared at them as if they held something she had never seen before.

'Was it your brother?' Case asked gently.

She nodded, then abruptly dropped her head and began to sob. Case took her by the elbow, led her across to the steps and sat her down. He took a dirty handkerchief from his pocket, wet it with water from his canteen and began to wash the blood from her hands. She sat like a stunned child, not protesting, while the tears rolled down her face and she was racked with deep wrenching sobs. Maynard watched them for a moment, amazed at the gentleness with which Case handled the grief-stricken girl, then, feeling inadequate, he went back to join Garrick and Kamar just as Cabrolini and Polo arrived.

'Who knows anything about wirelesses?' he said.

Polo had slumped down against the end of the wall. Above his head Mara, the demon, fought with snakes of vines; the demon's three daughters eyed the crippled Australian seductively. But Polo knew nothing of Buddhist mythology, was too exhausted even to have taken notice of Mara's daughters had they been living creatures. 'Ask Musso. They invented the bloody thing.'

Cabrolini had already noticed the field set. Without a word he put down his gear and crossed to the transmitter. The others watched him without a word till he at last looked up. 'It's only the tubes, that's all. They are burnt out. The batteries are all right.'

'The tubes? The valves, you mean?' Maynard gestured hopelessly. So men had come to rely so much on the things they had invented; a shilling radio valve was the barter price of their rescue, their attempt to warn Australia of the impending danger. 'What good is the damned thing without them?'

'The set is perfectly all right,' Cabrolini said. The outsider was the one with the most optimism: 'Perhaps we could find some tubes.'

'You want your bloody head read.' Polo looked around the temple, then saw Case and Elisabeth still down at the bottom of the steps. 'What's the matter with her?'

Maynard told him and Polo nodded his head sympathetically. 'She's had a bugger of a time. It's about time her luck changed.'

Kamar said, 'I know where we could get some valves, captain.'

'Where?'

'There is a town—Sinjambi——'

'I'm not going anywhere near any more bloody towns!' Polo said.

'We don't all have to go,' said Maynard. 'How far is it to this place?'

Kamar shrugged. 'Perhaps a day.'

Garrick slumped down beside Polo, exhaustion all at once overcoming him. 'Is that all we're going to do, hike around this blasted island for the rest of the war?'

'What other ideas have you?' Maynard, too, was suddenly exhausted; he turned his sarcasm on Garrick. 'Do you want to set up house somewhere? We're not at home on the Yorkshire moors, lad.' His accent was as thick as his sarcasm. 'Perhaps you'd like Saturdays off to go and watch Bolton Wanderers play.'

Garrick looked up, hurt and shocked by the rough edge of Maynard's tongue; he had not been arguing, had spoken only out of hopelessness brought on by fatigue. He did not argue now, just said quietly, 'Bolton is in Lancashire.'

Maynard was suddenly aware of the pettiness of what he had said. 'I'm sorry, Reg. I didn't mean that. It's only——'

He stopped and looked about him. The sun had gone down, burning the tops of the hills as it went. The guerrilla night was creeping up out of the valleys; its scout shadows were already in possession of the corners of the temple. Flying-foxes, like a creaking chair, swung through the air above his head; from somewhere on another ridge there came a roar that he guessed might be a tiger's. This wild country could soon defeat him and the others; it was a part of the enemy. The enemy: the Japanese, the nationalists, the country. And now despair, the worst of the lot. He looked back at the others, dug deep into himself for some optimism, flashed it like a bribe; 'If we can get those valves, we'll be all right. I found their code book——' He brought it out, another bribe: he was like a man pleading at a border for a visa. 'Miss Brinker can translate it, it's in Dutch. We'll get in touch with Australia ——'

'Then what?' Polo's voice was flatly unenthusiastic. 'Look, skipper. We've had nothing but a bad trot of luck all the way. Not one bloody thing has gone right for us. I was with you at the start, but now I think it's time we pulled our heads in.'

'Our luck has to change some time.' Maynard could see the demons smiling at him from the walls: he turned and faced away from them, superstition creeping over him again.

'I think Jack was right,' said Polo, still unconvinced. 'Maybe we should go back down to the coast, try for another boat. Do you know where we could get a boat, sport?'

Kamar blinked, not sure at first that he was *sport*. 'Oh yes. I can get you anything. For a price, of course,' he said, keeping his eyes averted from Garrick's suitcase. He had learned last night from one or two remarks dropped by the others what the suitcase contained. He did not know how much money Garrick had, but it was obviously not just a few Straits dollars. Men only joked about a lot of money or a lot of debts: an ordinary man's ordinary wealth was not worth comment. And Garrick was just an ordinary man. He had seen his type often in Malaya, the little man who grew two feet taller because his skin was white, because he was British and the Empire was God's own kingdom. But Garrick did seem better than most. He was just an ordinary little man, but so far he had not tried to masquerade as anything else. All that set him apart was the suitcase and whatever it contained. 'The people value their boats. They would not give one away.'

'We'd buy it,' Garrick said, as if he had recognised a cue.

'All you have to do is find us a decent big boat and as much petrol as it can carry.'

Maynard struggled for words with which to continue the argument, but he had none. He looked at Cabrolini, but the Italian had decided to take no sides; he would be as neutral as the others would allow him to be. Maynard turned away as Case and Elisabeth came up the steps on to the terrace. It was dusk now, the short tropical twilight that would soon be gone.

'How's the radio?' Case asked.

'It needs valves,' Maynard said dully, resigned.

'Then we better try and get some,' said Case, and everyone looked at him in surprise, even Elisabeth.

But Maynard's surprise was part suspicion: was Case trying on a bitter joke? Maynard felt an enormous tiredness pulling him down; he couldn't fight all these people any longer. 'Do you have any ideas?' he said; and as if his voice belonged to someone else, heard himself cross over to the other side: he was with the sceptics, Polo and Garrick.

'No,' said Case with no argument in his voice; he was just a vague shape now in the dusk, it was impossible to read his face, 'But Kamar might.'

Then Maynard knew he had an ally. He threw off his tiredness, said almost with excitement, 'There's a town—what is it?'

'Sinjambi,' said Kamar, ready to leave at once, sure that in the swiftly gathering darkness the spirits were coming out of the walls, grouping to attack the intruders here.

'It's about a day from here. You and I could go down there——' Maynard stopped. 'Would you come with me?'

'Not tonight,' said Case, fumbling in his brocaded bag for a tin of meat. 'But tomorrow, sure.'

'I'll go with you, captain,' said Cabrolini. 'I would know the right sort of valve.'

'You don't have to.'

'No, I don't have to,' the Italian said. 'But that is why I'll go. So far I have had no chance to volunteer for anything. But I am just as keen as any of you to survive. And this——' He tapped the transmitter. 'I think this is the only chance we have.'

CHAPTER 8

In the morning Elisabeth said, 'Do we have to leave them just like this?'

Case looked around at the dead guerrillas still lying like sleeping men on the steps and among the undergrowth in the temple. The half-light of the early dawn was gentle to them: none of them looked as if he had died in agony or pain. 'If we stop to bury them all, we might finish up digging our own graves, too. The other guys could come back.'

'The nationalists, you mean?'

He looked at her sharply. 'Who told you it wasn't the Japs?'

'I guessed.' The sun came up at that moment, striking into the temple with fierce red rays, and in its harsh light she looked old and disfigured: the scars of grief showed plainly. 'That man down the hill, on the path—what was he doing there? And if the Japanese had killed my—my brother and these men, why would they have not still been here when we got here? I've been awake all night, Mr. Case. I had plenty of time to put everything together.'

There was no point in trying to tell her otherwise. 'Okay, it was them. Your brother told Maynard just before he died.'

'But why? Why? They could not have wanted us Hollanders here—I can see that now. But most of us have gone, or have been captured by the Japanese. Why hunt down my brother and these men and kill them like this?'

He could not answer that. National independence was no longer an ambition for Americans but just an old habit. He wondered if, after Yorktown, there had continued to be acts of revenge in the boondocks against the British and those who had remained loyal to them. 'I wouldn't know. Maybe they felt they owed them something. Not your brother and these guys, but all the Hollanders who have ever been here. In three hundred years there must have been one or two sonsofbitches.'

She was not convinced, but she said nothing further. The other men had already gathered up their gear and were ready to depart. Maynard had been around the dead guerrillas and had found two hand grenades and about two hundred rounds of ammunition; the Sumatrans' fear of the spirits of the temple

145

had evidently not been strong enough to prevent them steal-
ing into the temple and collecting what weapons they could
find. They had missed the grenades and the ammunition,
which Maynard had found cached in one of the stupas; they
had also missed the Thompson gun which Elisabeth's brother
had taken into the monument with him. Maynard held up
what he had collected.

'It's not much, but we're a little better off than yesterday.'
He nodded at the transmitter, was almost jaunty in his
optimism: he was like a politician promising the voters a
better world that he knew in his heart he could not deliver.
'Once we have the valves for that——'

Don't try so hard, Case thought. He had become aware at
once last night that Polo and Garrick wanted to go near no
more towns. Polo had been exhausted physically and of
spirit by his suffering yesterday as he limped up and down the
rugged tracks on his crutch; he was prepared to settle now for
the simplest form of escape, no matter how short-lived it
might be. Garrick, for his part, had always had the simple
approach: run, run, run all the way. That attitude might
have been enough if Garrick, or any one of the others, had been
on his own; it was always easier for one man to hide himself
or to ask to be hidden. But it was not easy when there were
six of them; seven, if one counted Kamar, though Case was
not sure how long the Javanese would stay with them. He had
not stayed with them last night but had slept somewhere
outside the temple; he stood waiting for them now up on the
terrace at the entrance to the temple. The simple approach to
escape was not enough when there was a party. Seven
different capacities for endurance, seven different urges to
survive, seven different brands of courage: the lowest common
denominator had to be found if they were all to get out of
Sumatra and through to Australia. It was no use Maynard
trying to sell everyone a false bill of hope.

Case was not sure when his own attitude had changed.
Perhaps it had been when Elisabeth had come out of the
monument after seeing her dead brother; he had not spoken to
her while he had washed her hands, but he had been aware of
the shattered feeling of defeat in her. Not just grief, though
that was deep enough: the manner of her father's and
brother's deaths had been like an axe blow on her. But there
was something else that had happened to her, an awakening
as if to find that some dream, or even reality, had turned into

a nightmare. Life, that had promised so much, had without warning and cruelly broken all its pledges; but more than that, it had, also cruelly, taught her that history was a continuing event. And she, so proud of the past, had learned how unpredictable and degrading the present could be.

Case himself had only just begun to realise that history was a continuum. Pearl Harbour was only a little over two months old, but it was already history; in a dozen places throughout the world, at this very moment, history was happening. He might never learn of the events that were taking place, but he was beginning to realise that he was part of the web they spun. For two years he had ignored the war, looked upon it as something that did not concern Americans: it was the Europeans, not the Americans, who had bred Hitler. Even when Pearl Harbour had happened the effect on him had been delayed: he had been on a bender *that* week, too. Stone cold sober one night in a ring in Bangkok he had had another moment of awakening. There he was, one of the best middle-weights in the world in the late Twenties and early Thirties, making a fool of himself while a young Siamese, fighting Thai style, had kicked, punched and slapped him to the huge delight of the local crowd. He had lost his temper, at himself more than at his opponent, and lashing at the young Siamese with more savagery than he had shown in his hey-day. He had almost killed the youngster, while the laughter of the crowd had turned to shouts of horrified anger, and in the end the referee had stopped the bout. Case immediately afterwards had gone out and got drunk. Next day the Japanese had bombed Pearl Harbour, but he had not known about it till the following Friday. By then, and he would never know who had put him on it, he was on a ship a day out of Singapore. In Singapore itself the British had had enough to talk about without worrying about what had happened to Pearl Harbour. The *Repulse* and *Prince of Wales* had been lost; 'a damn' bad show,' he had heard one Englishman remark without much anger, as if he were complaining about the loss of some harbour launch. Singapore had still been smugly confident then and not prepared to offer any solace to a down-and-out American suffering from a hangover. And Case, though he did not like the Singapore British, had been infected by their smug narrow outlook. He had not gone near the American consulate, had avoided Americans, had increased his own particular personal isolation. He was a bum, he knew it, and the world was no longer a place for bums. He started drinking again, heading for oblivion, the only destination he had ever had.

But now he also knew that his isolation, like the mould of Elisabeth's life, had been shattered. Or not shattered, rather eaten away. As he was trapped in the web of world events, so he was trapped in the web of these people who were with him. The group had but one life and he was part of it.

'What d'you reckon, Jack?'

He realised Polo had repeated the question. 'Reckon what?'

'The skipper says we oughta split up. You and him and Musso oughta go ahead on your own and we'll catch you up.'

Case looked at Maynard. 'I think we oughta stick together.'

Maynard said nothing for the moment. He could sense that the American had undergone a change of attitude over the last twenty-four hours. He did not understand why, nor did he know how he could discuss it with Case. But he also sensed that, at least to a degree, Case was now on his side. He could not afford to argue with him. He said, 'If that's the way you want it——'

Case also recognised that he and Maynard had got closer together. This time yesterday morning the two of them had been at odds with each other, almost enemies. In his turn Case was puzzled by Maynard's acceptance of him. Compromise, which each despised, had trapped them both.

Maynard was examining the weapons they now had. 'I'll take the Thompson and the grenades. You'd better take these.' He handed Case and Cabrolini machine-carbines. 'Do you feel up to carrying a rifle, Polo?'

'My word, I do.'

Maynard gave Polo one of the rifles. Garrick still had his. 'That leaves one over.'

Elisabeth said, 'May I have it, captain?'

'It's too heavy for you to carry if we have to march all day. I was going to give you my pistol.'

'That will do. Just so long as I have something.' She took the pistol, handling it gingerly at first, then closing her fist firmly on the butt of it. She attached the holster to the belt of her skirt and put the pistol in it. The holster sagged on her hip, giving her a lopsided appearance; she looked comical, but no one made any joking remarks. The look on her face told them she would not tolerate any jokes this morning.

'May I have the extra rifle, captain?' Kamar said.

Maynard hesitated, then shook his head. 'I'm sorry, Kamar. If we should run into anyone, you'll be better off without a gun. You can duck into the bushes. But if you're carrying a gun, that would put you down as one of us. And I wouldn't fancy your chances after that.'

'Perhaps you are right, captain. You will not think I am deserting you, then, if I duck into the bushes if something happens? Discretion is the best value, captain.'

Maynard grinned, wondering if Kamar had intended a pun or just got his clichés mixed again. He turned away, put the barrel of the rifle in a cleft between two large stones, bent it, then threw the rifle into some nearby bushes. 'Time we were on our way.'

Cabrolini had taken the batteries out of the field set, put them in a rough sling he had made of vines and handed them to Kamar. The Javanese looked for a moment as if he was going to demur, but he saw Maynard watching him carefully. He forced a smile, took the sling and hitched it over his back. Cabrolini slung the field set over his own back, carrying it by its leather strap.

'Now it is just a matter of getting those valves,' he said.

They filed up the steps out of the temple. Elisabeth did not look back as she had done when they had left the bungalow yesterday. Case did look back, saw the crows already coming in to pick at the dead; he turned hurriedly away, caught up with Elisabeth and walked with her down through the lalang grass between the tall kenari trees. They walked in silence for a while, then she said, 'My brother and those men should have had their graves.'

'I don't think it worries them.' Case tried hard not to sound unkind.

'A woman likes to see her menfolk buried. Call it housekeeping, or whatever you like. It's the way we are.'

They walked all that day, descending out of the cool hills, passing through steaming jungle and in the early afternoon coming out on to a wide plain of yellowing grassland. They had passed several small kampongs, giving them a wide berth, and several times they had had to drop quickly into the grass as they saw groups of peasants passing. But they saw no Japanese.

'Maybe the Nips ain't around these parts.' Polo was stretched on the bank of a narrow rivulet. It looked as if it had been dry for months, but yesterday's rain had brought a trickle down from the hills. They had been reckless with their drinking water as they had marched, expecting to be able to fill their canteens anywhere along the way, but once they had come out on to the plain they had found that the few streams they had come across were just dry rocky breaks among the thorny scrub and the coarse yellow grass. This tiny rivulet beside which they now lay seemed to be the only stream that had not been dammed by the peasants higher up.

Case looked out across the yellow glare of the dryly whispering grass. It reminded him of the Middle West: he closed his eyes and remembered the silos coming up out of the brassy haze, the first hint of the town that lay there, like a dried out oasis, in the desert of wheat. He could feel the sun beating down on him, more humid here than in Iowa or Kansas but just as fierce. But he felt no nostalgia. The Middle West had been a place of defeat for him; he might have won all his bouts, but they had still been symbols of defeat; he had been on his way down when he had fought in Topeka, Wichita and points west. This wide Sumatran plain might also be a symbol of defeat. It certainly offered no hope.

He opened his eyes when he heard the whistle, a faint higher-pitched echo of that loneliest of sounds, the whistle of a train crossing a great deserted plain. Everyone stood up, forgetting the heat and their exhaustion, and Elisabeth said, 'It's probably coming down from the rubber plantations.'

Far away to the east they could see the train moving like a toy snake across the metallic landscape. Its smoke lay smudged against the faded sky, suggesting the shadow of its passing. It blew its whistle again, as if for no other reason than that its driver wanted to proclaim that he at least was alive in the vast dead plain.

'Where is it heading?' Maynard asked.

'Palembang, perhaps,' Elisabeth said.

'Would it pass through Sinjambi?'

'Oh, it passes through Sinjambi,' said Kamar quickly, as if he did not want Elisabeth cornering the market on his information. All he had to sell was information, and he needed these people, his buyers, as much as they needed him.

'How far is it then?' said Garrick irritably. 'I think you're leading us on a wild goose chase.'

Kamar put his hand over his heart, looking hurt. 'Oh, I am no liar, sir. Sinjambi is just over there.' He waved his other hand in the direction of the disappearing train. 'Another two hours' walking, sir. Not very far at all. Just a small stroll.'

The small stroll was another three and a half hours' walking. They crossed the plain, limping through the yellow countryside, progressing and yet making no progress, for distance seemed to have been dissolved in the great cauldron of blinding light. Their skin was baked tight on their bones and their tongues turned to leather in their mouths. They drank sparingly from the canteens they had filled at the rivulet, the water drying up almost at once in the dusty suède pockets of their mouths. They walked strung out in a thin file, with Polo sometimes a couple of hundred yards to the rear. Occasionally Case or one of the others would turn as if to wait for him, but the little man would wave an angry arm and they would move on. Of the others Elisabeth was the worst affected. Her feet, unaccustomed to walking more than a quarter of a mile up till last week, were now raw swollen lumps of meat in the leather baskets of her shoes. Her head, shaded by a hat Case had taken from one of the dead guerrillas and forced on her against her protests, felt like a great balloon that would at any moment lift up her desiccated body into the arid vacuum of light that enveloped them.

They came to the railway line, turned south along it. The light began to lift, the countryside creeping in under it to take on shape, colour and distance again. Then the railway lines were running like a long shining spear into the green flesh of low hills and soon the party had escaped the sun, were bathing in the sensual shade of trees. By then the sun had almost gone, turning the vast plain for one last moment into a sea of fire. They sank down against the trunks of the trees feeling that they had escaped only just in time: another few minutes out on the plain and they would have turned to ash.

Kamar, eager to keep his place in the group, had been ferreting about in the bush amongst the trees. He came back with some wild pineapples, cut them with the parang, and handed the slices around. Their tongues turned to flesh again in their mouths, their powdered blood once more became fluid, and they gave up thought of dying. Even Polo, wooded and spare as the crutch on which he leaned, managed a smile. Or at any rate his face cracked, like a brittle dried-out rind.

'This was the missus' favourite.' His voice was just a croak that must have torn his throat, but he could still be garrulous. He'll die talking, Maynard thought, he'll talk them blind in Heaven, if he gets there. 'Pineapple with custard, pineapple with trifle. Once, for Christmas, we had pineapple with ham. I'd never tasted that before. It was bloody good. Ah, she's a good cook, old Vi. My oath.'

Elisabeth, who had known banquets and never appreciated them, taking them for granted, sucked on the slice of pineapple, the juice running down the dust on her chin, giving her the gullied jaw of an old woman. 'When we get to Australia, Polo, we must all go out to dinner. All of us and your wife, too. And the children. We'll have pineapple with everything.'

An hour later it was night, completely and utterly black. By then, they had climbed the first of the low hills and Sinjambi lay below them, a broken pendant of lights hanging on the slopes and down to the floor of a narrow valley. They had stopped in a thick stand of bamboo, moving off the track till they had come to a small clearing from where they could see the town below them.

'No blackout there,' said Garrick.

'Why should there be?' Maynard said. 'They'll never have any bombing up here.'

'It's going to make it harder for us to go in there,' said Cabrolini.

Maynard looked at the dim shape of the Italian. 'I told you, you don't have to come in with us.'

'I know, captain.' The darkness seemed to point up the acid in Cabrolini's voice. 'But aren't we all in this together?'

'Indeed we are,' said Maynard, catching the other's unspoken point. 'And if it means anything to you, I stopped thinking of you as an Italian two days ago. Back there on the beach.'

'*Grazie*,' said Cabrolini, all at once perversely not wanting to be anything but Italian. Despite what Maynard had said, he knew he was still the outsider. Beside him he felt Kamar, the other outsider, move awkwardly, as if he, too, felt that he was an odd man out. Maynard and the others, Case, Elisabeth, Polo and Garrick, were all united: they had a common enemy: the war had made them relations of a sort. Cabrolini felt that even if he were not an Italian, if he had been a neutral Swede or a Swiss, he would still not have been fully accepted. Perhaps by Case and Garrick, even by Elisabeth; but certainly not by Maynard and Polo. The two soldiers drew their own lines of complete acceptance.

'I shall come, captain,' Kamar said. 'I know a man in Sinjambi. Perhaps he can tell us where we can get the valves.'

It will be better than looking around for a bird in the bush.'

Maynard wondered where Kamar had got his clichés, if they had come to him in a package without instructions. 'Yes, it would be better. But if there are going to be four of us, we'll need to be more careful. No improvising.'

'Improvising?' said Kamar. 'I do not understand that, captain.'

'The captain means we all do what he tells us.' Case chuckled in the darkness; there was no rancour or sarcasm in his voice. 'You don't have to worry, skipper. This is one time when knowing your business might help.'

'Thank you for your vote of confidence,' said Maynard with good-humoured mockery. 'I'm touched.'

2

'What the hell is going on?' asked Case.

'It is a Wayang Kulti,' said Kamar. 'A shadow play.'

'Why are we stopping here?' Maynard said.

'The Darlan is the man we have to see, captain.'

'The Darlan?' said Cabrolini. 'Who's he?'

'He is the one who handles the puppets, who tells the story and also conducts the orchestra. He is the director. Like Cecil B. De Mille.'

'Now I've done everything,' said Case. 'Sitting here on my ass in the mud waiting to meet Cecil B. De Mille. Why do we need him? How long does this show go on?'

'Sometimes an hour, Mr. Case, sometimes four, sometimes ten hours. But it is better to wait for this man. To be patient is to be virtuous. No offence, sir.'

'Let's all be virtuous then,' said Maynard. 'Difficult though it may be for some of us.'

'Did they teach you to be virtuous at Sandhurst?' Case said.

'Only if approached by Guardsmen,' said Maynard; but the others, not being English, knew nothing of the supposed habits of Guardsmen. 'We'll give the Darlan chap an hour. Then we'll see what happens.'

The four men, Maynard, Case, Cabrolini and Kamar, had come down out of the hills and into the outskirts of Sinjambi without meeting any trouble. Several times they had seen Japanese soldiers, some on foot, others in trucks, but it had been easy to avoid them. The Japanese had taken over Sumatra and already they seemed to look upon this part of the island at least as a backwater of the war. Maynard wondered if the Allies were as relaxed and careless as this in Syria or Italian Somaliland, the only two places he could think of where the Allies, in this catastrophic war, could claim to be victors. He did not think any the less of the Japanese for their careless attitude; he knew he might have been the same in Homs or Asmara. He had the professional soldier's habit of looking at the business of war from the enemy's viewpoint. But he did not mention his observation to Case. The American, he suspected and hoped, was becoming too committed to the war to be objective about it.

Camouflaged by a pattern of shadows they squatted now behind a line of ox-carts on the edge of a small square. Sinjambi was a town of mixed buildings: atap-roofed huts stood next to small houses and shops with corrugated-iron roofs, a row of solid two-storied Dutch houses ended at a church that might have been transplanted whole from Amsterdam. This open space was a market square and on the other side where Maynard and the others were hidden the line of ox-carts was backed by a row of stalls, all of them closed now for the night. The screen for the shadow play had been set up no more than twenty yards from the hidden men and they could see the Darlan preparing to begin his show. On the other side of the screen a crowd of perhaps two hundred, men, women and children, was seated, murmuring with quiet excitement as the Darlan turned up his lamp and began to manipulate his puppets to see if they worked properly. At the back of the crowd stood half a dozen Japanese soldiers leaning negligently on their rifles.

'What's the play about?' Maynard asked.

Kamar shrugged. 'The Darlan makes it up as he goes along. This man is very good. He comes from Java, like me.'

The Darlan was an elderly man with a wisp of beard, like a fog of breath around his chin, and long supple arms. He had arranged his flat leather puppets, each on a pointed stick, into a thick banana stalk at the bottom of the screen. Behind him half a dozen musicians had begun to play, two of them on percussion instruments like a xylophone, the others with gongs, cymbals and a drum.

'The gamelan, that is the orchestra, plays what the Darlan tells it.' Kamar sat with his back against the wheel of one of the ox-carts; he looked as if he was there for the night.

'Very beautiful music, is it not? To soothe the chest of the savage.'

'This savage is gonna get savager,' Case said, wriggling his back uncomfortably against the spoke of a cart wheel, 'if we stay here too goddam long.'

The Wayang had begun, greeted with shrill cries of delight by the audience. The Darlan, moving with extraordinary grace and speed, was passing his puppets across the screen, always keeping himself out of the direct glow from the pressure lamp behind him. Despite his impatience, Case sat up and began to watch the skilled performance. The puppets, intricately carved grotesque caricatures, went through their attitudes, striking poses that at once expressed their characters. The Darlan, never fumbling a move, gave a voice to each of the puppets; at the same time, with gestures of his head, he conducted the gamelan. It was an exhibition of dexterity and co-ordination that Case, whose living had depended on the same skills, had to admire.

The Wayang had been going for almost half an hour before Case began to get the gist of it. He looked at Maynard and the latter raised an eyebrow. They then both looked at Kamar.

'What's the play about, Kamar?' Maynard said.

The Javanese hesitated, then said, 'Oh, it is very mixed up, captain. Too much to tell.'

'It is a story about Indonesian independence,' Cabrolini said quietly. 'The big fat puppet, the one he has in his left hand now, is supposed to be a Dutchman.'

On the screen a bloated shadow-figure stood with its back to a smaller figure that was making rude gestures at it. The audience was shrieking with laughter, and at the back even the Japanese had begun to laugh.

'How do you know all this?' Case said.

'I saw one of these shows when I was here several years ago. Even when the Dutch were here, these Wayangs used to poke fun at them.'

Case looked at Kamar. 'Why didn't you tell us that?'

'I did not wish to offend, sir.' Kamar had sat back in the depths of a shadow, just a vague shape in the darkness.

'Offend who? We're not Dutch.'

'I was afraid you might tell Miss Brinker.'

'I think you're much too concerned for everyone's feelings,' said Maynard. 'From now on, when I ask you a question, I want a straight answer.'

'Oh, I shall give it, captain.' Kamar leaned forward, bringing his face into the light. The bastard's too eager, Case thought, like the pimps and touts you met around Times Square. 'Straight from the shoulder, sir.'

Maynard looked at his watch. 'The hour's not up, but I think we've been patient enough. We should——'

'Hold it,' said Case. 'I think it's intermission.'

The Darlan had stuck his puppets back into the banana stalk, had turned out his lamp and was sitting back, massaging his arms and shoulders. The gamelan had put down their instruments and were lighting cigarettes; beyond the screen the audience was standing up and moving over to buy food and drinks from some stalls on the far side of the square. These people, Case thought, are just ordinary folk enjoying the routine of their ordinary humdrum lives. He had seen how careless they were of the Japanese soldiers behind them; they had exchanged one set of masters for another; it was part of the routine of their lives. But if we're discovered here, all hell is going to break loose. What right had he and the others to import violence into the lives of these people? He went to protest, but Kamar had already slipped out from between the ox-carts and gone across to the Darlan.

'I don't trust that bugger,' Case said, watching the small Javanese whispering into the ear of the older man. 'I get the feeling he's using us, instead of the other way around.'

'It's his smuggling background,' said Maynard. 'I don't trust him, either. But if we keep the reins tight——'

He looked across at Kamar, wondering what was going on between the two Javanese. Trust was both a luxury and a necessity; he would rather have done without it. But without Kamar they would have to wait till the whole town went to bed and even then they might never find a store that sold wirelesses or wireless valves.

Kamar came back, slipped in between the ox-carts, became part of the shadows again. 'The Darlan will come to see us. But not here. Follow me.'

He slid out behind the ox-carts, keeping against the walls of the closed stalls. Case and Cabrolini looked at Maynard; the latter shrugged. The three of them stood up and followed Kamar. He led them round the end of the row of stalls and down a narrow alley that was no more than a tunnel of black shadow. A cat spat at them, exploded beneath Cabrolini's legs and went up the alley on a black flicker of legs.

'We wait here. The Darlan will come.'

The three white men waited tensely, fingers on the triggers of their guns. They stood in a dense shadow that was thick with the smell of decayed rubbish and open drains; Cabrolini felt that he was wrapped in a dark shroud that smelled of death. They had smeared dirt on their faces and arms to darken them and now they were itching as the sweat ran down them, gullying the dirt. Something rustled in the darkness, then three rats shot across a patch of light at the end of the alley and disappeared.

'Is this a sinking ship?' Case whispered; then brought his gun up as the figure appeared at the end of the alley. The barrel bumped against Kamar's arm and the little man started.

'Do not shoot, sir! It is the Darlan.'

The old man came down the alley, tall and thin and moving with such light grace that against the light he seemed to float. He stepped in to the shadow and, like the other four, was at once invisible. He said something in a high soft voice that was far different from any of those he had used during the Wayang; in the darkness he sounded like a young man. Then Kamar said, 'The Darlan says there was only one shop in Sinjambi that sold wirelesses. But all its goods have been confiscated by the Japanese.'

Maynard cursed. 'Do any of the people here own wirelesses?'

Kamar spoke to the old man, then said, 'No, captain. All wirelesses have been confiscated. But he says the Japanese have a big wireless in the centre of town. It broadcasts news and music through amplifiers.'

'Where is it?'

Kamar and the old man whispered together in the darkness, their voices sounding like a dribbling faucet. A figure passed across the end of the alley, stopped and looked down towards the shadows; Maynard, his finger on the trigger of his gun, could see the peaked cap and the rifle slung over the back of the silhouetted figure. Then the Japanese moved on, and out of the darkness Kamar said, 'The wireless is in a house next to the Japanese headquarters.'

'That's handy,' said Maynard.

'It's also the end of the line,' said Case. 'It's back to the hills, men.'

'We should not give up so easily, sir,' said Kamar. 'Nothing ventures, nothing wins. The Darlan says the place is not heavily guarded.'

'How does the Darlan know só much?' Case said.

'He knows everything, sir. Darlan means "teller of wisdom".'

'Is he suggesting we should go in there?' Maynard asked. 'There's not much wisdom in that.'

'I think it might be worth the risk,' Cabrolini said. 'Without the valves, the radio is worth nothing. And without the radio, what are our chances worth?'

'Fine Italian logic,' said Case. 'I still think we oughta head back to the hills. For the time being, anyway.'

Maynard, still hidden in the darkness and doubly glad of it, knew now that the decision must be his. Instinct told him Case was right. Their position was not so urgently desperate that they had to go courting disaster by—— 'It would be going into lion's den, captain,' said Kamar, supplying the right cliché. 'But what else is there to do?'

'It depends how important you think that information is about the Japanese and their ships at Belawan Deli.' Cabrolini, the outsider, spoke quietly, but it sounded like the voice of conscience to Maynard. 'You will forgive me if I say I'm not very concerned with what happens to Australia. But perhaps Polo and his countrymen might be.'

Maynard said abruptly, 'I think we'll try for the valves. Do you want to come, Case, or do you want to head back to the others?'

'Christ,' said Case, 'how do I get myself into foul-ups like this?'

'Perhaps it's an American talent,' said Maynard, then looked in the direction of the invisible Kamar. 'Get the Darlan to tell you where the Japanese headquarters are. Then thank him for his help.'

There was further whispering between the two Javanese, then the old man stepped out into the light. He looked back at the men in the shadow, then without another word went up the alley and turned the corner. Just before he disappeared he stopped and looked back. Against the light he looked like one of his own flat leather puppets; there was something in the stiffness of his body that sent a sudden chill through Maynard. It was as if the Darlan, the teller of wisdom, knew something that he had not told the foreigners.

'This way, captain,' said Kamar, again sounding like an usher, and led the way farther down the alley, picking his way along the side of an open drain as if his feet were being guided by his nose.

Fifteen minutes later they were coming up a dark street between rows of whitewashed houses that had the stillness of tombs. A dog came growling at them out of the shadows, was kicked by Kamar and curled back whimpering into the darkness. They passed the ruin of a garden where oleander stalks stood like the broken spears of a defeated army. There was an air of decay about the street, one that could be felt as much as smelled.

'The Hollanders lived in this street,' Kamar whispered. 'The rich men of the town.'

'Why haven't the townspeople moved in here?' Maynard asked. 'Are they expecting the Dutch to come back?'

'Not likely, captain.' Kamar grinned in the gloom; he was no longer afraid of offending anyone. 'The people are staying in their own houses till they are sure about the Japanese.'

'Are they going to collaborate with the Japs?'

'Collaborate? You mean work with them? I would not know, captain. But while in Rome, one does as the Romans say. Eh, Mr. Cabrolini?'

'I'm from Torino. No one from Torino ever takes any notice of the Romans.'

'One has to take notice of the Japanese.' Kamar drew his hand across his throat. 'Or else.'

'Was it like that with the Dutch?' Case said.

But Kamar had held up his hand. 'There are the Japanese. We must be careful.'

Ahead of them the street ran into a large square. Stalls and shops were open, their owners trying to take as much money as they could while they could: armies were always welcomed by store-keepers, Maynard thought. Japanese soldiers strolled by the stalls, sat outside some bars and cafés; Maynard had seen British soldiers relaxing exactly like this in Singapore and Kuala Lumpur. It was something of a shock to him: one never thought of the enemy without his gun. He stood in the shadow of a doorway and said, 'Where are the headquarters?'

'On the other side of the square,' said Kamar. 'It used to be the Dutch Resident's offices. This way.'

He led them back down the street and up a side alley. They went right round the square, keeping to the dark back alleys. Several times they had to stop and press themselves into the shadows as people came out of houses and headed towards the square. Then they had reached the intersection of an alley and a wider street. They stood in the shadows of a long corrugated-iron building from which came a delicious smell.

'Coffee,' said Case. 'We oughta help ourselves to a pound or two of that.'

'We're in here just to get those valves,' said Maynard. 'No diversions.'

'A little food and drink wouldn't harm us. All that tinned meat has gone. Polo could do with something solider inside him than wild bananas and pineapple.'

'We'll try for food somewhere else, find a kampong where there are no Japs. Just now, all we want are the valves. We'll get those and get out of here as fast as we can. Understand? No side trips.'

Case shrugged and said nothing further. He was prepared to admit that Maynard was probably right, but the smell of the coffee on the other side of the corrugated-iron wall had had a siren effect on him. He could not remember when he had last had a hot meal and a cup of coffee or tea; it could have been a week or even a month ago; his belly had no memory, only its awareness of how empty it now was. So far they had been fortunate: no dysentery, no hint yet that any of them had caught malaria. But these two sicknesses, and perhaps even worse, were sure to strike them eventually. Once they had got the valves, they should see about getting food and medicine as soon as possible.

'I shall go ahead and spy out the land,' Kamar said. 'When you see me signal, you can approach. You will understand, captain, if I do not come into the building with you.'

'Of course,' said Maynard, his smile hidden in the shadows. 'Get all the value you can out of your discretion.'

Kamar was about to move off when suddenly right above them a voice spoke. The four men started; Cabrolini fell back against the wall and it boomed like a drum. Maynard whirled, his gun coming up to shoot at the man on the roof above them. Then he giggled silently, leaned back against the wall as the amplifier, fixed to a bracket above their heads, increased its volume. The voice, speaking in Malay, sounded as if it was calling attention to itself.

'What's he saying?'

'They are broadcasting the news, captain.'

'Let's find another spot,' said Maynard. 'Just in case this draws a crowd.'

The four of them moved swiftly, crossing the street and coming to a fence and an open gate. They slipped in through the gate, found themselves in a compound in the middle of which stood a one-story brick building. In front of the building a white flagpole glowed like a tall stalagmite in the light of the moon that had just risen above the hills.

'This was the Dutch school,' said Kamar, and added with unexpected bitterness, 'For Dutch children only.'

'Were there no schools for Sumatran children?' Maynard said.

'Some, captain. But not enough. A little knowledge is a dangerous thing. So is too much education. It breeds revolution. So the Dutch never gave us too much education. They were like the British, captain. No offence.'

Of course not, Maynard thought; and noticed there had been no mangled clichés this time.

They stayed within the shadow of the compound fence. Out in the street the voice droned on through the amplifier, but they could hear no sound of any movement. 'The people do not care,' Kamar said.

'What's the news?'

'Japan is winning the war everywhere in the Pacific.'

'Have they bombed the States?' Case asked the question without any anxiety. America was a long way off, part of another life. It was difficult to think of it as home: home was more than just a succession of hotel bedrooms. Far, far back in his memory was a shack on the road from Beaumont to Port Neches. But that would be gone now. He had been born in that shack and lived there for six years, the longest he had ever lived in one place. His old man had destroyed home more than the Japanese ever would be able to.

'No, Mr. Case. But they say they have bombed Darwin in Australia. Mr. Polo will not like that.'

'No,' said Case, wondering how he would have felt if the Japanese *had* bombed San Francisco or Los Angeles or Seattle.

'Is there any news of the war in Europe?' Maynard asked.

'No, captain. There never is,' said Kamar, and Maynard thought he detected a note of satisfaction in the voice of the Javanese. 'No offence, captain, but the people here do not care about Europe. Not now.'

'Did you ever?'

'You mean when the Dutch were here?' Kamar scratched his armpit. Out in the street the voice droned on, lethargically, as if it knew no one here in Sinjambi cared about the war in the Pacific either. 'No, captain. Some went to Holland to the university, but most of the people——' He shrugged.

'When you know that you can never be anything but a peasant, you don't look farther than the end of your own rice paddy. Does the mill worker in Lancashire think very much about the outposts of Empire, captain?' He moved towards the gate. 'I shall go and clear the coasts.'

When Kamar had gone out into the street Maynard said, 'Where did he learn about the mill workers in Lancashire? And the outposts of Empire?'

'He went to school in Singapore, remember?' said Cabrolini. 'Was that not an outpost of Empire? Or was it a bastion?'

'Save your sarcasm,' said Maynard, but he knew the Italian had scored off him. He looked towards the school building, imagined he could hear the chanting of Dutch children's voices, wondered what the Sumatrans passing in the street outside had thought. Had signs ever been scrawled on this fence: For Imperialists Only? And wondered about the British schools in India, Malaya, Africa. Were they as segregated as this one, were they designed to keep education within a fence so that it would not get out and infect the local people? He realised now that while he had been in India and Malaya he had walked about with blinkers on. He had sworn to defend the Empire and he really did not know what the Empire stood for.

The gate creaked open and Kamar had returned. 'There is a back garden to the house where the wireless centre is, captain. There is a soldier on guard at the gate, but he is not very alert. I just walked by him and he took no notice of me.'

'But you look like one of the locals,' Maynard said. 'We don't.'

'You might pass for one if you wore a sarong,' said Case.

'You're right. Take off your sarong, Kamar.'

'But, captain——'

'Take it off!'

Kamar slipped off his sarong, stood with his thin legs showing like dark sticks beneath his shirt. 'Do not lose it, captain. This is very undignified.'

Maynard had rolled up the legs of his trousers and wrapped the sarong round himself. His normally dark face had been burnt even darker by the sun and in the night gloom he might pass for one of the local townspeople. His only handicap would be his height. There were few Sumatrans who would stand six feet two. He looked at Case and Cabrolini. 'You chaps stay in the shadows till I've taken care of the guard.

Then move quickly. As soon as we have the valves, we head back the way we've come. That way we shan't get lost.'

'We don't know where the valves are,' said Case.

'They'll be somewhere in that house. We'll have a closer look once we're in the back garden. You'd better stay here, Kamar.'

'Naturally, captain,' said Kamar, and drew his shirt-tail about his legs.

Maynard, Case and Cabrolini slipped out of the gate. The amplifier down the street was still blaring away, but with music now: Maynard recognised the strains of *Tai Hei Yo*. He remembered the massacre at the bridge in Malaya, then quickly put it out of his mind. This task was not going to be as easy as that had been.

The night was sticky, but Case knew that the humidity was not the sole reason for his sweating. He had never been lacking in physical courage; if he had he would never have taken up boxing. But there was a difference between a disregard for being hurt and a disregard for being killed. All the careless capitulation he had felt in the last few days of drunken depression in Singapore had gone; he had no more to live for now than he had then, but now he was afraid of dying. The realisation had come to him as they had sat beneath the ox-carts watching the shadow play. He had seen the Japanese soldiers beyond the crowd and though they had been relaxed and laughing with the audience, he had been uncomfortably aware of their rifles. For the first time it had come home to him that he and the others might not get out of this town alive.

When he had been in the ring, when danger threatened he had had a heightened awareness of everything immediately around him. Even though his face might be bloodied and his eyes almost closed, he had seen his opponent with a startling clarity: the flicker of the eyes as the man sensed an opening, the slight shifting of the shoulders as he prepared to drive home the punch: everything about the man would be magnified and slowed down. It was this seeming sixth sense that had enabled Texas Jack Case to ride out even the fiercest onslaught, had been the talent on which his famous footwork had been based. He knew that if his instinct to kill had been as great as his instinct to survive he could have been the champion.

Now he was experiencing the heightened awareness again. It had happened on the beach when the Japanese had landed from the patrol boat; it was happening once more, but this time more acutely. It was as if he were undergoing some sort of experience by drug. The music coming from the amplifier down the street was split into single notes; he could hear every individual voice coming from the crowd in the square. Maynard had gone ahead, but beside him he could hear Cabrolini breathing heavily, was as aware of the Italian as if he himself were in the latter's skin. He could feel the sweat on Cabrolini's arms, even though the Italian was not touching him; when Cabrolini stopped suddenly, he felt the stiffness in the other man's muscles. The shadows in which they walked had all at once lost their opacity and he could see everything as clearly as if it were in a bright light.

Up ahead he saw Maynard had stepped out of the shadows and was approaching the Japanese guard who lounged outside an iron gate set in a tall stone wall. To Case's acute eye Maynard looked like nothing but what he was, an Englishman doing a poor masquerade of a Sumatran. His usual long stride was hampered by the sarong so that he seemed to be mincing along. His left arm was held stiffly against his side as it carried his gun hidden against his leg. His head was down, trying to make his face darker, and he had stooped a little to disguise his height. But to Case's too sharp eye he looked nothing like a Sumatran. Any moment now the guard was going to bring up his rifle and challenge him.

But the guard was still lounging against the gate, his rifle leaning against the wall beside him. He looked up as Maynard approached him, nodded, then abruptly straightened up and reached for his rifle. Oh Christ, Case thought, this is it. But Maynard, stumbling a little, had taken two swift paces forward. His right arm came up and Case saw the knife flash in a streak of light coming from a rear window of the house. The guard went down, falling against Maynard with open arms as if welcoming him. Down the street the music had changed to a lively tune, one that reminded Case of a Japanese *Alexander's Ragtime Band*.

Case and Cabrolini ran quickly up the street, grabbed the guard from Maynard and carried him through the gateway and into the garden. They dumped him beneath a large shrub, tossing his rifle in beside him. When Case straightened up Maynard was wiping his knife on the sarong. Only then did Case feel the blood on his own hands.

'Messy,' said Maynard in a low voice. 'It would have been cleaner if I could have strangled him.'

His voice was calm and matter-of-fact: he had just done a job of work. Case felt both revolted and admiring at the same time; he was still very much an apprentice in the business of war. He wiped his hands on his trousers and said, 'Where do we go from here?'

'Let's do a little recce.'

They moved up through the garden towards the house. Above them the moon glowed like a large bloom on the branch of a tree, shadows and shrubs grew out of each other from the ground. A gravel path crunched beneath their feet and they stepped off into the long grass again. They moved in beside the back wall of the house, heard a flushing noise, then water gushed down a pipe right beside them.

'Just like us,' whispered Case.

The house was two-storied, a solid home that had probably once housed a solid, stolid Dutch family. Kids had probably played in this garden, Case thought; in the rooms of the house people had eaten, made love and thought they were safe forever. But they were quite possibly all dead now; and he felt the Japanese's blood congeal on his hands. He said irritably, 'Well, what's next?'

Maynard had moved ahead, but now came back. 'There's a back door into a kitchen. Next door to it is a dining-room—that's where they've set up the wireless centre. I could see through the window. Our luck looks as if it's in. They're using captured equipment. The set is the same as ours, a wx 62.'

'Anyone around?'

'Nobody in the kitchen—that's dark. Three men in the wireless room.'

'How do we take them?'

'I'm afraid it has to be the knife. Do you know how to strangle a man?'

'I fought Queensberry rules,' said Case, more nervous than he sounded. He had never been like this before a fight, not even his first. 'I'm just an old-fashioned gentleman at heart. And if you want to know the truth, I don't like the idea of using a knife. In any case I haven't got one.'

'Neither have I,' said Cabrolini.

'The kitchen looked to have lots of pots and pans. It should have some knives.' Maynard's voice softened a little. 'I'm sorry. I know this may not be what you're used to, but I'm afraid there's no other way. We have to be as quiet as possible. Okay?'

Case and Cabrolini did not look at each other, but each was aware of waiting upon the other to make up his mind. Then Case said, letting the word out like a hiss of air, 'Okay.'

They moved along the wall of the house, came to the back door. It opened when Maynard turned the handle and pushed against it; the three of them stepped quickly into the kitchen and Maynard closed the door. A door into the dining-room was ajar and enough light came through to show the three men the furnishings of the kitchen. It was a room not unlike the one at the Brinker plantation, but with even less concession to the East: it reminded Maynard of interiors he had seen in old Dutch paintings. Some people never really leave home, Maynard thought; and remembered the planter's bungalow he had visited once near Port Swettenham. The living-room had been shipped straight from the Home Counties: the brown tapestry lounge suite, the upright piano and the cabinet gramophone, the photograph of the plantation manager in his Masonic robes: one could almost hear the 5.40 from Paddington going by at the bottom of the garden. Suddenly he thought of Ruth, tried to picture her amongst her surroundings and couldn't. He had written home to her every day till the campaign had started; but there was really no home. They had not had time to start one.

'Here are some knives,' Cabrolini whispered.

He had cautiously pulled open a drawer in the big table in the middle of the room. He took out two knives with pointed blades, handed one to Case. He held the other tightly in his right hand, trying to force some strength into his fingers. He all at once realised how frightened he was, knew that he was not going to be able to kill anyone with this knife. He was more frightened of the thought of bloody violence than he was of the thought of death. He hated the Germans and the Japanese, he hated even Mussolini and the Fascists, for what they had done to the world; but they were abstracts, even Mussolini, on whom he could vent his hate without any blood-letting. But the Japanese in the next room were *men*, and he could not get past that image of them.

Case was thinking similarly. His hands were slippery with sweat; he clutched at the knife to prevent himself from dropping it. There was no strength in his right arm, the one that had held his only good punch; he felt he would not be able to drive the knife into even a rotten fruit. He was not revolted by the idea of bloody violence as Cabrolini was, though he did not know how Cabrolini felt: it was the

Italian who had searched for the knives, found them and now looked calm enough with the glittering blade in his hand. He had had sixteen years of violence, seen enough blood to stock a blood bank. He thought now that, if he had to, he could shoot a man. But to drive a knife into him, be close enough to him to have his life's blood gush out over you . . . He felt his stomach begin to flutter and he thought he was going to be sick.

Then Maynard, unaware of the fact that he was the only one prepared to kill the men in the next room, moved towards the half-opened door. Music was coming from a small speaker hung on a wall; below it a young Japanese sat in front of a field transceiver set. The set was on the dining-table and at the far end of the table another Japanese, an older man, looked to be writing a letter. There was no sign of the third man Maynard had seen when he had first reconnoitred the house.

Case was closest to Maynard, and the latter put his lips to the American's ear. 'You take the young chap. I'll take the other one. It'll have to be quick.'

Case could feel the sickness now in his mouth, the trembling in his hands. He shook his head, tried to say No, but his tongue wouldn't work. Maynard drew back his head, looked puzzled; then he jerked his head round as there was a movement in the dining-room. The older Japanese stood up, said something to the younger man, and went out of the room into what appeared to be a large hall, closed the door behind him.

'Now!' Maynard hissed. 'I'll take the young chap. You bar that door. Cabrolini, get the valves you want. Now!'

He pushed back the door, went through in a rush, his gun slung over his back, his knife raised for the death blow. The young Japanese looked up and Case, even while moving swiftly towards the far door, saw the whole thing in slow motion and with the same magnified awareness. He was surprised at how large the Japanese's eyes became in their shock; they opened up till they were almost round. The young man had been looking at a magazine full of photographs of nude girls; he died clutching a handful of breasts. Maynard pulled him out of the chair, dropped him to the floor, looked up and nodded appreciatively at Case. Everything was going well; the young Japanese had not uttered a sound. Case leaned back against the door into the hall and stared down at the dead man lying now beneath the table. He could hear the music coming from the speaker, imagined he could hear the scratch of the needle on the record. Then the music stopped and a Japanese voice spoke. He jumped, his head jerking up and in that moment his awareness shrunk, his reactions became normal again. It was as if his body recognised that the worst moment was over, that they would be out of this room and this house before they were discovered.

Cabrolini was feverishly searching through some cardboard boxes on the large sideboard against one wall, emptying them out like some vandal intent on creating a mess. Filing cards, balls of fuse wire, screws—everything but valves. Cabrolini was cursing in Italian, becoming more agitated every second. He flung open the cupboards of the sideboard, but they were full of chinaware; the Japanese evidently had not yet got round to looting the houses they took over. There *had* to be some valves somewhere in this room . . .

'Try these!'

Maynard had ripped open the back of the transceiver. Cabrolini moved swiftly across to the table. 'They will do! But if I take them out——' He nodded up at the speaker. The voice was droning on, unctuous as a bishop reading a commercial.

'We'll have to risk that!'

Cabrolini, in his agitation, grabbed at one of the valves and burnt his hand. Hastily he snatched at the half-completed letter lying on the table, wrapped it round the valve and jerked it out of its socket. The voice coming from the speaker stopped as if the broadcaster's windpipe had been chopped off; the room was suddenly silent. In that moment Case felt someone at the door behind his back.

He had locked the door and now someone, probably the older man who had left the room, was furiously rattling the knob. Maynard looked at the door, then at Case. 'It'll hold. Get out the back!'

Cabrolini had grabbed the other valves, dropped them into one of the cardboard boxes he had taken from the sideboard. Case moved quickly by him towards the door leading into the kitchen, just as a Japanese soldier appeared in the doorway. Case stopped in mid-stride, the knife in his hand but as useless as a peppermint stick.

'Get him!' Maynard snarled.

Case's limbs were leaden; he couldn't move. Then suddenly the urge to survive went through him like a current; but it was too late. Maynard had dived by him, his knife flashing down. The Japanese fell back into the kitchen, his finger jerking convulsively on the trigger of his automatic carbine, the same sort of Solothurn as Case and Cabrolini carried. Maynard, tripped by his sarong, had gone right over the fallen Japanese into the kitchen, was sprawled there on the tiled floor; Case was flattened against the wall by the doorway. But Cabrolini was right in the line of the spray of bullets. They smashed into his body and face and he was dead before he knew that his life was coming to a sudden end. He reeled back, utterly disfigured, hit the table, spun round, then fell forward again to land with a dull sickening thud at Case's feet.

'Grab the box!' Maynard had scrambled to his feet. 'The valves, man, the valves!'

Case had dropped on one knee. He reached out a hand to take the cardboard box from Cabrolini's grasp, but he was staring at the ugly mess of the Italian's face. Then he looked up as Maynard stood over him, snatched the box from him.

'He's dead!' Later he would recall the obviousness of his remark, but now he was suffering from a greater shock that he had ever before experienced.

'Whose fault is that?' Maynard snarled.

3

'They're taking a helluva time,' said Polo. 'I hope that little Javanese bastard hasn't put 'em in.'

'Why should he do that?' Elisabeth asked.

In the light of the bright moon Polo looked at her with gentle pity. 'You still can't believe what's happened here, can you, love? These Indonesians or whatever they call themselves, they've given you away, love. You Dutch, I mean.'

'Perhaps you're a bit premature,' Garrick said. 'Writing the Dutch off like that.'

'Don't you think you're all gunna be written off? The Dutch, you Pommies, the French up there in Indo-China where Musso was. Even if we ever clean the Japs outa there, the locals ain't gunna be glad to have you back. You're kidding yourself, mate, if that's what you think.'

They were still in the small clearing where Maynard and the others had left them. Above them the tall wands of bamboo rose like exclamation marks against the whey-faced moon; below them the dark country-side was punctuated by the yellow lights of Sinjambi. Here in the cool hills the mosquitoes were not too bad, though occasionally there would be the sound of a slap as Elisabeth or one of the men smacked one of the insects. Twice they heard the grunt of a wild pig and they could hear him moving around in the undergrowth, but he was down the hill from them and did not appear to be coming any closer. There were other sounds in the dark jungle, sibilant hisses, a silken rustling, a choked gasping; but they had become accustomed to these now. They were fitting into the country or were being absorbed by it; their levels of optimism or pessimism decided for each one how to accept his surroundings. Elisabeth, the native, felt the most alien. The country had changed in her mind, if not in her eye and ear, and she was afraid.

'Perhaps they will need us,' Elisabeth said. 'They must see how much more we know than they do.'

'I think you've had your chance, love. That young bloke back there at your brother's place, he didn't look as if he felt he needed you. I ain't arguing the rights or wrongs of it, but I think the whites have had their day out here in the East. You've all had a fair whack.'

'Do you think we were right to come here in the first place?'

'Me first inclination is to say no, you had no right to come barging in here. But then I gotta be realistic. If the Poms——'

'The Poms?'

'The English. Reg and the skipper and their mob. If they hadn't come out and took over Australia from the abos, then where would I be? I'd of been born in bloody Ireland and there ain't any future in that. No, I'm dead against the white bloke barging in and taking over the darkies' country. But how else would I have been an Aussie?'

Garrick decided to stay out of the discussion. Like most Englishmen of his class and generation he took the Empire for granted. He had learned at school that England ruled some six hundred million people throughout the world, and his banking experience, lowly though it was, had told him that England would not be as rich as it was if it were not for its Empire. When he had first arrived in Singapore he had been infected by the superior attitude of the local white people towards the Malayans and the Chinese; after he had been there a while he had noticed that it was people like himself, the white-collar lower middle-class, who were the rudest in their treatment of the Malayans and the Chinese. And, remembering his father and the latter's respect for George Lansbury's principles of brotherly love, he had been ashamed of himself. He had not rushed out and embraced the Malayans and the Chinese; he had too much of his mother in him for that. But he had begun to wonder if the trumpeted idealism, the divine sanction for the Empire, was not just a camouflage for self-interest, for getting rich at the expense of others. He had not found any answer because he had not dug deep enough, because he had not cared enough. But he knew in some vague way that the old days of Empire were over, that, if he survived this war, he would have seen the end of an era. And he was not sure what his reaction would be. Unlike Elisabeth, who had lost her home as well as her homeland, he would have lost nothing. Nothing but the prestige of being English and white in a coloured man's world. And, despite his sense of shame, he had enjoyed the sense of hierarchy. It was more than he would ever have achieved at home.

Elisabeth, for her part, had never had any sense of empire. If she had thought of status at all, it was as a member of the ruling class in her own land, one that had been conquered centuries before she was born. This was the way the world had grown. Holland itself had had a number of foreign rulers: The Franks, the Burgundians. She had never been naïve enough to think that Sumatran Hollanders would ever allow the Sumatrans themselves equal status. The Hollanders were masters and that was the way God and economic judgement thought best; her father and his friends had believed honestly in the rightness of their paternalism. She had heard vague talk of independence for the local people, had heard of men like Soekarno and Hatta; but she had also heard her father speaking at an official dinner before an audience that had wholeheartedly agreed with him: 'If we Hollanders moved out, someone else would only move in. Politics, like nature, abhors a vacuum. The Indonesians should realise that we are here as much for their good as for our own. This is our land as much as theirs. Three centuries gives us more than a leasehold, it gives us a freehold right.' She had applauded as loudly as anyone else at the dinner.

But the arrogant certainty of that past, only so recent, gave her no comfort now. She did not have Polo's suspicion of Kamar, but that was because she had lived for so 'ong in complacency; she was still too deep in the habit of taking people at their face value, which was another form of arrogance.

Like most people of calcified position she could not take easily to disillusion; it was an insult to her past assurance. But she was not unintelligent and now reason, overcoming habit, told her that perhaps Polo was right. No one was to be trusted from now on. And she began to worry about Case, Maynard and Cabrolini.

'Do you think one of us should go down into Sinjambi and see if anything has happened?'

'It's just happened!' Garrick exclaimed; and far below them, in the town, they heard the shots. There was silence for a moment, then there were further shots. 'What the hell do we do?'

'We sit and wait,' said Polo quietly. He was sitting on the field transceiver set, gazing steadily down into the valley below them. The wound in his thigh was still hurting and he had noticed when he had taken off the bandages late this evening that the edges of the wound had begun to fester. He was also painfully aware of the chafing under his armpit; that, too, had begun to fester. If Maynard and the others did not get back with the valves for the radio transmitter, he knew that his chances of getting back to Australia and old Vi would be practically nil. He was not a man who surrendered easily, but he had always been practical. He would give himself up to the Japanese before he would let himself become a burden to the others. In the meantime he would sit and wait.

They waited for another half hour, then they heard the sound of someone coming down through the jungle towards the clearing. Maynard and Case, both breathing heavily, came into the clearing and slumped down. The others sat waiting, ears strained for the sound of Cabrolini and Kamar coming down through the undergrowth. Then at last Polo said, 'Did the Nips get both of them?'

CHAPTER 9

Maynard looked across at Case, then he said, 'Only Cabrolini. He's dead.'

Elisabeth drew in her breath sharply with something like a sob. Garrick knitted his brows and squinted as though he were sitting in a bright light instead of the moonlit gloom of the clearing. Neither of them quite believed what they had heard; they had feared the worst but not expected it. Only Polo, who had expected the worst but never feared it, who was pessimistic but not afraid, took the news matter-of-factly: 'Poor bugger. How'd it happen? Did the little bloke give you away?'

Maynard looked up, surprised. He had taken off Kamar's sarong, had it draped over his shoulder. He pulled it off and looked at it, then looked across at Case as the latter said, 'Could have. Kamar must have seen that guy coming in the back way. Why didn't he warn us?'

Then in the darkness almost at Case's back a voice said, 'Captain, may I have my sarong? Modesty is the best policy when a lady is present.'

Maynard bunched the sarong in his hand, stared across at the dim shape of Kamar in the barred prison of the cane brake. 'Where have you been, Kamar?'

'I heard the shooting, captain. As you advised, I decided to be discreet. I ran away.'

'Did you see that second Jap soldier come in the back gate to the garden?'

Kamar hesitated for just a moment, then he said, 'What second Japanese, captain?'

Maynard said nothing, but there was a snort of disgust from Polo. Then Case said, 'Give him his sarong.'

Maynard threw the sarong into the cane brake, stood up and said, 'We'd better move farther back up in the hills.'

'It's gunna be a bit bloody difficult, skip, wandering around in the dark,' said Polo. 'I thought you said the Nips didn't like the jungle at night? They won't find us.'

'Not unless someone told them where they *could* find us.' Maynard looked across towards Kamar, but the Javanese, busy wrapping his sarong round him, appeared not to have heard. 'We'll just make it a little more difficult for them. Righto, Kamar, grab those batteries.'

Kamar stepped out of the cane brake, modestly clad now and his dignity intact once more. 'Where are we going, captain?'

'For a short walk,' said Maynard curtly and picked up the field set.

Kamar looked for a moment as if he were about to persist with his questioning, but then he changed his mind. He picked up the sling containing the batteries and fell in behind Maynard as the latter led the party out of the clearing, through the cane brake and up on to the path.

Case waited for Polo as the latter got painfully to his feet. 'You feel up to it, old-timer?'

'Old-timer?' Polo's shrunken face looked green in the moonlight, a mildewed skull. 'Do I look that far gone? Yeah, I guess you're right. I'm buggered, Jack, my word I am. Those bloody valves better work——' He looked up, suddenly apprehensive. 'You got 'em, didn't you?'

Case nodded, handed the Australian his crutch. 'We'll be in touch with Australia before morning. You'll be home in a week.'

'I hope so. I bloody hope so.' Polo tucked the crutch under his armpit. 'Pity about poor Musso. He wasn't a bad sort.' He did his best to struggle free of his prejudices: 'I didn't think I'd ever have a good word for a Dago, but he had his points.'

Case said nothing, began to walk ahead of Polo up the path, glad of the darkness that hid his expression. He still felt physically sick at Cabrolini's death; it was a solar plexus blow for which he had been completely unprepared. But there was also something else: rage. Rage at himself, for he knew that Maynard had been right: it was *his* fault that Cabrolini had died. If he had moved quickly enough, as he would have in the ring, if he had used his knife as it should have been used, the Japanese would never have had time to fire his gun. He who had wasted so much of his own life stormed now at the waste of another man's life. He had not thrown away the knife as soon as he and Maynard had escaped from the house, but had, for some reason he could not name, thrust it into the hip pocket of his trousers. He could feel it there now, the blade pricking against his buttock; it was a poor place to carry one's conscience, but perhaps it was the best place for it. To have had the knife in his breast pocket, pricking against his heart might have brought on thoughts that were too morbid. Full of wrath and despair as he was, he was still not so wasteful of his own life that he should want to sacrifice it as some sort of recompense for Cabrolini's. If he was to repay the ghost of Cabrolini, then he had to do it constructively. But how? And his uselessness only made him rage the more.

Maynard kept them walking for another hour, climbing all the time higher and higher into the hills. Then at last he called a halt. 'We'd all better sleep. We'll get to work with the wireless first thing in the morning.'

'Why not now?' Garrick was exhausted but impatient:

he knew he could summon up from somewhere enough strength to keep him walking another fifty or a hundred miles if the wireless would only give them some hope.

'We'll have to code everything,' Maynard said. 'If we get in touch with Australia, if they tell us they can help us, we don't want the Japs to know everything that's going on.'

Garrick offered no further argument. He and the others sank down into the long grass, heedless of any insects or snakes that might be there, and almost at once fell asleep. All but Case, who lay awake staring up at the moon in which was mirrored the sadly reproachful face of Cabrolini. Across from him Maynard also lay awake for a while, but he soon dropped off to sleep. Eventually both men slept, each tied to the other in his sleep by their antagonism. But their antagonism now was of a different order from the early difference between them. It was an antagonism that hurt each of them; each man knew now that he needed the other, and the knowledge was painful and resented. So each hated the other for his necessity.

They all came awake in the first light of morning, wakened by the dawn and by hope, and found themselves in a clearing on a rock-warted hill high above a wide rolling valley. It was cooler this morning and a breeze blew up the hillside, tracing its passing with rippling shadows across the tall lalang grass. A line of kapok trees stood above the clearing like a queue of old men; a spring bubbled out at their feet and trickled in a small stream down past where the party lay. Maynard and the others refreshed themselves at the stream, ate some of the fruit they had collected yesterday along the way, then everyone looked expectantly at Maynard as he opened the field set and replaced the batteries.

He took the valves out of the cardboard box, fitted them carefully into the transceiver as if he were setting jewels. Everyone held their breath as he switched on the set and waited for it to warm up. Then they saw the light glow on the panel; the soft light of the dawn and their own heightened expectancy seemed to make it flicker more brightly than was actual. A moment later a Japanese voice broke like a small thin explosion into the silence of the clearing.

Maynard turned down the volume, looked around at the excited faces about him, five suns in the dawn. He could feel the trembling running through his body and the hand resting on the field set was quivering like that of an old man with the ague. He wanted to weep, he felt so overjoyed.

Everyone started to exclaim at once, till Polo said impatiently, 'Don't muck about! Get Darwin or somewhere!'

Maynard had taken the code book from his string bag, handed it to Elisabeth. 'I'll try and pick them up in the clear at first. Then if we get on to them, we'll start coding. I'll explain how to do it when we get to it.'

He studied the dials, trying to remember all the drill he had seen done so many times by signallers; he was aware of the others watching him, but particularly Case. *This* was part of the business of war and he had neglected it. He switched over to short-range transmission, looked at his watch, then at Polo. 'What would it be in Darwin now?'

Polo, no mathematician, did some awkward calculating. 'About seven ack emma.'

'Well, here goes.' Maynard began to speak into the microphone: 'Waratah, this is Frangipani calling Waratah. Can you hear me? Over.'

He worked for ten minutes on the dials, alternately calling and listening, while the others began to swear with impatience and the warmth of the rising sun. Then abruptly a voice broke in, flat, nasal, crackling with static: 'This is Waratah. Who is that calling for Frangipani? Over.'

Maynard gave his name, rank and number. 'I was with the 13th Hampshire Rifles in Malaya. There are six of us, none from Frangipani. Frangipani was wiped out two days ago, no survivors. Over.'

There was nothing but static on the set for several moments, as if some sort of conference might be going on in Darwin. Then the Australian voice said, 'We need more identification than you have given us. If you are British, who won the last cricket Tests before the war? Over.'

'Oh, for Christ's sake!' Case slapped his thigh in disgust.

Maynard looked at him coldly. 'It's ingenious. No Japanese would know anything about cricket. But they might know who won the last baseball World Series or whatever it is called. I believe they play baseball in Japan.'

'Well, who did win the last cricket Tests?' Garrick said.

'I was expecting you to know that,' Maynard said. 'Your father was the cricketer.'

'I told you, I hated cricket.' Garrick screwed up his face in desperation. 'I can't remember a thing about the last Tests, except I think Len Hutton scored a lot of runs.'

'I thought all Englishmen knew all about cricket,' Elisabeth said.

'Do all Dutchmen grow tulips? Tennis was my game,' said Maynard, and felt a sort of hysterical anger seeping through him. Suddenly he did a mental about-face; the question Darwin had asked wasn't ingenious, it was stupid. Why couldn't they have asked an intelligent question, such as . . . But what would be an intelligent question in a situation such as this? One that the enemy could also answer?

Then Polo said with sardonic appreciation of himself and his countrymen, 'I never followed cricket. But I reckon Australia must've won. No Aussie would ever bring up a year when we lost.'

Maynard looked at him with quizzical admiration. 'That's a nice reading of national character, Polo. Personally, I've always felt Australians were big-headed—no offence, of course.' He glanced at Kamar, who smiled. 'Let's hope we're correct in our reading of them.' He switched over to transmission, said, 'Frangipani to Waratah. Australia won the last series. And please don't fool around, Darwin. We have an important message for you. We have to code it. We shall be back on the air in ten minutes. Over and out.'

Maynard wrote out the message he wanted to send on the inside of the cover of the code book. Elisabeth translated it into Dutch, then encoded it from the book. It was a laborious business, and Case and the others, frustrated by their uselessness, fumed impatiently. Case got up and walked away, moving up through the grass to the large rocks that formed a bastion at one end of the clearing. He sat down on a rock and looked out over the countryside.

The morning air was still clear and the valley and the hills had the unreal clarity of a modelled landscape; one looked for cardboard houses and metal animals and people that never moved. Birdsong hung as single notes, like pearls of music, on the strings of shining air; far away at the other end of the valley smoke rose straight and thin as a pale grey pencil line. Between two bushes behind Case, a spider had spun a crochet of sunlight; the web glistened with the poignancy of tears. The whole landscape was wrapped in peace as it was in sunlight, and Case suddenly was infected with it. After his troubled night he had woken with very little strength left, drained by the long physical day yesterday and by the emotion that had attacked him last night after Cabrolini's death. Now what remained of his strength ran out of him and he gave himself up, as he might to deep water, to the peace that surrounded him. He lay back, in his mind the ridiculous hope that the others might forget him and go off without him.

But the hope was of course ridiculous. People do not forget each other, especially those upon whom they have placed some dependence. Garrick came up through the lalang grass, moving so quietly that when he spoke Case jumped. 'Sorry, Jack.' He sat down on a rock and looked out over the valley. 'I wonder if Tahiti is as peaceful as this?'

Case was resentful at being claimed again; he had been on the point of drowning in the morning's peace. But Garrick, sitting bent like an old man on the rock, skeleton-like in his sherry party suit, could not be snarled at. 'You still reckon you'll make it there?'

'I have to, Jack. Hope, I mean. I couldn't walk to the top of that next hill if that was as far as I thought we were going to go. The others are thinking of Darwin. If we make it to there, I think I might make it to Tahiti.' He looked down at Case, said hesitantly, still afraid of prying too much into the American's life: 'What's your aim?'

Case sat up, accepting that he had been rescued, even if against his will. Garrick and the others wouldn't let him go. Maynard might, but he would never ask the Englishman for a decision. Not after last night. Maynard had already made up his mind about him, had already dismissed him. He opened his fingers that had gone stiff as he had thought of Maynard, looked down at them as if expecting to see the knife still there that had been there last night. But there was nothing, only the dried blood of the dead Japanese whom Maynard had killed in the garden. He turned his hand over, wiped the palm on the grass, but when he looked again the blood was still there, black in the cracks and scars on his hand.

'What's the matter?' Garrick asked, drawing Case farther back to the group.

'Nothing.' He looked down towards Maynard and the others grouped about the transmitter. 'What does Darwin say?'

At that moment Polo looked up towards them and waved them to come down. When they reached the group Case at once sensed the argument that was about to blow up. He could feel it in the stiffness of Maynard, Elisabeth and Polo, and he tensed, waiting for the first verbal blow. Maynard must have told them about how Cabrolini had died.

But Maynard looked up from the de-coded message he held, said, 'We gave them the message about the Jap task force at Belawan Deli.' He drew in a deep breath, as if he did not quite believe himself what he was about to say: 'They want to know if we'll volunteer to go in and blow up the main oil refinery at Palembang.'

'They're outa their bloody heads!' Polo stood up, began to limp up and down on his crutch. 'Five of us——' He stopped, looking at Kamar. 'You wouldn't be in it, would you, sport?'

Kamar sat very still. 'No, sir.'

'So there you are.' Polo stumbled a little as he waved a hand around him. 'Five of us. A woman, a cripple, and you three, skipper. It don't make much of a raiding party.'

'Tell them to cut out the jokes,' Garrick said, 'and tell us where they can pick us up.'

'They've already told us that,' said Elisabeth. 'They can pick us up in Timor.'

'Another coupla thousand bloody miles from here!' Polo looked as if he might snap apart at any moment. He stood on his good leg and thumped his crutch into the ground. 'They got that flyingboat up here once. Why can't they do it again?'

Maynard shrugged. 'Perhaps it had a rendezvous with some ship in the Indian Ocean.' He looked down at the scribbled message he held in his hand, the dialogue he had had with Darwin. 'They say it's too far for our planes now. All our bases must have been evacuated. It stands to reason, I suppose. If they could get a plane this far to pick us up, they could send planes to bomb Palembang.'

'But if we can make it to Timor,' said Elisabeth, 'they promise they can pick us up.'

'But what sorta bargain do these jokers want?' Polo demanded. 'They're asking us to shove our necks out, go right into the—the——'

'The lions' den,' said Kamar.

'Yeah. The lions' den. We go in there and practically ask the Nips to chop our heads off. Then we gotta find our own way out, grab a boat from somewhere, paddle another coupla thousand miles. Not on your bloody life! I was never much good to Mum when I was alive. With me throat cut I'd be a dead loss to her!'

Now that contact had been made with Australia he had had a sudden revival of strength and hope. There was nothing much left of him now but skin and bone and the terrible pain in his thigh; but hope knotted him together, prevented him from falling apart. Timor might be two thousand bloody miles away, but he could stay alive that long. *If* they did not have to shove their necks out . . . 'Tell 'em to forget Palembang, skipper.'

Case spoke at last: 'Why do they want *us* to go in and do this job?'

Maynard looked at him without expression, gave him the information like a window clerk giving out details of train schedules: 'The guerrillas, Frangipani Force, it was called, were to have done the job. They can't get anyone else in here in time. They want the oil installations blown up before that task force reaches Palembang. Once it has re-fuelled there, it can go straight on to Hollandia in New Guinea. We are the only ones close enough to do the damage.'

'Where are all the Dutch who were here before the Japs came? They couldn't all have got away.' Case hesitated, not looking at Elisabeth, then said, 'Or been killed.'

Kamar said, still sitting very still, 'They are in prison camps, sir. The oil engineers are in Palembang at the refineries. The Japanese are making them work them.'

Maynard jerked his head round. 'How do you know all this?'

'I heard it on the grapevine, captain. Bad news travels fast in this country, sir.'

'In any country,' said Case.

'What else do you know?' Maynard demanded.

Kamar's face was stiff, almost unfriendly; he's not the eager beaver he was yesterday, Case thought. 'The Hollander women are in separate camps, captain. They are—hosts?'

'Hostages,' said Maynard, and began to realise the situation even before Kamar had finished explaining it.

'Yes, sir. Hostages. If the engineers try to sabotage the oil installations, the Japanese will kill their families. Very simple, very clever.' Kamar looked around the group. 'Very bad for us. I do not think we should blow up the installations.'

There was silence for a moment, then Elisabeth said quietly, 'I think we should try to blow up the installations.'

All the men looked at her in varying degrees of astonishment. Each of them had his own reasons for not wanting to go into Palembang: Polo and Garrick because they were concerned only for their own safety, Maynard because he thought the task was beyond them, Case because he had since last night lost all interest in the war or, indeed, in life at all. None of them was accustomed to a woman making any decision for him, and now this Dutchwoman was telling them quietly but with a touch of her old imperiousness what they should do. It was more than Polo, at least, could stand.

'You stay outa this, love. This has got nothing to do with you!'

'I think it has a great deal to do with me.' Elisabeth's chin had come up; she was not used to being told what to do. She wanted to remind this ignorant coal miner what his place was; but she remembered in time that her own place no longer existed. This small group on this hill-top was a society in which she had never been instructed: democracy had been a word forbidden in her father's house. She struggled to remain calm while she said, 'If we go in and blow up the oil installations, the Japanese won't shoot the engineers. They will need them to help them rebuild them.'

'They could shoot the engineers' families,' Case said.

'I don't think you know the Hollanders of Sumatra,' said Elisabeth, and three centuries of pride made her voice a little stiff. She did not know, herself, all the Hollanders of Sumatra, least of all the oil engineers. Most of them were not natives like herself but Dutchmen out on tours of duty from Holland. But she knew what *she* would do, what her father and brother would have done, and her pride in her heritage committed the absent, unwitting Dutchmen. 'If the Japanese did kill the families, which I doubt, then they would have to kill the engineers too. Because no Hollander would take a thing like that lying down.'

Case stared at her in quiet amazement. She's like something out of a book, he thought, she believes in dying for a cause, in draping a flag over a group of men and expecting them all to act in the same brave, blind way. Christ, he thought, hasn't she heard of the Quislings of Norway, the collaborators of France, the fifth columnists of Greece? Like the words of half-forgotten songs, phrases came back to him out of the newspapers; they had been planted subliminally in his mind, without having any real meaning until now. Or what of the ordinary people in those countries and others who, though not traitors, were content to suffer occupation by the enemy? His amazement began to turn to anger. What right had she to make heroes of men who might have no more ambition than to stay alive, no matter what the cost in pride? Patriotism wasn't necessarily endemic.

'And the Japanese would never kill the engineers,' Elisabeth said finally.

'They killed your father,' said Case, and even the other men looked at him, shocked by his cruelty.

Elisabeth flinched a little, but said, her voice still quiet, 'My father was of no further use to them.'

'The argument is academic, anyway,' Maynard said, trying to prevent Elisabeth's being hurt any further. He, most of all, had been shocked by Case's blunt argument. He despised the American for his weakness, but that same weakness, the inability to kill another man in cold blood, intimated a certain sensitivity. But perhaps he had been entirely wrong about Case. He had been wrong about him last night. 'The job is impossible.'

'Why?' Elisabeth's very quietness had an irritating perverseness about it.

Polo said, 'Look, love, we can see why you'd like to have a go at the Nips. Get your own back for what they did to your dad and your brother. But it would be no go, love. We're not demolition experts.'

'We know nothing about oil installations,' Maynard said.

'Mr. Case does,' said Elisabeth, and looked up at the American.

Case shook his head, backing off from her challenge. 'Now wait a minute! Don't start nominating me as any hero.'

'She'd be a fool if she did,' Maynard said, not looking at him but at Elisabeth. 'It's out, Miss Brinker. We could never make it. Would you code this message for me? I'll tell Darwin we can't do the job.'

'Code it yourself!' Elisabeth stood up and walked away, her limbs those of an old woman. In her heart she knew the men were right, but they were robbing her life of purpose. Her future stretched ahead of her like a desert; escape to Australia would not lessen the bleakness of the future. To have tried to destroy the oil installations in Palembang would at least have been something constructive; she forgave herself the contradiction because she was in a mood to forgive herself anything. But not the men: she could not forgive them.

She did not turn when she heard the footstep behind her, but she knew who it was. 'I'm disappointed in you, Mr. Case.'

'You're not the first,' said Case amiably. 'Look, honey——'

'Don't call me honey!'

'I'll call you what I like,' Case said, his voice still even. 'Where I come from, to call a girl honey isn't an insult. I think that's your trouble. Your world has been too small.'

'Yours wasn't very big. A boxing ring.' The sarcasm curdled on her tongue.

'You'd be surprised. It's a bigger world than you think. One thing, it's more democratic than any you've ever known.'

She looked sideways at him, beginning to realise that he had not come up here to the edge of the clearing to attack her. 'Whose side are you on, Mr. Case?'

'I'm trying not to take any side,' said Case, aware of how difficult neutrality was. 'But you and I are the only two with nothing to go back to, I mean if we get to Australia. But the others, even Garrick, they've all got something. Maynard and Polo have their wives. Reg has——' He stopped, honouring Garrick's foolish dream of Tahiti. 'Well, he has something. You can't blame them for not wanting to be dead heroes. And chances are that's what they'd be if they went into Palembang.'

She was silent for a while. Her world was opening out and for the first time in her life she was feeling defeated. She was not frightened by her growing knowledge of other people and their circumstances; she had been mollycoddled, but she had not been made incapable of readjustment. But it was one thing to try to readjust her own thinking; but did not the others owe her some concession? 'If the Japanese invaded America, what would you do? Run away?'

Case considered for a moment. 'No, I wouldn't. But there I'd be among another hundred and fifty million Americans. You're on your own here. I don't know what the population of Sumatra is, but I'd bet you wouldn't find one in a hundred who'd want to back you in a fight against the Japs. That's the difference between us. You want to fight a war, or anyway this *part* of the war, for a country that doesn't even belong to you.'

She didn't argue with him about whom Sumatra belonged to. 'You have to stop and fight somewhere. I don't think this war concerns just Sumatra, Mr. Case. The Japanese must be stopped *somewhere*, otherwise the war is lost altogether. The Germans are winning the war in Europe because the English and the French gave away Czechoslovakia at Munich. If we had said we'd fight then, perhaps the war would never have happened.'

'And what if they'd called our bluff?' He didn't know much about Munich. He remembered the name of Chamberlain, but couldn't remember what Frenchman was there. He had been fighting in Topeka, Kansas, that month of that year, and you might have been hard pressed to find someone in Topeka who could point out Munich on the map to you. Europe was nobody's business in Kansas in that year. 'I don't know what state of preparation the British and French were in back in 1938, but I don't think they'd have gone one round with the Germans. Seems to me we're not too well prepared even right now. We're outmatched all along the line.'

'You're speaking in boxing terms, I take it—wasn't there some time in your career when you were out-matched, as you call it, but you managed to beat the other man?'

He shook his head. 'Sorry to disappoint you. Every time I was out-matched, I knew it from the first round. And it never worked out against the odds. It's only in movies that the little guy gets up off the floor and wins.'

She turned angrily away from him, stared out over the countryside, now losing its peaceful look as the sun rose higher and hardened it with harsh glare. The valley, that had looked so green and lush, now was seen in its truth, a baked crust whose greenness had been the deception of morning shadows. The hills glittered like ranges of quartz, smarting the eyes like grit. But, unlike Case, she was not looking for peace, so she was not disappointed. She knew this country and had come to terms with it. Or so she had told herself, but was now beginning to have doubts.

Then Maynard came up to them, carrying the code book in his hand like a clergyman with his prayer-book. He had had to scribble all over the cover and some of the pages; he held out the book, the long argument with Darwin. 'They're bribing us now. If we go down into Palembang, they have a contact there, a Chinese. They say he should be able to get us a boat. That would get us as far as Java at least.'

'Who translated the code book for you?' Elisabeth said.

'Kamar. He speaks Dutch as well as he speaks English. Better, perhaps. Less clichés, or perhaps I don't know any Dutch clichés.'

Polo, Garrick and Kamar had come up the slope, as if wary of some decision being made without their consent. Polo said, 'Well, do we go into Palembang? For that boat, I mean.'

Everyone looked at each other, then finally Maynard looked at Case and said, 'How much do you know about oil installations?'

'Look—skipper——' Polo began.

'Shut up for a moment, will you, Polo?' Maynard said irritably, still looking at Case. 'Nobody's asking you to shove your neck out.'

'Are you asking me to shove mine out?' Case said.

'I suppose that's what I am doing,' said Maynard. 'How much do you know?'

Case hesitated. 'I worked on the oil fields in Texas as a kid.'

Maynard also hesitated, as if he wished that there might have been someone else but Case on whom he had to rely. 'Would you know the set-up in a refinery?'

Again Case hesitated. One man did not want to ask the questions, the other did not want to answer them. But again they were trapped by each other and by the situation that each of them knew had to be faced. Then Case said, 'I could find my way around in one. But what have we got for explosives?'

Maynard gestured at the two hand grenades hanging from his belt. 'Just these.'

'Then forget it,' said Polo. 'We'd need at least a box of dynamite.'

'Would we?' asked Maynard.

Goddam, thought Case, is he trying to make me make the decision? He looked at the Englishman with the first genuine hatred he had felt for him, but he heard himself say, 'No. If you set up the right chain reaction, all you need is a match.'

Maynard looked steadily at him. 'If we go in, you're the one we'll have to depend on.'

You sonofabitch, Case thought; but then remarked that so far Maynard had not told the others how and why Cabrolini had died. Is he giving me another chance or is he using me, making me just a part of the business of war? 'Once we're in Palembang, how do we get into the oil refinery? They will have guards all over the joint.'

'There is a pipeline that comes in from the fields up-country,' Elisabeth said, arguing eagerly. Maynard looked at her, unaware that his thinking was paralleling Case's. God, he thought, when women take up war, they get intense about it. Had Boadicea, never one of his heroines, been like this? 'Then there are oil trains that go down to the Sunda Strait. Perhaps we could get into the oil compound on one of the trains.'

'How?' said Polo, and his impatience with a woman's lack of logic was plain. Vi had been like this, always telling him how to run a coal mine.

Elisabeth gestured helplessly; all her life she had never had to worry about details. Then Kamar said, 'I know the goods manager at Palembang railway yards. Perhaps he could get you into the oil depot.'

Case looked at the Javanese. 'Goods? You mean freight manager? How come you know him?'

Kamar smiled, but tentatively; he seemed to have lost all his self-confidence and was back to his original timidity. 'My father was a smuggler, sir, remember? He knew *everybody*.'

'What made you change your mind about going into Palembang?' Maynard asked.

Kamar looked around them all before he answered. 'I do not want to be left alone in these hills, captain.'

'Who said we were going into Palembang?' Polo said, and beside him Garrick nodded at the question.

'I'm afraid this is another time when majority rules,' said Maynard. 'Kamar doesn't have a vote, so that leaves five of us. And three of us——' He looked at Case, who hesitated, then nodded. 'Three of us vote to go in and try and do the job.'

'Before or after we've picked up this boat from this Chinaman?' said Garrick.

'It might be best to split up,' Maynard said. 'You, Polo and Miss Brinker can get the boat. Case, Kamar and I will try to do what we can to the oil installations. Then we'll rendezvous—and heigh-ho, Timor!'

'Heigho-bloody-ho the cemetery,' said Polo.

2

They boarded the rubber train as it laboured up the incline. The jungle was thick on either side of the single track and they had remained well hidden till the ancient engine, a museum piece, had gone gasping by. Then in the deep dusk they had run along beside the wagons and swung up on to them, keeping low so that they would not be observed by the guard in the van at the rear of the long line of wagons. Maynard and Kamar had, with some difficulty, swung aboard with the transmitter and the batteries. Garrick had been burdened by his suitcase, but he had refused to abandon it and had some-how clambered up on to the wagon. Elisabeth, showing sur-prising agility, had hauled herself aboard. It had been left to Case to help Polo and he had slung the Australian up into a wagon as if he were a sack of wheat; the little man had screamed in agony for a moment as he fell on his wounded thigh. But when the others came clambering back to the wagon in which he lay there was no complaint from him; he was stretched like a small silent ghost on the sheets of raw rubber, his hands holding his thigh. Case moved to him, lay down beside him to keep his own head below the top of the wagon.

'How is it, sport?'

Polo retched with pain, but still managed to shake his head. 'She'll be jake.' A glimmer of the old independence flickered for a moment: 'Don't you worry about me.'

Case sat back, looked around at the others as they sprawled on the thick sheets of rubber. It had been Kamar who had suggested they should jump the train into Palembang, and had known exactly where to catch it. 'My father used to use it, sir.'

'What exactly did your father smuggle?' Maynard had asked with wry curiosity.

'Everything, captain.' Kamar glowed with filial pride. 'He had the widest range of any goods in the Indies.'

'How come he didn't leave you a rich man?' Case said.

Kamar shrugged. 'When he was shot, the British and the Hollanders confiscated everything he owned. Smugglers are without profit in their own country. No offence, sir.'

Now they all lay in the wagon as the train reached the top of the incline and the old Krupps engine, taking the bit be-tween its teeth, bolted away down the other side. Smoke poured back uphill, choking those that were in the wagon, and sparks raced back through the dusk like frantic fireflies. The wagon swayed and rattled as, a link in the chain of thirty or forty, it was whipped down the hill and into the night. Then the engine, running out of steam, arthritic in its iron joints, had reached the floor of a valley and, defeated by the purely horizontal, slowed back to its normal chug-ging pace. The smoke lifted, everyone sat up and tried to clear their noses, only to breathe in the thick smell of rubber.

Garrick lay at one end of the wagon, his head resting on a sheet of rubber laid over his suitcase. He was frightened by the prospect that lay ahead of them, but once the decision to go into Palembang had been made he had said nothing more. They had eaten only some rambutans and wild bananas today and now he was hungry; the empty feeling in his gut only added to the weakening effect of his fear. The train clattered its way past a kampong and Garrick raised his head and looked out, saw the fires outside the huts and imagined he could smell the cooking food. Worn out, his young thin face aging by the minute, he fell asleep, his empty skull bouncing on the useless fortune beneath the sheet of rubber.

Maynard and Elisabeth lay side by side with the stiff formality of bride and groom who had been introduced to each other only at the wedding. Once Maynard rolled towards Elisabeth as the train swayed round a bend, but he hurriedly pushed himself away, muttering *Sorry* with such emphasis that it was as if he had tried to molest her. Elisabeth giggled inside, mistaking his stiffness for awkwardness with a woman; she had the foreigner's usual misguided view that no Englishman was ever at ease with a woman. But his stiffness was that of faithfulness. All day he had been thinking of Ruth, walking with her flesh wrapped round him, aware in memory's eye of the secret places that were her gift to him. Sensual though the day-dreaming had been, it had somehow purified him. He was more in love with her tonight than he had been on their wedding night. Tomorrow he might be dead.

Elisabeth was watching Case sitting up in the wagon now, the train's wind blowing his ragged hair about his face. There was no moon but enough starlight to carve out the bones of his face. His eyes were hidden by a mask of shadow from his brows, so that she could not tell whether he was watching her. But she did not mind. In an hour or two they might all be dead and time had run out for any pretence of modesty. She was frankly interested in this American drifter and she wanted to find some answer in him. Three months ago, in the cocoon of her stylised life then, she would never have given him a second glance, unless it was one of contempt; but then in that particular life, as irrevocable now as lost virginity, she would never have had the occasion to meet him at all. There had been drifters, of course, slipping in and out of her social circle, but they had invariably been men of some background, the unwanted sons of some rich families in Holland, and, occasionally, Englishmen, Germans and Frenchmen with titles that were as meaningless as many nicknames. She had overheard her father, who could be crude when no women were around, describe one of the latter as 'the last of a long line of European aristocrats in which the human sperm has finally been reduced to bladder-water.' She had been interested in none of them; nor would she have been interested in a drifting prizefighter (bum? Was that the American word for him?) if he had somehow strolled into her circle. But that circle no longer existed: one person didn't make a circle: at least two people were needed if social standards were to have any value. And none of the men in this wagon, not even Maynard, was interested in social standards now.

She stared at Case, aware of the self-deluding deceptions that a romantic heart could play on one—and she had never attempted to disguise from herself that she was romantic: her old life had given her little else but time in which to torture herself sweetly with fantasies of love. But she was not going to fall in love with him; she was romantic but she was not foolish. But their lives had become interwoven in a way that wasn't quite clear to her; she was involved with the other men as well, but somehow they were outside her relationship with Case. That relationship, as water hyacinths grow, meet and form an island in the middle of a river, had been spun by odd words and glances, by gestures and even silences, ever since they had first met on the beach. She, who had been nurtured on omens in this land of omens, remembered that it was Case whom she had first seen when she had opened her eyes after collapsing on the beach.

She looked up at the stars now, searching for an omen. Though the men had made their own decision about going into Palembang, it had been she who had prompted them. She felt a certain guilt and she looked for a good omen among the stars. But any pattern that might have been in them was wiped out by the flowing smoke of the train. She turned towards the rising yellow light about the eastern hills; but what could one read in the smile of the moon? She looked back at Case, saw him turn his face towards her and imagined, because his eyes were still hidden in shadow, that they winked at her. She smiled at him and saw the creases in his cheeks as he smiled back at her. But his smile was as inscrutable as that of the moon, and she felt a fierce annoyance course through her. If only she had more time to understand this man . . .

Case saw the kampong coming up on either side of the line ahead, a bigger village than any they had passed so far: they must be getting close to Palembang. He felt none of the nervousness that had attacked him just before they had gone into the house in Sinjambi. He was not apathetic, drugged by any guilt over Cabrolini's death; rather now he was calm, sensible of what lay ahead of him. Twice during his boxing career he had attempted a comeback into the big time and each time had failed; this was another sort of comeback and he knew this time he could not fail. The others were depending on him.

While they had waited in the jungle for the rubber train to come along he had said to Maynard, 'Just to get it straight. Once we get into that oil depot, we do things my way. Okay?'

Maynard had hesitated while Elisabeth and the others had watched him carefully. Then he said, 'I'm not stupid, Case. I'll always give way to the chap who knows what he's doing.'

Case said, 'Up till now you don't think I've known what I'm doing?'

'Have you?'

'Yes,' Case had said slowly. 'I may have been wrong once or twice, not been practical the way you see it. But I've known what I been doing. I'm not punch-drunk. A bit humane, soft-hearted if you like. But not punchy.'

'If there's any killing to be done, I'll do it,' Maynard had said coldly, but had still not mentioned Cabrolini. Case had been aware of the puzzled looks on the faces of the others, as if they sensed there was some secret between himself and Maynard. But none of them had voiced a question and he had been relieved when Maynard had gone on: 'All you have to do is fix things so that we can blow up the refinery. You do that and I'll stamp a medal for you myself.'

Now Case was trying to remember every oil refinery he had been in. He hadn't been inside one since he was eighteen or nineteen; he wondered how much they would have changed in the past eighteen years. He looked up ahead at the engine illuminated by the glow from its own firebox; Kamar had told them that it was a pre-World War One locomotive and it looked it. If they still used railroad stock as ancient as that here in Sumatra, it could be that the oil refineries had also been built years ago and not changed. For the first time since he was a boy he wished for the company of his old man. Joe Czeicinski would have known exactly how to blow up an oil installation.

Then he saw the lights of Palembang rushing towards them as the train curved its way round a dark bend of jungle. No bright lights, no rash of neon as you would meet on the outskirts of an American town; he wondered if there was a blackout these nights in San Francisco, Los Angeles, Seattle; Americans did not like the dark, his father had told him. There was probably a blackout in the main section of Palembang, they were still some way from it, but here on the edge of town lamps still hung outside stores, glowed through open doorways and windows. The Japanese must be having trouble trying to explain to the local people why the town should be dark. Or maybe there was no need for a complete blackout: maybe the Japanese knew Palembang was beyond the range of any Allied bombers. All at once Case realised how isolated he and the others were.

Then Kamar said, 'The river! We are getting close.'

Case crouched down, only the top of his head showing above the side of the wagon as he looked out at Palembang slowly beginning to grow around them. He could see the river with the floating homes, small wooden huts on bamboo rafts moored along the near bank, their cooking fires reflected as writhing pits of golden snakes in the oily water. Long poles hung out from each raft, each holding the black spider's web of a fishing net; on one larger raft two goats stood like iron garden ornaments outside the front door of the hut. On the far bank there were no lights, but he could see the angular outline of brick warehouses and, glowing in the moonlight like an illusion, the silver dome of a mosque.

Then the train was clanging its way over a bridge, riding over the moon on the yellow river. It bumped over some points, switching on to another track, and then it was rumbling to a stop between two large corrugated-iron buildings. The wagon pulled up in a well of black shadow and at once a thick smell fell on them, clogging their nostrils like a dark fog.

CHAPTER 10

'This is the rubber factory,' said Kamar. 'The train will probably stay here till morning.'

Up ahead the engine was blowing off steam that in the humid night air lay low and came drifting back between the sheds. Maynard cautiously raised his head and looked back to the rear of the train. The guard had dropped down from his van and stood talking to two Japanese soldiers who were silhouetted against the light coming from a small shack beside the line. The train was still settling after its long haul and the narrow space between the two buildings was loud with the harshness of metal noises.

'We can't stay here,' said Maynard. 'Perhaps this is where we should split up. How far to the railway yards from here, Kamar?'

'Not far, captain. Perhaps ten minutes.'

'Okay, you can show us the way.' Maynard looked at Elisabeth, Polo and Garrick. 'Do you think you can find your way to this Chinaman's, Lee Chin's?'

'I know where it is,' Elisabeth said. 'It is not a part of town where I ever went, but I can find it.'

'Darwin said they would get in touch with him, so he should be expecting you. Make sure he gives you a decent boat, one that will get us at least as far as Java.'

Then Case, who had been watching the Japanese soldiers at the rear of the train, signalled them all to be quiet. They lay flat again, their bodies awkwardly tensed, while they waited for the soldiers to come down the length of the train, pass the wagon and go on towards the engine. Maynard sat up again, conscious of how tensed he was; his joints cracked as if he, too, were made of metal. He could feel the sweat running from him, coldly clammy on his back where he had lain on the rubber. He was aware now of how weak he was from hunger and he would have felt more capable of the job ahead of them if he had a good meal inside him. But there wasn't time to go looking for food.

'Try and get some food from the Chinaman,' he said, and he imagined that even his voice sounded weak now. I'm becoming nervous, he thought; and over-compensated, making his voice grate: 'Don't stand any nonsense from him.'

'We ain't gunna be in any position to force any bargains, skipper,' said Polo, pessimistically realistic. His leg felt a little better for not having walked on it most of the day, but he knew that if he did not get medical attention for it soon he was going to lose it. Or maybe worse; but he tried not to think about dying. He would not have bet on their chances of getting out of Palembang, but so long as there was some hope, no matter how skinny, of getting back to Vi and the kids, he'd keep going.

'I think we could do with a couple of porters,' said Garrick. Now that danger lay so close ahead of them he was becoming a little light-headed he giggled nervously as he pointed to the transmitter, the batteries and his suitcase.

'I'm afraid you're going to have to leave something behind,' said Maynard, and said no more because he wanted the boy himself to make the sacrifice.

For a moment Garrick did not catch the point of what Maynard meant. Then he shook his head furiously, almost crying as he said, 'No, I'm not leaving *that*! I've lugged it all this way—this far——'

'It'll be a bloody pity,' said Polo.

'I know,' said Maynard gently. 'But what's worth more right now? The transmitter or the money?'

Garrick looked at Case, who was still watching the front of the train for the possible return of the Japanese soldiers. 'Jack, don't let them make me leave it! It's not just that it's money——' He could see his dream, the only source of strength that had kept him plodding on for mile after mile over these last few days, fading away like the steam of the train. The dream had begun to have various shapes, not always Tahiti, but sometimes London, Darwin, even Leeds; but always with the sun shining and food growing on bushes like flowers. Yesterday he had walked for a whole hour not conscious at all of the others or of the country through which they were tramping; he had woken from the dream sweating and frightened that perhaps he was going out of his head. While the others had been brushing aside branches and leaves, he had been walking through women's hair that swept across his face with a perfume that had made him reel; the others had climbed through long lalang grass, but he had waded uphill through a green sea in which fish swam against his legs and coral had glowed like frozen fire. He had not even felt the weight of his suitcase, it had been as light on his shoulders as his own head. 'Jack, you know why I have to keep it! Don't let them make me throw it away!'

Case looked at Maynard, but it was impossible to see the Englishman's face in the darkness here between the buildings. But Maynard hadn't sounded harsh and unreasonable. 'I don't think anyone's gonna make you do anything, Reg. But like the skipper says, how much is the dough worth to you right now? You got just a load of old paper there.'

'I thought you'd be on my side,' Garrick said accusingly.

'For Christ's sake, stop choosing sides! All along the goddam way it's been *your* side or *my* side——' Suddenly he stopped, reached out a hand and squeezed Garrick's arm.

'I'm sorry, Reg. I take that back. But you gotta decide for yourself what you're gonna do with that suitcase.'

'Once we get to Java,' said Elisabeth, 'we shall need the radio to get in touch with Darwin again. Your money won't send any messages.'

'It's all right for you,' said Garrick, his arm clutching his suitcase, sounding frighteningly young now. He's going to be no use at all to us, Maynard thought; and began to despair. 'You've always had money to do what you wanted——'

'I don't know how much you have in your suitcase,' Elisabeth said, 'but I'll buy it from you.'

'What with?' said Garrick with a schoolboy's cunning logic. 'A cheque on a bank here in Palembang?'

Elisabeth said nothing, aware again of her poverty and still not able to comprehend it. But Case said, 'Elisabeth is poorer than you, Reg. She's dead broke.'

'So shall I be if I throw this away,' said Garrick doggedly.

'You may be broke, but you can always go home. Even Leeds must be better than no home at all.'

'She can come back here after the war.' Garrick's voice was only a young boy's now, almost on the verge of weeping: he knew he had lost his argument.

'We're not even out of here yet,' said Maynard, his tone still not unkind. 'It's a little early to start talking about coming back.'

Garrick sat shaking his head, his arm still clutching his suitcase as if it were some dead pet. Exhaustion and hunger had hollowed him out till he felt that he was transparent, that even in the darkness the others could see through him and recognise the selfishness in him. But he was past being ashamed of what he felt; he knew the dream was the only strength he had left. He sat in silence, staring sullenly into the darkness. In the past he had been able to unburden himself of any problem just by talking; whatever it was that had worried him had flowed out of him with the words. It had not *solved* the problems, but somehow they had become unimportant; or perhaps *he* had become unimportant, he was not sure which, and whatever might have happened would not have mattered. But now his tongue was like rope in his mouth, dry and twisted, and he knew this was one problem that would not go away, would be solved neither by talking nor by silence. It would only be solved by downright Yorkshire commonsense, something his father had tried to teach him as he had tried to teach him to bowl an inswinger or play a cover drive. Charlie Garrick had failed on the last two points, but now, almost too late but just in time, the lesson of common-sense was learned.

'I'm not giving it to any Wog,' he said, staring resentfully through the darkness at Kamar. He had never had any colour prejudice, but now his mother and father were warring with each other in the shell of himself; his father, like George Lansbury, had believed in brotherly love, even of Lancastrians, but his mother had had no time for darkies, even the cricketing Indian princes such as Duleepsinjhi.

'No offence taken,' said Kamar before anyone could apologise to him. 'But if we sit here all night talking, captain——' He gestured in the darkness, threw in another of his minced clichés: 'All talk and no play, you know.'

'All right,' said Maynard, eager himself to be on the move now; he wanted no more time to think to become despairing. Now they were so close to their target, he had begun to realise how slim their chances were of succeeding. But it was too late to retreat. At Sandhurst he had always got high marks for his attack tactics, but he had been hopeless when he had come to planning a rearguard action. Yet that was all he had been doing for the two years of the war, though not always with success. If he had planned a decent rearguard action out of Dixmude, perhaps the Germans would not have captured him. He stood up, saw that the Japanese soldiers had now disappeared from the head of the train, then dropped over the side of the wagon and down beside the track. 'Come on, move!'

Garrick was the last to get out of the wagon. He sat looking at his suitcase till Maynard spoke sharply to him again; then suddenly he began to move. He ripped up the sheets of raw rubber, throwing them aside; then he almost reverently lowered the suitcase into the hollow he had created and covered it with the rubber sheets. Then he stood up, stood for a moment looking down at the burial spot, then quickly turned away and dropped down over the side of the wagon. Without a word he picked up the transmitter and slung it across his back.

Maynard was saying, 'We can't make any rendezvous time, but we'll give you an hour to find Lee Chin and get the boat. From then on you'll have to wait on us. As soon as you see the first tank go up, come up-river to the oil depot's

195

jetty. If we're not there when you get there, don't hang around. You'd better head down-river, make for Java—and good luck.'

Case shook hands with Polo. 'How's the leg?'

It was remarkable that Polo could even stand up. Burdened with his rifle and the string bag containing the batteries, he seemed staked like a limp straggly bush on his crutch. 'She'll do. You just look after yourself, sport. If things get too chancey, chuck in the towel and start running.'

'I'll practise my footwork on the way in there,' said Case, and turned to Garrick. 'Good luck, Reg. If we don't meet up after this, give my regards to Tahiti.'

Garrick was unsmiling; all his humour seemed to have drained out of him with his strength. He just nodded, put a handful of thin bones in Case's grip. 'Good luck, Jack.'

Case stared at the dark shape of the boy in the shadows, then he turned away and said good-bye to Elisabeth. Their fingers met in the darkness, formally at first, then with intimacy; they said good-bye by touch, with fingers stiff with a sadness that neither of them could have expressed in words. Words, in any event, would only have made them formal again.

Then Elisabeth, Polo and Garrick left the train, disappeared into the shadows and began to head for the river. Elisabeth was in a section of Palembang that she had never visited before; it was as unknown to her as the poorer districts of Rotterdam or Amsterdam. But she knew the way the Musi River curved through the city and she knew that the Chinese, as they always did in the kampongs and towns of Sumatra, lived together in the one quarter. Lee Chin, Darwin had said, could be found in the Chinese shopping centre in the water-street of rafts near the main bridge.

The last time she had been in Palembang she and her father had been guests at a dinner in honour of the Governor-General, who had come up from Batavia. That had been six months ago and the talk had been of what was happening in Holland now the Nazis had taken over, not what might happen here. She came out from the shadow of the rubber mills, tramped her way through a large pile of evil-smelling rubbish, and wondered how many of those who had been at the dinner were still alive. It was a measure of her growing acceptance of the utter defeat here in the Indies that she could not see any of them still living. The guests, some of them girlhood friends, were as remote in her memory as characters seen in some old, half-forgotten film. Her old life had already begun to assume the shape of fantasy.

They were moving down a narrow alley, no more than six feet wide, that ran down towards the river. Tiny huts, cells of bamboo, lined each side of the alley, their crudely-hung doors closed tight against the rats that slid like grey fish among the glistening heaps of rubbish. Then a door opened and an old man stood there outlined against the glow of a lamp behind him. Elisabeth, Polo and Garrick pulled up sharply, but the old man just looked at them with dull indifference, then closed the door again. He was too old, curiosity having gone dead in him like his sex, to wonder at the sight of a white girl and two white men here in this back alley at this time of night and with the Japanese in possession of the city. The war, Elisabeth thought, hasn't touched *everybody*.

Then they had come out of the last of a series of alleys and the river lay below them. The bank below them shone and glittered like dew-wet flowers in the brightness of the moon; but it was a garden of decaying rubbish among which goats, like obscene caricatures of fawns, picked their whining, complaining way. On the river itself small boats stitched the moonlight into patterns and a large sampan, gliding by with the dignity of a black swan, went down-river on the ebbing tide. The smell coming up from the refuse on the bank made Garrick heave and he clapped a hand hurriedly over his mouth.

'I wouldn't go for the chunda, sport,' said Polo, keeping a careful eye on him.

Garrick looked at him blankly. 'Chunda?'

Polo mimed a vomiting motion. 'Hang on to it, mate. You ain't got much left in you. You can't afford to start heaving it away.' He grinned, a horrible grimace that seemed to peel the last of the flesh away from his moonlight-green skull. 'We're almost there. Right, love?'

'Yes,' said Elisabeth. 'There are the river stalls.'

She nodded along towards where the stalls, built on bamboo rafts, were moored below an embankment on which were perched a line of wooden huts that suggested the flimsy walls of the city. Lamps burned brightly on the stalls and people moved like milling birds against their glow.

'Looks a bit busy,' Polo said. 'Maybe we better wait till closing time.'

'We can't,' Elisabeth said. 'We don't know how soon Mr. Case and Captain Maynard might get into the refinery.'

'What are you going to do about the Japs, then?' said Garrick, and pointed to the half a dozen Japanese soldiers moving casually, like gawking tourists, among the stalls.

2

'This is a very old city,' said Kamar, leading Case and Maynard at a run, like a headlong guide, through a maze of alleys beside the railway tracks. 'We had a university here before anyone had heard of Oxford or Cambridge.'

'How about Texas State?' said Case; and felt an unexpected relief and warmth when, in the moonlight, he saw Maynard smile. The two men had not spoken to each other since they had left the rubber train, trotting along behind Kamar like strangers caught up in the same guided tour. Kamar had been flinging bits of information over his shoulder as he ran, all at once garrulous again, as if fear loosened his tongue like drink. But Maynard had said nothing, running with the dogged strained look of a marathon runner, and Case had begun to despair. If he was going to die within the next half hour or so, he did not want to die beside a man who hated him, who was only using him to do a job that he himself could not do. If life had to end, it had to end better than that. Otherwise he might just as well have died on that garbage dump outside San Francisco, consigning himself to the flames along with the scrapbook of another life that was already dead then.

Maynard, for his part, had been silent, not because of any feeling he still had against Case, but because he was worried about what lay ahead of them. He did not like going into anything for which he could not plan, and he could not plan this attack because he knew nothing of the lay-out of the refinery. Guerrilla tactics had not been taught at Sandhurst in his time, but this was not even guerrilla warfare. This was fighting blindfolded.

Kamar led them out from the alleys and now they were in the railway yards. A delta of tracks spread out, silver in the moonlight, and wagons and ancient carriages stood in the yards like moored, ungainly ships. They moved swiftly down through the shadows of the wagons, stopping once to hide between two wagons as an engine, rickety and asthmatic, came panting by them.

Maynard looked at Kamar. 'Where does this friend of yours, Ahmat, have his office?'

Kamar nodded across towards the far side of the yards where stood a long low corrugated-iron shed. 'That is the goods shed. He has a small office at the other end.'

Maynard looked at him. 'For a man working on an up-country estate, you seem to know an awful lot about this part of the world.'

Kamar shrugged, smiling blandly. 'When you are smuggling, captain, you need transport. And where is one of the best places to find transport?' He spread an expressive hand towards the railway yards.

'Don't let's look a gift horse in the mouth,' Case said to Maynard. 'He could have been a piccolo player or a card sharp. Where would he have led us then?'

Maynard nodded, and again Case felt the lessening of the antagonism between them and felt better for it. He hitched the automatic carbine farther up on his shoulder and followed the other two men as they began to cross the tracks, running swiftly from shadow to shadow. Then they were in the shadow of the goods shed itself, pressing themselves hard against the cold tin of its walls as they saw the Japanese guard come out of the open doors farther along. The guard stood looking about him, for one moment staring hard down towards where Case and the others were doing their best to make themselves invisible. Then he moved out of the oblong of light thrown from the doorway and into the shadows. A moment later there was the flare of a match, then the tiny glow of a cigarette.

'What now?' Case whispered.

'I'll see if there's another way in. Stay here.' Maynard slipped away, moving through the shadows with the silence of another shadow. He was back in a couple of minutes. 'The other entrance is guarded. Two Nips there. It's got to be this chap.'

'He'll see us before we get within thirty feet of him,' Case said.

He could feel the heat coming out of Kamar as the Javanese huddled close to him, imagined he could smell the sweat of fear on him. He was sweating himself, yet his lips and mouth were as dry as when they had been crossing the plain just before Sinjambi. Part of his mind welcomed the presence of the Japanese: if they couldn't get past them, then there would be nothing to do but turn back and forget all about blowing the oil tanks. Then he remembered Elisabeth, Polo and Garrick. They were probably out on the river somewhere now, waiting for the first explosion of flame from the refinery. The longer they had to wait there, the more they would be in danger.

He looked around, straining his eyes, then saw the water tower, its long thick hose hanging like a dead elephant's trunk, on the other side of half a dozen wagons parked opposite the shed doors. He touched Maynard's arm and nodded towards the tower.

'Let's see if he's curious.'

They left Kamar in the shadow of the goods shed, darted quickly across the narrow open space towards the wagons and came up behind them and beneath the water tower. Case slung his carbine over his back, put his foot on the iron ladder that hung down the side of the tower, and began gingerly to climb towards the platform thirty feet above him. As he came up over the level of the wagons he glanced across towards the shed; the guard was still there in the shadows beside the doorway, his cigarette glowing like an angry watchful eye. Case paused, flattening himself against the ladder.

Then he began climbing again. The ladder creaked, a cold metallic sound that seemed to go right through Case's blood, freezing it. He stiffened, not turning his head, only his eyes, waiting for the Japanese to come out of the shadows and challenge him. He saw the cigarette go out, a narrowed suspicious eye now, and he poised, ready to jump down behind the wagon as the Japanese came running towards him. Then the cigarette glowed again and, straining his eyes, he imagined he saw the guard relax and lean back against the wall of the shed.

Slowly, moving his arms and legs like a man crippled by arthritis, he worked his way up the ladder. Every time a rung creaked beneath his foot it was like a sharp crack in his ears; he could not understand why the Japanese did not come out into the open and shoot him down. Then he was only a rung or two from the platform on which the water tank stood. He reached up, put his hand over the edge of the platform and felt something cold and slimy slide out from under his fingers as he lost his grip and swung back on the ladder. He saw the frog, like a small stone, plummet past him as he hung, like an exhibitionist trapeze artist, out from the ladder. Then he had swung himself up on the platform, reckless now of how much noise he made, and lay flat and breathless on the wet planks.

He waited till he had got his breath back, then cautiously stood up. Pressed hard against the cold wet iron of the tank, his shoes slipping occasionally on the wet platform, he inched his way round towards the thick pipe that hung out above the tracks and from which the rubber hose drooped, its mouth dripping water into a pool below. He reached the pipe, paused and looked down towards the shed. The guard had finished his cigarette, come out of the shadows and now stood with his back to the yards, looking into the shed through the open doorway. Case reached far out hoping the pipe would support him as he leant on it, and grabbed the chain that worked the valve on the pipe. Then he backed slowly round the curve of the tank, looked down and saw Maynard's hand come up in a gesture of acknowledgement. Then he jerked on the chain.

Water vomited out of the hose, then abruptly cut off as Case eased his pull on the chain. Round the curves of the tank he saw the Japanese guard turn in the doorway and look across the wagons at the water tank. Again he jerked on the chain; there was another cascade of water. The guard looked around him, as if looking for some support, then he began to move towards the wagons. He came round the end of the line of them as Case jerked on the chain for the third time.

The Japanese jumped aside as water splashed at him. He was off-balance when Maynard hit him with his knife; he went down with no more noise than a short gasp of shock. Then Case had swung hurriedly down the ladder and helped Maynard drag the dead guard under one of the wagons. Maynard wiped the blood from his knife on the man's trousers and stood up.

'Number one,' he said, and he looked uncertainly at Case. 'Let's hope we don't have to do this all the way into the refinery.'

Some of the Japanese's blood was on Case's hand. He wiped it on his trousers and said, 'So long as you use the knife, I'll put up with it.'

'I didn't mean it that way,' said Maynard; and Case all at once realised that it was the other man, and not himself, who was on the defensive.

They went back and rejoined Kamar, who had moved up into the shadows beside the doorway. 'Ahmat is in his office,' he told them. 'You can see from here.'

Maynard risked a peep round the edge of the doorway. The shed, perhaps a hundred yards long, was piled with stacks of freight all down its length. Half a dozen low-wattage globes hung like weak stars in the gloom beneath the roof, where bats drifted like paper ash among the girders. At the far end of the shed was a small glassed-in office. A man sat beneath another dim globe, his head bent over as he worked at a desk. A dozen or so workmen squatted in one corner of the shed behind some big packing cases, eating their evening meal. There was no sign of any Japanese guards inside the shed.

Maynard jerked his head, and the three men slipped round the edge of the doorway and into the shed. Crouched over, they made their way down one side, keeping the stacks of freight between themselves and the workmen. The freight itself was almost an inventory of what a rural country like Sumatra could produce: timber, great piles of fruit, stacks of rubber, crates of chicken, even half a dozen goats bleating like distressed commuters at being kept waiting. There were also a dozen or more bundles of rags lying among the packing cases. Maynard had passed three or four of them before he realised they were humans, the flotsam of Palembang who had crawled in here to escape the night rain which was already beginning to fall in heavy steady drops on the tin roof. The Japanese guards must have known the beggars were here, but had turned a blind eye to them. They would probably know, even more than Maynard himself had learned in his short time out here, that in the East misery was a flood you could not hold back. His hatred of the Japanese was such that he found it incredible that they might possess pity.

By the time they had reached the far end of the shed and were only a few yards short of the office, the rain was pelting down, turning the shed into a great reverberating drum. Maynard stopped behind a pile of rubber and looked anxiously at the closed doors at this end of the shed. Where were the two Japanese guards he had seen? When were they going to push back the sliding doors and come in out of the rain? He held Case and Kamar back, waiting; but the doors remained closed, there was no sign of the guards. Only half-satisfied that they must have found shelter somewhere outside the shed, but knowing he could not waste any more time, he moved quickly towards the office door, opened it and stepped inside.

The man at the desk looked up, his mouth falling open as he saw the European officer covering him with a pistol. A gold tooth gleamed for a moment before Maynard found the light switch and turned it off; then the office was lit only by the dim glow from the lights in the shed itself. Case and Kamar came quickly into the office, closing the door behind them.

'Do you speak English, Ahmat?' Maynard said.

Ahmat nodded, his mouth still hanging open as if his jaw was too heavy to lift. He was thin, balding, middle-aged and looked as if responsibility was something of which he was afraid; he had been promoted despite himself, the sort of competent man whom his superiors knew they could trust because he had no ambitions. He looked now as if he wished his superiors, Japanese or Dutch, anyone at all, were here instead of him. He found his voice, croaked in a thin falsetto, 'What are you doing here? What do you want?' He looked at Kamar, cleared his throat, said in a deeper, but still querulous, voice, his accent guttural as if he had learned English from a Dutchman, 'Why did you bring them here? The Japanese will kill us all.'

The rain was pounding on the roof; the shed seemed that it must burst its walls with the thunder it contained. Kamar had to raise his voice: 'They made me bring them.'

Maynard snapped his head round. 'You bloody liar! You volunteered——'

'Don't argue with him.' Case was watching the workmen in the far corner of the shed. They had finished their supper and were congregated in a tight circle, bent over some sort of game. 'Ask this guy about the oil trains.'

'What trains?' Ahmat stood up, looked wildly from one white man to the other. There was a small bamboo cage on his desk and in it a tiny green bird was fluttering nervously, hitting its wings against the bamboo strips. He put out a hand and patted the cage, trying to soothe the bird. But there was no one to soothe him, he was more terrified than the bird. 'You are not going to wreck the train?'

'Not the trains,' Maynard said. 'We want to get into the oil refinery. Is there a train in there tonight? Can you smuggle us in on it?'

Ahmat shook his head wildly, his eyes white with fear; beneath his hand the bird had begun to fling itself against the cage bars. 'No, no!' He shouted to make himself heard above the pelting of the rain; Case looked towards the workmen, but they were still intent on their game. 'You cannot ask me! The Japanese would kill me!'

'They wouldn't know.' The noise in the shed, the fluttering bird, the frightened Ahmat, all were getting on Maynard's nerves. 'All you have to do is tell us where to find the train, what time it's going down to the refinery——'

Ahmat stared at him a moment, then he swallowed. 'They're not my responsibility, not the oil trains. They cannot blame me. There is one going in in twenty minutes—empty——' He looked at Kamar, raised a hand that was trembling as much as the bird in the cage. 'You will not tell them what I've done? You brought these men here, not me——'

'Tell who?' Case turned away from the window, looked hard at Kamar. 'Tell the Japs?'

Kamar said nothing, his face suddenly set in stiff, hard planes. He stared impassively at Ahmat as the latter said, 'No, not the Japanese. The PNI, the Communists. Didn't you know?' Ahmat saw the surprised looks on the faces of Case and Maynard. 'He is one of their leaders. He used to lead strikes against the railways.'

'So that's how you knew Ahmat,' Case said. 'I don't suppose your old man ever was a smuggler.'

'He was a smuggler,' said Kamar, unsmiling. 'But not a bourgeois one. He smuggled men.'

'Agitators, you mean?'

'Workers for the cause,' Kamar corrected, not mangling his cliché this time.

'It doesn't matter,' Maynard snapped. 'Where do we find the oil train?'

'Go to the end of the yards, near the signal box.' Now that he thought they were going to leave him alone, Ahmat was only too willing to give the foreigners all the information they wanted. 'The oil tankers come in on a branch line ——' He shook his head, spoke to Kamar as if Case and Maynard were not in the office. 'But it is a pity. The refineries belong to us now. The Japanese have told us they want us to help them run Sumatra—the Hollanders will never be back——'

Kamar moved so quickly Maynard had no time to defend himself. The Javanese hit him a blow across the back of the neck and Maynard slumped across the desk, knocking the bamboo cage to the floor. Before Case could bring his carbine up to cover Kamar, the latter had grabbed Maynard's pistol.

'Drop your gun, Mr. Case! I don't want to have to shoot you.'

Case hesitated, then he clicked on the safety catch and dropped the carbine to the floor. Kamar stepped across to Maynard as the latter, still groggy, raised himself from the desk; he grabbed the Englishman's Thompson gun and slung it by its strap over his own shoulder. Ahmat still stood behind his desk, shackled by fear and shock. He said something in Malay, his voice high and quivering with near-hysteria, but Kamar determinedly shook his head.

'What's that all about?' Case was watching Kamar closely; the Javanese looked nervous enough to start shooting. 'Do us a favour—speak English.'

'Why should we do you any favours?' Kamar stepped back as Maynard slowly straightened up and turned round. The bird fluttering in panic in its cage and Kamar put a gaitered foot on the cage, tapping soothingly. But the bird continued to beat its wings wildly. 'None of you whites ever did us any favours, not in three hundred years.'

'I don't know anything about history in these parts,' Case said. 'Let's keep it just in this room——'

'Never believe history, Mr. Case. History is just the propaganda of the victors.'

'That another of your clichés?' Maynard was rubbing the back of his neck.

'No cliché, captain. Ernest Toller said that, a very great playwright. But from now on we are the ones who are going to write history.'

'Will we be expected to believe it?' Case said.

Kamar's face darkened with quick anger, but Ahmat said, 'Please get them out of here. Or are you going to hand them over to the Japanese? There is a price of four hundred guilders for each European.'

'That's more than I'm worth at home.' Case could see that Maynard was quickly recovering from the blow he had received. He could see Maynard's hand moving slowly towards the knife in his belt, and he kept talking, trying to hold Kamar's attention: 'Four hundred guilders? How much is that? A couple of hundred bucks, maybe? That's all I got for my last fight in the States. You oughta do all right with the two of us——'

'Money is not everything,' said Kamar. 'I don't want to

have to hand you over to the Japanese. I don't want to kill you. But you cannot be allowed to blow up the refineries. Not if the Japanese are going to let us govern ourselves.'

'Who said they are gonna do that?' Case said, not looking at Maynard but aware that the Englishman's hand was only inches now from his knife. The bird had suddenly stopped fluttering and Kamar took his foot off the cage.

'They will, if we co-operate with them.' Ahmat was still paralysed with fear; he waved his hands as if to try and brush the others out of his office. 'It will be a partnership ——'

'You don't believe that, do you?' Case said to Kamar. Maynard had his hand on his knife, was starting to straighten his leg, ready to leap at the Javanese.

'Time will tell, Mr. Case. But we are not part of your war with the Japanese—our war is with the Dutch—— Take your hand off that knife, captain!' He stepped back, swinging the pistol round to cover Maynard. 'You deserve to be killed for trying that!'

Then Ahmat hissed, "Jippon!' and glanced through the windows of the office towards the rear doors of the shed. Out of the corner of his eye Case saw one of the big doors sliding back. He was slightly behind Kamar, looking over the Javanese's right shoulder: he saw the door slide back, saw Kamar stiffen, saw the knife suddenly flip out of Maynard's hand towards himself. His right hand went up in a reflex action, caught the knife; later he would recall that his mind was a blank as he drove the blade hard into the back of Kamar. The Javanese let out a moan, fell forward, the knife still in his back, into the arms of Maynard, who lowered him to the floor. Maynard grabbed his pistol and gestured with it at Ahmat.

'Down!'

Ahmat dropped flat as if he had been pole-axed or had fainted. Maynard leapt across to him, put his hand over the Sumatran's mouth. Case had dropped to his hands and knees, crawled across the floor and locked the office door. He lay in the shadow of the half-door, hidden from the weak illumination of the shed's lights coming through the glass upper half of the door and walls. Maynard and Ahmat, locked together, were just a dark heap on the far side of the desk.

The rain had stopped completely now. Case, lying flat on the floor, his perception heightened again, could hear every sound in the echo chamber of the shed: the dripping of water, the bleating of the goats and clucking of chickens, the chatter of the workers as they hurriedly got up from their game, the steady tread of the Japanese guard as he came across the concrete floor towards the office. He had stopped breathing, a band tightening across his chest, and he could feel the beginning of cramp in his tautened muscles. His head was resting against the bottom of the door; it seemed that the guard's boots came to a halt only six inches from him. He felt the door shudder as the Japanese tried to push it open; then the glass panel creaked in its putty as the guard leaned his face against it to peer into the office. Case waited for the glass to be smashed in as the Japanese caught sight of Maynard and Ahmat and brought up his gun to shoot at them. He brought up his knee, poised himself to leap up and shoot the guard as soon as the glass was smashed. Across the office, beneath the desk, he saw Maynard move slightly, his hand coming up with the pistol in it. For a moment it seemed to Case that he went deaf: there was no sound at all in his ears as he waited, stretched as on a rack, for the explosion of both guns.

Then the Japanese muttered something that sounded like a curse, his boots grated on the concrete and he turned and walked away. At once Case eased himself up into a crouch, looked across at Maynard as the latter pushed Ahmat ahead of him out from behind the desk. 'What do we do with him?'

'I could be practical,' said Maynard, 'but the poor blighter hasn't done us any harm.' He looked at Ahmat in the dim light coming through the dirty windows. 'What the hell *do* we do with you? Your friend Kamar was wrong, Ahmat. I'm afraid you *are* part of our war with the Japs.'

'No, no,' Ahmat protested. 'Please—all I want is to be left alone! I have a family——'

Maynard looked at him sadly for a moment, then abruptly he lifted the pistol and clipped Ahmat behind the ear with it. The Sumatran went down without a sound, falling beside the dead Kamar. Maynard, on his knees as if at prayer, looked down at the two men with immeasurable pity.

'Poor devils,' he said. 'All they're against is the idea of empire.'

Case, whose only empire was himself, looked with surprise at the Englishman. 'I thought you were in favour of empires?'

Maynard shook his head. 'No, Case. All I said was that they did *some* good. At least one of us, the Dutch or the English, whether we meant it or not, taught Kamar the meaning of nationalism. There was no India before the English got there and there was no Indonesia before the Dutch came here.'

'Maybe that wasn't a bad thing.'

'Perhaps. But don't forget—if it hadn't been for us English there might not have been a United States of America.' He raised himself cautiously above the level of the wooden partition of the wall, looked out through the windows. 'The Jap has gone. Time we were gone, too.'

He unlocked the door, then moved quickly across to the dead Kamar, unslung the Thompson gun from the Javanese's shoulder. He stood up, still crouched over, then looked down in puzzlement as Case picked up the cage and murmured comfortingly to the bird.

'Oh, for Christ's sake, don't tell me you're a bloody bird-lover!'

Case said nothing, but, still holding the cage, stood up and stepped over Kamar. He stopped for just a moment and looked down at the dead man, the *tumbok lada*, the knife of love, still sticking out of his back. He reached down, pulled out the knife and handed it to Maynard.

'I did it that one time,' he said, his voice dry in his throat, 'but I'm not gonna make a habit of it.'

'Once was enough,' Maynard said, wiping the knife on his trousers and tucking it back in his belt. 'I gambled on you acting like a boxer. The reflex action—the counter-punch, I think you call it——'

'Did they teach you psychology at Sandhurst?'

'Nothing as subtle as that.' Maynard grinned. 'That was a ploy of my own. Shall we go?'

He stood back and let Case slip ahead of him out of the office. They went swiftly down the aisle behind the stacked freight, past the goats, the chickens and the still-sleeping beggars and out through the front doors of the shed. They swung right and began to run across the yards, moving from shadow to shadow through the long lines of parked wagons and carriages. An engine came bearing down on them and for a moment they stood confused in a maze of tracks; then they moved to one side and the engine clattered over some points and swept by right above them. They kept running, Case holding the cage delicately in front of him like a woman her vanity case, then they saw the signals looming up ahead of them like broken crucifixes, saw the engine coming round the curve of a branch line and, behind it, the unmistakable silhouettes of a long train of oil tankers.

They splashed through a large pool of water, dropped down to crouch beneath the overhang of a coal wagon as the oil train came rumbling in on the next track. They heard the brakes go on, the wheels screeching a little on the wet rails. The empty tankers clanged their buffers together, the sound going down the length of the train. Then the train had come to a halt and above them was the long cylinder of an oil tanker.

Case stepped swiftly across the space between the two sets of tracks, swung up the ladder to the top of the tanker. He lifted the lid of the opening, looped a torn and dirty handkerchief through the top of the cage and lowered it into the tanker, tying the other end of the handkerchief to the handle of the lid. He slipped off his shoe, propped open the lid with it, then swung back down the ladder.

'Okay,' he said as he rejoined Maynard under the coal wagon. 'Our best bet for getting into the refinery is *inside* one of those tankers. But we'll have to find out how bad the fumes are. If that bird lives for ten minutes, then so should we.'

'How would you like a job as an instructor at Sandhurst after the war?' Maynard said, and both men smiled at each other, all their antagonism now forgotten.

'A bum from Texas State? England would never survive it.'

3

When Case climbed back up on top of the tanker and raised the lid he could hear the bird fluttering around inside its cage. He undid the handkerchief, lifted out the cage, opened it and took out the bird. He held it for a moment, then he threw it up into the air and the bird was gone into the night. He watched it for just an instant, envying its freedom and its mindlessness; he was burdened now by his imagination, the thought of what lay ahead. He unslung his carbine, squeezed himself down through the opening into the tanker and a moment later Maynard was scrambling after him. Case reached up and pulled down the lid, propping it open once again with his shoe. The two men stood close together in the impenetrable blackness, each holding on to the rim of the opening above them. The tanker, fortunately, was one of the long shallow type and by stretching their arms they were able to reach the rim of the opening.

'Once this thing starts moving,' said Case, 'we're gonna slide all over the place. Hang on tight, but don't hang on to me. I'm ticklish.'

'You have areas of sensitivity I never suspected.' They were whispering, but their voices in the black chamber of the tanker had the hollow sound of sepulchral doom in them. 'I hope we don't have to stay in this thing too long. I'm a fresh air man myself.'

Case could feel the inch or two of oil lying in the rounded bottom of the tanker. The one shoe he wore was already full of it and the bare other foot was having trouble in retaining a grip on the tanker floor. The smell of the tanker's interior was already beginning to sicken him and he could feel revulsion welling up in his throat. He lifted the lid a little and turned his face towards the opening.

'Better not talk. And don't breathe too deeply.'

They stood silently there beneath the opening, arms raised above their heads, faces upturned, like some religious believers waiting for a vision to guide them out of the black limbo that surrounded them. Sounds came to them from outside, the hoarse shriek of an engine's whistle, the iron clangour of a moving train; but here in the tanker there was dead silence but for the occasional dull scrape as Maynard moved a booted foot out of the oil and rested it on the slope of the floor. Their arms began to ache as the blood flowed down out of them, but they had to keep their grip on the rim of the opening because they knew the train might start without any warning at all. If one of them should finish up face first in the oil in the bottom of the tanker he would be useless for the job that lay ahead of them. In a military sense they were already going in blind; it would be disastrous if one of them should be physically blinded, even if only temporarily. So they bore the ache in their stretched arms and hung on to the opening above them.

Case was concentrating on trying to breathe the air that crept down through the opening. There seemed in his mind to be an invisible battle between the rising fumes and the outside air, and the fumes were winning. He felt that his nose, his throat and his lungs were slowly filling up with oil; the sickness kept heaving up into his mouth every minute or so now. He began to appreciate his hunger, even though he was weakened by it; with no food in his stomach, the worst that could happen to him would be to dry retch. But it was little comfort, not enough to sustain him if the train did not soon begin to move.

Beside him Maynard had his eyes fixed on a star that had appeared through the breaking bundles of cloud. He concentrated on the fantasy that perhaps Ruth last night had gazed at the same star; but the thought was too much and the star disappeared behind the tears that clouded his vision. Oh God, he thought, how much love I've missed! And did not think of the physical pleasure of his wife but just of the presence of her, the kindness and comfort of her that now brought on a sadness more weakening than the rising fumes. He closed his eyes, looked into hers in memory and saw the secret beauty of her more clearly than he had ever seen it when he had been with her. Suddenly he hated the war, wanted it finished, regardless of who won it.

He turned his head in the direction of the invisible Case, was about to say 'Let's get out of here,' when the train abruptly started to move. Both men's feet slipped from under them and they swung by their arms from the opening. Oil sloshed up their shins, and a gust of fumes seemed to rush up past them. Case retched, then reached up and pushed the lid right back, grabbing his shoe before it could slide off. He tucked the shoe into the front of his shirt and went back to hanging on to the rim as the wagon began to sway a little on its bogie. The train picked up speed, though it was not moving fast, and air was scooped into the opening, pushing down the fumes. The two men stretched their necks, trying to get their faces closer to the air that, though tinged by smoke from the train's engine, seemed to them to smell so wonderfully of open spaces.

The train rattled on, but they could see nothing of what they were passing. Once the moon swung into view above them, grinning mockingly at them through a veil of thinning cloud. Then the train began to slow, crept forward, then halted.

Case tensed, tried to pull himself up through the opening; but there was not enough strength left in his arms. A gasp, almost like a whimper, burst from him and he tried again; but again he could barely lift himself off the floor of the tanker. Then he felt Maynard's mouth against his ear.

'Use me as a ladder. Just watch where you put your feet.'

Case felt with his bare foot for a hold on Maynard's flexed

leg. Then he sprang up, calling on the last of the strength in his arms. He hung for a moment, every muscle in his arms and shoulders burning, the sickness once more heaving up from his stomach into his mouth; then his head had emerged above the rim, his elbows had got a hold and he pulled himself up and lay along the top of the tanker. He vomited a dribble of thick spittle and lay gasping, his whole body trembling as if he might shake himself off the rounded top of the tanker. Determinedly he steadied himself, gingerly swung himself round and looked down into the opening.

'We're inside! But make it quick!'

It was much more difficult for Maynard to get out of the tanker. The opening was narrow and there was barely room for Case to get a grip on the other man. It seemed to Case that, perched on top of the tanker, it was impossible that he could not be spotted at once by the Japanese guards. But the moon had gone behind clouds again and here in the refinery the Japanese were enforcing a strict blackout. The two men struggled, expecting any moment to be challenged or shot at, but luck was with them. At last, spent and breathless, Maynard swung himself up out of the opening and slid down the slope of the tanker, only saving himself from tumbling headlong to the ground by grabbing at the rungs of the tanker's narrow ladder. Case slipped down after him and in a moment both men were on the ground, leaning against the platform of the tanker and gulping in the night air. They could hear shouting voices up at the head of the train, but for the moment they were heedless of their danger. There was no strength in their trembling legs, no breath in their aching, sickened chests. They were utterly spent and if the Japanese had come down the track at that moment neither man would have resisted.

Then Case reached down, wiped the oil from his bare foot and slipped on his shoe. He emptied the oil from his other shoe, then put it back on. Both shoes felt as if they might slide off his feet at any second, but he would have to risk that. He was not going to run around in here barefooted.

They ducked under the buffers of the tanker, came out on the other side of the track opposite a row of low sheds. The moon appeared again, and along to their right they saw the camouflaged oil tanks, their brown and green paint glistening dully from the night's rain. Beyond them was the refinery plant itself, tall towers and a spaghetti-mess of pipes coiled endlessly through a chiaroscuro of shadows and camouflage paint. Steam blew out of valves, something pounded like a gigantically magnified pulse; but there was no sign of any human activity. In the pale green moonlight the oil depot looked unreal, a city of the future with man already dead.

'We're gonna need a wrench,' Case muttered. 'We gotta find a tool shed.'

They inspected the sheds in front of them, moving from shadow to shadow with the ease of men who had quickly learned their own best camouflage. They could see figures at both ends of the oil train, but the men, whoever they were, Japanese or Sumatrans, were not looking for saboteurs: once again Maynard thanked Providence for the careless complacency that easy victory could give to the enemy.

The door to each shed was a wooden one, bolted by a rusted padlock. In each case it took Case only two or three minutes to prise away the plate of the padlock with his parang, open the door and take a quick look into the shed. The third shed was the one they were looking for; Case stepped into the dark interior and at once fell over a stack of crowbars. He blundered around in the darkness while Maynard stood outside in the shadows keeping a watchful eye on both ends of the train and wondering why he had volunteered for this foolhardy job.

All his training had been based upon the principle of preparedness. That the means of preparedness, as he had learned within a week of meeting the German Panzers, were twenty-five years out of date did not matter. It was the psychological prop of *feeling* prepared that counted. No professional should ever have allowed himself to be talked into taking on a job as unplanned and unpredictable as this one. He was even more rash than the missionaries, his father's heroes, who, prepared only with a bible and an umbrella, had gone out to win the savages for Christ and the Empire. At least they had had faith.

Case came out of the shed with a large wrench. 'This will do. Let's go.'

They began to move towards the line of squat tanks, each sunk in its own shallow moat. Case could feel his oily feet slipping uncomfortably up and down in his mocassins; with every step he took his shoes threatened to slide off. The air had turned steamy after the rain and he could feel the sweat soaking his shirt and the inside of his trouser-legs. During the day he had developed a rash on his legs and in his armpits and the sweat was making it prickle like a nettle sting.

He was hungry, weak and uncomfortable, and his stomach was still queasy from the smell of the oil fumes; if he had ever felt like this in his fighting days, he would have thrown in the towel before the first bell went. He felt no confidence at all about the job that lay ahead of them, indeed was pessimistic and apprehensive. He glanced sideways at Maynard and, unaware of the latter's own anxiety, cursed him silently. The Englishman, and the others, had cracked open his isolation and dragged him headlong into this crazy, hopeless act of sabotage. I should never have left home, he thought. But the thought was doubly bitter in his mind: there was no home.

Maynard stopped suddenly, putting an arm across in front of Case, who pulled up in mid-stride, his left shoe slipping off his foot into a pool of water. They had halted in the shadow on a low tower that carried pipes across the road that ran beside the line of tanks. Case, bending cautiously down to find his shoe and slip it on again, saw the Japanese guard come out from between two of the tanks, look up and down the road, then turn and walk down towards the end of the compound.

Maynard whispered, 'The jetty's down there. You can see the river.'

Case saw the high wire fence, a long silver cobweb in the moonlight, and beyond it the silhouette of two ships riding at anchor out on the broad, moon-streaked sweep of the river. Somewhere out there were Elisabeth, Polo and Garrick. He hoped . . .

He moved quickly out from under the shadow of the tower, crossed the road on the run and slid down into the moat of the nearest tank. He lay flat on the sloping side of the moat, in the shadow of the tank, and waited for Maynard to follow him. But the Englishman did not appear. He was about to raise his head above the rim of the moat when Maynard came over it in a rush, sliding down to land heavily on his back. Case looked at him curiously, but Maynard shook his head, got to his feet and, crouched over, ran quickly across behind the tank. Case followed him.

'The Jap came back,' Maynard whispered. 'There's another one down by the far tank.'

Case nodded pessimistically. He looked up at the wall of steel looming over them, then began to edge his way round the huge circular tank, Maynard keeping close behind him. It occurred to the latter that he was now the junior man, the other rank in this two-man army; he did not resent it, because Case so far had not attempted any retaliatory show of authority, but he smiled inwardly at the irony of it. Case himself was oblivious to the reversal of their roles.

He stopped by a large pipe that ran out of the bottom of the tank, across the moat and disappeared towards the next tank. He patted the valve-cock, a wheel about six inches in diameter mounted on a vertical spindle about three feet high. 'All these tanks are connected and they can run oil from one tank to another. This here controls the flow.' He took hold of the wheel, tried to turn it. 'Give me a hand. But don't turn it all the way.'

The two men struggled with the wheel, but it was stuck fast with rust. 'Someone around here ain't been doing his maintenance.'

Maynard said nothing, but he was conscious of a new air about Case. The American looked more purposeful than at any time since Maynard had met him; it was as if he had returned to a job he once used to enjoy, in which he had taken pride. Maynard wondered how purposeful he had been in his job as a boxer, but that was a question he might never get to ask the American.

They froze, hands together on the wheel like two men posing for a photograph of a heartfelt reunion, and stared across at the Japanese guard as, rifle slung across his back, he came round the rim of the moat. The squat hunched figure stood there staring down towards the river, a young boy dreaming of Hiroshima and home; then he began to saunter on, whistling softly and sadly. Case and Maynard strained again on the wheel.

Abruptly it gave; Case quickly whipped it back. Then he picked up the wrench he had put down, crouched beside the large circular plate that covered the valve itself. He fitted the wrench over one of the bolts holding the plate in place, began to loosen it. Maynard watched him, once again remarking how competent and purposeful Case looked. The hands that had chopped at a hundred chins, some of them famous, seemed just as familiar with the wrench. The last bolt was removed, Case prised off the plate and stood up.

'When you open that cock, the oil should shoot out of here about thirty or forty yards. Don't get in its way or you'll go with it—it's got the pressure of that whole tank behind it. I'm going down to the end tank. When you hear me whistle, I'll whistle twice, open the cock and toss your grenade into it. Then get the hell down to the jetty because from then on it's gonna be pretty hot around here.'

Maynard took one of the grenades from his belt, held it out. 'Here's yours. I'll see you down at the jetty. And if I don't—well, good luck. You're not all bastard, Jack.' It was the first time he had used the other's first name.

'You're not all sonofabitch.'

The two men grinned, then Case turned swiftly, as afraid of sentiment as the Englishman, ran across the moat, up the slope and across the intervening space and down into the moat of the next tank, running crouched down behind the connecting pipe all the way. Twice he had to fall flat in the moat as he saw a Japanese guard, once landing in a pool of mixed oil and water and almost choking as it splashed up into his open mouth; but at last he had made the end tank, crawling on hands and knees along the length of the pipe across the moonlit moat. He stood up, trembling a little now. Sweat was oozing out of every pore of him and he was having trouble focusing his eyes. Exhaustion and hunger were at last calling their payment on him.

He leaned against the pipe and looked down towards the river. If there was no gate at that end of the compound, he would never have the strength to climb the wire fence. Christ, he thought, it's all so goddam useless! He saw the guard come out from between two tanks farther back along the line, and he straightened up, took a step out into the moonlight, feeling relief run through him like a fever as he went to call out to the Japanese, to give himself up.

Instead he let out a sharp gasp of pain. As he took the step his foot had slipped out of his shoe and he had trodden on a sharp pebble. He flinched, bent down for his shoe, and in that moment reason came back. By the time he had straightened up again he knew he could never surrender. In a split moment he had committed himself totally to this act of sabotage, to the war.

He stepped quickly back into the shadows. He grabbed the valve wheel almost savagely, as if some sort of anger had now taken hold of him, turned it, then quickly shut it off. He put down his carbine, fitted the wrench over the first of the bolts on the plate and began to loosen it. Out of the corner of his eye he could see the guard still standing down the road. He strained on the bolt, felt it give and quickly he unscrewed it. Down the road he heard the guard begin to whistle again and he stopped, watching the young Japanese as the latter suddenly began to dance slowly up and down the road. Case watched in amazement as the guard, still dreaming of home, moved in slow motion through some intricate steps, bowing to an invisible partner, then gliding away, like a performer at the end of his act, into the shadows between the tanks. Case shook his head and went back to work on the other bolts.

The last one was badly rusted. Case strained on the wrench, but the bolt would not budge. He cursed it, the sound bubbling out of him almost like a whimper. His hollow arms ached with the effort of trying to shift the bolt; the sweat blinded him and stung his already sore eyes. Abruptly he stopped levering the wrench, ripped off his shirt and wrapped it round the wrench, giving it a rough padded handle. Then he picked up the carbine and using the stock as a hammer began to thump the wrench.

As soon as he hit the wrench he heard the sound quiver past him down the empty pipe. He turned his head quickly, every nerve strained, imagining he could *see* the sound dying away along the pipe. He waited for the guard to emerge again from between the tanks, but there was no sign of him. Perhaps he was still dancing.

Case thumped the wrench again, felt his stomach contract as the pipe vibrated against his legs as he leaned on it. The sound went thrumming across the moat, dying quickly away but still lingering like a long drawn-out flat note in Case's ear. The bolt had not moved and he hit the wrench a third time, harder this time. The sound seemed to ring out like a cracked bell note and Case, head turned, following the diminishing sound as he might have a disappearing bird, saw the guard come out now from between the tanks and look curiously up the road.

Case stood stock still, the carbine now pointed down the road towards the guard. The latter stood a further moment looking up the road, then he turned and slowly began to stroll down towards the opposite end of the line of tanks. Case hit the wrench again, harder still. The sound seemed to boom away down the pipe and Case saw the Japanese stop and look back. Then he had turned and was coming up the road, unslinging his rifle.

Desperately, careless now of any noise, Case hammered at the wrench. He knew the guard, running up the road, would not fire at him for fear of an explosion. He thumped at the wrench with the stock of the carbine, cursing loudly. The sound boomed along the pipe, great hollow flat notes. Then suddenly the bolt gave. The wrench slipped off, Case grabbed it, whipped it back on the bolt and spun it furiously. The bolt fell out, the plate slipped to the ground with a loud clang, and Case wrenched at the wheel.

The oil shot out in a great jet just as the guard came down the bank of the moat. It hit him and sent him sprawling. Case, both shoes slipping off his feet as he took his first steps, grabbed up his shirt and raced across the moat and up on to the road. He let out two piercing whistles, pulled out the pin of his grenade and tossed it as far as he could towards the end of the jetting rush of oil. Then he started running as fast as he could down towards the wire fence and the jetty. He felt the explosion go off behind him. He was sent sprawling as the whole night turned red around him. He felt the heat sear over him, all the sweat on him gone in an instant; then he was on his feet again, running away from the roaring blaze behind him. He ran over stones and gravel, but his fleeing feet felt nothing. He heard another explosion and another, but he did not look back. Night had abruptly fled and he was running through bright red daylight. In his jagged vision he could see Japanese appearing, but they were running around aimlessly, not seeming to know what to do. A siren was wailing somewhere, but it sounded more like a cry of helpless despair than a warning. Case could feel his heart pounding, his mouth was open gasping for air, his legs felt as brittle as burnt sticks; but somehow he still kept running. He saw the gate in the fence leading to the jetty, was only thirty yards from it, when the two Japanese came running up the jetty towards him.

He did not stop running. He brought up the carbine and fired through the wire of the fence, saw both Japanese go down in tumbling heaps. He reached the gate, wrenched it open and went running down the jetty, leaping over the dead guards. He had reached the end of the jetty before he could pull himself up; it was as if his legs had wanted to carry him right off the end of it into the river. He stopped, looked around, then began to yell at the top of his voice, 'Polo! Polo!'

But there was no sign of Polo or the others with their boat. He looked back towards the compound, saw the desperately running figure of Maynard come through the gate. Behind him flames were leaping at the moon; a great cloud of smoke billowed up and the moon was devoured. The end tank had already buckled with the heat of its own fire; even as

Case watched it, it folded in like a deflated rubber toy. There was a thunderous roar as another tank exploded. A tempest of flame and smoke blew upwards; the whole scene seemed to jump like a badly-sprocketed movie. The air itself seemed to turn to fire in Case's lungs and he turned his face away, gasping like a dying man.

And saw the boat, a large launch, coming across the river, Elisabeth standing in the bow of it.

4

'We want our bloody heads read,' said Polo. 'But somehow, now, I don't mind.'

Maynard said, 'A poet named Dryden once wrote, *There's a pleasure sure in being mad/That none but madmen know.*'

'We'll have a ball then,' said Case. 'We're gonna have plenty of time and opportunity.'

'All the way to Timor.' Garrick shook his head, but not dolefully, only with a sort of wonder at their optimism. 'But we'll make it.'

'Of course,' said Elisabeth. 'Is not the worst behind us now?'

They were well down river, already beginning to sense the open sea ahead of them. The sky above them was clear, the stars so bright that they lent some sort of perspective to infinity; only when they looked back could they see the black cloud, solid as a mountain against the peeping eye of the moon. The base of the cloud was red, the glow every now and again widening for an instant as if there had been another explosion. They were beyond any sound now, but each in his mind's eye could see the inferno that had once been the refinery. The crazy, hopeless task had been done and done well.

Garrick patted the transceiver on the seat beside him. 'Lee Chin gave us some extra valves, just in case.'

'Did you have any trouble getting to him?' Maynard asked.

'None at all,' said Polo, sitting by the tiller, his bad leg stuck out in front of him and, amazingly, giving him no pain now. He knew it would be hurting again in the morning, but tomorrow could look after itself. The Chinaman, a fussy little old bloke, had given them the boat, food and medicine —and hope. He had told them he had already got six Dutchmen away, that he had heard on his wireless that they were now safe in Australia. With the same amount of luck, they could achieve the same. A Chinaman's luck, he had told them with a boy's smile, incongruous on the wizened yellow face, was not necessarily always bad. 'No trouble at all. We just had to show a bit of patience, that was all. Ran into some Nips, but we sat on our behind and waited till they had gone.'

'In the middle of a rubbish dump,' Elisabeth said. 'Surrounded by goats.'

'Which was what I thought we were,' said Garrick. 'But you soon change your mind.'

'How about Tahiti?' Case said.

Garrick grinned. 'While there's life, there's hope. As Kamar would have said.'

'What d'you know, eh?' Polo shook his head. 'Him turning out like that.'

'Don't hold it against him,' said Maynard, and looked at Elisabeth.

'I'm not going to, captain,' she said. 'It won't be easy, but then perhaps nothing is going to be easy from now on.' She looked back at the glow beyond the trees on the curve of the river; it could have been her life going up in flames. 'One will just have to start learning all over again.'

'Learning what?' Case said.

'To look at people differently,' she said, and marvelled at the sweet, unaccustomed taste of humility.

Case, sitting in the bottom of the boat, lay back against a seat. His feet were cut and had been bleeding and he might be shoeless all the way to Timor; the rash in his armpits and on his legs seemed to have spread alarmingly within the last hour; he had vomited up the rice and fish Elisabeth had given him, the taste of oil still in his mouth and throat; but he was not dead. That was the important thing. He was alive, still afraid, still uncertain, but alive. And with a destination.

Where are you going? someone might have asked; and he could not have named any definite place. But he had stopped running away, was turning back. Perhaps to the heart of himself; that was a destination. For, like Elisabeth, he knew now the time had come to look at people differently. And that could only come if he looked at himself differently. Time had run out for non-involvement: America had discovered that at Pearl Harbour, he had discovered it when the knife had gone into Kamar. He would never have the killer instinct and he would regret the death of Kamar till the day of his own death. But this war, as Maynard had said, was not a war of which Kamar or anyone else was not a part. Maybe no war was. For any thinking man, no matter how remote from the battlefield, no matter what his conscience thought about the rights or wrongs of the struggle, must be wounded when man fought man.

'What are you thinking about?' Elisabeth said.

'About you and Maynard and Reg and Polo. And about Cabrolini and Kamar, Sitanala and Chairil, the Japanese officer on the beach, Singh and Hutton, Old Turkey Bones, Josef and Maria Czeiciniski.'

'I'm glad,' she said, and in the starlight he saw her smile.

'Why? Why are you glad?'

'Because,' she said, 'I need someone to think about me. We all do. Is that selfish?'

'No,' he said, and wondered why he had kept the knowledge from himself for so long. 'It's human.'

Then the sea opened up before them. Sumatra dropped back astern, a silhouette of black mangrove against a strangely impassive moon. Ahead of them lay the darkness, Timor and Darwin.

'Only another two thousand miles to go,' said Maynard.

'We're with you all the way, sport,' said Polo.

Alistair MacLean

His first book, *HMS Ulysses*, published in 1955, was outstandingly successful. It led the way to a string of best-selling novels which have established Alistair MacLean as the most popular adventure writer of our time.

Desmond Bagley

'Mr Bagley is nowadays incomparable.' *Sunday Time*

THE ENEMY £1·25
FLYAWAY £1·25
THE FREEDOM TRAP £1·25
THE GOLDEN KEEL £1·25
HIGH CITADEL £1·25
LANDSLIDE £1·25
RUNNING BLIND £1·25
THE SNOW TIGER £1·35
THE SPOILERS £1·25
THE TIGHTROPE MEN £1·25
THE VIVERO LETTER £1·35
WYATT'S HURRICANE £1·25
BAHAMA CRISIS £1·50

FONTANA PAPERBACKS

Fontana Paperbacks

Fontana is a leading paperback publisher of fiction and non-fiction, with authors ranging from Alistair MacLean, Agatha Christie and Desmond Bagley to Solzhenitsyn and Pasternak, from Gerald Durrell and Joy Adamson to the famous Modern Masters series.

In addition to a wide-ranging collection of internationally popular writers of fiction, Fontana also has an outstanding reputation for history, natural history, military history, psychology, psychiatry, politics, economics, religion and the social sciences.

All Fontana books are available at your bookshop or newsagent; or can be ordered direct. Just fill in the form and list the titles you want.

FONTANA BOOKS, Cash Sales Department, G.P.O. Box 29, Douglas, Isle of Man, British Isles. Please send purchase price, plus 8p per book. Customers outside the U.K. send purchase price, plus 10p per book. Cheque, postal or money order. No currency.

NAME (Block letters)

ADDRESS